GLAMOROUS DISASTERS

A Novel

Eliot Schrefer

SIMON & SCHUSTER
New York London Toronto Sydney

SIMON & SCHUSTER
Rockefeller Center
1230 Avenue of the Americas
New York, NY 10020

For information about special discounts for bulk purchases, please contact Simon & Schuster Special Sales:
1-800-456-6798 or business@simonandschuster.com.

Designed by Melissa Isriprashad

Manufactured in the United States of America

10 9 8 7 6 5 4 3 2 1

Library of Congress Cataloging-in-Publication Data
Schrefer, Eliot.
Glamorous disasters / Eliot Schrefer
p. cm.
1. Tutors and tutoring—Fiction. 2. SAT (Educational test)—Fiction. 3. High school students—Fiction. 4. Rich people—Fiction. 5. Manhattan (New York, N.Y.)—Fiction. I. Title
PS3619.C463G58 2006
813'.6—dc22 2005056325

ISBN-13: 978-0-7432-8167-6
ISBN-10: 0-7432-8167-5

for my mother and brother,

foundations both

chapter 1

Dr. Thayer will pay $395 an hour for Noah's services. Only the classiest prostitute could charge as much and, to any doorman glimpsing Noah stepping out of his taxi, Noah might indeed seem a well-kept callboy. Though brandless, his cobalt shirt is pressed as flat as paper, and the flesh exposed at his throat is Hamptons-tan. Diesel sunglasses dangle from a buttonhole. He has carefully chosen his pants: pin-striped dark linen, to denote a youthful vitality bobbing beneath a surface respect for decorum. His headphones are both inconspicuous and expensive. The guise is complete.

Noah pauses in front of a Fifth Avenue building, appearing dumbstruck that there should exist an environment so ideally suited to him. But he is neither favored son returned from the Hamptons nor callboy. He is an SAT tutor, paid those $395 to ensure that Thayer Junior attends the same Ivy League school as Thayer Senior. He has made himself appear as one of his students—attractive, complacent, glassy-eyed—and he will work at them stealthily, from within their world. They don't stand a chance to resist him.

When Noah feels tired—and tonight is such a night—he mouths, *Three hundred ninety-five dollars,* throughout his commute. Dr. Thayer called to ask him to come a half hour early; the family would pay the cab fare. And so, when Noah flagged the solitary yellow car arrowing between the gray brick buildings of Harlem, his meter started running along with the cabby's: twenty-five minutes' travel time added to a hundred-minute session, plus the fare itself, will run the Thayer family $835.

The doormen snap to attention when Noah appears behind the etched glass of the entrance, but then they slouch when the better interior lights reveal Noah's youth, his $30 sandals, the headphones in his ears. The doormen are white, of course, but not White—Noah listens for the trace of an Irish or Russian accent, reads the bleariness of a Brooklyn commute into their late-night eyes. They regard Noah warily, as if girding themselves to cast him back outside. The biggest snobs of any building, the doormen.

"I'm here for Dylan Thayer," Noah says.

A doorman nods in reluctant civility, picks up the handset, and dials. His console is gold and velvet blue, like a presidential lectern. Nine-four-nine Fifth Avenue is, like its Park Avenue neighbors, an essentially ugly structure with the artless lines of a Monopoly hotel, but the interior is done up in fleur-de-lis and *chinoiserie*. The doorman glances at Noah.

"Noah," he says.

"'Noah' is on his way up, Dr. Thayer . . . You're welcome." He hangs up and turns a key. "Eleven F."

Noah crosses to the mahogany doors of the elevator. He feels the doorman's gaze on his back, and wishes he were wearing loafers, that he looked more like someone who would live here. But at least the whole doorman interchange has earned him $30. He is $81,000 in debt. Or, after today's session, $80,700. The doors open.

Eleven F is the only button that will light. This is to prevent Noah from infiltrating any other apartment. The elevator is fast, but even so the ride up grosses $5.

The *F* in 11F stands for the front half of the floor: the doors open directly into the foyer of the apartment. A woman slides over the partially opened secondary door, frail hand extended. A pair of gold bracelets tinkles.

"Susan Thayer," she says.

Noah takes the bony hand and rattles it once.

"A pleasure, Dr. Thayer." One key to the first meeting is to get the titles right—if he's talking to a mother and she works, "Doctor" is a likely choice.

"Come in." She opens the door and floats into a mirrored vestibule.

She could be the mother of any of Noah's students: her hair is highlighted and lowlighted and then carelessly pulled back, as if to belie the weekly appointments required to maintain it. Equine eyes and dark eyebrows prove the dishonesty of the sun-streaked hair. A string of pearls rides her emaciated shoulders, rests in the gorges between her clavicles.

She smiles sweetly as her eyes dart over Noah's form. Dr. Thayer has been monstrous in her initial phone conversations, obliquely accusing Noah of overcharging her and disliking her son, whom he has not yet met. But in person she gives every appearance of fighting back the impulse to hug him. The Fifth Avenue hostess urge is hardwired.

"I wanted to be sure to be home the first time you met Dylan because, if not, who knows what could happen?" She throws her arms into the air and laughs, and Noah laughs too, mainly because she looks like a whirligig. He can't decide whether her joke is cautionary or just nonsensical and suddenly it comes back to him, strong, that he should be in front of a classroom instead.

"Well, I'm excited to meet Dylan," Noah says jovially. He

knows he is rushing this particular phase of the introductory ritual. He should take a few more moments to make the mother feel desired, but the responsibility of the money ticking away propels him. Noah grew up in a town with street names like Countryside Lane and State Road 40, not Park or Madison or even anything ending in Avenue. While a $200 chitchat on the stairs is nothing to the Thayers, to him it is unconscionable: the scale of money looms here, is too large to be comprehended, like geologic time to a human life span.

She gestures at a door upstairs. "He's in his bedroom."

Noah starts up, swinging around the flare of a shabby-chic banister and ascending into a darkened second-floor hallway. He wonders why Dr. Thayer isn't leading him up.

"Noah," Dr. Thayer calls after him. Noah stops and looks down. He can see her hard breasts where her shirt pouches around her narrow shoulders, and dutifully concentrates on the banister, even though the idea of Dr. Thayer's being exposed vaguely excites him.

"Look, I know there are problems here," she continues. "He just hasn't learned this stuff. I don't know why."

It is a familiar first-meeting move. The guilt deflection: my child may be stupid, but that doesn't make me any less intelligent.

"The test is teachable," Noah declaims from the landing. He can't remember if he has already given her this speech on the phone. "All it measures is how well one takes it. In some ways students from the best high schools are at a disadvantage, because they are taught to think abstractly, to voice opinions and argue nuance. The kid in the public school in Arkansas has been taking multiple-choice tests his whole life. Standardized tests are the first resort of low-income school districts, and the last resort of high-income ones."

The closing bit (Arkansas!) always gets a world-weary

nod from parents. Dr. Thayer peers up and smiles as if they were best friends just reunited and meeting for coffee. Despite the disingenuousness of the gesture, Noah is charmed. He finds himself wishing that he and Dr. Thayer *were* at a coffee shop somewhere. "That's very interesting, but it's not really the issue here. You'll see," Dr. Thayer says.

And with that, Noah reaches Dylan's door. It is as white and silver as the restroom door of an expensive restaurant. There is no construction-paper "Keep Out!" sign. Noah knocks and simultaneously glides the door open. The good tutor is polite, but need not ask to enter.

Dylan's bedroom is actually a suite of rooms. Noah passes through a spare and obviously unused study complete with antique globe and rolltop desk, then a marble bathroom, and finally reaches the bedroom. Tightly shaded windows dominate two walls. Dylan is slouched over an Empire desk, clacking into a laptop. His back is to Noah.

"Hey," Noah says.

"What's up," Dylan says, without turning around. Noah stands in the doorway. He breezily walks in. If he wants to get perfect 10's on his evaluations he has to prove from the start that he is cool. Perfect 10's will get him a raise. Perfect 10's will help his brother pass high school. If he doesn't gain each kid's admiration from the start, all that is sunk.

He has forgotten that Dylan is captain of the lacrosse team, but is reminded by the fact that Dylan doesn't turn around. Team captains don't do such things as acknowledge newcomers, of course, since their image is based on the burden of already knowing too many people. Noah became a cool teenager only late, and is a cool twenty-five-year-old through constant effort. And yet here he is, tutoring the kid who beat him up in high school.

"So what's up?" Noah asks. Do cool kids say "What's up" to a "What's up"?

Dylan swivels. A bright white T-shirt, still creased from

the package, stretches across his chest. His hair looks like he has just taken a nap, or has been licked by a goat. His eyes are glassy and widely spaced. He is the breed of seventeen-year-old who turns the heads of adult women.

The first-meeting monologue is all about pretending that the friendship has already begun. Never ask, *What are your interests?* Rather, *So what have you been up to today? Oh, really? What else? Did you drive? When do you get your license?* Noah and Dylan's $200 getting-to-know-you half hour passes, and Noah learns that Dylan likes to sleep when he has spare time, has a quiz on *The House of Mirth* the next day, prefers the club Pangaea to Lotus on Wednesday nights, thinks lacrosse is "okay," and goes to school at Dwight. Dwight, one of Noah's students once informed him, stands for Dumb White Idiots Getting High Together.

"How did you choose Dwight?" Noah asks.

"They made me transfer from Fieldston."

Dylan goes to the bathroom, which costs $35. After he returns, grunts, and throws himself on the bed, Noah asks him why *they* made him transfer.

"Whatever, it's not on my record," is the crafty response. Not that Dylan seems generally clever—he scored 420 out of 800 on the writing portion of his SAT, which Dr. Thayer (the monstrous phone Thayer, not the smashing hostess Thayer) informed Noah would need to become at least a 650 for the lacrosse recruiter at Penn to be satisfied. A 650 would put Dylan among the nation's brightest students. Or at least among the nation's bright students.

Noah swivels in his leather chair and faces Dylan, who is reclining on his bed and massaging a foot, the sweaty fragrance of which carries across the vaulted bedroom. "Dylan," he says, his tone carefully nonteacher, "we have two months, man, until your test. That's eight sessions. We're going to talk about the essay today, and then focus on grammar. Then you take a practice test each weekend."

At the mention of weekly practice tests Dylan suddenly looks glassy and cross, like a miffed sultan. Noah barrels onward:

"So! How would you respond to this prompt?" Noah asks. "The more things change, the more they stay the same."

Dylan's eyes drift over Noah's long frame. Noah can see the blunt calculation in Dylan's head—is this guy worth trying for? After another introspective moment Dylan laughs. "You messed up."

"What do you mean?"

"Say it again."

Noah does.

Dylan snorts. "Yeah, that makes no sense."

Noah's usual stratagem is now to impress the student by reciting the original French. This is quickly abandoned. "Okay," Noah says, "let's work your resistance into the essay."

Dylan eyes Noah warily. "That's fucked up. If something changes, then it's *different.*"

"Right, but it becomes the same thing as everything else at some point, right?" Noah falters. Suddenly the quote makes no sense to him either. Dr. Thayer's admonition that too much abstract thinking is "not really the issue here" taunts him.

"Whatever," Dylan says. "I don't care about all of this shit, I just need my score to go up."

Noah gives a manly chuckle and pretends there was irony in Dylan's voice. Will Dylan's score go up much? Based on his diagnostic test results, probably not: he capitalized neither proper names nor the beginnings of sentences, and spelled *introduction* with an *e.*

When the session is over, Noah deploys a "Later, man" (*later:* I'm chill, I don't need to waste the energy on a proper goodbye. *man:* I like you, but not *that* way) and exits down the hallway. It's too late in the evening for maids and personal assistants, so no one is waiting to see him out. But on his way down the stairs Noah passes a dull glow from Dr. Thayer's open bedroom door. She is ensconced in the opulent gloom, cradled in a voluminous satin duvet, reading a copy of *The House of Mirth.* Her gaze flickers to Noah. She shoots him one long-lashed, meaningful look, and then returns to her book: he has allowed himself to leave six minutes early, which puts him at a $40 deficit.

~

Noah had thought his new job would make him extremely wealthy, that he would become, in some small way, of the same class as the rest of Fifth Avenue. Three hundred ninety-five an hour: what a treat for a guy whose friends from high school are mostly earning minimum wage or trading WIC checks. On the subway ride home from his job interview he had computed what $395 an hour would earn him, were he to work forty hours a week: $822,000 a year.

He missed his stop and had to backtrack half an hour to get home.

On that walk he realized that his actual income wasn't going to be nearly as high. First, he only actually receives one-fourth of the $395; the agency keeps the rest. Second, he would be lucky to get six students, which would make for significantly fewer than forty hours a week. Third, there was the matter of taxes. He drafted a budget on the back of a receipt when he returned home:

Monthly Budget (STICK TO!):

Income:	
Salary	$3354
(if get up to six students—call office twice a week, beg if necess.)	
Interest from savings	2.65
Total:	$3356.65
Deficits:	
Federal Tax	$412.50
NY City Tax	68.75
NY State Tax	137.50
Social Security	275
Medicare	61.30
Rent	760
Utilities	55
Subway Pass	70
Health Ins.	375
Dental Ins.	10
Cell phone	45
(required by office—get on group plan?)	
Stafford loan	355.61
(if get on 20-year payment plan)	
Perkins loan	301.50
(ditto)	
America's Bank Loan	600.72
Total deficits:	$3527.88
Monthly savings:	$-171.23

Consider: Nix H. Ins.? Would result in $200 surplus a month! Woo-hoo!
Ditto dental.
Second job?
Add'l expense: food.

When Noah signed promissory notes at Princeton the amounts of his loans seemed so small, fractions of the university's endowment; school was free. But now the numbers aren't some insignificant eddies of money within a larger pot of billions of dollars. They are his alone. The triplets, Perkins, Stafford, and America's Bank: $25,000, $16,000, and $40,000. These kinds of numbers belong to the Thayers, not to him. He has pushed too hard in trying to compensate for his impoverished beginnings, to propel himself into the upper class.

The money comes out of his bank account on the fifteenth of every month. Having automatic withdrawal is like having a parasite, a tapeworm passively feeding off whatever sustenance Noah brings in. He makes a trip to buy furniture at Ikea, and in that cavern, all blond wood, chilled air, and high ceilings (a microcosm of Sweden, Noah imagines), he fingers his credit card gingerly, as if to prevent further hemorrhage in the plastic. He is eager to browse, to choose between the round red kettle and the sleek aluminum one, but at the cash registers he is smiling and forlorn, hollowed out, wistful that shopping in this fairyland should inevitably conclude with a return, not to a house in the woods, but to a sixth-floor tenement room. In New York there is no escape from money. There are prices everywhere, no end of costs to meet or flee.

Noah can think of a number of reasons for Dylan to have been unhappy at Fieldston. Foremost among them is that all of Noah's students from that school have been both artsy and intelligent. He meets with a favorite Fieldston student the next day: Cameron Leinzler, who is playing Audrey in the school production of *Little Shop of Horrors,* obsesses about food and boys, and shoots glances at the mirror throughout their sessions. Even though she scored fantastically well on her diagnostic test, it is not odd that she has a private tutor. Most of the students in the Upper East and Upper West Sides have one. Tutors are to Manhattan teenagers, Noah is beginning to realize, as ponies are to ten-year-old girls.

"Dylan??!!" Cameron squeals. "You teach *Dylan Thayer*??!!"

Noah nods.

"He's so hot, but a total asshole. My friends were totally in love with him, but I don't like him."

"Why don't you like him?"

"Well, he hooked up with all of them, but it was like his timing was off, you know? They all sorta overlapped."

They navigate into the safer terrain of reading comprehension. Cameron snaps her head up in the middle of a treatise on Gregor Mendel.

"You know he's a total druggie," she says.

Noah figured as much.

"He's like what the rest of the world imagines we are, you know?"

"In what way?"

"Screwed up. Totally warped."

"And why don't you like him?"

"I told you."

"You told me why your friends don't like him."

"Oh. Dylan thinks I'm annoying. He just wasn't ever any nice to me. I guess that's it. Um . . . because 'predictable traits are inherited by subsequent generations.' "

"Good."

"You know," Cameron says. She smiles and avoids Noah's eyes; she is tattling. He can see the flush of blood in her plump cheeks, the twisting corners of her smile. She might be in love with him. "He got kicked out because his mom wrote his essays for him."

To get to Dylan's building, Noah takes the subway through Harlem to 79th Street, and then boards a crosstown bus from the ironic affluence of the Upper West Side to the less reflective wealth of the Upper East Side. Dylan's doormen are a little warmer this time, and the one who opens the door even flickers a smile. Perhaps, since Noah has now entered twice without carrying dry cleaning, he has gained in status.

Dr. Thayer answers the door in an outfit that hasn't declared itself as either an evening gown or a high-end bathrobe. The tanned hand that grips the robe closed glints gold and silver.

"Hello, Noah," she pronounces. "How did last week go?"

Noah detects a desire for straight talk in the doctor's voice and tries to match it. "Well, there's certainly plenty of work to be done . . ."

"You've got a month left—as long as he gets a 650!" she calls out far too loudly, as if to browbeat her exclamation into a joke. The toned flesh on her stick arms shakes as she pinwheels through a broken laugh. Surely she realizes that a 650 isn't going to happen. A 500 would be a stretch.

"I'll try!" Noah responds, with a wink in his voice: *Ha-ha, we're in on the same joke!*

Noah adds a touch of a pimp roll to his walk as he mounts the stairs. Dylan and he are friends, Noah decides, and Noah will be that cool tutor kids swap rumors about at parties. The tutoring hierarchy replicates high school—raises are based on student evaluations, and the cooler, better-looking tutors get better evaluations. Noah's and Dylan's thought patterns are probably fairly similar: *Am I hot? Am I cool? Do they like me?* In Dylan's case coolness is an end in itself. But in Noah's case, coolness means financial solvency.

"Oh, before I forget," Dr. Thayer calls after a calculated moment. She has followed him upstairs without his realizing.

"Take this card. It tells the doormen that you're allowed in here, in case Dylan doesn't answer the phone and I'm out."

Noah glances at the scrap of heavy paper. There are two printed boxes below his handwritten name: "social" (a stencil of a martini glass) or "staff" (a stencil of an iron). He has been marked "staff."

"I didn't know what to put!" Dr. Thayer laughs. Noah laughs too.

Dr. Thayer floats back into her bedroom and Noah crosses through Dylan's suite. He collects himself before the doorway, runs a hand through his hair.

"What's up?" he asks as he saunters in.

But Dylan isn't there.

Puzzled, Noah sits on Dylan's bed and surveys the room. The duvet is coarse white linen. Dylan's backpack, draped with a pair of discarded boxers, lies next to the bed. Noah scans the bookshelf. The books range in difficulty level from *Maxim* to the first *Harry Potter.* The closet door is open, and reveals only overstuffed dry-cleaning bags. Noah imagines his Dominican neighbors ironing Dylan's underwear.

He realizes that he has already allowed $65 of empty time to slip by. He should be doing something. But what?

A teenage waif flits into the room. "I'm Tuscany," she whispers. "You're from the agency?" From the agency. As if he were a model, escort, or actor. Granted, the tutor's job is to be all three. She allows her long fingers to graze the duvet and adds: "Dylan's on his way. He told me to tell you not to tell *her* that he's not here. You should do what you want, though."

She stares at Noah blearily for a moment, and then vanishes.

Now Noah has just bought himself complicity. He is unsure of where his allegiances are supposed to lie in such a situation. He stares intently at the window shade and imagines scenarios and excuses, hopes he won't get fired.

Then he hears a door slam below, followed by Dylan's baritone grumblings amid Dr. Thayer's higher-pitched squeals. Dylan thumps up the stairs and then splashes onto the bed. He smells like lacrosse.

"I'm in deep shit," Dylan says.

"I met your girlfriend," Noah says.

"That's my sister! She's fifteen. You're fucked up." Dylan slaps his pillow with pleasure—Noah has somehow blundered his way into a cool-kid joke. Score.

"What happened?" Noah asks.

"I had to go downtown to buy something from a friend before tonight. It wasn't supposed to take so fuckin' long."

"I can imagine what kind of something you had to buy," Noah says. He intended to sound like a hip friend, but the words come shrilly, as if ejaculated by an inappropriate governess.

"Whatever, it's not like I'm that different from her or anything."

"Her," meaning Tuscany? "Her," meaning Dr. Thayer? "Not different," meaning we're all druggies? Noah pulls out his tutoring books.

"I mean, Tuscany and me used to go into my mom's office and her bedroom all the time and steal her shit." Dylan smiles crookedly. "She has all this crazy shit."

Dylan is only seventeen, Tuscany is even younger, and the lengthy expanse of time implied in the way Dylan says "used to" makes Noah shift in his seat.

"She's a pediatrician," Dylan says by way of explanation.

Of course. Dylan was raised by a child doctor.

~

That night when Noah returns home, while deliberating between a dinner of Progresso Lentil or Campbell's Black

Bean, he notices a flyer beneath his door advertising Harlem Fitness, *The Homeboy's Home for Being Jacked,* for only $15 a month.

None of his students' parents know that he lives in Harlem. Living above 96th Street is, like gambling debt or an alcoholic father, a secret one simply doesn't reveal. He used to live nearer to Fifth Avenue: after Noah graduated from college he moved in with his girlfriend on First, only blocks away from the Thayer apartment. He didn't have his tutoring job yet, and would set himself up to write his Ph.D. application essays in a corner of her bedroom while she was in law school classes. Tabitha would return home after spending the day in the library and find Noah in his boxers, eating her cereal and watching sitcom reruns. She kicked him out after a few weeks, but not before she landed him a job at the agency that had tutored her for the law school entrance exam. They have remained friends, and whenever Noah visits Tab's apartment he sees that the only impact of his moving out is fewer crumbs at the bottom of the toaster, and that the toilet paper supply declines at half rate.

The question for Noah had been where to move. Tabitha led him to a "totally reasonable, totally hot" apartment her real estate broker father found off Gramercy Park. Noah loved the apartment but discovered that, factoring in his loan payments, the monthly rent was two thousand dollars too many. He turned to the *Village Voice* instead. Most apartments he found were in the Bronx, a few were in Harlem ("Columbia University is making that area totally hip"), and one was a room in a houseboat off the coast of Hoboken. And so Noah moved to Harlem.

This is the chip on his shoulder, Noah knows, his big insecurity: he could be part of the elite world he works for, if only he had wealth. But he grew up poor and introverted, and neither is of any benefit in Manhattan.

Noah's father, a trucker away for months at a time, died

shortly after Noah's younger brother was born, and the modest insurance settlement permitted his mother's freedom from labor even as it set a strict $1,500-a-month boundary around her boys' existence. The money gave her, Noah's mother later told him, a sense of omnipotence, that she was landed gentry, unmoored from practical necessity and concerned only with location and lifestyle. For a woman obsessed with nineteenth century literature ("I would have been an academic," she once said, "if I finished high school. But I missed those first steps"), her situation seemed enviable—she was a Pip, an Isabel Archer. To the rest of the world she was slightly above destitute, a step above trailer trash. She moved to a rural Virginia town that had one excellent public school, bought a tract house ("a cottage," she always called it, though it had arrived from Alabama wrapped in plastic, its aluminum sides creaking), and purchased a small plot for it that backed onto the county reservoir. The reservoir was bounded by swaths of forest that circled the glowing pool of water like eyelashes, and which lent a dreamy, fantastic quality to Noah's childhood.

Noah's mother entered on a quest of self-improvement, which for her meant extended time reading, swimming in the reservoir, writing strong and candid letters for local environmental causes, and making sure her sons grew up to share her focus on helping others, on getting beyond just their own satisfaction.

As a child Noah happily followed his mother on her walks through the woods, made handicrafts out of paper towel tubes kept in tubs beneath the sink, and embarked on parallel reading projects of his own, stretching from *Peter Rabbit* through *The Wind in the Willows* and culminating in the two weeks he had chicken pox in second grade and read all fourteen *Oz* books in a row, one for each day. At age ten he went through a spell of reading only "serious, adult" books, and after contemplating *The Drama of the Gifted*

Child solemnly asked his mother if he might not have learned too well how to please her and never developed desires of his own.

And indeed, it wasn't until late that he had any rebellion: at age sixteen the scrap to get his hair cut at the strip mall instead of at the card table out back, at seventeen the fight to work at the grocery store after school, and finally, during the combative summer of 1999, the successful push for a television. Kent sat in the background, quietly reaping the benefits of Noah's struggles.

In middle school Noah had a tendency to start conversations with such prompts as "Did you know Alaska was purchased for nineteen cents a square mile?" and found himself friendless on the weekends. But by high school alternative had become cool, and he cultivated a certain mystique around his quirkiness. It helped that he also grew tall, and broad and narrow in the suitable places. Girls started to follow him home after school, and he'd read them poems he'd composed, with titles like "Tortured Roses" and "The Violent Thrusts of Rainstorms." Then he started to throw parties while his mother was away at Sierra Club conferences, and skyrocketed to outright popularity. Poetry fell to the wayside, replaced by Rolling Rock. He became (and he knew it at the time, enjoyed the hot splash of his villainy) something of a jerk, bouncing between girls, ignoring his outcast brother except for their tutoring sessions, and rejecting the few kids who had stuck by him during his trivia phase. During college, his first and second selves converged, he liked to think, into a cool guy who remembered what it was to struggle.

Regardless, he reminds himself, he has graduated now, and no longer has the luxury of thinking about himself in such terms. Twenty-five-year-olds who are shouldering $81,000 in debt and trying to send money home don't try to define themselves. They just are. They fight.

Wealthy Manhattan is scentless year-round (even the tended daffodils in the Park Avenue median seem other-worldly, like holograms), but the smell of the asphalt in Harlem at the peak of summer is akin to cat food: a combination of dried spit, secretions from distended garbage bags, and a softening accumulation of smog. The apartment Noah eventually found was a small dingy (*Trendy!* he reminds himself, *dirt is in!*) room in the attic of a Harlem tenement building.

The front door suggests a museum entrance—thick beaten wood, a medieval portico. The skeleton of the neighborhood is fascinating, articulate and worn architecture, ornate entranceways, and exposed brick. But it is also swaddled in neon signs, and the wide sidewalks are covered with litter and greasy puddles.

The wooden planks of Noah's apartment floor have blackened and warped over the decades and taken on the dry and gnarled appearance of witches' staves. The molding around the tin ceiling has turned a pumpkin color, except where an undercoat of iridescent blue peeks through. The rest of the walls have recently been painted in a glossy white that beams like new copy paper. The paint is thin, however, and doesn't mask a bizarre water stain that circles the walls just below the ceiling. It appears as if the room has only recently been drained of seawater.

During the summer the apartment is roasting hot and, square and virtually unfurnished, gives the same impression as the inside of a microwave oven. Noah throws off his shirt as he reads the Harlem Fitness flyer. It lands on his bed, though the collar reaches the edge of the kitchen table; a sleeve rests on the lip of the grayed porcelain bathtub. The apartment is very small. Noah reads the flyer sitting on the edge of the tub.

A dream surges in Noah's head: most days he doesn't work until four P.M.—he can spend all day at the gym! He will be broad, really impressive. He will box in the mornings, lift weights with the local boys all afternoon, gallantly stride on the treadmill for a few hours, shower, and then go teach. Getting his body nearer Dylan's movie-hero proportions can only help him win his students' admiration. It's worth the money, and he can afford the gym fees if he switches to generic granola.

Harlem Fitness is found up a dozen rusty, mossy steps from the Dominican bodega on the corner of 145th Street and Broadway. The rubber-coated stairs seem to have melted in the afternoon sun. Noah's sneakers make sucking sounds as he hauls himself up. As the door thuds closed he can still hear the street altercations conducted in Spanish and the excited cries of children tossing a ball. Noah ascends through bacterial, close air, through the humidity of years of workouts. He creaks the interior door open to the hums and thumps of treadmills, to grunts as musclemen swing weights above their heads.

A large-framed and dark-eyed man reclines at the front desk, bouncing a plastic pen against his biceps and toying with the sound system. The music is bluntly mixed electronica from a few years previous, all Cher and pounding beats, the breed of techno one might hear issuing from a gay bar in Kansas.

"Whaddup?" the man asks.

"Hi, I just wanted to enroll," Noah says.

"Oh yeah? Come over here."

The man stares at Noah's eyes. Noah smiles back dumbly, fighting a sudden attack of nerves. *Enroll?* Surely there's a less fussy verb. He wishes he hadn't worn his "Division of Princeton Athletics" track pants, hadn't streaked his hair red a few months before. The guys here all wear wife-beaters, and their hair products seem attributable more to Crisco than Kiehl's.

"You can pay by like cash, or whatever."

"Is credit card possible?"

"Yeah, I think." The guy rummages below the desk and pulls out a dusty card reader that looks like an old *Star Wars* toy.

"Look at you," the guy mutters derisively, staring down at the contraption but pointing his finger at Noah.

"What?" Noah asks. He quails, suddenly very aware that he is one of the few white people in his neighborhood.

But when the man looks up he is grinning. "Look at you! Spiky hair, vintage tee, cool sneakers, it's like this is fuckin' Park Slope."

Noah laughs in spite of himself. "Yeah, I know, I've never felt so pasty."

The man encloses Noah's hand in his and at the same time a play of air in the gym forces over a blast of sweat vapor. "I'm Roberto. They like call me Rob, but not in that holdin'-up-a-bank way."

"I'm Noah. But not in that two-animals-at-a-time way."

The skin of Roberto's face is tan, dry, and draws tightly across his face as he laughs; even though he speaks like a local eighteen-year-old, Noah guesses he is in his thirties. While his neck is massive, it seems barely able to support the broad planes of his face. His shiny square forehead and gelled hair reflect an impossible amount of light.

"Welcome to Harlem, Mr. White Man."

~

Noah doesn't see Dr. Thayer at all over the next three weeks. And neither, apparently, does Dylan.

"She's in the Hamptons with my dad," Dylan explains. They sit perched on his bed, workbooks open on their laps, a basketball game on mute. Noah hasn't considered that Dylan even had a father. "She calls all the time, like once a day sometimes. She leaves money stashed in all these crazy places, and when I run out I call her and she tells me where to find more."

He pulls a wad of bills out of his pocket. On top is a fifty. "This was below the bathroom sink. She doesn't know I found it yet, so I'm going to Bungalow 8 after we finish tonight. There's some party Justin Timberlake's throwing. Crazy."

Noah and Dylan watch the MTV Video Music Awards and discuss dangling modifiers during the commercials. Dylan's interest in pop music seems more a duty than a pleasure. He had a ticket to the awards show but didn't use it because he didn't want to go alone. Noah, though he feigns indifference, would have given anything to say that he had gone. This is their equation, their dovetailing strengths and weaknesses: Dylan is effortlessly cool, and Noah is effortlessly smart. Each gift is the other's limitation.

Dylan passes the session sending instant messages on his laptop and text messages on his phone, making a few calls that end with "I'm with my tutor, gotta go," and are followed by another call, and every so often answering a grammar question Noah throws out.

The laptop dings. "Check this out," Dylan says.

He pivots his laptop so that Noah can see. He scrolls through a list of potential interview questions and answers e-mailed by Dylan's college admissions tutor (he has seven tutors in all—one for each academic subject and now Noah). In bold: **What three adjectives would you use to describe yourself?** Then: "tenacious—I have excelled in academics even as I mastered the playing field." The list goes on for pages.

"I'm really good at memorizing," Dylan says. "Like for essays. He sends me what I need to write, I remember it, and I spit it out on the exam."

Dylan seems more reflective than usual and Noah is feeling bolder. "If you had it all to do over," Noah begins, "would you do it this way? Have all these tutors?"

"*Yeah!* This is awesome. Who wouldn't love this? I don't have to do *anything*."

"No, I mean, you seem kind of frustrated that now you can't work at all without a tutor here. What if we *weren't* all here, you know?"

Dylan looks pissed off. Noah is relieved to realize that he is just deep in thought. Finally: "Well, I'd be alone. That'd suck."

Dylan is right. He would be alone, and that would indeed suck. His parents are largely absent; if the choice is either tutors or solitude, why not opt for tutors? Noah is warmed by the implication: that he's doing a kid good by being there.

"So what about you, then?" Dylan asks. "Are you a tutor?"

Noah considers how to answer.

"I mean," Dylan continues, "is this all you do?"

"No. For now. I want to go get my Ph.D. in comparative literature."

"Oh, okay, cool. I mean, I was thinking, it'd be sad if you went to Princeton and just become a *tutor*!"

Dylan switches over to a *Sex and the City* rerun. Noah doesn't know how to respond: he did go to Princeton, and did become a tutor. He would feel more at home hanging out in front of the old Virginia middle school or drinking in a local diner with his friends, now all mechanics and cops; tutoring in Manhattan suddenly seems an incomprehensible choice to him too. But Princeton came in the way, with its increased expectations and increased debt. Going home stopped being an option long ago.

Noah harbors a vague plan of communicating his worry to Dylan that eventually he won't have tutors, that he'll be unable to pass university courses or hold a job. But he realizes there will be tutors in college to help him through, more men like Noah. Dylan's parents are well connected, so he's sure to land a low-responsibility glamour job. Dylan is rich, good-looking, hypersocialized. Why is Noah even there? College admissions seem so pale next to Dylan's easy smile and nonchalant popularity—his wealth and coolness bear more capital than a college degree.

Dylan's phone rings again, and Noah can tell from Dylan's barked reply that it's one of his parents. Dylan hands the phone over. "She wants to talk to you."

"Noah, hello," monstrous phone Thayer says. "There's a file on Dylan's desktop, Collegeapp. It needs work—his college advisor and I've already glanced at it, but I'm not sure what to do. Would you mind taking it home to look over? Just for grammar, of course."

~

Noah reads Dylan's college essay under the fluorescent lights of the M4 bus as it winds through Spanish Harlem. The first paragraph:

> *When I was fourteen, such a tender age, my teacher called me a "dumb jock." What struck me, then, was a certain vague profundity behind her offhand manner; a slippery significance I have only recently come to grasp: I was no longer an individual but a thing; an other.*

Noah blinks in the hard light of the bus as he reads the essay. He stares out the window as he glides under the dark steel overpass of 125th Street. Dylan's essay contains references to contemporary philosophy, to being alienated from one's own identity. "Slippery significance"? There are semicolons! This essay from the kid who thought "The more things change, the more they stay the same" was nonsense—it's impossible. Noah wonders who did write it; this essay has an academic pretension beyond Dr.

Thayer. She must have known that Noah would realize the essay wasn't Dylan's. It's almost as though she's trying to give evidence of her own deceitfulness—why? Noah feels a rush of shame. He's been trying to stay legal. Is she tempting him, teasing him? Does she know what he did for his old student? How will he approach her about all of this?

Plus ça change, plus ça reste la même chose.

~

Noah has brought his gym clothes, and stops by Harlem Fitness on his way home. Roberto receives him with a bewildering mix of friendliness and street aggression. He puts Noah off guard—how does one respond to a smiling thug?—and Noah finds it difficult to reconcile Roberto's barrio toughness and his earnest desire that Noah like him. "Get the hell outta my face," Roberto says to a girl hanger-on wearing hot pants and a chain. "*Noah* is here!"

"Hey, Rob, good evening," Noah says. He leans nonchalantly against the desk and promptly knocks a stack of back issues of *Muscle & Fitness* to the floor.

"Good evening to *you,* man," Roberto says. "You should have seen it earlier," he continues, craning over the counter to watch Noah's back as he picks magazines up from the industrial carpet. "There was like ten hot bitches here at once. All of them sprung in the ass, you know?"

"Oh yeah?" Noah calls up from the ground.

Roberto crosses around the counter and leans next to Noah. "Yeah, I mean I used to live in L.A., cutting hair? And there were so many hot bitches there, man. But now I'm here 'cuz my mother and sister came here. Supposed to be saving. I'm set up good, workin' here is just my second job, I've found like a good chair at a good cutter on the East Side, so I pull in some mad dough. L.A., though, man, there were hot bitches there. Not like here. They're too skinny and white. Or like tubby and black."

"Oh yeah?" Noah repeats. The magazines are old and slick with grease—he finds them nearly impossible to stack. Roberto has picked one up, as if to help, but just holds it slackly in his meaty grip.

"Yeah, I mean there are some hotties here too, especially the Ricans, but shit. L.A. was the *place.* I got so much pussy there. Badass music, and—oh, sorry, man—"

Noah has returned the magazines to the table, at which point they cascade back to the floor. He returns to the carpet. Roberto bows down next to him again.

"You go out a lot?" Roberto asks.

"Yeah," Noah lies.

"You like hip-hop?"

"Umm, yeah, totally." Noah's mind races as he tries to think of the name of a hip-hop singer; he's sure to need one soon. All he can think of are folk and country stars.

"I know some totally wasted clubs, I'm at them like all the time. We can cruise over sometime. I've got my own rig. You look like you could use a good time, and I think it's crap that people here don't like talk to their neighbors, you know? So you should totally come out."

Noah returns the magazines to the counter and positions himself a few safe feet away from the teetering stack. "Yeah, that'd be fun sometime."

"I'm goin' out tonight. I'm goin' with some hot bitches. You can ride shotgun. It'll be like us guys in front and the hot bitches in back."

A little laugh leaks out of Noah.

"What's funny?" Roberto looks honestly worried.

"No, nothing, it sounds cool."

"I mean, these aren't like sex clubs or anything."

"No, it would be fun."

"Then come tonight!"

"I'm working."

"You're *workin'*? What the hell work you do? We're leaving at like midnight."

"Yeah, but I'll have to work tomorrow too. You know how it goes."

"Okay, whatever, next time. Just come back here to find me. I'm like never sure what's goin' on but maybe you'll catch somethin' anyway."

"Thanks, yeah, we'll see."

Noah pauses before he mounts the treadmill. Roberto seems so eager to get to know him, so why did he say no? He doesn't have plans tonight; what is he going to do with himself? He long ago made it a conscious goal to meet as many people as he could. And Roberto is certainly different from his intellectual Princeton friends. But Noah is afraid he wouldn't be up to the challenge. Of course Roberto's friends would like him, right? But maybe they would think him boring: too mediated, too thoughtful. Noah starts the machine and begins running.

~

"Hello?"

"Hey! What's up? It's Noah."

"Oh, hey."

"How's it going? What're you up to?"

"Nothing much, just kind of sitting on the couch." Noah can hear his brother string out the words, imagines him searching around the room, looking for something to comment on. Kent always sounds depressed on the phone. Maybe he is depressed. Noah tries to muster the effort to break through his brother's silence, to reach in and draw him out. But Noah is tired of always leading the conversation. He keeps silent and waits for his brother to speak.

"So," Kent says. "What're you doing?"

"I'm on the bus back from working out."

A pause.

"Is Mom around?" Noah continues.

"No, she's not here."

"Okay, cool, give a call when she gets in, okay?"

"Yeah, sure."

As he hangs up Noah wonders how it would feel to move back to Virginia, to live in the little house with his mother and younger brother again. On the bus back from Harlem Fitness, he grips the plastic handle of his gym bag and stares at the dark and dusty emergency bar of the window and feels a surge of fear that he is losing them, that their lives and concerns are disappearing into the distance, that his love for them, the strongest attachment in his life, can fade just as any other bond can fade. Although he can't imagine life without them, he also finds it hard to envision them.

His brother: sixteen now, a skater, jeans as voluminous as a hoop skirt, pierced ears and sweet smile. The day he left for college, Noah sat at the kitchen table watching his mother pull a dish out of the microwave while Kent was at the sudsy sink, his sweatshirt sleeves bunched at his elbows, his arms half in the suds, Bic pen graffiti running up his arms. His sweatshirt sported a skull and flames and safety pins. At that moment—Noah remembers it so clearly, since it is the time he turned from being Kent's brother to being Kent's father—Kent seemed about to retreat into his own body, like he was backing away from some invisible aggressor stalking up through the soap suds.

In one important way, Noah knows, he works for the same reasons as the solitary middle-aged Dominican men who crowd into shared rooms in his Harlem neighborhood: he has headed into the great city to send money back home. Kent's GPA isn't much above a 1.2, and unless he starts passing foreign language this year, high school will be a memory. Noah's mother would never say as much, but if Kent is to pass high school, it will pretty much be up to Noah, and whatever money he can send home.

Noah can remember the nightly homework sessions with his brother, when Noah was a senior in high school and his brother was in third grade. He would corner Kent on the couch, and they would prop a textbook between their thighs. Noah hated those sessions, the moment each evening when his mother would say, "Helping time!" Tired from his own schoolwork and impatient with his brother's reluctance, Noah would bully Kent through his problems until Kent learned the right answers. Noah softened as the years went by, and sometimes he got past his preoccupation with his own achievement and began to see the hours during college breaks that his mother forced him to spend tutoring his brother as something almost satisfying. But for the most part Noah's tacit obligations to help "the slow one" weighed on him. Noah sometimes hated Kent, was frustrated by his thanklessness, his lack of drive. Noah would try to help but mostly just watched his brother's placid sweetness fossilize into stubborn apathy. With the eventual diagnosis of Kent's dyslexia (in eighth grade! Why hadn't he realized earlier?), the reason for Kent's failing academics became clear. His mother tried to help him with homework but found herself even less equipped than Noah to scale Kent's disability. And being suddenly named Afflicted rather than Slow sapped what remained of Kent's ambition, pitted his problems as the inevitable consequence of some outside force. He would refuse to do his homework altogether.

Kent doesn't want to go to a good college. He doesn't want to go to college at all. And Noah's tutoring has taught him that some people just aren't meant for university, and bridle under the expectation. But Kent has to at least pass high school, and it looks like he won't, not without help.

But Noah has his own life, and can't stomach the idea of going back to the confinement of Virginia. He broke out, and would never seriously consider going back. So help for Kent will have to come from a specialized private high school—financially impossible—or counseling with a learning disability specialist. And that costs two hundred dollars a week. His mother hasn't said so—she would never say so—but Noah is the star of the family, the one who broke free of Virginia and went away to college. If someone is going to help Kent, it has to be Noah. And the only way to do so is with the kind of money he makes from tutoring. And so he tutors in Manhattan in order to pay another tutor to help his brother. If he makes enough, if he keeps his expenses down and does well enough to get raises, he might even enjoy himself at the same time.

He is lucky to be teaching, to be doing his chosen profession at all. He could do a lot worse than be an SAT tutor. He's able, by living cheaply, to pay down his debt and send a bit home and go out when he wants to. He'll get his Ph.D. next year, maybe the year after. But he wonders: Wouldn't someone whose main plan is to be a "real teacher" care a little more whether his own brother succeeds? He loves his brother, but hates the dull weight of his obligation. As the bus stops and Noah steps onto the dingy Harlem pavement over the squeal of the bus's pneumatics, he grips the nylon strap of his gym bag over his chest and imagines the day that he will be able to live farther downtown, closer to where the Thayers live.

~

Dr. Thayer surprises Noah by answering the apartment door at the next meeting. She has returned early from the Hamptons. Noah grips The Essay Said to Be Dylan's in his hand. The doctor leads him into the kitchen.

It is spare and expensively severe, all tall cabinets and brushed-steel appliances. Tuscany is seated at the counter wearing what looks like a gossamer potato sack and watching the maid scoop flesh out of a melon. She doesn't look up.

Dr. Thayer leans against the doorway and stares into Noah's eyes. She appears to have gotten no sun in the Hamptons, nor any sleep.

"Have you read the essay? What do you think?"

"It's very well written. Excellent choice of topic."

Tuscany looks up incredulously. "You're talking about *Dylan's* essay?"

Dr. Thayer and Noah stand with their backs to either side of the doorjamb, and as she leans forward he suppresses an urge to trace the topography of brown and pink lines on her face, to satiate his curiosity about what her watery skin would feel like beneath his fingers. "So what would you change?" she asks.

"There are some punctuation errors. Misplaced semicolons, mainly."

"Mmm-hmm," she says.

"I don't think Dylan should even be using semicolons," Noah ventures.

"Oh, it's that moron college advisor at school. She suggested changes and just *compelled* Dylan to make them. She's such a twit."

"She's black," Tuscany offers.

"So what should we do?" Dr. Thayer asks. "We have to mail out his applications next month."

"Wait a second, Mom," Tuscany says. She chews a mouthful of melon, swallows. "Did *you* write the essay?"

"No, *Tuscany*," Dr. Thayer says. "Of course not."

Tuscany returns to the fruit bowl. Noah stares blankly at her, loses himself for a moment. She dangles her spoon over her melon absently, unfazed and maybe even bored by her mother's obvious cover-up.

"Let me talk to Dylan about it," Noah offers after a moment. "We'll see if we can come up with something more genuine."

Dr. Thayer drapes her clawed hand on Noah's arm. "Thank you," she mouths.

~

"So how do *you* feel about this essay?" Noah asks as he strides into Dylan's bedroom.

Dylan shrugs.

"Does it feel accurate to you?"

"I dunno. I haven't read it."

"Who wrote it?"

"My mom. Or maybe my college tutor. She's kinda dumb, I think. Is it any good?"

"It's really well written," Noah says. "But I don't know, like this . . ." He points to the second page. " 'Labeling can be as dangerous as any form of terrorism; in fact, merely associating oneself with a group is the first and primary act of violence.' "

"That makes absolutely no sense," says Dylan.

"It's your essay."

"Well, I dunno. I guess it sounds smart."

"I want you to take a look at it and then we'll try to make your own voice come through."

"No way. I don't know how to do that."

And he won't. The only way they gain ground on the essay portion of the writing test is when Noah finds a paper on Harriet Tubman that Dylan has previously memorized. The ex-slave becomes their crowning achievement. The "most important quality in a leader" is rebelliousness, as in the case of Harriet Tubman. The "national holiday you would create and why" is National Harriet Tubman Day. The "greatest invention of the twentieth century" is the documentary, because it allows us to learn about women like Harriet Tubman. Dylan possesses a true virtuosity at working in Harriet Tubman. He is fluent in the dead black woman; this is his greatest gift. But there is no place for Harriet Tubman in his college essay.

"I just wish I didn't have to *do* this shit," Dylan moans. Then he sits straight up, and in this new pose Noah suddenly doesn't know him. "There was this kid at my school," Dylan begins. Noah swivels in his executive chair to better listen. "He's at Yale now. He got like a 2340 or something when he first took the SAT. But then he took it like each month after."

"That's insane," Noah says. The SAT is composed of three 800-point sections—a 2340 is an almost perfect score.

"Wait, you don't know any of it. He took it for other people."

"How?" Noah forces his voice to remain under control.

"It's so easy. He just got a fake ID with his picture and some other kid's name, then he'd take the test for them, and the kid'd give him a shitload."

"How much?" Noah says. He says it quickly, sounds too eager, but Dylan seems not to notice.

"I dunno. A lot. So, he gets caught, 'cuz he takes the May test, and our *principal* is there, and she's like, 'Dude. You already got into Yale, why are you taking the SAT again?' So he got busted."

"Crazy."

"And the wildest thing? Get this—I was next! My mom had already written out the check! I would have been totally screwed."

Noah knows he should be outraged, but all he can think of is Dr. Thayer's firm angularity, the touch of her cool fingers on his arm.

"Isn't that crazy?" Dylan asks. "And now the check's just like sitting there."

Dr. Thayer appears in the doorway. Noah's breath catches; he suddenly has difficulty remembering where he is.

"What check?" she asks, her tone expressionless. The boys are silent. Noah studiously concentrates on the inner seam of his pants. "Noah," she says. "I need to talk to you before you go. Whenever you finish here."

"Get out of my room, Mom!"

"This isn't about you, Dylan. Unbelievable, I know."

"God! Get out of here!"

"Don't take that tone with me," Dr. Thayer says. There is no warning in her voice; this dialogue is for Noah's benefit. She leaves.

"Close the door!" Dylan yells. The door closes. He tosses a pillow at it. "Ugh, she's so annoying!"

"How's the practice test going to go tomorrow? Are you going to get us our 650?" Noah asks distractedly. Dylan's last four practice writing sections have been: 500, 440, 460, and 440.

"It's going to suck. It's too early in the morning."

For the first time, Noah is truly annoyed with Dylan. "It's at two P.M. The actual SAT will be at 8:30 *A.M.*"

Dylan, without taking his gaze off his laptop screen, waves a hand in the air. "Whatever."

The digital clock flashes 9:40. Noah already has his messenger bag over his shoulder. "Good luck, man," he says.

"'Bye."

~

Dr. Thayer is lying on her bed in a supine but stiff position, like a convalescent queen. Tuscany lingers in the shadows of the heavily curtained windows. Her eyes are large and wet.

"How is he doing?" Dr. Thayer asks as Noah steps into the doorway.

"Mom!" Tuscany wails.

"We'll finish this discussion later," Dr. Thayer says.

Tuscany bolts from the room, brushing past Noah. The door to the hallway bathroom slams.

"I'm hoping the pressure of the real thing will galvanize him," Noah says. He deploys an SAT word to shore up his defenses.

"He's not going to get our 650 on the writing portion, is he?"

"He might get close."

"There's a chance he won't need it after all," Dr. Thayer sighs. "We've got an in at the Sports Management Program at George Washington. Dylan's father's college roommate does their finances. I would prefer George Washington anyway. Dylan wants to stay in a big city. I think he's right in that. I can't imagine him anywhere else, frankly."

A hallway light turns off, and in the deepening gloom Dr. Thayer looks ill. She squints beneath the glare of her bedside lamp. "I have to do it all." Her voice catches. "He has no motivation."

"He's going to be okay," Noah says. His words sound pale, he knows. He is nervous and unsure of their truth.

"He would fail out without all of you tutors."

Noah shifts his weight. He thinks of his brother, and for a moment it seems impossible that anyone should get into college without an entourage. Dr. Thayer's eyes gleam at Noah across the room. She is baiting him, waiting for him to propose something. He isn't sure whether she wants him to kiss her or to offer to take the test for Dylan. He can't think of what to say.

"I just don't know what to do to make him work," Dr. Thayer finishes.

She is fishing for the hard truth, a confirmation that Dylan is totally hopeless. But Noah can't give it. Dylan is depressed and ruined but also pleasant, free of bitterness.

His life has a smooth glide to it; it is effortless. This will be Noah's job, to preserve a numb ruin that cannot be undone.

"We keep doing what we're doing, I guess," Noah says.

Dr. Thayer frowns and drums her fingertips on her breastbone. "There must be some other way for him to pass this test. Can you think of anything?"

"This test can be mastered," Noah says firmly.

Dr. Thayer shakes her head dully, as if to clear it. She smiles warmly into her bedsheets, and Noah can see on her lips the radiance that is lost inside her, the charisma she must have once had, that is now clouded by depression. She shifts her gaze to Noah and he is momentarily struck dumb. There is a question on her lips that is trapped somewhere. Pipes roar when Tuscany flushes the toilet.

"I'll see you next week?" Noah asks.

Dr. Thayer nods and picks up her novel.

Noah turns and slowly walks down the stairs. Was she going to ask him to take the test for Dylan? His heart races. The words *how much,* on the tip of his tongue throughout the conversation, now have nowhere to go.

chapter 2

Every Wednesday Noah buys the same groceries: one gallon of milk, a box of granola, oatmeal, toilet paper, seven cans of soup, and a bunch of bananas. The weekly totals vary from $24.50 to $24.75, depending on the size of the bananas. But now that he is a soon-to-be-jacked gym-goer, he figures he should shake up his diet. Near 130th Street, in one of the more menacing areas of Harlem, stands Fairway, a famous and fortresslike gourmet grocery store to which his students' parents take taxi safaris. These sallies are cloak-and-dagger: yellow cars intrepidly approach; couture couples scurry across the ten feet of Harlem asphalt, buy their groceries in the sanctuary inside, scurry back, and the cars retreat. Noah's approach, conversely, involves a brisk walk down Riverside Drive. He passes the Ralph Ellison monument surrounded by bleary-eyed homeless, and then follows Broadway to where the subway tracks surface at 135th Street. With the clacking rush of a train passing over rusty rails sounding to one side, Noah works his way between deserted and forgotten warehouses, along shattered windows papered with peeling posters for films that came out years before.

It is on such a street that Noah runs into Roberto. Since Roberto is wearing matching denim jacket and pants in late August, he is soaked in sweat. It is an odd sensation to feel underdressed on a Harlem street, but Noah feels insignificant in his T-shirt and ripped khaki shorts before Roberto's collected denim bulk. Should he say something? Noah is unsure if Roberto's all-welcoming manner is only maintained while he's on the job. But as soon as Roberto spots him, Noah's hand is lost in his.

"Noah, what you up to, man?"

"Oh, nothing, just buying food."

"That's cool."

They withdraw their hands and stare at each other, blinking in the sun, as if both struck dumb by their lack of common ground.

"What are you up to?" Noah asks.

"I'm off to work. You know. But tonight you wanna hang?"

"Yes." After his cautious refusal the week before, Noah is invigorated just by assenting; it is like plunging into a cold and bottomless lake.

"Awesome. I got a car, but I never wanna pay for parking so I'm always moving it, you know? Forget where it is right now. But why don't you just meet me when I get off work? I'll be on Ninety-first and Lex at like ten. We can go to one of the clubs you like."

"Right."

"Where do you like?" Roberto prompts.

Excited to have gotten to know a neighbor, Noah is reluctant to give up his in-the-know ruse just yet. Dylan will be his inspiration. "Lotus. Pangaea sometimes."

"Oh yeah? Wow. You're in some high circles, man."

"Oh, I don't know about that," Noah says, then adds "man" for good measure.

"No, this is real fly. I've been wantin' to change my scene, you know?"

"Cool," Noah says. The ruse has gone too far—he is suddenly nervous; his stomach tightens.

"Tonight, then!" Roberto draws his fist back as if to punch Noah. Noah dodges involuntarily, but Roberto only leads him through a complicated street handshake. Noah allows himself to be bullied through the steps like an incompetent dance partner, and misses Roberto's brown fist entirely when he tries to give it a manly swat at the end.

~

Tabitha's apartment is near Roberto's hair salon. Her parents (wealthy New Yorkers themselves, though of the Westchester variety) set her up in Yorkville, at the edge of the bubble of money in the Upper East Side, the border of the splash from the impact of billions of dollars flooding Fifth Avenue. Rents are lower here because Yorkville is farther from the subway and, although the occupants are similarly white and more or less well-to-do, many of them have to climb stairs to get to their apartments.

Tab's studio has been subdivided and partitioned into a two-bedroom apartment on the scale of a large dollhouse. She studies and sleeps on opposites sides of a temporary aluminum wall. The door opens right at the center of the partition, so when Noah enters he sees a riot of law books on one side, a metal beam in the middle, and Tabitha groggily rising from her bed on the other. Tab is wearing thick glasses that telescope her eyes, giving her face the aspect of a mole.

"Hey, babe," she says. She scratches beneath her T-shirt. Seeing her rise from the bed, lovely and laid back, gives Noah a pang of regret at not having fought for their relationship. He is tempted to sit beside her on the rumpled sheets—but after a year together they have managed to smoothly transition to a friendship, and he doesn't want to mess that up. She points to her eyeglasses. "Sorry, I'm starting torts reading. No time for contacts. Haven't had time to shower or anything for days, really."

Noah fixes her with a slow look and smiles.

"Um," Tab says, "that's pretty gross, huh? Oversharing. So what's up? Quit your job yet?"

"No," Noah says, jabbing his finger into her rib. "I didn't. Did you?"

"Hey, don't get all snarky. I'm just an idealistic student, or something. You're the one with the shady gig."

"What?" Noah allows his hand to remain on her lean torso, then removes it. "Bullshit. You had a tutor when you were in high school."

"Which doesn't exactly disprove my point. Who said I wasn't shady?" Tab says as she wades through dirty laundry to the kitchen.

"I do have huge issues with it," Noah calls. "But can I put my bag down before we go there?" Noah takes a seat at the foot of Tab's unmade bed, next to a teetering stack of law books with a rainbow of highlighters wedged between their pages. He hears the fridge suck open, and a beer comes flying at him from the kitchen area. He twists off the cap and takes a swig of foam while Tab approaches and sits next to him.

"Okay, important stuff first," Tabitha says. "I talked to my mom this morning. And it turns out the guy chairing the NYU American Studies Admissions Committee this year is an old friend of hers, and they take on tons of comp lit students."

"Really?" Noah asks, leaning forward. As he kneels in front of Tab, their knees touch. A remembered charge passes between them, and he pulls back an inch. "Wow." Tabitha's mother has always had an anthropological fascination for Noah, for the kid from rural Virginia who managed to make it to Princeton. She has a tendency to say, "Good for you," whenever Noah recounts anything he has done that involves money, down to going out to dinner. Tabitha's mother is third-generation Scarsdale.

"Only problem," Tab says, "is that the deadline has passed. She says you've got to get on this shit. Start applying. Or next year'll slip away too."

"Why is she so intent on this? I *will* apply. Just when I've paid down my debt. When my brother's taken care of."

"Let your brother take care of himself. You think you're doing him good, but you're just teaching him to depend on other people. Let yourself focus on yourself, you know? Indulge. Maybe it's this tutoring job," Tab says. "It's like sapping your karma."

"It's not like it takes that much time. It's just that I get mad sometimes seeing all that wasted wealth, I don't know . . ."

"It's just total bankruptcy of academic values."

Noah pauses before responding. Tabitha is relentlessly antagonistic, which added sexual chemistry to their relationship, but he often has to concentrate in order to tolerate her. He is rattled: he hates that she can make him question his convictions. "I don't know about 'total,' but yeah. This test is not meant to be prepared for. And yet it's the most important exam these kids will ever take, so their parents find a way. And it works. Going up three, four hundred points after a year of tutoring is huge. Who's Princeton going to take, some kid from a small town with an 1800, or the Manhattan kid with the 2200?"

"Neither," Tab snorts. "Twenty-two hundred. Please. Like either'd stand a chance. Try Michigan or Georgetown. But it's not as bad as you say, anyway. Princeton's only going to take, maybe, a hundred students from Manhattan. Your students are only competing against one another."

"But now it's obligatory," Noah says. "They all have to do it. I'm just filling two hours a week of these students' lives with crappy little rules that they'll never use again. They don't have time for their homework because they spend a hundred minutes with me learning strategies for a one-shot test. I just prime them to get unnaturally high scores for a short time. It's like I'm doping sprinters."

"So what? So you're not the cheerful little schoolmarm in the little red house," Tab says. "So you're not a professor yet, but a businessman. I don't accuse my banker or consultant friends, 'Money is the reason you're doing this, isn't it?' It's assumed—so get over it. You get paid absurdly well for a job that also gives you tons of crazy stories about people everyone loves to hate. Boohoo."

"Jesus," Noah says. "It's really sad too, Tab. This Dylan kid, I'm like basically his dad."

"You're no one's dad," Tab says. "You look eighteen. Try cousin."

"Whatever it is," Noah continues, "I'm his company. I'm all he's got. And that's a responsibility."

"Oh, he loves your company," Tabitha says, winking. She runs a hand down Noah's back.

Noah turns resolutely to her, tries to project to Tabitha how earnest he's feeling. He downs a swig of beer. "I'm a faker."

Tab lets her hand slip under Noah's shirt and play over his lower back. "You're not a faker, you're a player. And it's *hot.*" Noah can't resist the curve of her ass: his hand reaches into the back of her sweats.

"Tab . . ." Noah says after a moment. His resistance is halfhearted; his words get lost in the smokiness of Tabitha's hair.

She holds her hair back in one hand as he runs his hand around the length of the waistband of her pants so it rests at the front. His knuckles press into her abdomen. She talks into the base of his neck. "The real problem here is that you're just basically a servant, and that's what gets you riled up. This isn't about pity for Dylan," Tab says.

Noah gives Tab's head a long look, concentrates on the coolness of his beer beneath his fingers of one hand as his other hand slips farther into her pants. The reason he lost interest in her comes instantly to mind. She never knows when not to be honest. He shouldn't let this go any further, but . . . he's been lonely, and it's hard to turn down physical contact. If she wants to let him, he'll go ahead . . . "What I'm trying to say, here," Noah says, "is that I don't *want* Dylan to succeed. Because if he gets into school, that's one more spot that won't go to a kid who has had to fight to get opportunities, who has motivation and passion."

"So basically, you mean one less spot for *you,*" Tab says. Noah has untied the thick drawstring of her pants.

"Yes. I guess I do. Tutoring Dylan prevents another me from getting into school."

"This is great!" Tab says. "You're tutoring a kid that you secretly want to fail, and you're *jealous* of him too!"

Noah pauses, then nods and smiles. He stands still as Tabitha yanks his shirt over his head. Sex, for them, has always been about losing control, stopping thinking and just following the other's orders. Giving in was what brought him and Tabitha to bed again and again throughout college: two self-directed, ambitious kids allow the hand in their pants to take charge of pushing them forward. "I see what you mean by calling it creepy."

Tab takes off her glasses, leans her head against Noah's stomach, and wraps an arm snugly around his waist. She murmurs into the hints of hair at the top of his jeans, periodically cocking her head to look into his eyes. "Noah," she says. "Lawyers don't have to *want* their clients to win. Plastic surgeons don't have to *want* their patients to have fake boobs. Even academics don't have to *want* their theses about arsenic poisoning to be true. But they do it anyway, because it's their job, and they're good at it. Go out there, do the best you can. Just don't start *liking* these people. I see the gleam in your eyes, but you don't really want to become them. Go into these students' lives, learn what you can. Just remember to come back out."

And with that, Tab drops Noah's pants to his ankles.

~

Noah double-checks the address he scrawled down, because at 91st and Lexington he sees only what appears to be a nightclub, a midnight-purple doorway trembling to a pounding electronic beat. But the neon sign above reads "Space Hair," and when he opens the door he reveals a line of men cutting women's hair. The men are dressed as if in a downtown dance club, wearing platform shoes and stretch shirts. A couple of them dangle cigarettes from one hand as they cut with the other, all the time carrying on a furious conversation. The music is impossibly loud, and bright animations sparkle from TV screens. The women being attended to are brittle and blond, five Dr. Thayers of varying appearances of youth. A girl with spiked hair and dozens of leather accessories gives Noah a blank, appraising look. "Can I help you?"

"I'm just here to meet Roberto."

"Rob!" she shouts. The sound dissipates under the onslaught of the techno. "*Rob*!"

Roberto arrives from the back, dressed in black linen and silver chains. His hair is wet. He strides toward Noah with a broad smile, and engages him in another elaborate handshake. "Noah, how's it *going*? You look awesome."

"Yeah? Thanks." Noah is fairly certain that he does not "look awesome." He is still wearing the work clothes he put on that morning, and has rolled up his shirtsleeves in an attempt to look edgy. One of them has fallen back down.

Roberto leads Noah to his car, which is double-parked in front of a hydrant. He's "been runnin' out to check on it like every five minutes, but there haven't been any fires or nothing." It is a tiny Datsun that may have once been black but has sun-bleached to silver in broad stripes, giving it the appearance of an elderly metallic zebra. Noah is unsure exactly how old it is, but knows Datsun became Nissan in the early eighties. They fold inside.

"So where to?" Roberto asks. "Downtown? Lotus, maybe? The Coral Room?"

"Uh, I'm not sure about the scene on Wednesday nights, maybe we'd better go to one of your clubs."

"Oh man, I hoped you were going to show me the life!"

"What about *your* life?" Noah counters. He wonders: is it just that he balks at the $40 cover charges, or is he is embarrassed at the idea of showing up at one of Dylan's clubs in a Datsun, with Roberto in tow?

"My scene is like a total South-Central L.A. crossover, kinda lame for New York. Rowdy warehouse parties, sorta like raves but the crowd's older."

"Ah," Noah says knowingly.

As they race over the bridge into Queens, Roberto fishes around the backseat, one hand on the wheel, and retrieves a half-full bottle of gin. He hands it to Noah, who takes dutiful swigs, clenching his throat muscles to mask his tiny retches at each swallow of the warm poison. He wonders: if their lives up until then had been switched—if he had grown up in Latin America, and Roberto in Virginia—then would he be the one driving the bent Datsun, with the warm bottle of gin rolling in the back, and would Roberto be the privileged young man taking sips like a polite foreigner? He wonders at himself momentarily—why is he going anywhere with Roberto? But the question is instantly unimportant. Roberto represents something new. To someone rocketed from farmland into a university full of the nation's all-stars, the "new thing," the experience not yet lived, is always an improvement. Here he is, getting to know someone he would never have come across in Virginia or Princeton. Whatever he uncovers, however he might further the frontiers of what he knows, is bound to make him a better person.

They wind through broad empty streets, Roberto expertly navigating the bleak enormity of Queens. He stops before a warehouse in the middle of a deserted block. Music thuds from the building. One window is broken, and from another hangs a makeshift milk-crate basketball hoop. They get out of the car, and Roberto raps on a grate painted "Do Not Block Driveway." It rises, and they are admitted into a cavernous darkness.

Hundreds of bodies undulate to pulsing music, each outlined in blue neon light.

"It's a good scene tonight!" Roberto yells. Noah feels the words rather than hears them; the music is too loud. The beat fills his head and multiplies the effects of the gin; the world moves at an odd pace; he is already drunk.

Roberto darts to the bar and starts talking to a girl clad in vinyl. Noah approaches them nervously, as if joining a game of dodgeball. "I'm Noah!" he says, and makes a little cool-guy dance move that he instantly regrets. "No-ah. What's your name?" he shrieks to another girl.

The girl shakes her head savagely. She either can't hear him or, he realizes, perhaps doesn't speak English. She is wearing so much pink gloss that her lips join like two wet sticks of bubble gum, and slide over each other uncontrollably. She is pretty, but looks at Noah with such pliancy that, more than anything else, he is scared for her well-being. Roberto has led his girl to the dance floor, where they gyrate amid the crowd, in full body contact, the girl jerkily waving her hands above her head as though keeping her balance on rough seas. Noah stands by the other girl and sips his drink. *What do you do in the city?,* his usual cocktail party prompt, seems inappropriate here. He should be talking about indie electronica acts, or piercings. He sips again. The blue liquid seems to find the gin in his stomach a good playmate, and the two heave and frolic together.

After a burst of light-headed inspiration Noah and the girl are on the dance floor, flailing and surging and soon splattered with other people's sweat. In his intoxication he allows his intellect to surge forward, doesn't check his pretension: the music, Roberto, the girls surrounding them, all start to take on profound implications, bear layers of meaning and insight. He is suddenly obsessed with the clinging but forlorn manner in which a worn tank top sits on the shoulders of the girl with whom he is dancing. He puts a hand on her shoulder and the room spins slightly around the cotton strap, as though it were the axis at the center of the pivoting club. Emboldened by the alcohol, he fingers the fragile fabric, the loose threads at the seam where some factory worker in Ecuador inserted her stitches, the softened holes of the jersey material. The girl smells like sprints, of saline and sweat and human oil. He tugs gently on her hair and she pulls her head back and stares up at him as they dance. Then she lowers her gaze to his chest and he realizes that she is nervous and at that moment it seems sublime, that they should both be shy and unsure of what to do next. The world continues to pivot, and as his thoughts further fragment he experiences the abstract, disembodied sensation that he will need to throw up soon.

Noah watches the broad triangle of Roberto's back disappear into the crowd. He and the girl press into the corrugated aluminum wall of the warehouse and alternate watching the crowd and making out. She is smooth and slick in his arms; he is aroused but the weight on top of his head is getting heavier and his eyelids creep toward one another. The party goes dark whenever he blinks, only slowly reappears after he opens his eyes.

He doesn't know how much time has passed before he next opens his eyes, but he is in Roberto's car, his face pressed against the polyester felt of the backseat door. The Datsun seems impossibly full of girls, all giggling and yelling. He feels them on all sides, enjoys the pressure of their legs against his. Two different-color arms are draped across his lap. He wants to speak, but that would require him to focus his eyes, and he can't quite manage it. When the car door opens, a girl separates from the group and she and Noah take turns dragging each other up the stairwell to his waiting bed.

~

Noah's next-day appointment with Dylan isn't until two, but even so, he has difficulty getting up in time. He wakes up alone in his unairconditioned attic apartment with sunlight flooding his bed. It is a hot September afternoon, and although he is red-faced and radiating heat, he isn't sweating at all: hangover. He creaks out of bed and smacks his dry tongue around his mouth experimentally. The fluids in his brain seem to have a rhythm to them, and jostle when he moves, like a wave pool. Noah quaffs a half gallon of water that he just manages to keep in his stomach, downs a handful of aspirin and a multivitamin, and at the last moment remembers to grab Dylan's practice test results before he rushes out the door. There is no trace of the girl from the night before, except that the toilet seat is down.

The heated pavement is hot enough to have softened, and seems to stick to Noah's feet as he passes along it. He is relieved to throw himself into the crisp air of the bus. He pulls out Dylan's score report: this weekend, after two months of tutoring, he got a 450 out of 800, up a pitiful 30 points from his diagnostic test, still 70 points below the low national average and nowhere near the 650 Dr. Thayer is set on. Dylan is a senior, and so the last test he can take in time for college applications is next week. In the sentence improvement section Dylan has elected to change the sentence

Classical musicians are putting alluring portraits on their recordings, increasing sales through both musicianship and sex appeal.

to

Increasing sales through musicianship and also through sex appeal, and now putting alluring portraits on their recordings, they are classical musicians.

Noah rests his head against the cool blue plastic of the bus as he watches the 99¢ stores and bodegas pass by the window and imagines that he is instead off to the breezy tree-lined reservoir behind his house in Virginia, his notebook and a girlfriend in hand.

It is a Sunday, so Dr. Thayer is sure to be away. The doormen call up to the apartment but no one answers. "Ya know," one of them says, "Dylan's probably home and just sleeping or watching TV. Doesn't want to get up."

The "social/staff" card Dr. Thayer gave him at their first meeting is folded into Noah's wallet, but he can't will himself to flash his stenciled iron at the doormen. "Dr. Thayer told me to call her on her cell if he doesn't answer. I'll just try her."

Dr. Thayer doesn't answer her phone, but her voicemail prompt, in sultry and practiced tones, instructs Noah to leave a message.

Hi, Dr. Thayer, this is Noah. I'm supposed to meet with Dylan at four, and it's four-fifteen. I know you're in the Hamptons, but if you get this message and can try reaching Dylan, that would be great. Thanks!

Noah sits on a leather bench to wait. He presses his hands against the marble of the wall, relishes its smooth coldness against his throbbing fingertips. He remembers he was supposed to call his family the night before. Crap. He yawns as he leafs through Dylan's test. Dylan has elected to replace

> *The jazz singer was famous because of his father's enduring popularity.*

with

> *In that his father was popular, and enduring, the jazz singer being famous was due to the fact that his father was also the same way.*

On the essay, when prompted to "Agree or Disagree that Dreams Hinder Reality," Dylan has chosen to argue what Noah loosely deems the negative:

> *To often we dont allow people to hinder there dreams. Hindering can be the only thing that gives a person hope. When we take that away, with recklessness the dreams, their no longer hindered but killed. In her speeches Harriet Tubman spoke on her own hinder~~ing~~ance and inspires women in America too emanceapate.*

Mental note: Model the verb *to hinder* during the session.

Noah yawns again. The doormen's phone rings. One of them answers and then nods at Noah. "Go on up."

The front door of the apartment is open. Noah cautiously wanders through, his arms clasped behind his back like a respectful museum patron's, until he finds Dylan seated on his bed, eating sesame chicken with a heavy silver fork and watching a baseball game.

"Hey," Noah says.

Dylan looks at Noah accusingly. "I got totally nailed."

"What were you doing?"

"I dunno, I was totally here, I dunno what happened. But my mom's like, 'DYLAN! You asshole, go get the door.' " Dylan is pissed for one more moment but then smiles. "She's so wack," he laughs.

Noah puts his bag down on the floor, and his head takes to renewed throbbing.

"You look like hell," Dylan says.

"Thanks. Thank you."

"I'm just saying." Dylan looks at Noah with friendly admiration. "What did you *do* last night?"

Noah pauses—are teachers allowed to go down this road? "I went to this party with a guy from my neighborhood. It was in some warehouse in Queens, really crazy."

"Wait, a guy from your neighborhood, like from Harlem?"

"Yeah," Noah says.

"*Cool.* What was the party like?"

"You know, they had a bar just sort of thrown together against the wall. Really strong drinks." Noah pauses. For the moment the drinks are all he can think of. He wonders about the name of the girl he took home.

"What kind of scene?" Dylan asks, leaning forward. He hands Noah the discarded chopsticks.

"Um, mixed. Lots of ages. Pretty chill." Noah pinches a clot of chicken.

"That's awesome. I'm so tired of all the petty crap I go to, you know? Every night I'm like, 'No, I don't wanna go,' but I go anyway and it sucks, but I guess it's fun too."

"You want to know how you did this weekend?"

"What do you mean, like if everyone at the parties was into me?"

"No, on your test."

"Oh. Yeah, I guess."

"You got 450 out of 800."

"Is that good?"

"No, not really."

Dylan laughs. "I told you I sucked."

"Aren't you nervous? The test is in a few weeks."

Dylan thinks about it for a moment, then begins writing a text message on his phone. "No, I don't *think* I am. Should I be?"

"Well, it all depends on how well you do in sports this season, I guess."

"If I was someone else I would be pissed that I'm going to get into George Washington just 'cuz I can play ball."

"If I *were* someone else," Noah corrects.

"Mmm-hmm," Dylan says, distracted. He finishes his message. "If you were someone else you'd what?"

Noah can't help but smile at the small success of the afternoon. Dylan has not only used the word *petty* but also has used the subjunctive, and put himself in someone else's shoes to boot.

A girl's voice carries down the hallway. "Dylan? Did you like see the money Mom left?"

Dylan smiles and smirks in the direction of the voice. "Yeah," he yells, "but I went out last night. Getting a table cost two hundred and fifty dollars."

The door opens and Tuscany is standing before them. "You jerk-off! That was for my stupid printing fees."

"The money in the fruit bowl?"

Tuscany emits a squeaky growl, then adjusts her shredded couture T-shirt.

"Well, whatever, give her a call. I'm sure there's more somewhere," Dylan says.

"*You* give her a call, ass-wipe. You're the one who spent all my money on your moron friends."

"I don't even remember spending any, it just kind of disappeared." He stares down Tuscany, as if daring her to find a hole in his counterargument.

Tuscany plucks the portable receiver from the fax machine on Dylan's desk and hurls it at him.

"Jesus," he says, "does this mega-bitch act turn all your boyfriends on?"

"Call her. *Call her.* I'm serious, Dylan."

Dylan toys with the buttons and then, somewhat cowed, dials. Tuscany looks around the room in outrage and then notices Noah. "Oh, hey," she says.

"Mom? Yeah, it's Dylan . . . no, I don't know where Dad is . . . but Tuscany's got like a problem she's too scared to tell you about. Yeah, she's outta money."

"Ooh! I hate you!" Tuscany squeals.

Dylan grins into the phone and runs a hand through his dark hair. "So anyway, she was wondering if there's any more . . . I don't know where it went—" He puts a hand over the receiver and looks pointedly at Tuscany. "She wants to know where it went, *trouble—*" he whispers, then returns to his mother. "Actually I think I prob'ly spent it. You should really leave separate piles, it's fucked that you never do that. Whoa. Whoa! Jesus." He turns to Noah and Tuscany, a broad smile on his face. "You gotta hear this."

He clicks on the speakerphone.

"—not just un*limited,* you can't just keep on like that, I don't know why you think you can get away with this, just always *asking for more,* but it's *rude,* Dylan, it's rude to me, it's rude to yourself, it's rude to Tuscany, it'd be rude to your father if he knew about it. You don't understand how lucky you are that we have enough money for you to go out to these places every night, how *impressive* that is, how *grateful* you should be. Put Tuscany on. Tussy, are you on the line?"

"Yes, Mom," Tuscany says.

"I'm telling you this so that you can get it before Dylan. There's some more money in the second master bedroom hallway chandelier."

"That one!" Dylan yells, punching the bed in mock frustration. "I never thought of that one."

"Thanks, Mom!" Tuscany calls. She grins flirtatiously at Dylan. "Asshole." She darts out of the room.

Dylan, a finger over his lips, turns his laptop toward Noah. He has typed: *T's strting a mag for local slutz momz paying.*

"That's so unfair, Mom," Dylan says into the speakerphone.

"What's unfair?" A pause. "Why can I hear myself? Am I on speakerphone?"

"Yeah, Noah's here, I wanted him to hear."

"Oh, Jesus Christ, Dylan." Dr. Thayer hangs up.

Dylan laughs. "She's hilarious," he says, as a frat brother might say about a new rush who puked in the bushes.

Noah leafs through his tutoring papers as Dylan picks at a scab on his knee. Today they are to cover verb tense. He isn't sure that Dylan can even tell him what a verb is, much less a verb tense, but plunges in anyway. "At the party Jamie noticed that she forgot to put socks on," he prompts.

Dylan scratches his chest. "And?"

"And what's wrong with the sentence?" Noah writes it out on a spiral notebook and hands it to Dylan.

"At . . . the . . . party . . . Jamie . . . noticed . . . that . . . she . . . forgot . . . to . . . put . . . socks . . . on. Nothing's wrong. It's bullshit if you're going to tell me something is wrong with that."

"Well, you have to consider that—"

"Oh, wait, I think I know. Jamie's actually a guy?"

"No."

"Okay . . . Jamie's not really at the party, right? She's like somewhere else."

"No."

"Oh. Maybe, you have to say that Jamie is like being forgetful, before you say that she forgets something? So that it makes more sense? Like 'Jamie, forgetful, forgot to put socks on'? " To the end, Dylan is a resourceful kid.

"No, you have to put one of the verbs in the past perfect," Noah says. "You remember, we called it the 'really-past.' Which action happens first? Would you say 'had noticed,' or rather 'had forgotten'?"

"Who's hotter, Ashlee or Jessica?"

"Dylan, man, come on—"

"I know who you're going to say. Ashlee."

"No way. Jessica."

"Cool. Totally. Beyoncé or Ashanti?"

"Beyoncé, clearly. Now, what if Beyoncé had forgotten her socks at a party?"

"You never give up."

"That's my job."

Dylan lies face down on his bed. His voice is muffled by his duvet. "Yeah, why do you do this? This must be totally boring for you, always doing the same stuff with every kid."

"You're right, the material's always the same, but you guys are all different, you know? So that's what makes it interesting. I'm going be a professor. Helping you guys is enough for me." Noah kicks off his shoes and rests his feet on Dylan's bed, hoping to mask his uncertainty with a display of comfort. Is that really why he wants to be a professor?

"You're like a scientist, just studying all of us. That's what gets you off."

That doesn't feel too good. Particularly since Tab has already basically told him the same thing.

"I wouldn't do it if I was you—whoa, if I *were* you," Dylan says. "There must be something better to do."

"Umm, no, not really, unless I want to go into business and work a hundred hours a week."

"Yeah, like my dad."

Once again, Noah has forgotten that Dylan has a father. But the fathers are absent in most of the families he tutors—only the rare millionaire is also a family man.

"You could go to grad school," Dylan tries.

Dylan is giving him career advice. "I'm *applying* to grad school," Noah says. "But I have *loans,* man." Noah holds his tongue. He feels oddly comfortable around Dylan, and almost told him about Kent.

"Right, those," Dylan says. "Forgot." He spears a piece of sesame chicken and then lets it drop into the Styrofoam container. He clicks over to the Chinese delivery website. "It's gotta be fresh," he explains.

~

When Noah returns from teaching he realizes he has left the overhead light on in his apartment. For some reason that idea, that the solitary bulb has been needlessly shining in his empty apartment all day, induces a wave of loneliness. He props himself up against the counter and stares at his dirty cereal bowls, washes one and then puts it back into the sink, lies on his new couch. He stares at the blue-brown floral print of his exposed mattress. There is no history to anything in the room. An emptiness stretches between everything. Noah pulls out his phone and dials.

"Hey, Noah, Mom's not here."

"It's okay, what's up?"

"Not much. Just kind of sitting around." Kent offers nothing for Noah to talk to him about, and Noah knows he will only hold further attempts at conversation against him. He can imagine Kent complaining to his friends that his brother acts like he's his "fuckin' father."

"How was school?" Noah persists.

"Pretty good."

A pause. Noah just listens to the static of the Virginia–New York connection. Finally his brother speaks. "I met with that counselor for the first time on Monday. She's pretty cool."

"Oh yeah? Why?"

"She says it's not my fault. That I just learn differently. Like I'm a well that's perfectly fine, it's just missing a bucket."

"You're just missing a bucket?"

"That's what she said."

"Well, that sounds good."

"Yeah, maybe all this'll work." Kent takes on a distant, practiced tone, as if puzzling over how to light kindling.

"Talk to you later, okay?" Noah says.

Noah closes his phone and sits on his unmade bed. The sheet has pulled away from a corner and his knee rests against the bare coarseness of the mattress. He's angry at his brother and he doesn't know why. It is four P.M. on a Sunday—his friends are all either getting ahead at work or finishing up lazy brunches. He could read over his applications but he can't summon the will today. Studying literature seems like an inconsequential intellectual game. It takes Noah an inordinate amount of effort to pull on his workout pants and head out the door.

Noah decides to devote his thirty minutes on the treadmill to figuring out how to further his teaching career. He seems to remember having it all figured out in the past, but now he can't remember what his strategies for success were. His application essays all read like hollow gamesmanship now, scholarly sleight of hand. He was so excited about going back to school before; he would gush to his friends about again being part of the security of an institution. And there was always the looming, secret reason: professors are esteemed, part of the upper class. Since he had no inheritance coming to him and no desire for business, teaching at a university seemed the best way to make it into a more genteel world. But now all his energy is devoted to coping with Dylan, Cameron, and the rest. That very genteel world he craves to enter has made him a governess.

As he stares into the mirror in front of the treadmill, the drawstring of his CK athletic pants bobbing as he sprints, he realizes that he has redeveloped a preoccupation with coolness that he thought he had abandoned in high school. Perhaps it has come from hanging around teenagers all the time. He constantly thinks of social capital, wonders who has the most access to what. In his adolescence, coolness had seemed like a foolish goal—it was myopic, didn't offer anything beyond the rewards of being liked. Even as he became popular he saw it as an end in itself, and a delusory one at that. But here in Manhattan, a world through which live supermodels wander, and where those one sees on the streets are tackling not the intimations of success but rather the pinnacles of it, coolness becomes a valid objective. Investment bankers aren't ex-nerds—they are ex-partiers. The high schoolers here who are cool don't eventually show up fat and sunburned at the class reunion. These cool kids attend fundraisers, start magazines, date the children of their parents' influential friends. They are making connections, becoming urbane, adept at making people like them and also adept at seeing the Manhattan truth around them—that for those with the desire to further themselves, success *is* being cool. Dylan has mastered coolness, and for all of his knowledge about the SATs, Noah still has to work at it, and is jealous. Yes, he admits to himself as he mops his brow, he is jealous.

Noah speeds the machine up to 8.4 miles per hour and races along for a few seconds before the power goes out. One moment he is staring into the greasy mirrored wall of the gym, and the next the sudden stop of the treadmill has thrown him to the ground, flat on his face and struggling against a rush of pressure in his head. The lights have gone out, and around him Noah hears the moans of similarly incapacitated weighty Hispanic men. They all stand, groggily stare at one another in the fettered sunlight filtering through the dirty windows on Broadway, and file out of the building.

Roberto is in front of the door, massive and agitated, ineffectually guiding men into the street. "Noah, man, isn't this wild? How you feeling? You were so gone last night. It's amazing you didn't piss yourself."

"Was hoping the workout would purge the hangover. Didn't really work. What happened?"

"Dunno. I think the power's gone out. Did you see that bitch I was dancing with last night? So fucking hot."

"So what do we do?"

"I'm going out with her again. You could go out with yours again. We'll like all get our bang goin'."

The sun pounds against Noah's head. He can't process "Bang goin' "; it sounds like a phrase from an Asian language. "No, I meant what should we do about the power outage?"

"Oh, go home, I guess. You're near Riverside, right? We'll walk together."

They pass along Broadway, through a milling crowd of children playing stickball with a steel pipe, vendors selling sliced mangoes out of grocery carts, quartets of old men playing dominoes on card tables, bodega owners hawking melting ice cream. The power outage has imbued the street with a festive energy, as though an important parade is about to begin. Noah feels a sudden and intense affection for his neighborhood, its willingness to make anything out of the ordinary into a cause for revelry.

Noah and Roberto have been chatting outside Noah's building for a few moments when Roberto says, "Hey, you got any candles? It's going to be dark soon. You'll be like dark, too."

Noah doesn't own any candles. Already he is aware of the darkening rectangles of the apartment windows in contrast to the street glowing in the waning afternoon light, the groups of young men collecting outside—unknown, some of them disapproving. He feels a shiver of trepidation. He lingers on his doorstep, fingers his keys, imagines holing up alone in a corner of his apartment, watching the sky turn black.

"Do *you* have any candles?" he asks Roberto.

Roberto lives in a dilapidated brownstone a few blocks away. The buildings on either side of his are boarded up with graffitied plywood and hunch over the street like sullen gargoyles. Roberto jiggles the doorknob and then pounds on the door. "Mom!"

A series of thumps issue through the brownstone's thick door, and Noah can trace the progress of someone very heavy passing from the top floor to the bottom. The door swings open to a woman large enough to obscure the hallway behind her. Her housedress barely contains her spherical body. She grips the doorframe as if for balance; her corpulence is probably new to her—she bobs like a tethered balloon, and her features are still those of a very thin woman, sharp, almost crustacean.

"Mom, hey, this is Noah. A friend of mine."

"No-ah," the woman says. "I am He-ra. I am Roberto's mother."

"Oh, hello," Noah says.

Roberto says something to Hera in rapid Spanish. She responds, in tones variously furious and saccharine. Suddenly Hera steps back from the doorway and the three of them pass up a stairwell lit only by stray afternoon light. Dust bunnies and McDonald's wrappers glimmer from the corners. Noah trails Hera and Roberto silently, like a younger brother. They maintain an unbroken string of foreign exclamations. Hera swings open the door. She strikes her knuckles against the wall when she expansively sweeps Noah and her son inside. "Welcome. Please come in," she says.

Noah thanks her, and they pass into a shabbily furnished but very neat living room. Roberto disappears into the bathroom as Hera guides Noah to a frayed dusty-pink armchair. She lights a candle that illuminates a yellowed paper perched on the arm of the chair, its headlines in an eastern European script. "Oh!" says Noah, despite himself.

"Yes?" says Hera.

Noah points to the paper. "I assumed you were Hispanic," he laughs.

Hera looks stricken and raises a tremulous fist before her mouth. "Hispanic? I and Roberto?"

"Uh, yeah, I just figured, with the neighborhood and everything?" Noah can't quite determine why he feels like such an asshole.

"But our names! Roberto. No *Hispanic* should have this name. And Hera." At the mention of her own name, as if invoking the fearsome power of the goddess herself, Hera seems about to fly into a rage; her cheeks heave; she draws herself up to full height.

"Your names are very nice."

"I chose them so carefully. They have roots! Real classics."

Roberto surfaces from the bathroom and sees his brewing mother. "What's going on?"

"Nothing," Hera barks.

Noah smiles obliquely.

"Now it is my turn," Hera declares, and enters the bathroom. The door slams.

"My mom is like a total nut," Roberto says, wiping his hands on a towel slung over the top of a door. "You have no idea. She's like totally nuts. Olena talks to her, but I refuse."

"You've all lived together for a while?"

"Yah, we're saving money for my sister to go to school, and it's cheaper to live together in like one place, you know?" He looks Noah up and down and then nods approvingly as he throws himself on the couch. "You'd like her. Her name is Olena, even though Mom's gonna tell you it's Titania. You want a drink or something?"

"No thanks," Noah says, momentarily distracted by the ridiculous vision of a female Roberto.

"She never goes out. My mom. It's like she's completely unsocial. She just sits at home and plays cards with my sister whenever she's home. Which is like never, 'cuz Olena works all day."

"What does she do?"

"My sister? I dunno, waiting tables and stuff. I think she's working at a dry cleaner right now."

Noah reclines in his seat. Roberto proceeds to recount his day, which involved a lunch date with a girl who turned out to be (the epithet alternates throughout the telling) a bitch/snob, and then a full-body wax ("Man, I know it sounds swishy, but it's totally necessary for me, I'm furry like an animal, and I'm goin' on this beach trip with a hot bitch on Saturday"). The bathroom door finally opens and Hera emerges. A great cloud of perfumed air rolls over the room as she closes the door. She has done up her hair, and has splashed such bright circles of rouge and eye shadow that her face gives the impression of a painter's palette. She casts Noah an overly gracious smile, a caricature of Dr. Thayer's sophisticated hospitality.

"Noah," she declaims, wiping her hands on the ample material of her housedress. "What will you have to drink?"

Noah's three demurrals are refused, and Hera finally succeeds in pressing a tumbler of half-melted ice into his grip, which Roberto then fills to the brim with a grain alcohol from a ceramic jug rummaged out from beneath the sink. Noah's stomach, still testy from the abuse of the night before, lurches as he takes a sip. He holds the glass far away from his body.

"Do you like it?" Hera asks, eyes wide.

"Yes, very much," Noah lies. "Where is it from?"

"Italy," Hera says.

"Albania," Roberto says, his voice overlapping his mother's. He turns to Noah. "We are from Albania. Came here via Italy."

"Oh, *Roberto*," Hera sniffs. "We are prac-tic-ally Italians."

"My name isn't really Roberto," Roberto says. There is a naughty, charged smile on his face; he is baiting his mother, playing at something illicit.

"His name is prac-tic-ally Roberto," Hera amends.

"And her name isn't really Hera."

This is not too surprising to Noah.

"Why do you try to hurt your gentle mother?" Hera asks Roberto. "In America, we might as well be Italians."

To this Roberto simply turns away from his mother and sips his drink, hiding his face behind his glass.

"You are one of Roberto's friends?" Hera asks hopefully. "You are much better than these others, these dark-skinned men and these women with too many earrings."

Noah glances up quickly at Roberto, but he doesn't protest. In fact, he nods almost imperceptibly.

"All the time I am saying to him, I am saying, 'Roberto, why don't you spend your time with people of class, of *culture*?' Here in New York, those people are white! We don't choose this, it is true. So I wonder why he doesn't have more white friends." A pause. "You seem very nice. What do you work at?"

"Oh, I tutor for a college entrance exam on the Upper East Side."

"Roberto does work in the Upper East Side too," Hera says proudly.

"I know," Noah says, nodding slightly to acknowledge that, yes, this is indeed very impressive.

"Your job sounds very interesting," Hera says. "You must have rich clients. Are they raised well? Have money? Fifth Avenue, Madison Avenue, that is where the truly great live, not"—she gestures out the window disdainfully—"here."

"My students are wealthy, yeah," Noah says evasively.

"Yes," Hera says dreamily. She lays a hand on Roberto's muscular leg. "I have given up on my Roberto ever getting us that. But Titania—you should meet her, No-ah. So bright. Beautiful. A jewel."

Hera stares at Noah with bright eyes, concentrating all of her descriptive power. "Titania is lovely. We will be sure that you meet her one day, you will see . . ."

He takes another sip and is surprised to find that he has finished the glass, that his body accepted the cupful of toxin. Hera pours him another tumblerful.

The electricity returns just before midnight. A fringed lampshade leaps into glow above their heads, and they cheer its reentrance like an engagement announcement, sloshing their drinks together and yelling.

When Noah returns home, three new messages are waiting on the cell phone he left charging on his bed:

Noah, hi! This is Dr. Thayer, Dylan's mother. Call me, please. Have a request for you.

Noah. This is Dr. Thayer, Dylan's mother. Bad news. Call me as soon as you get this.

Noah. Call me now. Thank you. [A pause.] This is Dr. Thayer, Dylan's mother.

Noah hesitates: it is almost midnight. But he remembers that Dr. Thayer is always up and reading when he leaves Dylan late, recalls her indented, sleep-circled eyes. She'll be awake. He opens his address book and sifts through the Thayer numbers: office, office fax, home fax, Dylan/Tuscany/Dr. Thayer's cell, Dylan/Tuscany/Dr. Thayer's home lines.

"Hello?" she answers, her voice both husky and sharp, like a talking raven.

"Dr. Thayer? Hi, this is Noah, I hope I'm not disturbing you."

"Yes. Noah. I wasn't sure if you'd bother to call me tonight."

"Of course I would. You sound preoccupied. What's going on?"

"I don't know if you noticed, but Dylan hasn't been doing well at all on this thing. I just saw the pile of score reports in his desk drawer—I don't know if it was his idea to hide them from me, or if you came up with that brilliant idea together—but he's doing horribly."

"I've walked you through his test results each week, I know they're low, but—"

"The test is Saturday, Noah, not next month, not next May, but Saturday. What are you going to tell me when it turns out that I've spent $15,000 to have Dylan's score *stay crappy*? His whole future is riding on this. I know you're trying your best, I'm *sure* you're trying your best, but you're young, you don't have experience with cases like Dylan. He needs to be *motivated.*"

"He does need motivation," Noah says, trying to keep the dryness out of his voice.

"So what? It's his fault? You're what, basically telling me that Dylan is unteachable?"

"No, of course I'm not—"

"Because you wouldn't be the first. Everyone's given up on this kid. Sometimes I think they're right." She pauses. Noah listens to her breathe into the phone. "I hope you don't think I'm blaming you, Noah."

Noah lies on his unmade bed, finding tired comfort in the softness of the worn sheets. How different this conversation might be, he thinks, if Dr. Thayer could see where he was as she spoke, could know the tremendous rift between their apartments, their beds. She probably imagines him, at worst, in a Tribeca loft.

". . . I just think, well, I've done everything, and still nothing helps," Dr. Thayer is saying. Of course her concerns come back to her. For a moment Noah is furious that she is unable to focus on her children. But then his heart quakes a moment when he realizes that, otherwise, no one in the world would think of her well-being. Although she has millions of dollars and a phalanx of staff, she is still the classic single mom, like Noah's: fixated on helping her offspring, and no one with whom to discuss her own troubles. All the concern she sends toward her children dissipates, is absorbed and never returned. And then she spends her afternoons with her clients, taking on the woes of her friends' children without ever releasing her own troubles. But what can he do to help her? And what does she want him to do to help her?

"This test is hard for Dylan, yes, but he should do fine whatever he gets. He's got a lot of support." Noah crinkles his nose at some ineffable irony in the last bit.

"Well, that brings me to my request. He's had two SAT tutors before you, and unlike them at least you've stayed around. I want him to know I've done everything I can for him, that's why we've kept you around this far. You stick with him, you give him a sense that we're both there for him. I want each of my children to feel that. Which is why I want you to help out Tuscany."

"Tuscany!" Noah had been afraid Dr. Thayer was going to ask him to come over for a drink, or to take the SAT for Dylan. And he wasn't about to go back to that dark spot in his history.

"Yes. She's applying to boarding school this year and needs to take that test, what is it called, the ISEE, to get in. It's three months away, so that means we'll need how many sessions a week, three?"

Three sessions a week. That means unheard-of luxury: that means health insurance. Noah will start on Monday.

chapter 3

Tuscany Thayer, fifteen, attends Moore-Pike Girls Academy. Among the teenage men of Noah's acquaintance her school is known as Whore-Like Girls Academy. The doormen snort when Noah announces whom he has come to see.

"We have orders. No boys for Ms. Thayer without Dr. Thayer present."

"I tutor Dylan as well," Noah says, incredulous.

"Right. Head on up."

In the elevator Noah crosses his arms, plants his hands in his armpits. He removes them, inspects his dress shirt for wrinkles. Roberto has arranged a double date for that night.

Noah turns off his phone and has reached Tuscany's floor by the time the power-down graphic flickers off. The door swings open to reveal a mass of gray silk. Dr. Thayer has one hand hitched on the door; she wears an evening gown and slightly parted lips, as if a photographer has just called out, *now, you're a tigress!*

"Hello, Noah," she purrs. "Welcome."

Noah, momentarily speechless, rustles the manicured leaf of her hand.

"Come in, come in," she says with faux urgency, as if Noah were standing in a blizzard. "Poor thing," she tuts inexplicably.

In the few days since Noah has last been there, the apartment has been redecorated. The front hall is impossibly dark, silver candlesticks and a chandelier providing only meager, flickering illumination. The tile floor, glossy black and white, stretches in all directions. Giant ottomans, upholstered in a gray silk that matches the hue of Dr. Thayer's gown to an astonishing exactness, populate the adjoining living room.

Noah blinks, twice.

"H-how are you," he stammers.

"Look what we did! It's our winter changeover," Dr. Thayer replies, gesturing expansively.

"How are you?" Noah repeats.

"I'm sorry I didn't answer the phone at first . . ." Dr. Thayer starts.

Noah waits. Dr. Thayer smiles politely. There is no second half to the sentence.

"That's okay. How has your day been?" Noah's pulse is racing: there is something uncanny here. Usually he talks to a Fifth Avenue parent about their primary common experience, namely being stuck in taxis, then maneuvers the conversation rapidly and prodigiously to authors or philosophers, at which point the parent grows bored and releases him. But Dr. Thayer wants to Talk.

"Oh, it has *been*!" She laughs lightly, carefully tossing her hair. She has more vitality today than she has ever expressed before. She is decaying and gorgeous, like Snow White's Evil Queen if she had tanned and smoked a pack a day. "I've been taking it easy today. Canceled my Westchester sessions—I do some pediatrics psych consulting, did I tell you?—because I'm going out with my husband tonight. We're going to see *Love* on Broadway, have you been?"

Noah hasn't been.

"Oh, it should be good, I think. I still get starstruck to see those movie men on the stage." She makes an ostensibly sexy shimmy that is jerky and forced, painful-looking. "Bang. Get me going even after all these years."

"Any plans after? Are you making a whole evening out of it?" Noah swallows.

"Oh yes, we have reservations before and after. Two dinners." She makes an I'm-bloated gesture.

"Where is Tuscany?" he asks.

Dr. Thayer is taken aback. "Oh, Tuscany? Good luck with her!"

And, with a swift rustle of silk, Dr. Thayer is gone.

This is unexpected. Noah takes a step forward and stops. He pivots. On one side looms the brilliant white and silver kitchen. The maid, Fuen, is scrubbing the spotless wall. From the set of her face Noah has always assumed that she either doesn't speak English or pretends not to in order to avoid being subjected to guests who might ask her for service. On the other side is the wide, ottoman-overrun living room. Noah wanders in, among and through the monumental furniture. The silk tassels of the ottomans swish as he passes.

Noah starts down a long, obscure hallway, daunted but also feeling intrepid: he is wandering alone in an unknown land; it is as though he should be brandishing a torch or a sword. As he stalks down the hallway it comes to him that the doormen's reservations about letting him up aren't that bizarre—his questing for Tuscany could easily seem a seduction. A lean, large-framed man with the wholesome polar-fleece aesthetic of a summer camp counselor raps softly on the bedroom door of a fifteen-year-old beauty . . .

Noah hears a polyphonic cell phone ring. He raps his knuckles on the partially opened door. It opens fully to reveal Tuscany. "Oh, hey."

She wears tiny purple pants that don't quite make it to the top of her exposed hipbones. Her hair is moussed out into a grand arc that curves over her off-the-shoulder sweatshirt. She beckons Noah into her room. They stand in the center. She plays with a strand of hair, twirls it around an orange, fake-baked finger.

Tuscany sits in an executive chair. Noah is left with a quaint embroidered wicker throne that would comfortably seat a teddy bear. He folds himself into it, smiles, and tries to think of something interesting to say as he pulls out his materials. But his mind is full of the fact that the Josh Hartnett poster over Tuscany's desk has been set back into an ornately gilt eighteenth century frame.

"So, you go to Moore-Pike Academy?" he tries.

"Yeah." She is collected but nervous.

"Do you like it?"

"Yeah. It's cool. We get out pretty early in the day."

"You probably wish there were boys there, huh?"

She looks at Noah, startled. Her eyes are wide and very blue. Her eyelashes have been mascaraed into spider legs. Her lips slacken into a slight, breathless grin. There is a glimmer of conspiracy in her gaze.

"Girls' schools totally suck," she announces.

"It's a good school, though," Noah says.

"For dykes."

They begin by discussing how to memorize vocabulary ("I totally suck at vocab," Tuscany warns). Noah then teaches her about "plugging in numbers," a strategy that replaces even the most complex algebra on a standardized test with rote arithmetic. Tuscany is very excited by this technique.

"I can't believe they let this happen!" she exclaims. "It's like cheating."

There is no answer to that. It is like cheating, and it explains why the scores of Noah's students are three hundred and fifty points higher after tutoring.

Noah glances about the room. An alcoved queen bed occupies half of the floor. Swaths of fabric float over it and attach to the ceiling. It is a regal poop, Cleopatra's perfumed barge. Tuscany has covered the bed with pillows—raw silk, corduroy, some embroidered and sporting maxims such as "Keep on Shopping." Tuscany's teak desk has been pushed against the opposite wall. It is huge, fashionably worn, and could have served as the centerpiece of a museum collection if it didn't have an iMac on it.

Tuscany is staring at him. He has lost himself in his thoughts. "Tutoring is relationship-building," he remembers hearing during training; "spend at least a fifth of your time chatting about the student's life." The mathematical precision of that rule always seemed creepy to him before, but now he finds himself falling back on it. These hundred minutes are about Tuscany, not him.

"You're the coolest kid in your class, huh?" Noah asks. He asks this of roughly half his students. They dance around the question until eventually agreeing with him.

"Not the *coolest,*" Tuscany generously concedes. "I don't hang around with school friends much."

"Whom do you hang around?"

Tuscany smiles slyly. "I'm grounded."

"Why are you grounded?"

"I had boys over when my mom was away. I don't get it. She knows I'm a teenager. She knows I'm supposed to party. What does she expect?"

"Is that why the doormen wouldn't let me up?"

"They wouldn't?" she hoots. "That's so funny. They thought you were like my boyfriend in disguise or something."

Noah nods and smiles nervously.

"My boyfriend is *so* much older than you."

"How old do you think I am?" Noah asks after a moment.

"I don't know, like twenty."

"Twenty-five."

"Oh, you're closer to his age, then." She sighs. "My mom thinks I should hang out with guys my own age."

"She's probably right," Noah says.

"I know, of course, I'm not stupid. But guys my age are just so dumb."

"Did anything happen at your party? When you had those guys over?" Noah asks.

"I don't get what you mean. What do you want to know?"

Noah shrugs. What *does* he want to know? He was just trying to make conversation, though it has certainly taken an unexpected turn. How to segue to the volume of a cube . . .

"I can get anyone past the doormen." For a moment Tuscany is staring at Noah. He feels appraised.

"I didn't party much in high school," Noah confides. "I was a complete nerd."

"Oh, please, I can't believe that. You were totally a cool kid."

Tuscany's cell phone tinkles out Vivaldi's "Spring." She shoots a hand out and presses a button. "Sorry."

"Nice ring," Noah says.

"Yah, it's springtime something. I downloaded it."

The phone rings once more. "Ugh. I should just turn it off."

Tuscany opens a drawer in her desk and rummages through. She withdraws a cigarette and places it between her lips. "You want one?" she offers, the cigarette bobbing in her mouth.

Noah shakes his head. "Your mom lets you smoke in here?"

"Are you kidding? She knows I'd be eating if I wasn't smoking."

Tuscany pulls out an ashtray that reads "Party Girl" and is decorated by the kind of roughly sketched and impossibly slender women that appear on the covers of novels about Manhattan. She takes a pensive, almost Socratic pose, holding her cigarette far from her body. The filter is slick with pink lip gloss. "She's going to have to let me go to the gym tonight, I've been eating like a cow. I don't know when she thinks I'm going to do my homework."

Noah now makes Tuscany determine the average height of a certain baseball team. He then asks her what the reciprocal of the smallest prime number is. He stares about her room as she puzzles through the question. One pillow is centered on the bed, flanked by "I Stop for Visa" and "The Princess of Everything." This largest pillow is embroidered in a simple "Home Sweet Home" style. Tuscany purrs a number, but Noah misses her answer. The pillow on the center of Tuscany's bed reads: "Boys Like Girls Who Look Neat—When in Doubt, Just Don't Eat!"

Noah spends the early evening at a coffee shop, making guilty and uproarious calls on his cell phone. In the space of one week the pillow becomes a legend among Noah's circle. The forced, awkward rhyme takes on the dimensions of a couplet from a Greek epic. His friends Tim and Justin think it's a travesty; Tab thinks it's hilarious and wants to order one. His mother is saddened and his brother is titillated. Hera wonders how Dr. Thayer allowed the pillow into her house, while Roberto suggests that maybe Dr. Thayer *bought* the pillow.

Roberto voices this suspicion while they are on their double date. They are seated in the darkest corner a fluorescently lit Puerto Rican restaurant can provide. Roberto has arranged to meet up with a girl he met at the Queens warehouse rave, and she has agreed to bring along her friend. Noah couldn't invite the girl he took home: he was embarrassed to be unable to recall her name. Roberto's Warehouse Girl has smirked throughout the meal, leaning forward over jelly-braceleted arms, gulping beer like soda through her crooked smile. Every time she responds to Noah, her eyes are on Roberto. Her friend was apparently at the rave as well, though Noah can't recollect her face among the drunken images of the evening. A butterfly tattoo stretches across the nape of her neck.

"That poor pillow girl," moans Butterfly.

"Whatever, I'm not exactly sympathetic," says Warehouse Girl, who has a nose ring. "Little rich girl."

"I just think it's hella funny," Roberto says, after calling to the waitress for more *plátanos.* "Noah's got like the maddest job. I tell everyone I know about it."

Noah can't get the smile off his face (he rarely tells a story that can command a table; it is a thrilling success), but he feels a wave of cool melancholy behind the hot splash of pleasure. Tuscany makes him genuinely sad, but now she has become an anecdote. He finds it hard to attach emotions to the comedy piece she's become.

"Those people're totally fucked up," Warehouse Girl says. "It just makes you glad that you're not part of it all, you know?"

"I don't know," says Butterfly. She doesn't look up when she speaks, and wears a voluminous Yankees sweatshirt. "She's just a kid. It's not as though she asked for this. I feel bad even talking about it." Butterfly has worked her chair a formidable distance back from the table, her legs crossed, looking not only unhappy to be there but also not quite alive.

"You couldn't make this shit up, it's that fucked," Roberto proclaims. He dominates the airspace of the table with his arms, as though he might be dating all three of them. His hair is carefully oiled and gelled and falls back from his face like a swashbuckler's. Noah wonders if he has let his curiosity about Roberto take him too far, if he is now friends with someone he doesn't actually like.

Roberto runs a finger over Warehouse Girl's arm, traces small circles into the pit of her elbow. Noah looks to Butterfly, technically his date: her elbows appear to be covered by a long-sleeve T-shirt, a windbreaker, and a sweatshirt.

Warehouse Girl stares meaningfully into Roberto's eyes as she stabs a piece of *pernil.* "Is she a babe, this girl?" she asks.

"Umm, I guess," Noah says. He seems to have lost his charisma somewhere. "I think she expects me to drool over her."

"And do you? Drool? Wanna like spank her?" Roberto asks. Butterfly has begun to peel the label off her beer bottle, stares at it intently, as if hoping to banish the rest of them by dint of her concentration. "'Cuz she sounds totally fuckworthy. Her mom, too."

Butterfly rises and goes to the bathroom. She still has her sweatshirt on; there is nothing of her left at the table. Noah watches Roberto and Warehouse Girl giggle over the Tuscany anecdote. Roberto leans forward, suavely holding back his greasy locks to prevent them from sliding into the rice and beans. "Just wait until I get you home," he whispers to Warehouse Girl in a voice that is just loud enough for Noah to hear. "I wanna spread your legs and taste you."

He looks at Noah proudly—*Look at who I'm gonna be doing tonight!*—and Noah stares into the wood of the table in an embarrassed rage. He is furious at Roberto for being so blunt and predatory, furious at Warehouse Girl for accepting it and apparently enjoying it. And he's furious, Noah realizes, that Butterfly finds him so unengaging, has an instant aversion to dating him because—aha, is this the key?—he is white and college-educated. The topics he likes to talk about hold no currency here. He has served as the table's anchor; everyone listens to him, and is charmed. But they are fascinated by Tuscany, not him. He is transparent, an intermediary, useful only as a means to hear about the facile and ridiculous family that employs him. He has neither the glib immediacy of the Harlem streets nor the cultivated rarity of Fifth Avenue.

The ones who admire him for who he is, he knows, are his Princeton friends. But he doesn't want to be someone who went to Princeton and only carries on relationships with alumni. He came from a backwater, and wouldn't trade that "underprivileged" childhood for anything. This has been part of his ambition, he realizes (how often his very own feelings are unclear, and reveal themselves only after the fact)—to move to Harlem in order to connect with a world foreign to both his four years at upper-class Princeton and his white-bread home in Virginia. He is always searching for new ground.

But now his Tuscany anecdote is over, the beers have emptied, and Roberto wants to bring his date home, spread her legs, and taste her. Butterfly returns; the quartet fumbles outside; Butterfly splits; Noah leaves soon after, drunkenly picking his way over the cracked sidewalks of 150th Street until he throws himself onto his bed, alone. He could have invited her up; she was pretty enough. But he no longer wants the odd night of passion. Pretty is such a small part of it. Everything is such a small part of it.

~

By the time Noah has another meeting with Tuscany, he has told the pillow story so many times, has created such a mythology around her, that he is actually nervous to see her again, as nervous as one of his students would be taking the SAT. He can't taste his lunch: his fast-food meal passes into his gullet without taste. He compulsively pops Altoids all afternoon.

Noah misjudges his commute and arrives an hour early. He wanders up and down 86th Street. And then he sees her.

She is across the street, wearing a light peacoat and a black furry hat. Together with a friend, she stares into the window of Victoria's Secret. They stand at an odd angle, feet close but bodies apart, like halves of a split arrow—it is apparent that they do not like each other. They check out a pink teddy on a waxy pale mannequin, but are clearly not talking about it. From the looks of her gloved gesticulations, Tuscany is recounting something that recently happened to her, probably involving a boy, or a man. Nervous lest Tuscany should see him and think he is stalking her, Noah ducks over to Lexington and spends the rest of the hour chewing a stale donut in a coffee shop.

When Noah finally arrives at the apartment, he is led to Tuscany's room by the thuds of hip-hop music emanating down the hallway. She is holding court with two sullen friends. They are fogged in by cigarette smoke.

"Oh, hey," Tuscany says. She cracks a window open and waves smoke out with a vocabulary list.

"Hey," Noah says, looking at each girl in turn. They stare back frankly, gauging him, waiting for him to either light up or ask them out already.

"Outta here, guys," Tuscany declares. "I gotta tute."

"Tute," informal conjugation of "to tutor," Noah intends to tease after the friends leave. But Tuscany yawns and tosses her hair, and at the sight of her swaying hips Noah is overtaken by a sudden burst of nerves. His tongue catapults his breath mint out of his mouth. It lands with a ping on the hardwood floor.

They stare at each other through the smoke.

"Aha!" Noah says jocularly. It is all he can think to say.

"Hey," Tuscany sniggers. She is uncomfortable and suddenly fifteen again.

Noah puts down his bag, picks up the Altoid, stares at it for a moment, and places it in his pocket. More silence.

"I'm grounded again," Tuscany says.

"Oh yeah? Why?"

"This man," she replies. "My mom is crazy."

"Ah."

They go over the *A* words on the vocabulary list. Noah is disheartened: he doesn't expect his students to know *arbiter,* but he does expect *abduction.*

"So do you like this guy?" Noah asks.

"He's all right. He's pretty nice. And loaded. But, I dunno. Sometimes I want something more . . . deep? You know, intellectual?" She stares at Noah.

"Where do you want to go to school?" Noah asks, smiling solidly to enforce the shift in conversation.

"My mom wants me to go to Hampshire Academy. My aunt's a dean there, and my granddad built a library or something. But I'd have to get like seventy-fifth percentile—"

"You could get seventy-fifth percentile."

"And then, I just don't wanna go. It'd be lame. It's like, how about a party school, someplace easier or something."

Conventional wisdom would call for Noah to suggest aiming for Hampshire Academy, but he doesn't. He can't imagine Tuscany sledding in New Hampshire. Or studying.

The day's program is analogies. Noah gives her an easy start problem: COOP:CHICKEN. She moans, spits out a few inaudible curses, then ventures a guess. "Um, if you live in a co-op . . . you can't own any chickens?"

The third problem is PUEBLO:IGLOO.

"What the hell? I know what an *ig*loo is, everyone knows that, it's like a Canadian ice house, but how am I supposed to know what a *pueb*lo is? What the hell is a *pueb*lo?"

"You know, you studied it in eighth grade, probably, Native Americans—"

"Oh yeah! Totally. It's what African Americans live in."

"No! No, not *African* Americans, *Native* Americans."

"Oh, right, right, sorry."

They puzzle through the analogy for a few minutes. Finally:

"Okay, I get it," Tuscany declares. "IGLOO is to Canadian ice house as PUEBLO is to African Americans. But that's not an answer choice!"

Noah can no longer object. There is too much working against him. There is no difference between Native and African Americans, not for Tuscany, not here. She would expect Harlem to be full of pueblos and powwows.

Noah excuses himself to the bathroom, stares mesmerized into the vortex of the backlit glass sink as he washes his hands. Dr. Thayer is at the door when he comes out. She is dressed up, presumably to go to work, although she could just as easily be going to lunch at Sarabeth's. Dr. Thayer's afternoon sessions are lunch dates, coffee in a Madison Avenue apartment, finished off with a prescription for some kid's Ritalin.

"Noah," she whispers. "How is she doing? Better than Dylan, at least?" She has reapplied her makeup and glows bronze.

"Jeez! I can totally hear you," Tuscany yells from behind her door.

"Well, Jesus to you!" Dr. Thayer yells back. "How *are* you doing?"

"Fine!" comes Tuscany's voice.

Dr. Thayer turns to Noah. "Is she fine?"

"She has a very rational mind," Noah replies.

"Well, she has to do better than she did on that diagnostic test."

"I was totally hung over. I told you that!" comes the voice beyond the door.

"She says 'hung over' as if it's not going to bother me."

Noah is unsure of what to say: Dr. Thayer is, indeed, unruffled.

"How do you expect me to get better if you don't let us work?"

They are now all three in Tuscany's room. "It's my turn with Noah right now, honey. You've had him for forty-five minutes."

Noah sits next to Tuscany. Her "Party Girl" ashtray smolders between them. They stare at her mother, firmly planted in the doorway. Dr. Thayer is suddenly petulant, terrifying. Tuscany and Noah are both defiant children before her.

"Fuen!" she calls. Fuen arrives with a tea tray.

Tuscany is disgusted. "What are you *doing,* Mom?"

"I thought you and Noah would enjoy some refreshments. Keep you focused."

"You're so *weird.*"

"Apparently I'm weird," Dr. Thayer confirms resignedly.

Noah eyes the tray placed on the wide antique desk. The china is razor-thin and decorated with black swans, and the teacup handles are so small that they can only be pinched, not grasped. Two lonely cookies sit in the middle of the tray.

"You're being annoying," Tuscany says.

Weakly: "That's enough." Then, instructively, to Noah: "You need to make sure she gets more questions right."

"That's what we're trying," Noah responds.

"And you," Dr. Thayer begins to Tuscany. She pauses. Is she about to cry? "You need to realize that there are other people in this world beyond yourself. You don't think of me, do you?"

"No," Tuscany says. Her voice has lost all vitality.

"Work on this," Dr. Thayer commands them.

Tuscany has had enough of submission. She takes a long, angry drag on her cigarette. "I did all my vocab. Didn't I do all my vocab, Noah?"

"She did all her vocab," Noah lies. "Almost all."

"So. Are you done?" Tuscany asks her mother.

Dr. Thayer looks at Tuscany for a long while, as though sickened by her insolence. "I. Am. Done."

With an odd, questioning turn of her head, she is gone. She is a different mother than she was around Dylan. She has become aloof, defensive—competitive? With her daughter?

"She sucks," Tuscany says.

"She cares about you." Noah has no idea how much this is true.

"Bullshit. She's just worried about how I'll make her look. All her clients are my friends' families—'it's such a small world'—and whatever I do reflects on her. She's told me as much. I think it's the only reason she cares at all about me."

"Wow. That's harsh. Are you sure?"

Tuscany stares at Noah from beneath the prison bars of her lashes. She appears about to say something virulent and deeply felt. But the motions of smoking have pushed her hair forward and she is now more concerned with fondling the white-blond tips. "Whatever. Let's do some math."

Noah is concerned: it is the first time a student has steered the meeting toward, rather than away from, the test at hand.

The surface area of a cube, Tuscany learns, is $6s^2$. If a man has three dress shirts, five pairs of pants, and two belts, he has thirty outfits. If Carlos delivers twenty-seven pizzas in an hour, he delivers nine in twenty minutes.

"Our maid's husband is named Carlos," Tuscany remarks. "Which is weird, because she's Filipino. She's illegal."

"Oh."

"I've never dated anyone who wasn't white," Tuscany continues.

"Oh, really?"

"No, I think I should, I mean everyone should."

Noah takes a deep breath before responding. "Well, I don't think you should feel *obligated,* I mean, it would be a little strange to think it was your responsibility."

"Yeah, you're totally right. I should face it—I'm just attracted to white guys. That's who I like. White guys in dress shirts. And sometimes Hispanic guys in dress shirts."

There is something apologetic in Tuscany's tone. Noah looks down at his own sweater, sans dress shirt, and then clenches his jaw for having done so. It's as though fifteen-year-old Tuscany is letting her twenty-five-year-old tutor down easy.

"I could totally see that," Noah says.

"Yah, I have such a type."

"How do you meet these guys?"

"I dunno. The same way you meet girls. At a bar, a club."

"Do they buy you drinks?"

"Sometimes. But then it's weird, 'cuz it's like, I don't want to get a drink from him, but then I have it, and it's like I'm suddenly tied to this guy who might be gross. So I try and buy my own drinks."

The runner from Westchester, if sprinting at eight miles an hour, will overtake Laeticia in half an hour. The interior angles of an octagon total 1080 degrees. If, of the twenty women at a party, fourteen are blond and twelve wear high heels, six women are both blond and wear high heels.

I want to spread your legs and taste you.

Tuscany will not be able to meet at the usual time the following week since she has to go to the doctor, so she and Noah plan to meet during one of Tuscany's free periods, in the Moore-Pike Academy library.

It's supposed to be a quiet place, and other kids will be trying to study, and you two won't be able to concentrate, and further-

more I think it's just inappropriate, don't you, why don't you just come later, here, as late as it needs to be, just come here.

The voicemail is from Dr. Thayer.

~

Noah's meeting with Tuscany will have to be late indeed, as his seniors are cramming in sessions. The SAT can be taken multiple times and is offered roughly once a month—once students enter senior year, however, only a few administrations are left in order to make application deadlines. Noah's sessions with juniors, whose SATs are a year away, are comparatively carefree. He meets Cameron on the Upper West Side (she is having a down day; she complains throughout the vocabulary quiz that the lead in the school production of *Gypsy* went to vapid, vacuous, insipid, inane Maribeth Culbert), then grabs a cab back to the East Side to meet with a new Fieldston student, Rafferty Zeigler. Mrs. Zeigler agreed to Noah's tutoring Rafferty only after being convinced by Cameron's parents' repeated recommendations. Mrs. Zeigler is an anxious type, the breed of wispy-boned, fluttery Park Avenue woman whose apartment encloses her like a birdcage. Rafferty himself is as terse as most other boys his age, gets math concepts easily but doesn't seem to have ever actually read anything beyond his PlayStation manual. A fairly typical case, though when dealing with such a nervous mother Noah is always aware that dissatisfaction can be quick to bloom.

Noah arrives at 949 Fifth Avenue around ten P.M. Dr. Thayer is at the door when Noah steps off the elevator.

"It's late," she hisses.

"I'm sorry, you asked me to come when I could—I have other students."

"Come in," Dr. Thayer commands. She has traded in her gray gown for garnet. There are large gold earrings in her ears, instead of the usual pearls. She might have just returned from the theater.

"Sit down," she instructs, and suddenly Noah is perched on one of the ottomans. Dr. Thayer sits across from him and smiles. Her teeth are stained red with wine. She places a hand on the couch beside her, catching the fabric of her dress with her thumb and pulling it sheer across her firm abdomen.

"Tuscany," she intones, "has gone to bed."

"Oh." In the glowing evening light, Dr. Thayer's eyes look large and liquid, like Tuscany's.

"There's a twenty-four-hour cancellation policy?"

"Yes, I'm afraid so."

"Like lawyers." She smiles, so Noah does as well. "We should fill the time, then," she continues. "Listen, I'm concerned. I don't think Tuscany's going to do well on this. We really want her to go to Hampshire. Can she get into Hampshire?"

I just want to go to a party school.

"You know someone there, right?"

Dr. Thayer laughs. Noah has apparently just been very, very amusing. "Yes, we 'know someone there.' "

"Well, her chances aren't half bad. I've been concentrating on math; I think we'll make our biggest gains there."

"You should make sure she knows how to multiply well."

"Yes. I should."

Dr. Thayer pulls her teased-out hair back and smiles at Noah, as if apologizing for trying to do his job. "You know, I didn't have to take the ISEE."

"No?"

"No." Dr. Thayer cocks her head and looks at Noah inquisitively, like a bird or a bright child. It is a pose Tuscany frequently adopts: Dr. Thayer is wondering what Noah thinks of her.

The agency will bill them for one hundred minutes. He is here for one hundred minutes.

We should fill the time, then.

"Why," Noah asks, "didn't you have to take the ISEE?"

Dr. Thayer leans forward. Her bra is flesh-toned. "I," she says conspiratorially, "went to a *public* high school."

"Really?" Noah is shocked by his own reflexive reaction. He too, after all, went to a public school. And doubtlessly one a lot more "public" than Dr. Thayer's.

"Yes, really. It's strange, no? I go to parties, and the host will take my coat and ask where I went to school, and I'll smile and say, 'Providence Latin, can I still stay?' "

They laugh.

"Can I offer you anything?"

Boys Like Girls Who Look Neat—When in Doubt, Just Don't Eat.

"No, thank you, I have dinner plans."

"Oh, am I keeping you?"

"No, of course not." And she's not. He doesn't have dinner plans. He looks at her where she sits, reclined and smiling, on the antique couch. What's stopping him from staying?

"Can I offer you anything to drink, then?" She flashes her red teeth.

Noah glances at his watch. Ninety minutes left. Six hundred dollars. For a glass of wine with a woman who is, at the very least, fascinating. Noah accepts.

Dr. Thayer leaves him in the gray land of the ottomans. Noah searches his memory of training week for a situation remotely like this. He hasn't turned up anything before Dr. Thayer returns with two large glasses of wine.

"This is my husband's stock, we mustn't tell him."

Noah sips.

"Do you like it?"

"It's very good."

"So what do you do when you're not tutoring?"

"I fill out grad school apps."

"Oh, aren't you a dear! I knew you were planning on being a real professor, I think. Tuscany used to play teacher, back when she was in preschool. Always ahead of herself. Good thing she gave that up."

Dr. Thayer looks at Noah questioningly, gauging her attractiveness in his eyes. He debates whether he could get up from the ottoman and sit next to her on the couch, what it would feel like to talk to her from inches away, to lay his hand on hers. She has charmed him despite himself. Her gold rings flash in the candlelight—he is lost in the play of warm light as he muses that she could, after all, be the answer to all of his problems. He could just replace her absent husband from time to time, accompany her to the theater. She would take care of Stafford, Perkins, and America's Bank. He has never dated an older woman—maybe she would be able to hold his interest longer than girls his own age. He senses the exact question Dr. Thayer wants him to ask. He stares directly into her blond-framed brown eyes:

"So how do you feel in all of this?"

Dr. Thayer opens her mouth and then closes it. She smiles, then drops the smile, then takes it up again. The question behind Noah's—*Who is looking out for* you?—has stunned her. He wonders if he should apologize, although the actual question he posed was fairly innocuous.

There is only a foot of open floor between them. He makes to get up and join her on the couch but then changes his mind. He is collected and smiling and then suddenly he has spilled wine on the new rug.

He darts to his feet. "I'm so sorry. Let me get a towel," he exclaims.

Dr. Thayer looks at him coldly. All the light has gone

out of the room. Noah should *not* have sprung up. "It's *all right,* Noah," she says, exasperated. "I'll call Fuen in to take care of it."

Noah can't stop his leg from shaking. His eyes dart over the reclining form of Dr. Thayer, who is both languid and hostile. "I can really get it," Noah says. "Don't bother Fuen."

"Jesus. Fuen will get it. Stop worrying."

"Sorry."

Dr. Thayer tries to smile for a moment, but then the contrived expression breaks and she throws her hands on her knees and grimaces. She gets up. "I won't keep you any longer."

Noah is happy to get his coat. "You won't be billed for this session," he says, trying to sound lighthearted.

"Noah. You came, you bill for a session. What are you saying about yourself otherwise?"

"Okay, well, thanks for the tip, then."

"Good night. See you on Wednesday."

~

Since their double date, Noah has taken to avoiding Roberto. He walks back from the subway along Riverside Drive, which is scenic and not at all "happening"; he is unlikely to encounter Roberto there. He thinks of Roberto's crassness, and of his own failure to make an impression on his date. The experience that night, coupled with his recent brush with Dr. Thayer, leaves Noah defensive, with the sour impression that most people on earth are sexual predators in one guise or another. He yearns for simplicity, serenity.

Unfortunately, avoiding Roberto also means avoiding the gym. Although Noah gained pounds of muscle in the weeks after beginning working out, he is afraid that in recent days those pounds have softened into something dismayingly less firm. As he lies on the couch he pats his belly experimentally, passes his hand over it like a paddle over an air hockey table. Flab is new to him. It is kind of fun, he decides. He rolls over on the couch, sighs dramatically into the fabric.

From the bathroom comes the sound of a rock hitting porcelain—the exposed pipe has begun to corrode, and rust chips and bits of hardened insulation have begun to cascade into the bathtub. The latest chunk is quite large, and Noah has to hold it in two hands as he walks it down the stairs and out to the trash.

He pauses and savors the air. Or rather intends to savor the air, until he takes in the stench of the greasy streaks left on the road after the trash pickup that morning. He scans the block. Same monoliths of brick and concrete.

The mail-delivery woman is slamming letters into the mailboxes when he returns. Noah retreats inside with his mail: two offers for credit cards (Noah throws them away immediately; the temptation is too great; the glossy brochures slink in his hands like seductresses) and a letter from the Princeton loan office. The gray linen notice cheerfully informs him that, the postgraduation grace period being over, his loans administered through Princeton will now enter into repayment. They are not colossal but this will throw Noah's budget, just recently tweaked to give him a $30-a-month surplus, back deep into negatives. Noah frowns, standing in the middle of his bare room. He sighs once, and then again, louder. After a few moments his frown begins to tremble.

He hates crying, can't tolerate the selfish weakness of it. He will instead concentrate on ways out of his current situation. He powers up his laptop, opens his application essay, stares at the blinking cursor:

My life has always been one of contrasts. Much like a deconstructed text, my meanings do not give easily of themselves.

Crap. Total crap. He was proud of his opening yesterday, but today it feels awful. It has been faked; there is no passion in it.

He powers down the laptop and glances at his watch. It is six P.M., and since Friday is his day off he has no tutoring to do. He calls his friend Tim and makes plans, but their movie doesn't begin until ten. He knows he only calls his family when his life is slow, when he is not at his best, but he knows he should reach out to them, and he wants to speak to *somebody,* and they're sure to be there. The message clicks on, his mother's voice, her accent that guttural southern speech that fills him with reluctant shame, the inflection that speaks of boiled peanuts and bonfires and Jerry Springer, of everything Manhattan derides.

"Hey, guys, it's Noah. Just calling to check in. Everything's good here. Give me a call!" He closes his cell phone and stares at it. He's always careful not to give specifics in his phone messages, not mention the particular Princeton friends or Broadway plays that he's seeing, so they don't feel he's moved on from them, that he feels above them. Though, he acknowledges, he's proud to have moved beyond the sinking force of his hometown. And doesn't that mean that he thinks he's done better than them? The phone in his hand vibrates. "Hello?"

"Hey, it's Kent."

"What's up? I just called."

"I know. I was out mowin'."

"How's the lawn going?"

"Are you serious?"

"Just trying to make conversation."

Silence fills the line. "How's school going?" Noah tries.

"School?"

"Yeah."

"I figured Mom told you. I dropped out."

"What the hell?"

"I've got a job. It pays pretty good. I'm helping pay the rent here."

"You don't need to pay the rent. You need to pass high school."

"No, I don't, and I didn't. It's over, man. I'm out."

Noah knows he shouldn't push his brother any further, that Kent's guard is already up. "How do you feel about it?" he asks.

"Good, I really do."

Noah pauses on the line. His brother does sound good. Or, at the least, relieved. More comfortable in his skin. But Noah can't stop himself. "That was a fucking stupid thing to do," Noah says. Even as he says it he wonders: if it was indeed stupid, why does he feel a flood of relief?

"No," Kent says flatly. "It wasn't."

Noah throws his phone down on the bed. His brother has hung up on him. He's furious, but more at himself than at Kent, he suspects. If he's going to be some great teacher, how couldn't he even help his own brother succeed? Maybe being a good instructor means letting some kids go, but he's mad at the stupid reality of it, that he can control everything in himself but nothing of his brother. He can't stand the reckless self-promotion of banking or consulting, but he fears he doesn't have sufficient selflessness to be a good teacher.

Noah trudges into the kitchen. He remembers Hera's being aghast to discover that Noah didn't have a mother at home to cook him dinner; she seemed amazed that Noah managed to feed himself at all. There is no food in Noah's fridge, and he is hungry. He is tired of soup and Taco Bell—it may be time to renew his friendship with Roberto and Hera.

Noah rummages through his cupboard for something to offer. The only unopened food item he owns is a jar of Swedish spaghetti sauce he bought on a whim as he paid for his furniture at Ikea. He throws it into a plastic grocery bag and heads out the door.

At the sound of the buzzer Hera thumps downstairs. She seems overjoyed to see Noah, and he is thrilled to see someone so undisguisedly pleased to see him. Her smile is the earnest opposite of the hostess smile of Dr. Thayer, whose hospitality is convincing only to those eager to be convinced. She beckons him upstairs and he follows in the airless zone behind her bulk. She disappears into her bedroom for a few moments and then reappears in a slightly more elegant muumuu, this one with a silver lamé hem.

"How ahr you, No-ah?" She seems to be experimenting with accents—today her *a*'s are as long as the royal family's.

"I'm doing very well, thanks," Noah says.

"You have eaten?" Hera asks, moving toward the kitchen.

"I brought this," Noah says, pulling the jar of spaghetti sauce out of the crinkling plastic. Noah bites his lip; now it seems rude to have brought something, since Hera will be the one to toil over it. But Hera sees the offering and claps her hands, beaming in wonder and joy, as if Noah has just produced the baby Moses.

"Oh, *No-ah*! Thank you." She carries the jar reverently into the kitchen.

"You're welcome," Noah says, toying with the frayed threads of the couch.

"Mmm-hmm," Hera calls, her voice distracted. Her head and large bosom pop around the wall. "How much does your agency charge for you, No-ah?" Her head and bosom pop back into the kitchen.

"Oh, they charge plenty. It would pay better if they gave me more students."

"My lovely daughter Titania"—Hera's head reappears long enough to emphasize the word *lovely*—"she has always been so studious. She turns twenty this year. It is a hope of mine that she can to study, to go to college. Do you think she would be able to study well?"

"Yes, I'm sure she—"

"Because she is intelligent, not like Roberto, who is such a sweet boy but, you know, not *rapid.* I think she would do very good."

There is a beseeching quality to Hera's tone, as if Noah were sitting on an admissions council. "Your daughter sounds remarkable," he says.

"A jewel. Noah," she says, "you *will* love Titania." She punches the word *will* as though it were a command. Perhaps it's just because of her imperfect grasp of English. Noah involves himself in the tumbler of wine Hera has given him. "Titania!" Hera calls. "Come! Dinner will be soon!"

Noah coughs and stands. A girl enters from the hallway, drying her hands on an old towel. "Oh, hi," she says, wiping her hand one last time on the towel, then on her pants, and then finally extending it to Noah. "My name is Olena. My mother will tell you it's Titania, but it's Olena."

She is tall and slender, with a lovely scrubbed-pink face and a gleaming line of white teeth. Noah takes her hand. It is moist and cool.

"Noah is a tutor," Hera says. She overenunciates the words, a parody of a hostess.

"I know," Olena says. "I've been hearing all about it nonstop." She is tall enough that she must bend slightly to meet Noah's eyes. Her accent is faintly British.

"Your English is very good," Noah says.

Olena nods swiftly. Like many foreigners who speak English well, she takes being complimented as an oblique insult, an affirmation that she is not a native speaker. "Your English is good too," she says with a heavy wink.

Noah smiles. "Point taken."

"Very good." Olena yawns. Her fine hair has been pulled

back in a careless ponytail. Her features are large and striking; the broad planes of her cheekbones, which mark her so strongly as Roberto's sister, reflect the light of the exposed lightbulb above their heads.

Hera slaps another smudgy tumbler of wine on the table and then returns to the kitchen, not before flashing Noah a knowing smile.

Olena excuses herself, opens the fridge, and extracts a bottle of beer. She pops the lid off by sharply slamming the top against the counter. "You would like one, Noah?" she calls from the kitchen.

"Shut the fuck up!" comes Roberto's groggy voice from the other bedroom. Olena retorts with a yell in piercing Albanian.

She returns to the table, pushes the wine her mother has poured to one side, and clanks her bottle against Noah's wineglass. "Cheers. You," Olena says quietly to Noah, "have become friends with Roberto, no?"

"We've spent some time together, yeah," Noah says.

"I do not understand how we are even related. He is like a strange offshoot, proof of how diverse our genes must be, do you know what I mean? That we were both produced by, you know, the same gametes—it is amazing." Her lips curl sardonically as she speaks, as though she is perpetually disappointed by the limits of language. Noah stares at her mouth.

They take a gulp of their respective drinks. "Have you noticed," Olena asks, "that there are no books here? It is as if my family came to America and became simple. Perhaps"—she smiles thinly—"this is what your country does to people."

"Albania, I suppose, is full of intellectuals?" Noah smiles knowingly, as though he has any idea whether Albania is indeed full of intellectuals.

"There are plenty, yes," Olena says. "Although there is one less, now that I have come here."

"Well, we're glad to have you."

Olena nods. Noah becomes aware of the hardness of her shoulders beneath her T-shirt, the fatless rockiness of her body.

"My mother talks about you all the time," Olena continues. "Having you here is like having a crown prince for a nephew. I'm sorry, does that phrase make sense in English?"

"Yeah, it makes sense," Noah says. Why is he finding it so hard to formulate responses?

Olena smiles, and Noah is again charmed by its smallness, the gray sarcasm of her expression. She pulls her long legs beneath her so that she is sitting on top of them.

"So what are your plans now?" Noah asks.

"Well, I'm here to go to school." For a moment her tough tone falls, and she wipes her brow tiredly. "I'm trying to work and save money, but it's hard. Minimum wage is pretty minimum in Manhattan."

She looks up, and her steely resolve is back. "Albania has many wonderful things, but for universities, well, I have to hand it to you, there is no place better than the United States. I understand that you went to Princeton. You must be proud of this."

"I am, yeah, sure."

"That does, after all, make you intelligent." She stares at him teasingly. Noah swigs his wine.

"I am a little old to begin school," Olena says, "but so be it. I was not able to come earlier. I had some money in Albania, yes, but here"—she snaps her fingers—"I have almost nothing. A few dollars. But starting at the bottom is what your country is renowned for, no? The national cliché." She laughs.

Noah wonders where Olena plans to apply, but the prospect of asking causes some conversational mechanism to tiredly whir—this is a route he constantly travels, and he is weary of talking about tests and schools. "When I'm feeling smug," Noah says, "I think that I started at the bottom too."

"But you were born in America?" she asks. She laughs once, dryly. All her spoken language is ironic, yet she leans forward earnestly, is so obviously vulnerable to the possibility that she will always be trapped in a class to which she feels she doesn't belong. "This makes you not at the bottom. This is a definitional thing. You do not have constant diarrhea. Your hands are not bent by farming without tools."

Noah laughs. "I guess not, no, not at the bottom, then, but when you're here it seems that anything below millions of dollars is the bottom."

"We just have to redefine our bottoms, then," Olena says. She pauses, then winks. "Perhaps I will need to join a gym."

Hera sets a steaming pan on the worn table. Within are several meat pies, smothered in Swedish spaghetti sauce and freshly microwaved.

"What are you serving to us, Mother?" Olena asks. "What have you done to your pies?"

"This looks lovely," Noah says.

"These pastries are our favorites," Hera says. "I am certain they will only be better with this lovely sauce."

Hera serves them, and Noah takes a bite. It is impossible to tell if indeed the meat pie has been improved, for it is undetectable beneath the sugary tomato purée. This meal, at least, does not come from a can. Noah takes another bite.

"Your apartment must be very nice, if you earn so much money," Hera says.

"Mother is a little hyper-money-aware," Olena explains as she dissects a pastry.

"Actually, my apartment's sort of falling apart," Noah says.

"Oh," Olena says proudly. "*Rustic* is the word you are looking for. A lovely, falling-down type of building."

"Not really," Noah says around a wet slug of peeled tomato. "Last week I opened the front door to some guy shooting up in the stairwell."

Olena shouts a laugh. Hera nods benignly. Noah is fairly certain that she hasn't understood.

"I overheard two women in my building talking," Noah starts. He is surprised to hear a catch in his throat. The world seems impossibly lonely tonight. He is suddenly, viscerally glad for Olena and Hera's company. "They said that last winter the pipes froze and when they called the landlord he said, 'In two months it will be spring. When spring comes, ice melts. Then you get your water.' "

Olena laughs merrily, looks twinklingly at Noah.

Hera asks, "You are sad, no?"

"Ech, Ma!" Olena says.

Noah stares at her, alarmed. "Sad?" He hadn't thought himself sad, but being asked seems to make him so.

"In home," Hera says, her voice dropping to a momentary whisper, "in *Albania,* it would seem very strange for someone to live on his own. But here all of you do it. Why? Look at the past—never before did people do such a thing so often, live for themselves. Where is, for example, your father?"

"He's dead. My mother lives in Virginia."

Neither Hera nor Olena offers the typical condolences. "Why do you not live with your mother?" Hera presses. "If you stayed with her until you married, you would never be alone, no?"

"She lives in a little rural town. There's nothing for me in Virginia." Not true, he mentally amends. There are his old friends. His brother and mother. But at the same time he can't escape the conviction that returning home would be stepping down.

She leans forward, heaving her massive bosom to rest on the table, and takes Noah's hands in her own. "You carry a lot on you. Ambition, strength, yes, but you seem also . . . afraid. Forgive me, I come from an open culture, more than yours, you could say. Titania and I often spoke like this after dinner, in front of the fire. I hope I am not being disrespectful."

"What do you *really* want?" Olena asks Noah, momentarily letting her hand as well rest on Noah's forearm. The feeling of her fingers on the hairs of his arm lingers. But despite the pleasant sensation it makes Noah want to cringe, the banality of being another twentysomething who doesn't know what he wants. He removes his hands from Hera's.

"I want to be a teacher. Not the way I am now. A schoolroom teacher," he says.

Olena looks puzzled. "Are there still such things?"

"Do you want to be in love?" Hera asks, undeterred.

"Ma!"

"Sure, of course, that would be great too." Noah smiles shyly and swallows a gob of pie. Hera rises to get them glasses of water. Why is the world so preoccupied with falling in love?

"She doesn't mean to probe," Olena says while Hera is away, "but we both do enjoy the talking about *things,* big things. I get tired of this American obsession with talking only about minutiae all the time."

Noah nods. He is becoming drawn to Olena's manner of speaking—it is as though she has read thousands of books but has seldom spoken before; her language has more breadth than fluency. Roberto prattles easily, like a child; Olena weighs her language down, trips over her own intelligence.

Hera emerges; she has apparently overheard her daughter. "Who do you talk about your day with, Noah?"

"Umm, I guess it changes, one person one day, another the next."

"Mmm-hmm. You have considered to live with someone else?"

Noah laughs. "I did, once. But no girl has asked me since."

"You could to live here," Hera says.

"Live here!"

"Well, Roberto would enjoy your company, and I'm sure Titania does. You would be good influence on them both. I would make you meals, you would pay less rent, our building is not falling apart, why not?"

Noah's Princeton loans' going into repayment flickers through his mind—the tapeworm in his bank account has gotten bigger. A room here would be cheaper. And despite the addition of spaghetti sauce the meat pies are good, and carry within them a spiritual warmth not to be found in soup cans. He wouldn't eat every meal out of a bowl, here! And his home life would certainly be livelier, and perhaps he would pay off his loans faster if Hera were around to scold him. He imagines reading next to Olena on the couch.

But being roommates with Roberto, who is fun and dynamic but tells his dates that he wants to spread their legs and taste them? And Noah's mother was already nervous when he announced that he was moving into Harlem—what would she say if he told her he was moving in with the Albanian immigrant family in the tenement up the street?

"That's quite an offer!" Noah says.

"We would love to have you with us," Hera urges. Olena nods.

Noah says he will think about it, but there is a sudden formality in his tone that makes it clear to all of them that his answer is no.

But Noah returns home to the sound of running water. The warped planks of his floor glisten with moisture, and a small brook runs down the center of the room, culminating in a puddle beneath Noah's bed. He plucks his laptop from the mattress and secures it on top of the bookcase before opening the door to his bathroom. A brackish pond has formed. The corroded pipe streams a steady arc of brown water into the bathtub, which it has filled until the glistening surface expels sheets of foul water over the bathroom floor. The air is heavy, moist, brown-green, and permeated with the odor of dilute sewage—like rotten potting soil or concentrated body odor. Those old watermarks on his walls suddenly make more sense.

After standing ankle-deep in the fetid water and expelling a stream of curses, Noah takes almost no time to throw a few belongings into his suitcase and lug it outside. He takes a moment to collect himself and then makes a panicky call to Roberto on his cell phone. Roberto and Olena arrive shortly after, panting, and help Noah drag his furniture over the few blocks to his new home.

chapter 4

Noah pulls a worn chair to the table and eats another of Hera's pies for consolation while Roberto lugs his suitcase up the stairs. He can glimpse the room he will share with Roberto: his cot is neatly made with a soft and threadbare comforter, his laptop case centered at the foot. Olena has donated her bedside table, on which she has placed a cloudy glass vase containing a number of drooping but colorful carnations. It is a simple display of both squalor and goodwill, and Noah wonders if the tears wetting the corners of his eyes are from gratitude or frustration.

Roberto is bouncing on the mattress of his bed. "Check this out, man! Our new digs!"

Noah wanders into Roberto's room—his room—and puts his tutoring bag down next to his cot. From his vantage point he has a view of half a worn dresser, a construction site just visible through the cloudy window, and a ripped poster of Anna Kournikova. "Cool," he says.

Roberto starts doing chin-ups from the doorframe. Noah watches his feet lower and rise as he speaks. "This is going to be awesome. I've always wanted like a little brother to share a room with."

Tabitha used to snore all night long, and pressed the snooze button from six to nine each morning. Noah is a little leery of going back to sharing a room. He lumbers back into the living room. Olena gives his arm a little rub, as if to warm it. "Thank you," he says wetly.

Olena laughs and drapes her arm over Noah's shoulder. "Don't worry, Noah, you're going to be okay. This is going to be fun."

Noah nods.

"Stupid asshole slumlord," she adds.

Noah breaks into a little grin.

~

Noah opens the Thayer apartment door to Dylan's declaration that "that looks stupid." Noah glances around the corner. Dylan sits on a leather stool in the middle of the kitchen's chrome simplicity, his lower half wrapped as tightly as a wound in a plush white towel. An olive-skinned man takes quick snips at Dylan's thick hair. Heedless of the flashing scissors, Dylan raises his hand to his crown after each cut, perfecting his hairstyle in the mirrored surface of the fridge.

"Hi, Dylan," Noah says.

For a moment Dylan just stares blankly, seems not to recognize him. Then he smiles. "Hey."

"How did the test go yesterday? It was the real thing this time."

"Pretty good, I think."

"Pretty good?"

"Yeah, I dunno, it always seems impossible, and this time was as impossible as always. Not like *more* impossible. So I guess that means it was pretty good."

"What was the essay on?"

"Essay . . ." Dylan glazes over as he processes. Then his

eyes widen. The hairdresser retracts his scissors just in time as Dylan whips his head around to look at Noah. "Oh my God! The essay!"

"What's the matter?" Noah asks. For a horrible moment he is convinced that Dylan forgot to do it.

Dylan slams his hands down on his toweled thighs, scattering hair clippings. "You would have been so proud of me, Noah!"

"Why?"

"It was *so* hard to find a way to make it about Harriet Tubman."

"What was the question?"

Dylan sits up. The hairdresser twitches once in fear as, unnoticed by Dylan, a large chunk of hair is severed from Dylan's head.

"Here it is, and I'm not shitting you: 'Some say the twentieth century was a century of increased communication. The twenty-first century will be a century of *blank*. Fill in the blank and explain.'"

"And you wrote about Harriet Tubman?" Noah asks. He feels slightly sick.

Dylan nods proudly. "Yeah! First of all, I realized their trick. The *twentieth* century is all the years that begin with one-nine, not two-zero. They almost got me there."

Noah gives Dylan a little thumbs-up.

"So," Dylan continues, "here's how I filled in the blank: the twenty-first century will be the century of—get this—Harriet Tubman rememberation."

"Harriet Tubman *rememberation*?"

"Yup. So I wrote about how like, since the beginning of time, blah blah, we have always waited for the moment to rememberate Harriet Tubman, who emancipated all the slaves—"

"Led a number of slaves to freedom, you mean."

"Right, that, and now the moment has come—I think I

actually wrote 'the moment is upon us,' how cool is that—to finally achieve the human forever goal of praising Harriet Tubman for the rebellious leader she always was being!"

Noah blinks.

"Was that awesome, or what?" Dylan asks.

"Yeah, sounds great."

"Just wait'll we get the score!"

Noah nods. "Ten days, Dylan, we've got ten days until it comes." The words sound like a stay of execution.

~

"Your brother's getting his hair cut in the kitchen," Noah says as he enters Tuscany's room. He has found that one of the easiest ways to make conversation with teenagers is to say something stupid and nonintimidating and then let them run with it.

"Yeah, how lame is that?" Tuscany asks. She is reclined on her pillows, plucking frayed threads of gold from a tassel of her bedspread. She's wearing denim shorts that have been cut so high that the white cotton pocket hangs to midthigh. "He's so lazy he won't even go somewhere to get his hair cut. Mom has to get the guy to come here. But then it's weird, because Dylan doesn't care enough to go get his hair cut but when the guy comes here it's like all life in this apartment stops, like Dylan's downstairs being knighted or something." Tuscany smiles, a numbly amazed expression on her face: she is proud of her simile.

"Does this guy do your hair, too?"

"Cristos? No way. He would have to bring like fifty pounds of stuff."

"How'd your homework go?"

Tuscany swings her narrow legs together and runs her hands down them. She stares at their tan softness for a moment, then remembers why she began moving, hops into her desk chair, and pulls out her homework. "Not bad, take a look."

Noah glances over it. Tuscany is a hard worker, especially compared to her brother; Noah can't recall ever seeing Dylan's handwriting. Tuscany has nailed her percents worksheet, and although she has missed most of the distance problems, she displays a surprising penchant for right triangles. Noah gives her a vocabulary quiz. The word lists he provides are more in the genre of cheat sheets than glossaries: the agency tabulated the frequency of words that reappear in all the standardized tests of the last ten years, and because terms and entire problems repeat from administration to administration, the vocabulary lists are essentially forecasters of the exact words that will appear on the exam. Tuscany knows *quagmire, embolden,* and *nonentity,* but misses *circumlocution, laconic,* and *domicile*.

"Domicile?" Noah repeats.

"Umm, hold on," Tuscany says, pressing her fingers into her blond hair and scowling. She points to a small mountain of index cards. "I did my work, I know this . . . is it a type of apartment?"

"Sort of." Seeing Tuscany's crestfallen expression, Noah adds "Or yes, yes, that's fine."

Tuscany sits back and slaps Noah a high five. The acrylic of her nails glides against his callused fingertips. "Cool!"

"So, not bad! We'll get you into boarding school, no problem."

"Thank God. I can't wait to get out of here."

"Why do you want to leave so much?" Noah asks. He noticed something odd about Tuscany's room during their last session—while most girls her age paper their mirrors with snapshots of themselves and their friends, Tuscany's mirrors are bare.

"It sucks around here," Tuscany says. "I just want to get out, you know?"

"Is everyone just too shallow?" Noah asks.

Tuscany looks taken aback; no one has posed her a question like this before. "Yeah, that's it! It's like no one really cares, you know? They're jealous. Or maybe just mean."

Seeing Tuscany, weightless and friendless, depressed and yet probably planning her next date with an older man, leaves Noah with a desolating concern for her. He looks at her with as much sympathy and empathy as he feels he can express without seeming improper. She is, after all, a hot girl in tiny shorts. It is his job to look at her as little as possible. He learned that the hard way. Even so, it takes resolve to keep his gaze averted.

"The rest of the world isn't like this, you know," Noah says.

"What's that mean?" Tuscany asks.

Noah isn't sure where he wants to go with this. Tuscany's rarefied, privileged environment is no harder than the rest of America—it just isn't any easier. "There are completely different worlds than this. If you feel isolated here, it says more about where you are than who you are."

Tuscany stares out her window, tapping her fingers on the protective glass of her desk. Her mouth squirms, forms the beginnings of sentences, but eventually she just sighs, squeezes her thigh to gauge its leanness, and pulls out a cigarette. "So, what're we doing next?" she asks brightly.

"No more analogies," Noah announces.

"Yay!" Tuscany flashes an unclouded smile, so happy and unencumbered that Noah can see the allure she holds for her stressed businessmen boyfriends.

"It's time for reading comprehension."

Tuscany grimaces as she lights up. They take turns reading aloud a passage comparing the Hopi class system to that of the Maya. Tuscany is wearing a tiny pink "Wild

Grrls" T-shirt and twists a strand of white-blond hair around a finger: hearing her voice complex rhetoric amazes Noah. He is fascinated that the human brain can do it, exist on twenty-first-century Fifth Avenue and comprehend ancient hierarchies.

Tuscany finishes, leans back, and pushes the test booklet away like a plate of unfinished food.

"Did you get it?"

"It was *so* boring, but I got it."

And she does get it. The only question she misses asks her to compare gradated and tiered class structures. Tuscany breaks into a bright peal of laughter upon reading it. "Yeah, I don't think so. What the hell is *that* supposed to mean?"

Noah teaches Tuscany to paraphrase difficult sections, to focus on the first and last four lines of the passage. Tuscany punctuates Noah's lesson with observations about how much finals will suck and how bloated she feels. She politely returns her attention to the passage when Noah asks her to, but in the middle of a section about the Mayan jungle she glances sagaciously at her fingernails and observes that guzzling ice water burns calories.

"Time for a break," Noah says. "Want to run around the room screaming?"

Tuscany titters. "No."

"Oh!" Noah remembers. "Tell me about this magazine you're starting!"

"It's called *It's All You.* It's a fashion magazine, only it's directed at like girls around here. We don't have anything for *us,* you know?"

Noah grins. "Right. Because *Glamour* and *Vogue* are full of trailer park girls."

"What?"

"When does the first issue come out?"

"It already came out like a few months ago!" Tuscany says, beaming. She opens a drawer full of glossy magazines, extracts one, and hands it to Noah. Spread across the front cover is a glamour shot of Tuscany—not a booth-in-the-mall, girl-in-feather-boa photo, but one that could have been ripped from the cover of *Vanity Fair.* Tuscany reclines in a yellow sundress on the steps of the Metropolitan Museum—her skin has been airbrushed the color of toasted marshmallows, and her eyes have been doctored a cerulean blue.

"Isn't it awesome?" Tuscany asks. "Take a look. I have to go to the bathroom."

Tuscany leaves, and Noah begins a $150 perusal of *It's All You.* Tuscany is also centered on the second page, sporting a tutu and spouting a blurb outlining *The Ballet-SoHo Mega Style Crossover.* There are five articles listed in the table of contents, all followed with the byline of Tuscany Thayer. Tuscany offers to show the reader

and, finally, inexplicably (and perhaps cut-and-pasted from *Martha Stewart Living*):

"So whaddya think?" Tuscany asks on returning, flouncing onto the bed.

"You're a star. This must have taken so much work."

"Yeah. But it was like a labor of love."

"So how do you distribute it?"

"How do I what?"

"Who gets a copy?"

"You know, whoever wants. I've still got a bunch left." She points to a half dozen unopened cartons beneath her desk. "No one seems to really want one. You can keep that copy if you want."

"Uh, thanks," Noah says, wedging it in his messenger bag between vocabulary lists and *Invisible Man*.

Dr. Thayer appears in the doorway. "Did you tell Noah what I asked you to tell him, Tuscany?"

Tuscany groans. "No."

"Well, tell him now."

"Are you serious? You're right there! You tell him. Why are you being so messed?"

Dr. Thayer just stands there, fixing Tuscany with a look that was probably intended to be fearsome but comes off as simply baffled.

"Noah," Tuscany says, inflectionless, "my mom wants to talk to you."

"Thank you," Dr. Thayer says, spins on her heel, and walks out.

"What a bitch," Tuscany says after the door closes. "She's on like a total power trip."

Noah is unsure of how to respond. Dr. Thayer is behaving strangely, but "a power trip" means exerting control, and is, after all, what parents are supposed to do.

"Is everything okay between you two?" is the most diplomatic response Noah can come up with.

"That's a stupid question." Tuscany picks angrily at the furry end of her pencil. "Nothing can be okay with her. She's a monster."

There are still ten minutes left in the session, but Noah can't imagine delving back into standardized tests now. He decides he will just stay ten minutes longer next time, and gathers his things.

Noah has no idea where Dr. Thayer is in the apartment. Even after all the weeks he has worked there the Thayer residence remains labyrinthine, with an almost mythological power to make him lost. He wanders past the kitchen and finally finds Dr. Thayer dressed in a suit and seated on the oversized antique armchair in her bedroom, squinting in the half-light emitted by the shuttered windows.

"Dr. Thayer?" Noah says softly. She doesn't move.

He repeats his greeting. Her head turns slowly, laboriously, as though the temperature in the room were subzero.

"Come in. Sit down."

Noah gingerly inclines himself so he rests a minimum of weight on an emerald crushed-silk settee.

"'Harriet Tubman rememberation,'" Dr. Thayer announces flatly.

A silence floods the room. The marble clock on an armoire ticks loudly.

"Yeah," Noah finally says sadly. This is his wiliest defense for parent dissatisfaction, reserved only for the most dire situations, his "crazy world" routine: he tacitly commiserates with the disgruntled parent, emphasizes their united front in the face of the world's cruel onslaughts.

"Did you teach him that?" Dr. Thayer asks. "I'm fairly sure 'rememberation' isn't even a word." Noah can't tell if she is angry; her words limp out from within the fog of some narcotic.

"Uh, no, he came up with it himself. I've encouraged him to write on Harriet Tubman, but not in quite that way."

A wide and glassy smile spreads across Dr. Thayer's face. "It's kind of funny, really. Do they give points for humor?"

"I imagine they do occasionally, but I don't generally suggest going for it."

Dr. Thayer dismissively waves her hand from across a distance. "I've thought of so many ways around this test, Noah. But if Dylan isn't motivated, there's no point in any of it. You can hand him everything—I hand him everything—but he doesn't realize what he's got, what I've done for him. It's like I don't exist here."

"Tuscany is doing well," Noah says, in what he hopes is a guileless tone.

"Tuscany will do fine." Dr. Thayer yawns. "I'm not concerned."

"Her test is in a couple of weeks."

"I know. Dylan's test results will come at the same time. Do you have a lot riding on this? Personally?"

"Well, obviously the office bases our promotions on score increases, to some extent—"

"Because I have to say, when I first met you I thought, *He's too young, he'll never be able to do this.* I was about to send you back and get another." She pauses and stares meaningfully at Noah, as if waiting for him to realize the extent of her benevolence. "But the kids seem to like you. Which probably just means you're being too easy on them, but still."

Noah smiles blandly at Dr. Thayer.

"But my children don't see the dark side of Noah, do they?" she presses.

He forces a smile. "What do you mean?"

"Oh yes, let's keep up appearances: 'Why, Noah, I have no idea what I meant, silly me!' "

Noah stares at her across the darkness, clenching his throat against his rising fear.

"I guess on one level I'm saying thank you," Dr. Thayer says, shifting her skeleton in the chair. "For being there for them. For seeming so sweet to them."

"Thanks," Noah says, feeling a touch of vertigo, as though on the brink of a chasm. "That means a lot to me."

Dr. Thayer smiles condescendingly, as if amused at some yokel inanity of Noah's. "But that doesn't mean that I'm satisfied by this. Were you, for example, going to tell me you were leaving ten minutes early, or just hope I didn't notice?"

She doesn't sound angry, merely toying. Noah's voice quavers when he answers. He forces himself to speak slowly. "Of course. And I have to say, Dr. Thayer, I've stayed ten minutes late plenty of other sessions."

She adopts a puzzled tone, inclines her head. "But I didn't *ask* you to stay late those times, did I?"

"Of course not . . ." He can't stretch to anything else to say, so he just repeats "of course not" more curtly.

Dr. Thayer pushes her frame erect in the chair. "There you go, Noah, put your foot down."

"I'm sorry?"

"There's a real masculine vitality in you, that you're trying to hide from me. You've been pretty scrappy to make it this far, to Manhattan. Assert yourself. Don't worry about my feelings. This is no case for politeness. Now tell me, frankly this time, how is Dylan's score going to be?"

Dr. Thayer seems to be training him to defy her. She pulls her hair back to expose her long, smooth neck, and stares at him. "Not well. Not good," Noah says.

"There. Now tell me: why is that?"

"Too many tutors." He tries to stare straight into her eyes, but he can't. Despite the fact that he towers over her, has strength on his side, she makes him primally afraid; she is a gorgon playing with her powers.

She cocks her head even further. "What was that?"

"He's had too many tutors," Noah mumbles into the rug.

"Well, disregarding, for the moment, the fact that he *needs* all these tutors, answer this: you are one of these tutors, no?"

"Yes, of course, but you can hardly fault me for—"

Dr. Thayer makes a motion like an underwater punch. "Yes, lovely, go on!"

"I'm here at your request, it's hardly my place to deny you a service that you request of me."

"But you're still contributing to what you see as a destructive problem. A destructive situation, I should say."

"There's no other option now. Without tutors Dylan would be totally unprepared."

"Now? But there was *never* any option, Noah," Dr. Thayer whispers. "This all started in the sixth grade—there was never a time when he was willing to work. He's always been totally passive, a giant infant. Without tutors Dylan wouldn't even have been able to stay at *Dwight,* much less Fieldston. So what's the better parenting: get Dylan tutors, or watch him fail when I can offer him so much? I can tell you disapprove of all this, Noah—I'm a *doctor,* understanding what you're feeling is my *occupation*—but you need to realize that I'm not ashamed of any of the choices I've made here."

Noah nods, trying to cast himself as the supportive friend, not the misbehaving employee. But he wonders: if Dr. Thayer is so free of regret, why is she telling him all this?

"How does your husband feel about your kids' scores?"

"My *husband*?" Dr. Thayer throws her head back; she is about to say something truly virulent. But then her head nods, as if she has been taken by a fit of narcolepsy. "My husband does not know."

She stares at Noah. He's sure it is a trick of the gloom, but her eyes seem to blink one before the other, like a lizard's.

"How about Tuscany's magazine?" Noah says briskly. "That's pretty impressive."

Dr. Thayer snorts. "Have you *read* it?"

"Seeing the amount of effort that went in, I'm impressed. None of my other students have done anything like that."

"Well, you've just got a bumper crop of students, don't

you?" She has put on a country bumpkin accent—all that is missing is an "I reckon" at the end. Is she mocking his poverty, his slight southern accent?

"Even the best students won't work on their own like Tuscany," Noah says. "For a school project, sure, but not for the sheer pleasure of it."

There is a pause. Dr. Thayer screws up her face; she looks dissatisfied.

"Has she done something wrong?" Noah asks. Why does she constantly sell her daughter so short?

Dr. Thayer shoots Noah a warning glance. "No . . . and yes, it seems that she's dedicated to some things."

"Yeah, it's great," Noah says. His words hang feebly. The very word *great* seems timid and brittle here, a useless social convention in a chaotic land.

Dr. Thayer leans forward and presses her arms into the cushion of her chair. She looks as if about to pounce. "I believe Dylan told you about this SAT incident at Dwight last year. Nothing that made the papers, of course. No one wants a scandal."

They're back to the dark place. Noah's whole body clenches. He forces his muscles to relax. "Someone took the test for other students, right?"

Dr. Thayer fixes Noah with a slow smile. "Yes, Noah, that's correct."

"Whatever happened to the student?"

"Frankly, I don't care about that. What I do care about is this: you are very familiar with how this process works, no?"

Noah laughs. "Familiar with what process? With taking the SAT for a Dwight student?"

"Yours went to Dalton, I believe."

"I don't see what you're getting at."

"Interesting phrasing there. Not exactly denying it, are you? Tell me, how did that work out for you? How did the girl's score come out? Or did you never find out? Maybe the check was just, you know, left on the nightstand, and then you were gone."

"Who told you this?" Noah asks. He doesn't much care, but he can think of no better question to cover his guilt.

"I found out about it because I was looking for someone to 'help out' Dylan, way back. And your name, funnily enough, came up. See, Noah? We're both *so very evil.* Or maybe we just both want to see kids we care about succeed."

"What are you trying to do?"

Dr. Thayer falls back among her pillows. "I just want to make sure that we're relating to each other on the correct terms. We're not so different, you and I. That's why I chose you."

Flustered, fighting back panic, and desperate to alter the course of the conversation, Noah makes a mistake—he asks a "student question" of a parent: "Do you have plans tonight?"

Dr. Thayer puts down her book, glances to the bed, and then smiles thinly at Noah. "I do have plans tonight. I have work to do. Do *you* have plans tonight?"

"Yes," Noah says quietly.

"Good night, then."

~

At the Fifth Avenue stop Noah's crosstown bus is loaded with commuters, young men and women in business suits, those future executives willing to put in ninety-hour workweeks and return home at ten P.M. Noah stands crowded into their weary mass, listens to their clipped and irritated cell phone conversations. Half the calls seem to be to parents, and the other half to friends or lovers. Some calls complain about rent payments and negligent landlords, and other calls complain about friends' complaining. Noah is glad that Olena might be home waiting for him.

The subway train that pulls in at 79th Street is almost full. Noah wedges himself between a bushy-haired woman clutching a canvas bag and reading *The Prophet* and an elderly Asian man whose head bobs as he listens to his iPod. After 96th Street the white occupants of the car begin to trickle out, and minorities trickle on. The train that rackets aboveground at 125th Street is full of brown and black bodies, and Noah.

He exits the subway at 145th Street and tracks up Broadway, his tutoring bag bouncing against his hip. The sidewalk is littered with the detritus of the day's activities. Wrappers—primarily McDonald's and KFC, interspersed with a few Chinese takeout Styrofoam containers—combine with broken glass to form a local sort of low-lying scrub vegetation along the sidewalk. One of the local panhandlers has thrown up in the concrete median of Broadway, and he points out the orange splash to Noah as he passes, raising his brown-bagged bottle in a cheer. The local supermarket has closed, but a woman clutching a child has spread a few dusty cans of food on a blanket in front of it, hawking the goods to those who pass. For the moment Noah hates both Fifth Avenue and Harlem, that they can coexist, one so near to the other, and not crash together and equalize.

~

Noah pauses halfway up the building stairwell. He leans against the cinderblock wall and rubs his temples. Dr. Thayer knows about Monroe.

Monroe Eichler, his first and best student. Confident, aggressive, red curls, and tartan skirts fastened with safety pins. Now at Amherst, presumably. Noah would love to know where she is, how she is doing. He would love to just talk to her, like they used to do. But Mrs. Eichler made it clear that he's not to make contact at all.

For three hours a week, Wednesday evenings were bliss (one-hundred-minute session with Monroe, one-hundred-minute dinner with Mrs. Eichler and Monroe). Monroe was president of Dalton's Model United Nations Club, and would excitedly chatter about Argentina's tenuous position in world politics. She confessed to a guilty fascination with the Fibonacci sequence. She read Russian fantasy and was auditing advanced calculus courses at Columbia. Halfway through the year she was already scoring 2300s on her practice tests.

And then, one week before she was supposed to take the October SAT, her father died. Congestive heart failure, just like Noah's father. "His heart isn't pumping out the venous blood," Monroe had brokenly reported on the phone, in the detached and ironic tone good students take on for teachers. She was sorry, but she would have to cancel the week's session. As if that were her primary concern. Noah rescheduled his other appointments in order to rush over and spend the day with the family, made calls and performed whatever insignificant errands were necessary. He spent Friday and Saturday night there (he was breaking up with Tabitha at the time and grateful, secondarily, for a place to stay), and shared melancholy and emotional meals with Monroe and her mother. He joined in their unhappiness and yet, at the same time, couldn't remember ever having felt more content. He felt himself part of their family, an adopted member of their inner circle, as if he were Monroe's fiancé.

Monroe's mother, a polished and eloquent analyst for Deutsche Bank, pulled Noah aside on Sunday. She was concerned—Monroe was brilliant but also flighty, and in her melancholy she was hardly able to put the silver away in the correct place—how could she do well on her SAT on Saturday? And the October administration was her last option for her early application to Amherst. Would she be able to get a special postponement? No? What did Noah suggest, then?

Noah worked with Monroe throughout the week. But she was entirely unable to concentrate. Her scores plummeted to 1800s, nothing that would get her into Amherst. She sobbed over missed vocabulary words.

Noah's reverie about Monroe is broken. He raises his head. Music has begun to crackle from his apartment. He opens the door to Olena and Roberto dancing. The little tape player Hera keeps on the windowsill hums, wafting out a feeble Polish pop tune that sounds like Shakira interpreting a polka. Roberto, his large frame clothed like an eighties rock star, his hair slicked back in vain waves that reach his neck, turns his sister gracefully, and she stands and accepts him with poised generosity, circling her brother with bonny enthusiasm. They are oblivious to Noah, and the scene is so unexpected, so lovely and odd, that Noah is paralyzed in the doorway, entranced.

Roberto sees Noah and lets his hands drop.

"Hey, what's up?" he says.

Olena flashes Noah a sardonic smile. "May brothers and sisters never dance in America?"

Noah stammers in response, not because he finds it odd that they were dancing—he thought it charming—but because he is unable to find the words to prove himself not to be the prudish American.

Luckily Roberto, always an abundant source of distraction, starts to rummage through Noah's bag. He looks at the first page of a vocabulary list as he scratches a finger through his stiffly gelled hair. He hunches over in dazed concentration, as if he were reading a cereal box early in the morning. "I don't know any of these."

"Yeah," Noah says, "it's hard."

Roberto passes the list to his sister. "Do you know any of these?"

She squints at the list. She is wearing an old softened T-shirt that falls like gossamer over her breasts, and a patch of fair skin shows through a rip in the shoulder. "Yes, I know these. But I have read a lot, that's why, Roberto." She turns to Noah, then continues proudly: "Our family was of some importance back when Albania was communist. We had an English teacher who lived with us, a young guy like you. But then the communists were gone and under the new, capitalist *régime* we had to give up our teachers. Albania is no longer a good place to live, Noah. Not good."

"What's this?" Roberto exclaims. He has tossed a dozen word lists and *Invisible Man* to one side and has come upon Tuscany's magazine. "*It's All You.* I don't get it. What does it mean? And why do you have it?"

"It's my student," Noah explains curtly. Then he wishes he hadn't spoken; he doesn't like the sight of Tuscany's semi-clothed form beneath Roberto's broad fingers.

Olena inhales sharply as Roberto lets out a low whistle. "Your student has published a *magazine*?" Olena breathes.

"And this," Roberto says excitedly, holding the magazine out and pointing to the cover. "This is her?"

"Wow," Olena says amazedly.

"Wow," Roberto says libidinously.

"Yep," Noah says, wondering how difficult it would be to snatch the magazine from Roberto's grip.

"So costly, no? To put out a magazine," Olena says.

"Well, it's not exactly hard-hitting journalism," Noah says.

"But this is very high quality paper. Gosh. Think what that money could have gone to instead."

"This bitch is *hot,*" Roberto adds. "Seriously, Noah, you have to let me meet her."

"No," Noah says, his eyes flashing. "Absolutely not."

"You've got to be shittin' me. Why not, *cabrón*?"

"She's a kid. Stop it."

Roberto flips through the magazine and makes grunts similar to those he affected while working out. "Wow," he says again, then, "Jesus," and then various phrases in what

Noah has come to recognize as Albanian. Noah glowers across the table. Seeing Noah's annoyance, Olena plucks the magazine from Roberto and hands it back to Noah.

Roberto grins wickedly, crosses his bare arms over his chest and mouths the words, *Hot bitch.*

That night, in bed early, Noah's first thoughts are on Tuscany. Roberto's irresponsible desire infuriates him. Such attentions from men are what make Tuscany obsess about her body instead of her future. He punches a pillow. His fury is more complex than he realizes, he is sure, but he is unable to sort his feelings about her. He is alarmed by his flicker of attraction to her. After Monroe he promised himself never to be drawn to another student. He stuffs *It's All You* under his mattress.

He thought he had banished Monroe from his mind, thought he had healed, but suddenly he feels the shame and guilt afresh. The depth of his feelings for her was inappropriate, he knows. His intense affection led him to consider doing things he should never have done, for which he can't forgive himself. He distrusts his own feelings toward Tuscany, second-guesses himself: surely he isn't repeating history, allowing attraction to distort his sense of duty?

~

Monroe's score didn't go up all week. Friday afternoon, Noah got a call from Mrs. Eichler. She was at a loss. Monroe wouldn't get into Amherst if she performed the next day as she had performed all week. Would it turn out, Mrs. Eichler lamented a touch dramatically, that everything Monroe had striven for would be ripped away because of the timing of her father's death?

Noah proposed a solution which Mrs. Eichler accepted immediately, as if Noah were stating a foregone conclusion. He went to St. Marks Place and purchased a fake ID with his picture and the name of Monroe Eichler. Thanks to the faddish tendency of Fifth Avenue to give its children the last names of nineteenth century presidents (it is a two-mile gallery of tiny Grants, Harrisons, Jeffersons, Madisons, Monroes, Pierces, Taylors, and Tylers), he could take the test for a girl, for Monroe. He imagined plunging into Monroe's test on Saturday morning in an altered state, so wracked by guilt that taking the standardized test would become a visceral, animalistic experience. He knew there was no rationalizing what he was about to do, philosophically, but taking the test had an emotional necessity—he couldn't bear to see his Monroe miss her chance to go to Amherst. He would take care to miss the verbal questions Monroe would have missed (the hard sentence completions), and to miss no math. The scoring machine would know no difference between his bubbles and those of Monroe, and her score, when it came, should turn out to be what it would have been had her father not died.

But Mrs. Eichler called on Friday night. Monroe had a fit of compunction and demanded to take the test herself. Noah wondered if he could speak to her. Monroe was unavailable. Mrs. Eichler hung up. She and Noah would never talk again.

Three days later, an envelope arrived in the mail, inside it a check from Deutsche Bank with no sender's name and no memo, no little "thanks" or smiley face scrawled in the corner. The check was for $5,000.

Was it payment for his trouble, regardless of his not having taken the test, or a clerical accident? It was a cashier's check—Mrs. Eichler would never know if he deposited it or not. There was no moral high road here, no making a statement. He deposited the check. He had maxed out a credit card, and his brother's counselor's fees were due.

The next afternoon Noah travels from Harlem back down to the Upper East Side on a train full of blacks and Hispanics commuting with glassy, gloomy gazes; then the composition of the train gradually shifts, until he gets off at Fifth Avenue amid glassy, gloomy gazes of white women in pricey suits. Noah dashes into the Thayers' building just as sheets of rain begin to fall from the sky.

When Noah exits the elevator he exchanges places with the hulking form of Dr. Thayer's personal trainer. Dr. Thayer is propped against the foyer wall, carefully and meticulously breathless, dressed in workout clothes that are sleek, stylish, and not in the least sweaty.

"So, how were the scores?" Noah asks. The question bubbles out without preamble; he is excited to discover the answer.

"The scores?" Dr. Thayer pants. She tilts her head disdainfully, as if Noah has just asked her the latest football standings.

"Tuscany and Dylan. How did they do?"

"Oh, their scores! They did pretty well. Well, Dylan did awfully, actually, but we got this at the same time." Dr. Thayer hands Noah a letter addressed to Dylan from the George Washington athletics director. He scans it:

We were delighted to review your athletic performances over the last few weeks, and while the sports program has no direct say in admissions decisions, we do highly suggest that you apply to George Washington, and have the strongest hopes that you will join us in the fall for a challenging and successful season.

"So he's basically in," Noah says. He is conflicted: heartened to see Dylan succeed and his own pressures released, disheartened that it should happen this way.

"It looks like it!" Dr. Thayer beams and places a hand on Noah's shoulder. Her hard fingers are cool through his shirt. "And I'm sure, Noah, that he couldn't have done it without you."

Noah is quite certain Dylan could have done it without him. In fact, Dylan's score didn't rise at all.

"Thank you, Dr. Thayer."

"Didn't I tell you to call me Susan? I think I told you to call me Susan." She laughs and makes as if to playfully swat at her words as they hang in the air.

"And how did Tuscany do?" Noah asks.

"Oh, very well, I'm sure. She's never been the trouble case Dylan was." She positions a hand against the entranceway curio cabinet, bearing a look of exhaustion on her carefully made-up face.

"Do you have the score report?"

"Yes, somewhere here . . ." Dr. Thayer sorts through a pile of papers on the mahogany hallway table. "Oh, here it is."

She hands Noah an envelope. It is unopened.

"You haven't looked at it." Noah's words come out half beseeching, half accusatory—*You don't care how she did.*

"Well, not yet. Go ahead, you do it."

"Are you sure?"

"Yes, of course, go!"

Noah slides a finger under the seal of the envelope. The paper rips in jagged triangles. He pulls out the red and white letter.

He has never seen an ISEE score report—he always hears about scores secondhand, from the parents—and it is a mess of numbers and statistics. He stares dumbly for a few moments, trying to find patterns in the chaos. Then the results start to sort themselves into order. They're good.

"She did really well, Dr. Thayer," Noah says excitedly. "A really big improvement from her diagnostic test!"

"Really?" Dr. Thayer says, holding back a foot and stretching, her hipbone clearly outlined in the black spandex.

"Her percentiles are all in the upper 80s, and her math is a 92."

"And that's good?" Dr. Thayer sounds dubious.

"Good enough to get her wherever she needs to go. Don't forget that the percentiles are comparing her against other applicants to private high schools, not the whole nation. So it's a pretty elite category, and she's doing better than most of them."

"Well, good for her." Dr. Thayer's tone is ambiguous; Noah can read either smoldering elation or outright contempt into it.

"So she doesn't know yet?" Noah asks. Dr. Thayer shakes her head. "I'm sure you want to tell her," he says. "I'll just wait down here."

Dr. Thayer waves him on and winks. "No, no, just go ahead. I'm bound to run into her later today."

"So my scores are *good?*" Tuscany is sprawled on her bed, in a pair of sweatpants with "Moore-Pike" emblazoned across the ass.

"Yeah, really good. You're up a whole fifteen percentile points. Especially math. Ninety-second, really good."

"Awesome." Her voice rises to a screech as she scans the paper. "Awesome!"

"So where are you going to go? You could widen your net now—look at Andover or Exeter, even."

"*No!* No way."

"Well, Hampshire Academy certainly looks possible. Or you could go take a look at Choate, that's another good one. I think you might like it there."

Tuscany clacks a glitter pen against her teeth. "God, I really haven't thought about it."

"Where does your mom want you to go?"

"She doesn't really say much. That's so that she can complain about wherever I choose. If she doesn't like say anything now, it's easier for her to bitch later, you know?" Tuscany runs the pen back and forth across her teeth. Then: "I have to call a friend."

She picks up her phone, gives it a hard look, and throws it on the bed. "No, they prob'ly don't give a crap." She looks at Noah. "You asked me something, right?"

Noah nods. "Why do you want to go away?"

"People here suck. I just need to get out."

Tuscany has created a magazine that nobody seems to want (four cartons of it sit beside her desk), and she seems to detest her friends—Noah is desperate to see her leave New York before her determination to find something better atrophies.

"Well, this is your ticket away," Noah says. "I think you'll do well at boarding school."

"What do you mean?" Tuscany asks, suspicious.

"Just that some students aren't really suited to boarding school. But you're independent enough to make it."

"Yah, thanks. This is so cool." She lights a cigarette.

"You know, a lot of schools have rolling admissions—you can apply now and get in for the spring semester. You'd be at school within a couple of months." What impresses Noah about Tuscany is her drive for self-preservation. She has found her own ways to shine beneath the rotting stardom of her older brother. She has created a magazine because she wants to, not out of a desire to please her mother. She has enough self-possession to realize that she both dislikes and is disliked at Moore-Pike, and she has taken it upon herself to change schools.

"Yah, I thought about spring semester. So I should apply like now?"

"Yes, now."

~

Since Tuscany has already taken her test, there is no need for a session. Noah discusses her percentiles with her, then leaves her bedroom. Dr. Thayer stands at the bottom of the stairs and peers up, trapping him. She has taken on a cat-like pose, but in her tight charcoal spandex she seems to Noah like a length of knotted chain.

"How is she feeling?" Dr. Thayer asks mournfully, as if Tuscany has scarlet fever.

"She's thrilled. She's thinking of applying to schools for spring admission."

Dr. Thayer's eyes narrow. "You suggested that?"

"Well, yes, if she's unhappy where she is, I figured it was best that she move on. Plenty of students start boarding school in the spring."

Dr. Thayer laughs lightly and profusely. "Well, she's *your* daughter!"

"I'm sorry?"

"I wouldn't dream of inserting myself into this . . . process. What do I know about applying to schools? I'm just a mom." She pronounces "I'm just a mom" with leagues of saccharine self-effacement, as would any dissatisfied suburban mother. She is so unpredictable, adopting various half-hearted and intimidating personae.

"I'm sure Tuscany would appreciate your guidance," Noah says.

Dr. Thayer looks up at Noah bleakly. "Right."

"I've left my e-mail address with Tuscany, in case she wants to bounce any school options or application essay ideas off me."

Dr. Thayer raises a thin eyebrow. "That's very kind of you."

She lets go of the banister and stands to one side, indicating that Noah should now pass. He starts down the stairs. The stairs end right before the front door, but Dr. Thayer has not yet opened it, so they stand a foot apart from each other. For someone who has just heavily worked out, Dr. Thayer doesn't give off even a whiff of body odor. She seems to be wearing any number of fragrances. Again, Noah notices that she is significantly shorter than he. He looks at the part of her wiry blond hair during their awkward silence, observes the hints of steel-gray roots. Dr. Thayer tilts her head back. She slackens her mouth; the heavy lines around her lips broaden. After a moment of concentration she makes her smile lively and lovely.

"I guess this is it," she says. "I'd hug you, but I'm horribly sweaty." She laughs as if at the preposterousness of her statement, a goddess feigning mortality.

"It's been a pleasure," Noah says.

"They couldn't have done it without you." It is Dr. Thayer's stock phrase; she says it so often that Noah is quite certain it isn't ever meant to be taken seriously. He wonders what she is waiting for; he gets the odd sense that she wants him to fold her in his arms.

Noah glances up toward Dylan's suite. "I should probably say goodbye to Dylan."

Dr. Thayer turns the silver doorknob of the front door. "Oh, I'll say goodbye for you. Don't worry about that."

Noah nods reluctantly. He is saddened that she won't let him say goodbye, but he can't understand why he feels that way—Dylan won't care, and he won't miss Dylan. Will he? "Okay, then," he says softly.

"He's probably busy watching a game or sleeping. And you know how he gets when he's disturbed unnecessarily," Dr. Thayer says breezily.

"Right."

Dr. Thayer glides the door open. "Goodbye, Noah." Her

tone is tentative, both condescending and apologetic, as if she has just dumped an inferior lover. As he passes through the doorway she leans forward and, with a whiff of rose essence, kisses Noah on the space below his ear. The door clicks smoothly shut.

~

It is near impossible to divine the weather from within the Thayer apartment—most rooms are curtained so tightly that it might as well not have windows at all. When Noah exits the elevator he sees that the doormen are holding slick black umbrellas. The sky is a luminous gray, and Fifth Avenue is glossy black.

"Wow, it rained pretty hard, huh?" Noah asks the doormen as he leaves.

"Yeah," one answers. "You should have seen it."

"This is the last time I'm coming here, guys. It's all done."

The doormen shrug and hold the door open.

Noah has an appointment with Cameron in twenty minutes. The sky holds back long enough for him to walk briskly across Central Park to the Leinzler residence. A great gray building overlooking the Museum of Natural History, it stands starkly outlined before the stormy sky. Cameron has piled her masses of black hair on top of her head and covered them with a gum-pink Yankees cap. She sports a hooded sweatshirt that declares, "Drama Geeks Rule."

"Hey, Noah, what's up?" she asks as she guides him to her father's desk, their usual tutoring spot. Imported from North Africa, its plane is covered in black leather, and extends farther than most dining room tables.

"Not much," Noah says, sitting at a Moroccan chair and pulling out Cameron's assignments folder.

"You seem totally gloomy today!"

Noah forces a carefree smile. "Really?"

Cameron scrutinizes Noah, then tosses her head. "Or maybe not."

"How'd the vocab go this week?"

"Okay, I guess. List Eight was totally hard."

Cameron begins her quiz. Her mother is French, her father fluent in German, and she grew up with a Spanish-speaking nanny. It is a felicitous combination, and for a B student, she has a great vocabulary. Noah watches her fill in the worksheet.

"Gourmand," she says, reflexively putting a hand to her abdomen. "That's a fat person, right?"

"Close. Put 'one with an unhealthy obsession with food.' "

"Okay."

"I had my last session with Dylan Thayer's sister today." He can't get the Thayers out of his head.

"Oh yeah? Tuscany? Is she mean, or what?"

"No, she's totally nice. Why?"

"I don't know, she just always seems so"—she points to a word on the list—"lofty. Tuscany Thayer is lofty. And she—" Cameron cuts off her words dramatically and stares at Noah with falsely wide eyes, as though they were at the climax of a melodrama.

"And she what?" Noah prompts.

"Oh no, I totally can't say anything."

"Oh, I'm sure whatever you have to—"

"Okay, you know her friend Monica? Really tall, really skinny?"

Noah nods. That must be the girl he saw with Tuscany outside Victoria's Secret, the one whose posture simultaneously screamed best friend and mortal enemy.

"Well, they're totally not friends anymore." Cameron pauses, as if to finish the story there, but of course barrels on: "Monica has this totally hot doorman. Like, a little like Colin Farrell. And this one night Tuscany goes to Monica's but, well, the doormen call up from the desk to say that she arrived, but she never makes it to Monica's apartment—"

"All right, that's enough."

"You asked."

"To my chagrin."

"Whatever. I'm not going to say what I think, I'm sure she's totally nice, but my friends say she's a slut."

"They shouldn't."

Cameron shrugs. "Okay, fine, whatever you say. Wait, why have you finished with them? Dylan has to take the SAT again like next month."

Noah looks at her, confused. "No, he's done. Dylan and I have finished."

"I heard his mom tried to pay someone to take it for him, but it didn't happen. Is that true?"

Noah carefully considers his answer. "It didn't happen."

"And my friend Isabelle"—she points to one of five blonde girls holding hands in a snapshot mounted on the mirror—"went out with Dylan like last week. They talked for like hours, and he's definitely still working on his SAT. Weren't you tutoring him?"

"Just for the writing part. I think he's already fine for math and verbal." Noah's mind is racing. Dylan only needed help with writing, right? That's what Dr. Thayer told him.

"Um, *you think*?" Cameron laughs. "You're totally supposed to know these things."

"His family hasn't told me anything about it. So I guess they have something arranged." Noah feels a rising anger, that he has been obscurely betrayed. He can think of two possibilities—either Dr. Thayer has secretly gotten Dylan a new tutor, or she is still searching for someone she can pay to take the test for Dylan. Either possibility makes Noah uneasy.

After he finishes his session with Cameron, Noah walks up Broadway, peering in store windows, unwilling to return right away to the narrow room he shares with Roberto. He drinks a coffee in a Starbucks, gazes into the darkened displays of a closed Banana Republic across the street. He checks his cell phone—a message from Tab giving some encouraging feedback on his application essays, but nothing from Dr. Thayer. Of course not.

The call comes six weeks later. He turns on his phone after leaving a session, and hears the unmistakable rasp of Dr. Thayer's voice. But the message is not about Dylan, it is about Tuscany: she got into Choate, began the spring semester, and was removed from classes three days in for reasons Dr. Thayer is "not at liberty to name." She wonders: would Noah be available to teach her until they can find another school?

chapter 5

Dr. Thayer's message insists that Noah contact her at his convenience. He calls her immediately.

"Hi, Dr. Thayer? This is Noah." He stands in a crowd waiting for the walk light to turn at Central Park West, holding his phone tightly against his ear to make out her urgent rasp.

"Oh, thank God. I thought you would never call."

"Is this an okay time?"

"Yes, fine."

"Good."

A pause. Noah halts on the corner as the crowd surges across the street. He is unsure of how to segue into the issue of Tuscany's getting kicked out. "So. Tell me about Tuscany," Noah says.

"Well, yes, plans have changed a little there. I suppose I'm wondering: do you have any free time during the day? It turns out that Choate won't be happening after all, and, well, Tuscany wants to keep up with her studies while she's between schools."

The first question that springs to Noah's mind—*What the hell did she do?*—seems unsuitable, so he just holds his breath.

"Well, she still has riding lessons Tuesday and Thursday, and ballet on Wednesday and piano on Monday. So afternoons are shot. Could you come from, say, nine to two each day? That would give you five hours to work. She's got, let's see, she'll know her classes better than me, but I *think* she's taking chemistry, and some history, and God, she's bound to be taking French too . . . hold on a moment. Tuscany! *Tussy*!"

Noah hears Dr. Thayer's continued shrieks, then a thudding as someone heavy approaches the phone.

It is Dylan's voice: "Noah! Did you hear what happened? Aha! Can you—"

Then Tuscany, from a distance: "You asshole!" Noah smiles to hear her squeal as she wrestles the phone away from her brother. "Hello?"

"Hi, Tuscany, it's Noah."

"Hi."

"How's it going?"

"Fine. So I'm taking chemistry, world history, French IV, geometry, and English—"

"What are you reading in English?"

"Somerset something, I don't know. So do you think you're going to be able to come?" She sounds so hopeful, like a nine-year-old throwing a birthday party. She really, genuinely likes him. Noah smiles goofily into the phone; he has really missed her.

"I think so. But you have to put your mother back on for a second." He hears a squabble of static as the phone switches hands.

"Hi, so what do you think?" Dr. Thayer's words come at a clipped pace; she is rushing to get somewhere.

It all seems so nineteenth century, the bored young man responsible for the intellectual upbringing of a bright but reluctant noblewoman. Of course there are the extra twenty-five hours of work a week, which will solve his financial problems. His mind races.

"I'd be happy to. Of course, I'll have plenty of questions before I start."

"Wonderful. Of course you do. But I've got to run. Why don't you just come by tomorrow at nine? Get whatever books you need. We'll reimburse you, of course. We'll talk tomorrow, see you tomorrow, 'bye!"

Noah is left standing at the corner listening to a dead phone, wondering how to become a real teacher within twenty-four hours. He has done academic tutoring twice before—but both students were nerdy types who wanted to stay at the top of their class. Tuscany Thayer promises to be a different case entirely. How thrilling! He will be her sole intellectual guidance. He can do anything with her: if she takes an interest in factoring binomials, they can investigate higher theories of . . . binomial mathematical . . . discrete . . . abstract . . . something. Christ, he thinks as he swings idly around a light pole, it's been a long time since high school, since he studied science or history at all.

He stops at Barnes & Noble on the way home. He knows of no bookstores anywhere within Harlem, so he has to go to the Columbia University bookstore on 115th Street. The "Study Aids" section is all cheat-books, a massive wall full of course outlines and textbook summaries, made by a plethora of companies. Princeton Review, Kaplan, SparkNotes, REA, Barron's, Peterson's . . . each publishes its guides in a different gaudy color, and the wall is a riot of loud paperbacks, a circus of education. He opens one and flips through the pages of cartoons and "hot tips"—he can't teach from this. It is an abbreviation of knowledge, designed to replace the complexity of an original source with the reductive bare bones.

He stands at the corner with empty hands but a full head, dreaming of ways to broaden Tuscany, to explore together worlds foreign to her own. He remembers her blithe ignorance of the distinction between African Americans and Native Americans, of what a pueblo is. He imagines a unit on Native Americans in which they will make dioramas and imagine what their lives involved.

When he gets off the subway he has a voicemail from Roberto: Does Noah want to get a beer? Yes, Noah wants to get a beer.

Roberto and Noah drive downtown and double-park the Datsun outside Charlie's. It's Roberto's favorite place, the only bar in Manhattan with the bland catchall atmosphere of a suburban chain restaurant. The waiters wear buttons. Roberto and Noah plant themselves at a corner of the bar.

"So we hooked up that night, after we all ate dinner? And shit, it was hot, I mean, she was grabbing me right here"—Noah doesn't bother to look where Roberto is pointing—"and I was grabbing her, like right under there, and she has this like tiny room and her feet were hitting the wall and we were like all sweaty and shit."

Roberto looks at Noah expectantly, a huge smile on his face.

"And you liked that?" Noah dutifully replies.

"Uh, *yah!* And she liked it too. But they always do, man. If there's one thing I do right, it's the like bed play, you know? But I fuck up everything else." Roberto laughs and shakes his beer in the air ruefully. "How's like your love life?" he asks.

"Um, kind of nonexistent," Noah says. "I just don't fall in love too often. When I do, it's strong, but it just doesn't happen every day."

"But you must hook up with plenty of hotties. But it never goes anywhere? I guess you're like, what word is it? Really choosy?"

"Yeah, I guess you could say that." Noah has a distaste for the word *choosy*. It makes him feel like a snotty cheerleader, or a spinster with a pearl necklace and a poodle.

"What about the bitch from the magazine, that Tuscany girl?"

"She's my student, Rob. And she's fifteen. That's not going to happen."

"Yeah, but—" Roberto makes a lewd gesture the likes of which Noah hasn't seen since eighties teen movies. A couple of guys at the other end of the bar chuckle and roll their eyes.

"You don't know how wrong that is," Noah says.

"And you don't know how damn laced up you are. Just do things, don't worry about what's gonna happen, you know?"

Roberto goes on to enumerate Noah's options, which include sticking his hand in Tuscany's pants, and if that doesn't work kissing her first. Noah laughs despite himself. This is why he enjoys Roberto's company: he is such a stark contrast, the opposite of Noah himself.

"Yeah, I'll admit I could go crazy more often. Just not with my students."

"Have you ever gone to any of those hot clubs Dylan or Tuscany go to? Have you ever at least, you know, hit the town with them?"

"I don't think that would be too professional."

Roberto cracks his fist on top of Noah's head. "God, I got lots of work to do on you, man."

Noah downs the rest of his beer. He can party with his friends, he reminds himself. He doesn't need Tuscany and Dylan to become his social life.

"Truth is, Noah, man," Roberto says, "I really want to check out the hot bitches at one of those clubs. And you are going to get us on the guest list."

Noah laughs. But Roberto is just staring at him with earnest eyes. How strange to see him sincere and desirous. Noah bounces his cardboard coaster against the wood of the bar, presses the empty beer bottle to his lips, and then puts it down. A night with celebrities at an ultra-hip bar. Could be fantastic. Could be awful. Would certainly be out of the ordinary.

"Okay," Noah pledges. "I'll get us on the list."

Roberto stands, hugs Noah, lifts him off the barstool, shakes him once, and puts him back down. "All right! You're a cool kid, Noah. And now everyone's gonna see it."

Roberto orders them another round, and as Noah pays the bartender Roberto declares: "Pangaea Wednesday. 'Rich Bitch Wednesday.' That's the one I want. You got two days to get us in."

~

The next morning Noah arrives at the Thayer apartment clutching a stack of texts. Although he has been there dozens of times, he knows he has a big job to begin today: he feels as nervous as he did at first. He has worn a dress shirt for the occasion. He stayed up late preparing lessons, and his eyes prick with lack of sleep. Roberto had locked himself into the bathroom that morning to get ready for work, so Noah styled his hair at the kitchen sink. He used too much gel, and his hair has fallen against his head in slick lines. He clicks his pen nervously. With his concerned air and his creased white dress shirt he feels a bit like a salesman, or a Mormon missionary.

Fuen answers the door.

"Hello," Noah says. "Good morning."

Fuen retreats into the apartment. Noah follows her. He scans the foyer and the adjoining rooms, but Fuen has disappeared.

"Fuck, fuck, fuck!" he hears from the kitchen. It is Dylan. His hair is in disarray (clearly unplanned this time, rather than the usual carefully constructed chaos), and he staggers to his feet from a half-eaten bowl of cereal.

"Hey, Dylan," Noah says. "Late for school?"

"Fuck, fuck. Did you see a car service out front when you came?"

"There were a few cars out there. I don't know who they were for."

"Fuck." Dylan picks up a small handful of pills from the kitchen counter and downs them with milk slurped from his remaining cereal. Cornflakes stick to his chin. He lurches out the front door.

Almost as soon as it closes, the front door opens again. Dylan's hand reaches in, grabs his backpack, and withdraws. The door is left hanging open. Noah closes it. It gives a solid click. He slowly walks upstairs toward Tuscany's bedroom. The ebony of the stairwell walls has been recently polished, and the glints of morning light admitted through the heavily curtained windows make feeble, ephemeral designs upon it.

"Noah?" comes a groggy voice from Dr. Thayer's bedroom.

He enters. Dr. Thayer has wrapped herself in her silk covers. Only her head emerges from the duvet, and rests between two black satin pillows as if disembodied, cradled in emptiness. A pale and ensconced reading lamp is the only light in the room, and it illuminates her haggard face dramatically, giving it the elaborate shadows of a museum display. She must spend half the day in the bed, drugged and unmoving.

Noah stands at the entrance to the bedroom, nervously fingering the buttons of his shirt. It is as though he has entered the inner sanctum of a forgotten queen. As always in Dr. Thayer's bedroom, his very life seems to hang in the balance, could be snuffed out with a snap of Dr. Thayer's fingers.

"What time is it?" Dr. Thayer's head moans.

"About ten to nine."

"You were supposed to come at nine, no?"

There is a vague, groggy accusation in her tone, but Noah finds it hard to imagine that he has inconvenienced her, that she would have been up and ready for him had he arrived ten minutes later. "Well, I wanted to make sure to be here on time. It's hard to gauge the commute."

He was about to add *from Harlem,* but decides against it. He doesn't know whether his neighborhood would add charm or taint to his image in Dr. Thayer's eyes, and chooses not to risk it.

Dr. Thayer rises slightly in the bed. The two white lacy straps of her nightdress emerge from the satin. She places a pair of broad golden reading glasses over her large eyes. "Early's just as bad as late, or so they say! I'm sorry not to be more ready, but I suppose you know what to do, don't need my guidance. It hasn't been too long since you were studying this material yourself, right?"

Noah blinks, trying to follow the rapid twist of Dr. Thayer's words. "Not too long, really. Well, a number of years, but still."

She sits up further, and more white lace emerges from the satin. "You know, there's something I wanted to talk to you about. Since this is not, strictly speaking, *tutoring,* seeing as we're not preparing for a test, I think it's only fair that we do this just between us, and not through your agency."

Noah has predicted this tack—parents frequently balk at the high rates, and ask to arrange something under the table. He has always declined. But in this case he is not sure. He is not really tutoring here; he is teaching, right? It's as if he's doing an entirely different job. And how much more quickly would he be able to get out of his $81,000 of debt if the agency didn't take two-thirds of his pay?

"I'd be willing to arrange something like that," he says. "Some of the sessions through the agency, some between us, maybe."

Dr. Thayer squints under the light and her mouth pulls tighter. "Fantastic. What rates do you normally charge?"

Noah has precalculated this—Dr. Thayer is charged $395 by the agency, but has no idea what percentage Noah actually makes. Thus he should ask for something significantly lower than the $395 Dr. Thayer is billed, but higher than the $100 he actually makes. "I think two hundred twenty-five an hour would be customary."

Customary. Two hundred twenty-five! In three hours he would earn what his teachers in high school made in a week. And they were in their fifties, bespectacled, respected. He's just a kid from Princeton in Adidas sneakers, paid to be liked by fifteen-year-olds.

"Two twenty-five?" Dr. Thayer says. She puts her hands to her hair and pulls the dry blond mass behind her head, leaning back and pinning it against the headboard. "Let's go with that for now. I'm going to ask a few of my friends what is normal in these situations, but I need you, so I guess I'll pay it anyway!"

She emits a choked little laugh. It becomes clear to Noah that he could have asked for $1,025 an hour instead, if other tutors did the same—what matters to Dr. Thayer is not the amount of money she spends, but that she isn't taken.

"I don't mean to pry, but—" Noah begins.

"I'd rather you didn't ask Tuscany what happened there," Dr. Thayer says. "We're still dealing with the repercussions. Suffice it to say that she's going to be here for some time, until we can get her into another school for the fall semester."

"She can't just go back to Moore-Pike?"

"No," Dr. Thayer says wearily. "I'd push it, but Tuscany refuses to go back anyway. But I don't want her to feel left behind, so all I really need for you to do is keep her busy, keep her happy and out of my hair."

"Have you looked at Rothman? It's a school down in the sixties on the East Side, and they have a tutorial system and specialize in"—Noah was about to say *dropouts*—"cases like Tuscany's."

Dr. Thayer eyes Noah suspiciously. "We're looking into

Rothman." She crosses her arms, as if dubious that Noah could actually put Tuscany's education ahead of getting paid. "But for now it's all on you."

"Is Tuscany awake?" Noah asks. He is nervous about entering the bedroom of a sleeping hot fifteen-year-old.

"Agnès will get her up. Have you met Agnès? I suppose not, she's only here during the day. She's the kids' personal assistant. She'll be the one to get you your check at the end of the week."

"Okay, great," Noah says. He wonders if Agnès lives somewhere in the cavernous apartment, if they have been stepping around each other the whole time and just haven't happened to cross paths. He starts from the room.

"One last thing," Dr. Thayer says. Noah halts and cringes inwardly. One-last-things are Dr. Thayer's vicious specialty. He suspects she plans them ahead of time, waits breathlessly throughout the conversation for the chance to make her parting shot at his back.

"I've asked Agnès to prepare the dining room for you two to work in. I think it would be very improper, don't you, for you to spend all your time in Tuscany's bedroom?"

She shoots Noah an accusing look. He chokes down a number of indignant responses, then nods and leaves.

He hates her for a moment, with a tempestuous all-consuming rage; a bit, he admonishes himself, like a small child. And just like a small child, he is powerless against her. So he bucks up and starts down the hall. Dining rooms, Noah reasons, are rarely upstairs. So he walks down the dark stairwell and wanders the wide painting-lined hallway on the first floor. He comes upon two rooms that look like offices, both strewn with paper and receipts. The next room has a wide polished wooden table decorated by a pair of silver candelabras. Portraits of old men line the walls, and an antique serving table dominates one corner. This might as well be a dining room, although

Noah can't envision anyone eating here, can't picture a glob of mashed potatoes striking the thick gloss of the table. He can only see the room as part of a museum house, tourists peering over a velvet rope and then moving on. He sits at a high-backed chair whose cushions are a green fleur-de-lis brocade.

A few stacks of papers are scattered on the table, apparently overflow from the pair of offices next door. Noah glances at them as he pulls out his books. One is a legal-sized ream, bound with a giant binder clip. On the front are laser-printed gray and white columns, titled

Income and Expenses, December

Income:

Westfield Money Market, transaction:	$40,001.09
Blue Chip Mutuals, Shift:	$53,344.76
Dividends of Blaker Trust:	$3,905.50
Property appreciation, Wilmington, DE, est.:	$24,000.00

The list continues for pages and pages. Listening for the sound of approaching footsteps, Noah timorously and noncommittally lifts the corner of the report. He flips through the statement. Each entry is a holding company, a gift-in-kind, a transferred donation, or just a random sequence of letters and numbers, until:

Total Income, 12/01–12/31:	$747,842.42

Noah closes the stack of paper and pushes it away. Suddenly he feels significantly less contrite about his own $225 an hour.

He hears, from far away in the apartment, the strains of a conversation. "Where?" Tuscany is saying.

"The dine-ing rooom. Dine-ing roooom!" It is a woman's voice, the aspirated syllables unmistakably Parisian.

"Aargh. I can't understand you! Speak better," Tuscany says.

"The. Dine. Ing. Rooom."

"Which one is that?"

"It is after the three'd door in the hallway after the kitchen."

"Oh! The one with the big table?"

"Yes, that rooom."

"Okay, okay! We just never called it the 'dining room.' "

"What do you call eet, then?"

"Just let it go, Agnès," Tuscany says imperiously. She pronounces the name with a passable French accent.

The pair is at the door. Tuscany is wearing a clubbing shirt emblazoned with a sequined martini glass, the neckline dipping to the tops of her breasts. She saunters into the room and places her school materials, namely a glitter pen, on the table. She throws herself back in her chair and thrusts her hands into her lap, as if exasperated at the world's lack of compassion for her.

Agnès stands in the doorway. She is plump, with braided straw-colored hair and rosy cheeks, and the bonny but wary aspect of every heroine of European fairy tales. She can't be much older than Noah. "Hello," she says haltingly, "I am Agnès."

"Je m'appelle Noah," Noah says. *"Enchanté."*

Agnès bursts into a grand smile. *"Vous parlez français, alors! Bien, je vous laisse ici. Si vous avez besoin de quelque chose, n'hésitez pas à m'appeler!"*

After Agnès leaves, Tuscany leans to Noah and says in a whisper: "She's incredibly stupid. She barely knows how to talk."

"Actually, Tuscany, she speaks pretty well in French. English is, after all, her second language."

"Yeah, you two loved your little show-off moment, huh?"

Tuscany adjusts the strap of her shirt and looks at Noah

passionately, as though she has just accused him of messing around with another woman. He is unused to Tuscany's being unruly, and he is unsure of what to say. And when he thinks about it, Tuscany is right—he supposes that he was showing off. But the first job of a teacher is to illustrate his command of the subject, right? *Stop thinking,* Noah reprimands himself, *you're just showing doubt. And stop looking at the slender fingers playing with the bra strap, the butterfly wings of her breastbone.*

"We'd best start with French, then," Noah says. It is the material he is most unsure of, and figures he should take it out first.

"Right. What do you have there?" Tuscany has pulled one of Noah's textbooks from the pile and flips through it, lips parted, toying with her hair, as if scanning the latest *Cosmopolitan.* "'Confucian Ethics'? What are those?"

"It's one of our textbooks."

"That doesn't look like any textbook I've ever had."

"They're all from college."

"*Princeton* textbooks? Wow. I don't think that's going to happen. They'll be like hard."

"No, not really. Nothing you can't handle." Tuscany blushes. "I want to give you a chance to get beyond what you did in high school, where we can do some real abstract thinking, study more than just rules and words and dates and explore *why* things happen, and what knowledge means for you as a human being."

Tuscany—eyes wide—removes the pen cap she was chewing from her mouth and sets it neatly on the table. She nods solemnly. Noah isn't sure if she's being serious or flirtatious. She has picked up her mother's knack for rapidly vacillating between over-sexed and reproachful.

"You must be tired of test crap, huh?"

"No, I don't mind it. I'm looking forward to this, though."

Tuscany places both hands on the table, open-palmed, as if she were a mod guru on a mountain. "Showtime! Fill me up. Make me smart. I'm ready."

They conjugate a few verbs. "Anyway," Noah says, "I planned a full French lesson to do today, but that was before I knew you had a French au pair."

"Personal assistant. Mom says au pairs are outdated."

"She might be the best one to work on French with, so—"

"I told you, she's *stupid*—"

"I'm going to check in with your mom about doing your French with Agnès, so you can get a good accent. *Elle parle comme une parisienne.* I've got a Virginian accent, if anything."

"But I told you!" Tuscany wails. "She's awful. I bet she can't even *speak* French. You're not listening to me! No one ever listens to me! Ahh!"

"I am listening to you, Tuscany. What's going on here? Why are you being so contrary?"

"Ooh!" Tuscany says, throwing her voice into an odd pitch that might have been intended to simulate a British accent, "Look at me! I'm so smart! I went to Princeton! 'You are being so contraaary, Tussscany.' "

"Do you mind telling me what's going on?" It both amuses and horrifies Noah to be portrayed as putting on airs in this Fifth Avenue apartment.

"Do you miiind . . . giving me a spot of tea?" Tuscany cackles.

The door to the dining room opens. Agnès stands beyond. Her massive braids have been tied back by a piece of fabric, and she wipes her hands on her dress. "I forgot in telling you," she says in English. "Dr. Thayer asked me to get food for you in the day, in the morning, now, and at lunch, then, and a snack in afternoon. I am ready for you to request. What do you like?"

Tuscany orders a tofu salad and diet lemonade from two

different restaurants. Noah bites his lip. The employee hierarchy of the Thayer household is delineating itself, and he is uncomfortable to have both Fuen and Agnès at his service. "Oh, nothing, I'll be fine."

"What are you talking about?" Tuscany says. "Get food!"

Noah considers. Free food. From a place that offers nutrition! "Can I get a tuna sandwich? With vegetables?" Noah asks. "And a V-8?"

Agnès backs out of the doorway.

"I think," Tuscany says, smiling, "now you can see that she actually is stupid."

"That's really mean. Imagine if you were in France. It wouldn't be easy, right?"

Tuscany shrugs, then thinks of something of obvious interest: her face lights. "Agnès didn't used to be so big. She used to be like sorta skinny. Then she got to America and she just blimped out, you know? So she gets this *belly,* and at one point, this was like a couple months ago, Dylan and I talk about it and come up with this plan and then we go to Mom and he's like, 'Uh, do you know that Agnès has this boyfriend down in the East Village?' And I'm like, 'Yeah, and she's gettin' kind of large.' Preggers! Don't look at me that way, we really thought she was—we didn't know that she just got all obese."

"So what did your mom say?" Noah asks apprehensively. Agnès is hardly fat—he can only imagine what Tuscany would say about Hera.

"Well, she called Agnès into her room, and she *asked her*! Just straight up, 'Have you gotten pregnant?' Dylan and I were outside the door. And of course Agnès says no, of course not, only it's like, 'Nooo, of couuurse not!' 'cuz she's French, and Dylan and I are like rolling on the floor laughing."

"That's horrible."

"It was *so* funny. You would have laughed."

"That's really bad. I'm serious."

"It was like really funny. If you were there, you'd get it. I guess you had to be there."

"Think how that made her feel."

Tuscany catches Noah's expression. "What's up? Do you suddenly think you're supposed to be my morality teacher too? It's *funny*! Laugh!"

Tuscany's eyebrows knit closer than Noah has ever seen them, and there is a distance behind her eyes. He is losing her. His students will only do their work if they want him to like them. If he isn't careful, Tuscany will no longer want to impress him, and he will have lost control.

"You're terrible," Noah says. He layers a jovial tone over the reproach, so she might find it a compliment.

"Yeah." Tuscany smiles. "So, can we do something fun now?"

History is the only subject for which Noah was able to obtain Tuscany's former textbook. He slides the book out of the pile. He took an instant dislike to the text as soon as he glanced through—it is arranged not by geography or time period but by theme; Tuscany's current unit is on trade routes throughout time. Noah is tempted to reminisce about the simpler textbooks of yore, but suppresses the urge. Worst thing to do would be to come off as a curmudgeon. His students like him for his youth, not despite it.

"You know, we had a lot of girls here before Agnès," Tuscany says.

Noah glances at his watch—Tuscany's education can afford a few more moments of chatting, if it means that Tuscany will become excited again. "Yeah, what were they like?" he asks.

"Well, first there was Claude, who I don't really remember 'cuz I was too little, but Dylan hated her, and she left after like a month. Then there was Brigitte, she was nice I guess, she used to take Dylan and me to the park where she would meet her boyfriend. He was cool, it was fun, but then I got mad at Brigitte one day for messing up what I wanted—I hate coffee ice cream—and then I let slip to Mom about the boyfriend, so then Brigitte had to go. But the total worst one we had was Pascale. I mean, she would be like a total Nazi about getting us to bed, and if I hadn't finished my bath within like half an hour she would get all mad and say shit like, 'I want to go hooome, Tuscany, please feenish sooon,' like that was fair, I mean, Mom was paying her, right? But she was tough, and I think Mom liked her 'cuz she was older than the others, and wouldn't take much shit. But Dylan and I would find ways to get back at her, we'd like put salt in the sugar dispenser when she was baking stuff, or once Dylan dunked her loofah sponge in the toilet, this is back when he was like fifteen, that was so nasty. And then one time Mom and Dad were having like an anniversary dinner, so Pascale had to take us to dinner. She was such a freak, she was always like about to have a nervous wreck—"

"Breakdown," Noah corrects numbly.

"—and Dylan and I were laughing about something or other, I don't remember what, and my foot just taps, I mean taps, *so soft,* hers under the table. And suddenly she stands up saying shit like, 'I'm not going to take it anymore, you two are monsters, good luck with the rest of your lives'—and this is in the middle of a restaurant in like Gramercy—and Dylan and I just look at each other like, *What the fuck?* and she leaves and doesn't come back. Then Mom finds Agnès, who as I said we thought was pregnant."

"Wow," Noah says. "Now let's talk about the Turkish invasions! Yea, Turkish invasions!"

"Isn't that the craziest shit you've ever heard?"

There are a few possibilities for why Tuscany is misbehaving—for one thing, she is getting more comfortable with him. But beyond that, this might be how Tuscany behaves in school. This must be her Moore-Pike Academy (and short-lived Choate) persona: the girl who wears low-cut shirts, seems not to care about academics, draws focus to herself whenever she can.

"It is crazy," Noah admits.

Tuscany pulls her hair around the side of her head and pets it. "Okay," she says, "I'm ready to work. We were studying trade routes in the Middle Ages when I left."

Noah gulps. What does he know about medieval trade routes? "So what can you tell me?" he asks.

"Um, I don't know." She pulls a wadded piece of paper out of her back pocket. It takes a few seconds to extract the steam-pressed sheet from the skin-tight denim.

Noah peeks at the review questions printed at the end of the chapter. "So," he prompts Tuscany, "if you were to draw maps of both the major trade routes in the fourteenth century and the spread of the bubonic plague during the same era, do you think the maps would overlap? Why or why not?"

"Hey," Tuscany responds. "Do you like Lindsay Lohan? Don't you think she's so hot?"

Agnès, as if sensing the most opportune time for her reemergence, arrives with the late morning meal, and a box of Petit Écolier cookies. "I have also purchased some cookies. Would you care for some?"

Noah and Tuscany demur. Agnès exits with the cookies, not before glancing meaningfully at their meals. Tuscany looks at Noah with one eyebrow arched impossibly high: *Cookies?* Noah is unable to repress a laugh. Teenagers are cruel, and carry that cruelness like an aura, darkening those around them.

They finish early enough for Tuscany to get to the Connecticut house in time for her four o'clock riding lesson. Dr. Thayer comes into the dining room and orders Tuscany to her room. Tuscany lingers, toying with a filigreed statue of a groom in the center of the table.

"*Now,* Tuscany. The car service is downstairs. Go get your gear."

Tuscany contorts in order to look through the wide space between her mother's elbow and torso, pretending Dr. Thayer is merely an inanimate obstruction between her and her tutor. "Goodbye, Noah," she says.

"Same time tomorrow," Noah says.

"Yah, see you then."

Tuscany ducks around her mother and leaves. Dr. Thayer licks a finger and idly presses it into a smudge on the glossy table. "Hmm," she says slowly. "How was she?"

"She's fairly willing to work. Since we don't know what the curriculum is wherever she'll end up, I'm concentrating on more general study skills, reasoning abilities."

Dr. Thayer looks up. A gray smile puckers her features. "Reasoning abilities?"

What can he say to a parent who is selling her child short? "Umm, yes."

Dr. Thayer eases into a chair next to Noah. She places both hands on the table, rolls her fingers over one another. Her knuckles catch on the rings as they rise and fall. "It wasn't her lack of 'reasoning abilities' that got her tossed out of Choate."

Noah, distinctly remembering Dr. Thayer's not wanting to speak of Tuscany's being kicked out, simply leans forward and looks at the doctor.

"This has been a hell of a week, Noah," Dr. Thayer says. "I've been up to the school at least three times. Meetings with disciplinary committees, heads of the school, trustees that are friends of friends, everyone we could find. She got the short end of the stick here. Of course, there was a boy involved, but because Tuscany was new and he wasn't, it was easiest to place all the blame on her, make her an example without disrupting the social networks of the school."

"Can she go back next semester?" Noah asks softly.

"She got expelled, Noah. We're not going to try to send her back there."

Noah bites his lip, but he cannot resist. "What happened?"

Dr. Thayer raises her hands up to the flickering light of the Murano glass chandelier, as if praying to it for strength. "She e-mailed a picture of herself to a boy she liked, some guy she already knew in Manhattan, a picture she shouldn't have sent, on a school computer. Then they looked at her room, and found drugs I'm sure all the kids there are doing. Adderall, Nembutal, Dexedrine."

Not pot or coke, not drugs one gets from a pusher. These are prescription drugs. Pediatrician drugs.

"They accused her of selling to the other kids on the hall. I have trouble believing that, don't you?"

Tuscany as drug dealer does seem unlikely. Though certainly not impossible. "Do they know where she got the drugs?" Noah asks.

Dr. Thayer looks at Noah shrewdly. "I get deliveries at home; I know the implication, that Tuscany got the drugs from my supplies. Is that what you're asking, if I think those drugs were my own?"

"No, I wasn't implying anything."

"Do you know what kind of impact it would have on my practice if a scandal like that came out? Do you think people around here don't *talk*?"

Noah shakes his head. Dr. Thayer looks disappointed at his having given way. "I could see the disdain on the administrators' faces—here's another parent of another screwed-up Manhattan kid, her daughter all twisted and warped, leading all the fresh-faced country bumpkin Choate kids astray. As if I have any control, *any control,* over what my daughter does. None of these clubs around here ID, there's no taking away car privileges when the city is full of taxis. Other parents have to worry about their kid going to the wrong kind of tailgate party. Here, there's an endless supply of thirty-year-olds eager to corrupt them much more efficiently than any fellow teenager could. Not for one second, for *one second,* did any of those administrators put themselves in my shoes. Of course, they're not going to report anything to the authorities, but if they did, well, I have a high-profile practice, and I'd be sunk, just sunk."

Dr. Thayer pauses. Noah is dumbfounded; his mind wrestles with the slipperiness of her tone—he can't tell if she agrees with the administrators' disdain of her.

"I just hope I can get Tuscany through the next two years, get her to college without imploding first," Dr. Thayer finishes.

"She's grown up early," Noah agrees. Dr. Thayer looks at him. "But she's faced the full adult world for a few years now. There's nothing new that's going to be thrown at her. She's kept levelheaded"—*considering her mother,* Noah mentally adds—"so far. She's made herself a magazine, and sometimes she's excited about learning. I have high hopes for Tuscany."

"I suppose Dylan's made it to the end of high school, so Tuscany is bound to as well," Dr. Thayer sighs.

"That's true," Noah says. But comparing Dylan and Tuscany troubles Noah, for there is a major difference, he thinks—Dylan is hopeless. Tuscany stands a chance.

"But Dylan is a boy," she adds.

"I think social pressure here can be just as strong for boys," Noah says, thinking of Dylan's partying, his drug use and disaffection.

"But boys do not date older women. Dylan does not date forty-year-olds," Dr. Thayer says.

Noah's stomach sinks. He remembers Cameron's rumor about Tuscany and her friend's doorman. "Is Tuscany really dating forty-year-olds?"

Dr. Thayer sighs wearily. "She has in the past. I don't think she is now. But I was so happy to see her go to Choate, to get away from this. And now she's back. And it's going to be a mess. Whoever gave her those drugs is still here."

"Whoever gave her those drugs," whether you know it or not, is probably you. "Couldn't you just keep her at home?" Noah asks.

Dr. Thayer snorts. "You mean *ground* her?" She packs the word with condescension, as if Noah has suggested going to Dairy Queen and then to the town pasture to tip cows.

"Yeah, ground her." Noah hesitates—doesn't that just mean keeping Tuscany tied to this dark apartment, her only company her occasionally present mother, ruined brother, and multiple stashes of narcotics?

"It doesn't work. Whenever I try to enforce a rule I push her in the opposite direction." Dr. Thayer pushes her fists against her brittle thighs and makes to get up, but lowers herself back down. "No, it's just a mess, that's all there is to it."

"I'll do everything I can to help," Noah says softly.

Dr. Thayer snaps her head toward him. Her eyes blaze for a second. "Just teach her, Noah. Leave the parenting to me."

"Let me know if there's anything I can do," Noah persists.

"Oh, I will be sure to," Dr. Thayer says, her tone hollow. "But for now, just concentrate on making sure that she learns this material. You're all she's got. You're it."

Dr. Thayer moves around to Noah's back, places her chilly fingers over his shoulders. She kneads her fingertips deep into the muscle, once.

"I'm counting on you. You can do it!" Her words have a false effusiveness to them, like they are spoken by a predatory sci-fi alien only pretending to be the supportive gym coach. She glides from the room, leaving Noah to find his way out.

chapter 6

Between his morning sessions with Tuscany and his afternoon sessions with the rest of his students, Noah finds himself working full-time. Earlier that year his sessions with Tuscany would be followed by a bar with Tab or other friends. But today he follows Tuscany with Cameron and then three more students.

As happens to most tutors, Noah has become something of a one-school specialist. Cameron Leinzler's recommendation led to Rafferty Zeigler, and Rafferty Zeigler's recommendation led to Eliza Lipton, and so on, until Noah is tutoring a good chunk of Fieldston's junior class. He has even picked up a sophomore, Sonoma Levin, who wants to start early because "everyone else had a tutor, so I wanted one too." Tutor as puppy, or charm bracelet.

Noah's Fieldston students are all jocks or drama types, so they don't have time to meet on afternoons, and cram instead into Noah's evenings. He relishes his non-Thayer nighttimes, his only chance to occupy himself with students who aren't Tuscany or Dylan. It is midnight before Noah returns home. Although the sun has gone down, the streets of his neighborhood are full of light. The McDonald's at the corner of 145th and Broadway emits a fluorescent radiance, and the street lamps shine their yellow glow upon the men playing dominoes at card tables propped up on the pavement. They greet one another with effusive yells and hand-slaps, but Noah passes through them as invisible as always. His earlier fears about being a conspicuous outsider in Harlem have proven to be unfounded: he is neither liked nor disliked here. He is merely disregarded.

He thinks of Olena. Two aspects of her collude to make her seem magically unique—her dry narration of the world around her, and the gentle slope of her narrow back into her hips. The day before she was standing at the window, waiting patiently for the Internet connection to dial up, and her shirt rode up to reveal the elegant curve where the muscle dimpled in two pale hollows. He wanted to touch her, to embrace her from behind, but when she heard him approach she turned, made a joke, and the moment was lost.

Roberto is standing at the front stoop, surrounded by a group of local Dominican boys whom Noah doesn't recognize. "What's up, Noah?"

The boys stop speaking and stare at Noah. He stops short, and when he does his messenger bag swings off his hip and lands in front, so it looks like a handbag. He pushes it back, squares his shoulders. "Hello."

He realizes he is only looking at Roberto, so he makes a conscious effort to include the other boys in his gaze. They stare back. Noah swallows.

"Boys, this is Noah," Roberto says. He has affected a twinge of a Hispanic accent. One of the guys nods noncommittally. "Noah and I are going out tomorrow night, huh, Noah?"

Noah nods cautiously. He has forgotten to ask Dylan about the guest list.

"We're going to this really fly club," Roberto continues. "Like where there are celebrities. It's like made of gold."

Roberto's friends look categorically unimpressed. They resume their conversation in Spanish.

"Good night, nice to meet you," Noah says. He swaps a convoluted handshake with Roberto, just managing to remember the correct moves this time, and goes upstairs.

Roberto comes in a few moments later. "So, are we all hooked up for tomorrow?" Roberto asks.

"I'm sorry, man, I forgot to ask. I'll check it out tomorrow."

Roberto looks crestfallen. "You've got to work this shit for me!"

Noah nods. The best way to get Roberto back in high spirits, he intuits, is to feign profound nonchalance. *Of course, man, it's all going to work out—chill!* "Don't worry, Rob, I've got it under control," he says.

"Cool," Roberto says, smiling. Once someone has told you to calm down, there's no staying worked up, not in the realm of cool guys.

~

Noah arrives at the Thayer household early the next day, in hopes of catching Dylan before he lurches out the door to school. He finds Dylan staggering around the apartment, pulling on a shirt as he slurps a protein shake, in the peculiar state of groggy panic that only he has mastered. Dylan notices Noah in the front entrance and stares at him blearily. "Hey," Dylan says. Then he pauses, as if trying to remember Noah's name. "What are you doing here?"

"I'm teaching your sister."

"Oh, right, tutor to the porno druggie queen. This is so hilarious. My own kid sister, *kicked out of school.* It's kinda awesome, actually. Have you seen like a hat? It's beat up, has the Knicks logo on the front."

Noah shakes his head. Dylan blusters around the art pieces in the foyer. His backpack comes close to swiping a frosted glass fish off its pedestal, and then knocks a bronze geisha to the ground. Noah picks it up and replaces it. Dylan's hunt for his hat turns him in the direction of the fallen statue and he stares questioningly at Noah. "Whatya doing?"

"You knocked this down," Noah says.

Dylan nods. "Oh."

Then, with a last glance about the front hall, he says, "Fuck it," runs a hand through his hair and then holds it to his nose to smell for grease, and heads toward the door.

Noah steps in front of him. Dylan flashes Noah a look of pure irritation, which immediately relaxes into a casual smile. "What's up?"

"Hey, I was wondering something," Noah says. "Do you know anything about getting on the list at Pangaea?"

Dylan scratches his armpit. "Pangaea? Why?"

"I was thinking of going with a friend, and we weren't sure of the best way."

Dylan laughs, and then shifts his scratching hand to his abdomen. "You?"

"Yes." Noah looks winningly at Dylan, as if to say, *I know, how crazy, I'm so above that.*

"Yeah, I can get you on the list." Dylan claps. His tone turns from cloudy to elated. "This is so awesome! My *tutor* is going to *Pangaea*!"

"So you'll get me on?"

"Yeah, totally, it's the only scene that's worth anything on Wednesday nights, anyway. So what's your friend's name?"

"Roberto."

"Is that a girl?"

"No, why?"

"It's so easier to get in with a hottie. I can work it out,

though. Now"—he pulls out his phone and stares blankly into the screen—"who's on door tonight? Oh right, Malcolm."

Dylan begins to write a text message, his thumb flurrying over the lighted keypad. "That's cool, you're bringing like some Italian or something," he says distractedly. Dylan's phone pings. "Done, you're in," he says. "Make sure you wear something cool. See you later, or maybe," he adds, grinning as he closes the front door, "see you tonight!"

Noah hasn't even considered this possibility. Dr. Thayer wouldn't allow Dylan to go downtown on a school night, would she? But as soon as he poses the question to himself, Noah knows she would. He heads down the hall to the dining room.

Tuscany is fifteen minutes late. She has decided to dress casually today: she wears drawstring sweats and a tangerine polo shirt that would have been snug on a five-year-old.

"Good morning," Noah says.

Tuscany woefully shakes her head in response. "You're going to Pangaea tonight." She looks at Noah wide-eyed, overwhelmed, as if thrown into an existential crisis by her teacher's impending presence at a nightclub.

"How'd you find out?"

"Message from Dylan. He's excited. What are you *doing,* going there?"

Noah laughs. But then he sees real concern on Tuscany's face; she is genuinely upset. "I just want to check it out," he says.

Tuscany puts a hand to her temple and gives her head a little shake. "No, you can't go, you're *different.* You're like not a normal person."

"Tutors have social lives too."

"That's not what I mean. It's not 'cuz you're a tutor. You like don't own a TV, you don't say normal things, you're like unexpected, like someone rare, a philosopher or something. You're going to be miserable there."

Tuscany's eyes droop. She is truly saddened, as if she is protective of Noah, doesn't want his life to become like hers. He feels a tremendous urge to take her hand and pat it, to enfold her in his arms, but stops himself. "It's okay, Tuscany, it's only one night."

"I just don't get why you'd go."

"I'm curious."

"I figured that by the time people get to be your age they know what they like or not. But you're always taking everything that comes, like you haven't decided what you don't like." She flounces into an ebony-inlaid chair, grinds her head dramatically against the cushions.

"Wow," Noah says. He is astounded—not because Tuscany's words have hurt him, but because she thought them at all, because they come from the girl who didn't know the definition of *domicile.* He has been condescending to her, he realizes. "That's really insightful. What you're talking about is discrimination. It's the last thing to come when you're growing up. Some people never really attain it. You have to be really secure in yourself to know for sure that something isn't for you, instead of just fearing that *you're* not for *it.*"

"You mean, discrimination like racial discrimination?"

"No. Well, yes, it shares a root meaning—but I mean judgment, making distinctions between things."

"So you're saying that you're indiscriminate?"

Noah coughs. "I don't really think of it that way, but in a way, yeah. It's something I'm working on."

Tuscany smiles. "I don't think you should change it. It sounds good to me. It sounds like being nice."

The heat of Tuscany's smile makes Noah recall an admonition he received during training: *Never talk about yourself. Stay focused on the student.*

"How'd the homework go?" he asks chirpily.

"I made the maps, and it was totally true, the plague spread along the trade routes. Because that's where people were like traveling from one area to another? Kind of cool. If I was living then I would have just hung out in like a little town or something."

"If I *were* living then. Subjunctive clause."

"Sub-what who?"

Noah shakes his head: it was Dylan with whom he covered the subjunctive. Where is his head? He can't keep himself from smiling goofily, from losing track of his thoughts; it is as though he were on a first date. "We'll cover it later, don't worry. Just remember to use *were* after *if.*"

"Sure, whatever."

Noah assigns Tuscany a set of problems from her Algebra II workbook, and hurriedly tries to teach himself the material as she works through them. Matrices? What the hell are matrices? He got a scholarship to take college algebra at the local junior college one summer during high school. But that was his summer of girlfriends, when he baked on the rocks of the reservoir and shared a six-pack with buddies each day after leaving class. Maybe he was hung over the day they did matrices . . .

Soon it is lunchtime. They put their orders in with Agnès (a BLT on seven-grain bread with homemade potato chips for Noah, half a grilled chicken breast for Tuscany), and share an amiable meal before passing the afternoon discussing a Somerset Maugham story.

Noah doesn't have any students after Tuscany, so he naps in Central Park before going home. He knows he will be role-playing at Pangaea that night, and it will take some effort to prepare his costume.

~

Roberto enters the bedroom with a grim, determined expression, and solemnly plunges into the task of making Noah look cool. Noah cedes control, just sits passively on the bed as Roberto pulls all of Noah's clothing out of the closet, gradually immersing him in a dune of cotton and polyester. Noah dutifully holds shirt after shirt against his torso, and Roberto dismisses them one by one, until finally the last option has been vetoed. Roberto makes a grunt that sounds almost affirmative, as if conceding that perhaps a shirt isn't necessary after all.

They move on to pants. Shoes. Socks. And accessories (that goes quickly, as Noah only has one, a leather cuff his brother braided for him at some after-school program). After he upends Noah's wardrobe, the only clothes that pass Roberto's evaluation are a pair of black polyester slacks that flare slightly at the bottom, acceptably inconspicuous black socks, and a pair of Doc Martens. They still have no shirt. Noah proposes that maybe he can just wear a bow tie and go as a Chippendales dancer. Roberto, unfazed, asks Noah if he has a dress shirt he doesn't use much. Noah points to a charcoal shirt sent by his mother after she got her tax refund years before. Its sleeves are far too long. With Noah's permission Roberto hacks away at them with a Swiss army knife. The resulting tangle of threads reaches halfway down Noah's forearm. Noah is dubious, but Roberto works in a business of appearances, and when they look in the mirror Noah has to admit that the shirt looks great. The sleeves are like a jagged threaded jungle from which Noah's arms emerge like obelisks.

Roberto pomades Noah's hair into a mass of tight spikes, has Noah rub shea butter into the dry skin at the edges of his nose. They stand back to survey the results. Noah's hair, made shiny and dark by the pomade, contrasts dramatically with his white skin, and the black clothes give him a sleek, artful look. He looks like an aggressive and narcissistic poet. Success.

Roberto goes for a different look, donning an outfit that seems to be made mostly of blue plastic. He wedges his feet into a pair of white leather shoes and then completes the look with a pair of aviator sunglasses. He too looks aggressive and narcissistic, though nothing like a poet. Noah has always been contemptuous of poseurs who wear sunglasses during the night or in the subway, that they wear their vanity so openly. But for an evening at Pangaea, sunglasses make Roberto into the perfect sidekick.

They emerge into the living room. When Olena sees them she bursts into a laugh, and rummages out a disposable camera to snap an impromptu photo. She poses them in front of the window in awkward gentlemanly positions, as if they were about to pick up their dates for the senior prom. Roberto rolls his eyes and curses, makes as if to slap her, which only makes Olena laugh harder. Roberto bounds out the front door. Noah hugs Olena goodbye, his lips grazing her cheek, and soon he and Roberto are racing down the West Side Highway in the rusty Datsun.

It will be better, they agree, if they park the car somewhere out of sight from the club and walk the rest of the way.

They arrive at Pangaea's block at ten-thirty. The stretch of Lafayette Street that forms the club's backdrop is wide and dark. Prestigious venues recline alongside the road like dozing royalty. Noah figured ten-thirty would be a good time to arrive—not so early as to identify them as newbies, but not so late that the crowds would grow massive enough to raise the level of the bouncers' selectivity.

There is no one in front of the club, however, besides the bouncer himself. Noah has misjudged; they are clearly too early. But now they have made their approach. There is no turning back.

They have already agreed that Roberto will do the talking, since when Noah rehearsed saying, "Hi, we're on the Velvet List," in the car his voice cracked.

"Hey, things hoppin' yet?" Roberto asks the bouncer.

The large white man in a collared shirt stands tall. "Are things what?"

Roberto cracks his neck. "We're early tonight, I know, but is there anyone inside?"

"Are you on the list?"

"On the list? Yeah. It's Roberto. Noah." Roberto gives the bouncer a weary look, as if to admonish him that every other club has memorized their names.

The bouncer just gazes at them for a moment. Noah stares authoritatively into his eyes. "The list hasn't arrived yet, it's too early. But I'll take your word for it, go ahead."

First strike: arriving at the club before the guest list.

They approach the entrance. But there is not one door, but two. One is glass, rimmed in steel, with a flat piece of metal for a handle, like the door to a Wal-Mart. The other is textured, windowless, and made of bent tin. Which would be more likely? The first door is new and mundane, the second downtrodden and chic. Noah tries it.

"You can go that way," the bouncer says, "if you want to take out our trash. Use the other door."

Roberto looks at Noah sternly. Sweat dots his brow. He pushes on the glass door. It doesn't give. Noah pulls instead and it swings open. He and Roberto hurry into the club.

Another strike: attempting to enter through the service entrance.

Pangaea, once a singular prehistoric mass of land, now signifies a trendy nightclub. Moreover, "Pangaea" has been boiled down to "Africa." Crude wooden spears and shields line the wall, along with navigator maps, mounted animal heads, cave drawings, and any number of other props that might have come from a low-budget miniseries of *Heart of Darkness.* As if to remind patrons that this is not actually Africa, the owners have pinned elegant red swaths of silk to the ceiling that crisscross and float above the club like tangled sails. Oblong couches are carefully arranged beneath the fabric, and the floor is rimmed with votive candles. Drumbeats echo in the background.

The décor puts Noah at unease. He's galled at the underlying assumption that Africa is a modern representation of the past, that Africans form a link to the prehistoric world. And all of this in Manhattan! Look—you can escape to an exotic, savage, and beautiful place, and *still* drink Cosmopolitans!

"This is awesome," Roberto breathes.

The air is chilly to compensate for the body heat of the crowds to come. Five men in business suits are the only patrons. They cluster at the bar, where three bartenders sit idly, two men in tight silk T-shirts and expensive pants, and a girl in a halter top. The businessmen chat with the halter top.

"I'll get us drinks," Noah says, eager to give himself something to do.

Roberto nods. "A vodka tonic."

Noah approaches the bar. The girl abandons her conversation with the businessmen and swoops over. She checks Noah out, pauses on the undone buttons of his shirt, the ripped sleeves, the shine of his hair. She nods. Apparently, on prehistoric continents Noah's look would be acceptable; Noah has passed the hotness test. "What can I get for you?"

"A vodka tonic and a Stella," Noah says. After his night at Roberto's rave, he has sworn off hard liquor.

"I can give you the vodka tonic for free, but I'll have to charge you for the beer."

Noah smiles. She's giving him free drinks? Woo-hoo! "Make it two vodka tonics, then."

She prepares the drinks, and as she stoops to get ice Noah wonders what she has done to make her breasts disobey physics enough to stay inside the top. She slides the drinks over and winks. "There you go."

Noah tries to wink back, but since he hasn't had recent

occasion to wink it comes out as a hard blink. He tips her a couple of dollars and returns to Roberto, who has perched at a corner of the bar, staring about the room. Roberto takes his drink and sips. "Aren't too many people here, huh?" he asks.

Roberto is not making conversation, but is actually curious—Noah surmises he can't see any of the candlelit club through his sunglasses.

"No, not really . . . well, wait—what are those?"

Three blond women have emerged from the back of the club. They float through the shadows, gamboling and giggling like fairies, wearing gossamer white dresses that manage to be both flimsy and tight-fitting. When they reach the bar they disperse, flitting among the men at the front. One girl, tall and with the nondescriptly perfect features of a woman in a catalogue, plants herself in front of Noah and Roberto. Her hand is instantly on Noah's arm. He is dumbstruck—a model is flirting with him.

"How are you boys tonight?"

Roberto slides his sunglasses back against the broad planes of his face until they catch in his slick hair. "Doin' fine. Is it going to be a hot scene tonight, or what?"

The girl erupts into impressed laughter, as though Roberto has just spontaneously generated an Oscar Wilde aphorism. "I certainly hope so!" she says.

"Awesome," Roberto says, flashing a suave smile.

The girl, still tittering, turns to Noah. Her hand has remained on his arm. Perhaps, Noah thinks, Roberto's overpowering magnetism isn't successful everywhere, and Noah will hold more appeal here. He straightens. "And what about the silent, mysterious one?" the girl asks. "Do you think it's going to be a 'hot scene' tonight?"

"I'd be fine with warm," Noah says. He laughs deeply, trying to convince her that his statement has some profound meaning. She breaks into more peals of laughter. She seems more and more like an automaton, and suddenly Noah would happily leave Roberto to her.

"You're so serious-looking," she says. Her arm has crept up to Noah's elbow. "Isn't he serious-looking?" she asks Roberto.

"Yah," Roberto says darkly.

"Do you come here often?" the girl asks. It is as if she has memorized a dating manual.

"No," Noah says, gulping his drink. He inadvertently takes an ice cube into his mouth, and tries to swallow it surreptitiously. It won't fit in his throat. He instead tries to talk around it. "This isn't really my scene."

He aims to sound enigmatic, leaving it open that his "scene" might be Milan or Paris, not sitting in bed with a book. He coughs slightly. The ice cube rests somewhere at the base of his throat.

"To tell you the truth," the girl says—her eyes sparkle within her buttery tan face, and Noah is dumbstruck all over again by her physical perfection—"this isn't really my scene either. Pangaea is so '04."

Her arm has crept up again, hitched over Noah's triceps. He isn't naïve enough to suspect that there isn't some ulterior motive to her flirting. Beautiful women don't need to be aggressive. Noah wonders if she is hired by the club to serve as extra decoration, to add to its appeal. Or maybe she is an escort. He wonders how much she makes. They might be two highly paid hourly employees, she and he, both handed thousands of dollars just for being who they are and performing fairly mechanical duties. And even as Noah realizes he is being played, that the whole game is false and inorganic, he is transfixed by the woman's beauty. He isn't attracted to her, he tells himself. But the sheer fact that someone so gorgeous is speaking with him renders him unable to do anything but use all his resources to keep her around; it is like being asked to dance by the prom queen . . . you simply don't say no.

"Would you like another drink?" she asks. Noah looks down at his tumbler and is startled to see it empty. He also distantly notices that Roberto is gone.

"I'd love another drink." Noah starts toward the bar. "What can I get you?"

"Oh no, I'll get it," the woman demands. She takes Noah's glass and goes to the bar. Noah glances around. Undaunted at being ignored by a supermodel, Roberto has pulled a recent entrant to the club into conversation, his new quarry a young diva in a miniskirt and snakeskin stilettos. Noah watches his woman dressed in white. She is bent over the bar, chatting with the bartender. She is impossibly lovely, like an older Tuscany. It isn't just that girls like her didn't talk to him in Virginia; he couldn't *find* any in Virginia. New York is where the extraordinary flock. He is proud to be here, proud to be in this club. He shakes his head. Suddenly he senses the point of it, and even through all his ironic distance feels it deeply: being in a club like Pangaea puts him ahead, marks him as above the crowd. It isn't unlike getting a perfect 2400 or going to Princeton. Coming to Pangaea is just another means to set yourself apart. Why wouldn't this woman be excited to speak to him? He's well-dressed, articulate (though he certainly hasn't proven that to her yet!), and, above all else, he's at *Pangaea.* He's not just any ordinary guy.

The fairy in white returns with Noah's drink. She hasn't brought one for herself. "You're not drinking?" Noah asks.

"No," the girl says. "One drink and I'm under the table." She winks and laughs as she says "under the table," as if wishing she were under a table with Noah. It comes back to Noah, strong, that he's being played, and his heart starts beating faster.

"So," the girl says, her bare leg against Noah's. "What do you think of the vodka?"

Noah looks at his drink for a second, as if waiting for it to provide him an answer. "The vodka?"

The girl nods. Noah takes a sip. "It's very good."

"It's called Wolsyncha. It's from Poland, distilled and bottled at a chateau."

"Oh really . . . wow."

"It's a hard name, I know, but can you say it?"

"I think so," Noah says, his lips tight.

"Let's hear it. Wolsyncha. Vol-sync-ah." Her lips perform a voluptuous red dance around the syllables.

"Wolsyncha," Noah returns reluctantly.

"Very good!" the girl laughs, caressing Noah on the back with long, smooth strokes. "We're offering free drinks all night. We want you to really experience how great it tastes."

Noah raises his glass with a hollow smile. "Wolsyncha!"

The fairy removes her hand from Noah's back and gives a reserved little clap. "Wolsyncha!"

And she is gone.

She was an hourly employee, just not of the kind Noah imagined. Probably a model by day, a vodka promoter by night. It makes sense, Noah thinks, a marketing version of trickle-down economics: get your drink an image with the elite and influential and they will do the rest of your work for you, spreading it to the masses. And what better place to ignite the fire than here at Pangaea? The rejection burns a little, but business is business. He knows that from his own job, from those calls he gets from students who just want to chat after the test is over, those calls he delays before returning. Business relationships are much like friendships, only they come with a set "consume by" date. Getting to know one another, flirting, these are parts of a transaction, and eventually the transaction will be over. He thinks of Tuscany, of her unexpected disappointment that he was coming to Pangaea. Why has he thought of her? The connection is slippery, escapes him.

Noah sips his drink, surveys the club. It has filled somewhat and the conversations are louder; there are now probably a few dozen people here. He glances at his watch: eleven forty-five. After his experience with the vodka promoter he is feeling his role to be more and more anthropological; it is safer just to observe, he decides. He takes another ice cube into his mouth and savors its painful chill against his cheek. Roberto is still chatting with the same girl, who nods vapidly to each of his gesticulations. Noah tries to view Roberto through the girl's eyes. He should look ridiculous in his blue plastic outfit, his sunglasses black ovals in the semidarkness. But he carries himself with such confidence that he seems a true individual, some unique creature roaming the earth. The girl probably sees his narrow white shoes, muscled frame, and eccentric look and figures he's a music video producer, or maybe a high-profile DJ. As for herself, she has a rounded, tight figure, with both the hardness and extreme curves of a cello. Her eyes are a little buggy. Noah finds himself thinking that Roberto could probably do better.

Where did that thought come from? But as he looks around he realizes that he has subconsciously and pitilessly appraised everyone in the club. That is what one does here; evaluating image is the evening's entertainment. In some ways this mix of people is like that of any other nightclub. It's not as though everyone is a celebrity; not everyone looks like a model. In other clubs, however, there are always a few people that clearly don't belong—some girl in a beer T-shirt, or a guy with huge glasses and a ponytail—but at Pangaea misfits have been stopped at the door. Everyone who makes it in belongs.

It is odd to Noah that *he* should belong, that he could pass for a Pangaea-goer. But no one shoots him strange looks—in fact, he notes a number of admiring glances. Being here has turned him coquettish. But it has turned all the guys that way. Both men and women have posed themselves strategically about the club, intently gauging the amount of attention they receive.

Now that it is past midnight, a steady stream of people files through the front doors. The men are generally in their late twenties or thirties, their uniforms expensive dress shirts with the top two buttons undone. The girls seem to be in their twenties or often younger, wearing some version of a halter top. Each girl wears the halter but sports a different material and color, aspiring both to conformity and uniqueness. Groups of boys circle groups of girls; groups of girls circle groups of boys. It is like a school mixer, only everyone here knows what to say. There is no awkwardness, only varying levels of suavity and frankness.

Noah returns to the bar and gets another free drink. Roberto returns and, after making sure that none of his conquests are looking, displays for Noah the new numbers he has keyed into his cell phone. Noah nods encouragingly and carries on his conversation with Roberto as he continues his scan of the club. Music has begun to pulse louder from the back, and a pair of waifs dances on a platform. Their outfits are a convergence of bikini, formal wear, and underwear. They press out their hard, tan little bellies, their matching navel rings glistening as they sweat in the candlelight. Noah finds it hard to look away.

Noah and Roberto pass an hour or two at the bar, commenting on the "hot bitches." Roberto is in a frenzy and falls into recurring loops of conversation, centering on which girl he will call first, and whether to push his luck by going for more numbers. Noah had worried that Roberto might feel out of place here. But he is at ease and admired, shows a real fluency with any social situation. Roberto goes to the bathroom, then returns, excitedly reports that the urinals are made of steel and joined; it is like pissing into a fountain.

Then Dylan arrives.

He is surrounded by a bevy of men Noah's age, a swarm of Diesel jeans and rumpled European shirts that straddle the line between body-conscious and unkempt. Each of them aspires to look, not as though he just got out of bed, but like the platonic ideal of messiness—they aim for a verisimilitude of not caring, not for actual lack of interest. Dylan is in the lead, walking masterfully into the club, stepping around jutting couches and tables, dexterously passing between outflung limbs as if between tree boughs, swinging through the jungle like the Pangaean native he is. Groups of girls and boys cease their conversations to observe and comment. Dylan's entourage adopts slight, knowing smiles, affirming that Dylan is their friend, and that yes, indeed, that makes them as good as Dylan.

Noah turns toward the bar, stares into his ice cubes. He had predicted this might happen; his contingency plan should Dylan arrive had been to say hi and then leave. But he is enjoying himself. He doesn't want to leave. He turns his head slightly so he can watch from the corner of his eye.

Dylan is at the center of the club now. He halts and the crowd of men forms a protective circle, hovering around him like an aura. Dylan looks toward the waiting tables, all marked with "Reserved" signs, then toward Noah. Noah turns to scrutinize the wood of the bar, waits for his student to approach.

Suddenly Dylan is standing next to him, signaling to the female bartender. Then, without turning or acknowledging Noah, he speaks: "Hey."

"What's up?" Noah says.

Dylan turns his head slowly toward him. His eyes are dark and large. "You came."

"Yeah, what did you think, I'd wuss out?"

Dylan smiles, looks at the wood grain of the bar, then up at the bartender. "Yeah, actually, I did."

"No way," Noah says. "I'm not about to miss this."

Dylan just stares back at him. Noah rattles on amiably: "I mean, it's totally not my scene, but I'm having an awesome time. I'm not seeing this—that you're getting a drink—by the way." In truth, Noah isn't shocked to see Dylan drinking. Alcohol is probably the least potent of the substances in his system. Dylan is so outside the world of normal teenagers that Noah feels unable to attach any moral system to him.

Dylan rolls his eyes. "Okay, whatever, you're not seeing me drink." He raises his glass to his lips.

"Is this the time you normally arrive?" Noah asks.

Dylan picks up three imported beers and a mixed drink and drops three twenties on the bar. "You wanna meet my gang?" he asks as he turns around.

Noah turns with him. Three men circle them. Two are long-haired and handsome, leering and bored, what Noah has come to identify as the bad element of Upper East Side twentysomething aristocracy; the other is an eyebrow-pierced Asian kid about Dylan's age. "Guys, this is my *tutor,* Noah."

The guys nod as they accept their drinks. Noah gives his name to each in turn. They all say "Hey" back.

"That's so awesome," the Asian kid says to Dylan. "My tutor would never come to a club. This is so cool."

"God," one of the aristocrats says, "back when I took the SATs our tutors were all like forty-five and wearing sweater vests. Not club kids at Pangaea."

"Yeah," the other aristocrat affirms.

They haven't offered their names, and they speak to one another around Noah. He realizes that he has been cast by the group as an exhibit, not a peer. Noah latches on to an easy way to alter the dynamic. Roberto is nearby; Noah slaps the back of his hand against his arm. "Hey, guys," Noah announces. "I want you to meet my friend Roberto."

Roberto turns around, takes in the sight of the four well-heeled men. "Hey," he says, "what's goin' on?"

The guys look at Roberto doubtfully. Noah can sense what they're evaluating: the cheap scent of Roberto's cologne, his dropped consonant, the brandlessness of his clothing. Not in malicious judgment, necessarily, but because evaluation is the pleasure of being at Pangaea.

Roberto holds his open hand in front of the group. It is a ruse, Noah realizes, a means to force the men to recognize him: not even the haughtiest person could let someone's hand just lie outstretched in front of him. Roberto is larger than they by half, and the arm he has placed in the center of the group is thickly muscled. The men have no choice but to give it a clasp, one by one losing their puny hands inside Roberto's. And by this move Roberto turns the tide. He proves his confidence by initiating the handshake, and he simultaneously establishes his physical superiority. Dylan and his friends jostle one another, searching for ways to engage Roberto.

"So how do you know Noah?" the Asian kid asks.

"Yeah," an aristocrat says. "How do you know Noah?"

"Noah? Noah and I are from the same 'hood. We're like bros." Roberto puts an arm around Noah's shoulders.

"Yeah, Noah lives in Harlem," Dylan says proudly.

"Wow," the guys mumble.

"But you guys aren't even *black*," says one of the aristocrats.

"Do you come to Pangaea a lot?" the other aristocrat asks.

"No, man," Roberto says, "but we figured we should check it out. There are some hot scenes in Harlem, there's enough happening there that's really down. But we thought, shit, we should check out some other spots too."

Noah is impressed. He knows there is no real nightlife scene in Harlem, at least not any that Roberto is interested in—he has heard him complain to that effect. But now

Roberto has taken the doubt implied in the question (*Are you worthy of this place?*) and reversed it. The guys are now afraid that it is they who are missing out.

"Really?" says the Asian kid. "Like where?"

"No one place," Roberto says. "You have to be hooked in, find out what's hot. So, are there any celebs here tonight?"

Dylan looks around the room. "No, not yet. It's way too early anyway, it's like embarrassing to be here before one."

"I guess that makes us all embarrassed, then," Noah says. Roberto laughs, and therefore the other guys follow.

Shockingly, thrillingly, the six dissimilar young men engage in conversation. They talk about traffic delays getting there, and all agree that the West Side Highway is the best way to go (never mind that the guys directed their cabdrivers that way, and Roberto and Noah cruised the highway at forty-five miles per hour in the sputtering Datsun). They identify in minute detail which of the girls in the club might be worth talking to. Dylan sets his eyes on a group of black girls in high heels holding bright green drinks.

"They're like out of this world," he says. "Like not black, like African Americans, but black like daughters of kings from Africa, you know?"

Noah coughs.

Dylan then declares his mission that night will be to find a date for Noah.

"What about the one with the red hair and tiny skirt?"

"I don't think so, Dylan, man."

"Oh, that's right, you're into like philosophers."

Roberto bursts out laughing and gives Dylan a high five. "See any philosophers around with hot asses?" he asks.

"Yeah, Noah," the Asian kid asks. "See anyone you like?" Then, to Dylan: "Your tutor's the man. We're totally going to find him a babe."

Noah looks around. There are a few girls who interest

him—one with long arms, the hollow of her neck glistening as she stands by the bathroom door; another making liquid dance moves beneath a red banner. But he's not about to air his preferences before his student. He wonders what moral code he has bestowed on himself tonight that allows him to share drinks with Dylan, but not to discuss girls.

"I don't know, guys," Noah says. "No one, really."

"Hey, Dylan," Roberto asks, "where's your sister tonight?"

"My sister? She's like fifteen. She's at home."

"Come on, Dylan," an aristocrat says. "You know she's here all the time."

"Yeah," says the other aristocrat to the first. "Here with *you*!"

"That had better not happen ever again, asshole," Dylan says darkly. "Don't ever let me hear about you touching her."

"Dylan, Dylan." The aristocrat overenunciates, bathing the group in beer vapor. "Don't you remember? Maybe you were too coked up. *She* was touching *me*."

Dylan scowls, but there is little fury behind it. Whatever happened between the aristocrat and Tuscany must have occurred months previously. Or else Dylan has just taken too many depressants.

"Dude," says the Asian kid, laughing. "That's so fucked. That's like statutory."

"It's cool that you protect your sister," Roberto says to Dylan.

The conversation is getting too bizarre for Noah. He turns away and scans the room. There is a queasiness in his stomach; suddenly he hates the club. When he turns back, the group has shifted position. The aristocrats have closed ranks around Roberto, and Noah is standing at the bar with the Asian kid.

"That's so fucked," the Asian kid says. "The way they talk about Tuscany."

"Yeah, I just couldn't take it," Noah says.

"You teach her, right? It must be totally weird for you to hear shit like that."

Noah ponders that; it would feel totally weird, he decides, if he hadn't had half a dozen vodka tonics. As it stands, it's irritating more than anything else.

"She really needs help," the Asian kid continues. "See that guy in the business suit over there?" The Asian kid points out a man who might be thirty-five, one hand against his belly and the other holding an unlit cigar. "She was with him for a while. And you've probably noticed that she like doesn't eat? The problem is that she's way too hot."

"I'm sorry?" Noah says, surreptitiously spitting an ice cube back into his drink.

"She's too hot. Ugly girls can grow up in Manhattan fine. But the hot ones, the really gorgeous ones, get eaten alive before they even turn eighteen. Tuscany knows what attention she can get if she's hot, so she doesn't eat. And then she comes to places like this and all these guys are forcing drinks and drugs on her, and all the other girls are bitches and won't talk to her because she's so pretty, so all she can do is hang out with these guys. It's totally messed."

Noah nods. He feels horribly irresponsible, now, for his own moments of attraction, and for not having done more to help her.

"What were you tutoring her for, the SAT already?"

"No, no, the ISEE. She wanted to go to boarding school."

"Oh right, I forgot, she got busted for sending naked pictures to some guy and having like forty bajillion tabs of Xanax."

The Asian kid stares at his drink, trying to glimpse his reflection in the curved glass. He gives the silver spike in his eyebrow an experimental half turn.

Noah is the adult here. He looks at Dylan's friends, laughing and slapping Roberto on the back. Guys like that will mess her up. Manhattan will mess her up. Tuscany's mom isn't going to help her—it's up to him. Noah excuses himself to the bathroom, pisses in the steel fountain. He stares in the mirror as well-dressed and preoccupied guys jostle him on either side. He checks out his outfit and hair for a moment, but he doesn't actually see himself. All his thoughts are on Tuscany. She has luxury of which the rest of the world dreams, would be the envy of teen girls across America, and yet is barely staying above water. She's besieged on all sides. And what has he been doing to help, meanwhile? He knows that he has been self-absorbed, that he has focused on making money for himself and his family. But that has been okay, right? He's twenty-five; his big job is to figure his own life out. But now there's Tuscany, bright and plummeting, warped and under assault by men with millions of dollars. He wants to help her, but distrusts his own impulse. But he has to do something.

Noah stands and jokes around with the guys for an hour more but leaves early. He tells Roberto that he'll just take a cab, not to worry (not that, he suspects, Roberto would). He ducks around a gaggle of girls at the front of the bar and hails a cab, guiding the driver toward Harlem. As he slides on the slippery vinyl fabric, staring out the smudgy window at the diffuse city lights, Noah drunkenly comes up with a plan to save Tuscany.

chapter 7

March brings Spring Trip season to Moore-Pike Academy, during which groups of rich girls wander the globe under the protective tutelage of their professors, get some grit under their fingernails, and wash it back out before returning home. Each year, one trip ends up infamous. These notorious episodes in the history of Moore-Pike include the '00 trip to Los Angeles in which Ariel Pernstein spotted a man jerking off outside her hotel room and Professor Ganz stood in front of the window until he finished, the '01 trip to Valparaiso during which Victoria Roberts got tequila-induced alcohol poisoning but convinced Señora Mendez that she had simply eaten lettuce from a street vendor, the '02 trip when Brittany Lyon broke her ankle and was carried up a mountain by a sherpa, '03's trip to the Red Sea in which Ariana Burns got her hair caught in her snorkeling mask and slammed into a reef, breaking off a fluorescent chunk of coral and requiring a dozen stitches, and finally the '04 capstone, when Talia Illich-Murphy smoked in the airplane bathroom over the Pacific and got so nervous that she flushed the toilet while she was sitting on it, the resulting suction causing her to adhere to the seat until the plane landed in Seoul.

Tuscany excitedly narrates these stories to Noah, placing special emphasis on each girl's name. The key part to note is, clearly, to whom each disaster happened. While Talia Illich-Murphy was causing a ruckus on Korean Airlines, Tuscany moans, she was stuck in D.C. at the stupid National Air and Space Museum.

"The girls are going on the trips next week, right?" Noah asks as they eat their midafternoon snack of imported olives. Or rather, as Noah eats their midafternoon snack and Tuscany sucks on an olive pit.

"Yeah," Tuscany says.

"There's no way you could still go?" Noah asks.

"Uh, *hello*? I'm not a *student* there anymore."

"Okay, okay, I know. But it just seems like such a good opportunity."

"No, they're really boring, usually. The teacher like thinks they need to make a big lesson out of everything, like, you know, *This rock is called tufa, a volcanic blah blah.* Yawn."

"But if you could, you'd go?"

Tuscany pulls the pit out of her mouth and inspects the wet green felt before continuing. "Oh, yeah, totally. I had so much fun last year. We snuck out to this D.C. club. Everyone there was like, *Whoa, who are these girls*, 'cuz we went like buck wild. We got back at like four A.M., and we had to be up at seven-thirty to see some Indian reservation. I like fell asleep and drooled while we listened to some old guy with feathers on his head tell some story about Pocahontas. It was hilarious."

"Hey, is your mom around today?"

"Beats me."

Noah finds Dr. Thayer in the kitchen standing by the counter in a silk shift, picking through a china dish of raspberries. She hums softly to herself and plucks out the choicest berries with violent pecking motions. She looks up as Noah enters. Her hair has been freshly highlighted, so it appears that the sun has just risen on her head.

"Good morning," Dr. Thayer says.

"Good afternoon," Noah says. It is three P.M.

"Mmm," she says, glancing dazedly at the kitchen clock, apparently bemused to discover another paradox in the world. "How is Tuscany?" she asks.

"Tuscany's doing well. She was shocked today to realize that she won't be taking any tests."

"You're not testing her?"

"Well, no. I can tell if she's learned the material or not. You only really need tests for distinguishing students in groups."

"Oh! Isn't that funny?" Dr. Thayer squishes a raspberry between her fingers, flicks the wet red mess into the sink.

"Listen, Dr. Thayer, I had a thought."

Dr. Thayer stands erect, as if posing for a statue, holding the dish of raspberries aloft like a torch.

"As you probably remember, all the girls from Moore-Pike take spring break trips. I was thinking that maybe Tuscany could really benefit from going on one. Part of schooling is the benefit of interacting with peers, right? And Tuscany is here by herself a lot of the time, unless she's out at clubs, and I thought it might be healthy if she got out for a while, spent some time outside of Manhattan."

Dr. Thayer looks at Noah from a void, across some narcotic. "Tuscany doesn't go to Moore-Pike Academy anymore."

"I know. But there's no reason she couldn't still have a spring break anyway, take a trip somewhere."

Dr. Thayer has been scowling, but her expression lightens a shade. "It would be good if she got out of here for a bit . . . but what are you suggesting, that you jet off with Tuscany somewhere?"

Noah is irked by Dr. Thayer's insinuations, that this is all some gambit to get Tuscany alone. But getting angry now won't help Tuscany. He forces a smile to stretch across his face. "No, of course not. I'm not proposing that I lead it. You could take her, or a female chaperone."

Dr. Thayer chuckles. Her face is reflected in the stainless steel Míele appliances, and it seems that the whole kitchen is full of her sharp laughing face. "Spring break with Tuscany and all of her friends. Oh, you have big plans for me, don't you?"

"Maybe you could hire someone, send her off with an established program? I just think that it's really important that she get out of Manhattan for a while."

"She's not your daughter, Noah. I know what kind of trouble she'd get into."

"Well, what I was thinking was this: what if the trip were a hiking trip, away from big cities, just nature and camping and sleeping under the stars?"

Her expression hardens as she peers at Noah. "And you think Tuscany would go for that?" she asks.

The way Dr. Thayer phrases it, it does seem unlikely that Tuscany would pitch a tent. Or pee outdoors. But Noah presses on. "I think she would. She doesn't have too many options."

"It's true. It's either that or stay here. She'd be practically forced into going." She breaks into a fit of laughter; she is pleased with the idea of Tuscany being out of her hair for two weeks. "Where would you suggest she go? Not Central Park, I trust?"

"No, I think abroad would be a good idea. We've been studying French; maybe she could go to France."

"Hiking through the Louvre! Sharing a tent in the Jardin des Tuileries!"

"France is famous for its forests, Dr. Thayer. There are plenty of trails and parks once you get outside of Paris."

"I know, Noah, lighten up a little. I know."

Dr. Thayer pats her hair and stands against the brushed-steel fridge, holding the bowl of raspberries in her hand. She flashes Noah suddenly warm eyes, the look of a girl waiting to be asked to dance. Her mercurial mood disorients him, baffles him. Noah shifts his weight from one foot to the other. Finally Dr. Thayer shakes her head. "No, I'm sorry. I can't send her off into the woods with someone I don't even know." Her mouth opens wide, as if about to laugh, but no sound comes out. "I just couldn't. She'd see it as a reward, and what's she to be rewarded for?" Dr. Thayer's tone frustrates him: *Sign off,* it says, *she's not worth it.*

"Okay," Noah says. He bites his tongue. He wants this trip to work out so much—what else can he do for Tuscany? He is furious. "Let me know if you change your mind."

"Oh, Noah!" Dr. Thayer says softly after a moment. "You really wanted to see this happen, didn't you?"

Noah nods. "It's okay, though. Just do let me know."

Dr. Thayer looks at him with an unreadable expression, some ineffable mixture of scorn and compassion. She picks a seed out from between her magenta-stained teeth.

~

It is Friday, so Noah is due for his paycheck. He finds Agnès in Dr. Thayer's office, trying to sift through a broad binder stuffed with receipts and financial statements. "Oh, hello, Noah," she says in French as he arrives. "I am just trying to sort finances here. This is, I'm afraid, the part of the job I'm least good at."

"You seem to be doing fine," Noah says, or hopes he says, in French. It might have been more like *seeming fine to be you doing,* because Agnès blinks twice before responding.

"Thank you," she says in English. "How much this week?"

"Umm . . . twenty-six hours at two twenty-five. Whatever that comes out to."

Agnès whistles. "A lot. Let's see . . . five thousand eight hundred fifty. How does you spell your name?"

Noah tells her. She fills out the check, looks at Noah. "You must do great things, to make such much."

It is a tremendous amount of money. If it weren't for his huge loan payments and the money he still owes his brother's counselor, he'd be veritably wealthy. Even so, the thought of his wages makes him want to go skipping through the streets. "I'm trying to do greater things," Noah says. He has to talk to someone about this. "I'm trying to save Tuscany." His words hang in the air, sound ridiculously self-important, preposterous, as though he imagines himself a general rescuing a lost convoy.

"Save Tuscany?" Agnès asks, confused.

Noah decides to stick with slow French: "I'm trying to get her out of Manhattan for a while. She's on the road to ruin here, she needs to see the rest of the world." Of course, he knows he has said something more like: *Tuscany must Manhattan leave. She is weird here, will be less weird elsewhere.*

"Ah," Agnès says. "That's a good idea, to take her away."

Noah thanks her and walks down the hallway toward the front door. He is in the vestibule when realization hits. Agnès. Trip to France. Should he ask Agnès, or go straight to Dr. Thayer?

He finds Dr. Thayer still in the kitchen, numbly staring out the window.

"One thought," Noah says. His voice echoes. "What if Agnès took her? That way Tuscany would have someone to practice French with too."

Dr. Thayer slowly turns. Whether through drugs or rumination, she has come to a new, more open state of mind in the last few minutes. She nods, smiling, touched by something Noah has done. "I'll consider it. Ask me again on Monday."

~

Noah comes home to Roberto doing pull-ups from the living room overhead lamp. "Hey, you know who I'm going out with tonight?" Roberto asks. His pull-ups are slowing, and he emits a loud grunt each time he reaches the groaning fixture. "Siggy! From Wednesday night. He's got some party he's havin' out at his phatty-phat pad in the Hamptons. I've never been out there, man, it should be awesome. You wanna come?"

Noah is irked by the oddity of it, being invited to the Hamptons by Roberto. "I've got plans with friends tonight. I'm going to see a play."

"Oh, okay, that's cool. It's funny, I told Siggy how to get here and he was all nervous about driving into Harlem, he was like, 'I'll call you before I get there so you can come outside.' I'm like, 'Settle down, dude, it may be Harlem, but you're not gonna get killed.' "

Which one is Siggy? "Siggy's the one that . . . ?" Noah starts to ask, then trails off. He can't think of a distinguishing characteristic beyond "rich" or "asshole."

"You know, drinkin' Grey Goose. He bought the table for us. Oh, you weren't there for that part. He's cool, though, he's cool."

"Is Dylan going to be there?"

"Shit, I dunno. That would be awesome, though. Kid's hilarious."

"Yeah, be careful around him, you know? He is my student, after all."

Roberto heaves himself onto his bed and turns to gauge Noah. "What you think I'm gonna do, like corrupt him or something?"

"No, I just feel responsible."

"Don't worry man, He's like a big kid. Already been corrupted. Done more shit than I done. You should worry for me."

~

On Monday morning Noah makes all his train connections easily, and so gets off the crosstown bus early. He strolls along the forested edge of Central Park, enjoys the clear sunshine streaming onto the wide street. He crosses to Madison, buys a muffin and coffee, and sits on the stoop of a brownstone. A gregarious Old English sheepdog accosts him, and as Noah fends off its friendly assault he spies Agnès making her way down the block. She is hurriedly applying a shock of bright red lipstick as she walks, and pauses every few paces to check her progress in a compact.

"Agnès," Noah calls as she nears. The dog, scorned, huffs back to its owner.

"Oh, Noah." There is an iciness to her tone.

"Are you off to the Thayers'?" Detecting Agnès's distance, Noah has added an extra burst of pleasantness to his words. He can imagine her later complaining to her French friends about the artificial sweetness of Americans.

"Yes," Agnès says.

"I am too, I'll walk with you." Noah stands and joins her as they pick their way between tourists and sharp rectangular shopping bags clutched by the women parading between boutiques.

"So," Agnès says slowly, keeping her eyes focused ahead, "I understand that I am going hiking with Tuscany."

Crap.

"Dr. Thayer told you that? That you're taking her?"

"Yes. I have never been hiked, Noah. I have never spend the night in woods. I'm not sure I do *like* to spend the night in woods."

"I just suggested it to her as an option. I didn't think that she would decide without consulting you."

"I am her employee, Noah. That is what bosses do, no? To decide."

"Don't you think it might be fun? She'll pay you, you'll get a guide, it's a chance to travel."

"I'm sorry, I just usually stay in hotels, that's all." Agnès says sharply. For a second she seems furious, then the force of Noah's smiling resolve breaks through and she bursts into a laugh. "Yes, it might be fun," she concedes. "But the reason I said it would be such a good idea on Friday was because I thought someone else would take Tuscany away. Not that I would go! She is not kind to me. I did not think I would have to share a tent with her in the wilderness."

"If she's not nice to you, then perhaps alone in the woods is exactly where you want her."

Agnès laughs again. "A good point. But oh, Noah, *que ce pourrait devenir un désastre.*"

"I'm just hoping to show her that there's a world beyond all of this." He points down Madison Avenue.

"In ten days? Good courage to us."

Agnès continues to perfect her lipstick as they walk. "You care for her a great deal, hmm?"

He looks at her sharply. "I just figure teaching her is more than showing her how to bubble in letters."

Agnès sidesteps a nanny pushing a stroller. " 'To bubble letters' is safer than teaching them, I believe. But carry on anyway. Dr. Thayer says I am to purchase the plane fare today. I leave for Marseille in two weeks."

"I'm going *camping*?" Tuscany exclaims.

"Yeah, how cool is that?"

Tuscany looks unconvinced. "I guess it's cool. What does it involve?"

Noah describes his own camping experiences, in the forest around his Virginia house and on the Sierra Club trips he attended with his mother. He introduces Tuscany to the realities of foam-core sleeping pads, water-purifying pills, mosquitoes.

"I guess that'll be all right," Tuscany says, with an evident show of courage. "What do I wear, though?"

They go to Tuscany's bedroom and look through her clothes. Tuscany owns no fleece or wool, or even cotton. The majority of her shirts sit on only one shoulder, and her pants all require thong underwear. Despite having two full large closets, it becomes clear that Tuscany will need to buy more clothes.

This sells her on the trip.

"Awesome. Wait'll I tell Mom she has to loan me one of her credit cards."

Noah focuses the day's French lesson on Marseille. They learn the lyrics to "La Marseillaise," outline the city's history of sackings by French kings and foreign armies. Tuscany spies a picture of Les Calanques, the fjords that the Mediterranean has forged east of Marseille.

"Those are pretty. I think I should go there."

And so the trip is formed.

~

That night, after back-to-back sessions with a sadistically enthusiastic twin brother and sister, Noah is ready for a drink. He calls up Tabitha and they share a bottle of wine on the roof of her apartment building, singing songs to the night sky until a May-December gay couple across the street hurls open a pair of windows and shouts at them to fuck off. Noah and Tab are momentarily white-faced and then howl with laughter at their own immaturity. Once inside, they open another bottle, lie on the floor, and watch television.

"Um," Tabitha says after a long moment.

"Um?" He turns and finds her staring at him. "Um?"

"I don't know, man," she says, looking up at him with playful eyes. "I think you're lost."

Noah sits back, deflated. "Good thing I'm a cocky bastard, or that could have hurt. What does that *mean,* lost?"

"I don't think you have a direction. Do you know why you're doing what you're doing?"

"You know what? We're going to stop talking about this, right now."

"See? We're getting somewhere. I've hit a nerve."

"I'll do what I want. I'm a teacher, that's who I am, it's what I want to do, I want to help people learn, and no, tutoring's not perfect for me, but it's only for a year or two, till I've paid down some debt, okay?"

Tab slaps her leg, mocking his outrage. "Really, Noah," she says, running a hand over the top of his bare foot. "I don't buy it. Your ambitions are a lot more selfish than you're admitting to yourself. You want to be a professor because you get summers off and people will listen to you at dinner parties. Because it makes you classy. It's not for the good of the world. You're going to be teaching survey courses to kids who don't want to be there. Are you ready for that? I don't think so. You've got it easy now, you know? Don't forget that."

Noah takes a moment. "You're right. I'm incredibly lucky. But that's not enough. There's a lot more out there than my own satisfaction."

Tabitha shakes her head as she takes a large gulp of wine. "You're so full of crap. Yes, teachers are great. Sure,

I'm glad I had good teachers." Tabitha is really getting into it. She sits forward. Her eyes sparkle. "But you're not the heal-the-world type. You're out for comfort and prestige. And that's fine. But wanting to be a teacher, I don't know, it seems like you just don't really know why you want it."

"So you're what, complaining that I don't think about myself enough?"

"Oh, you're no altruist. You just want to help others because you can't figure out your own shit. Your own bizarre little paradox."

Noah leans back. He hates her and at the same time couldn't be more turned on. He wants to boil over into her, splash her with his heat. "And you're mean as all fuck."

Tabitha leans back against her body pillow, exposing the middle of her lean body, from the top of her panties to her rib cage. "This is going to hurt, but you have to hear it. What I'm telling you is why, Noah, you've never had a stable relationship."

"You're saying what, that I'm too self-absorbed?"

"Yes. And not at all. You're like every other extraordinary person—a mix of complete selfishness and complete selflessness. So beyond yourself and yet trapped in your own head. None of *this*"—she gestures to her room and, presumably, the rest of New York—"can compare to whatever larger questions are raging in your head. Sure, a girlfriend doesn't have anything to do with class structures, with philosophy. But she can make you feel good. She can support you, and you can feel good supporting her. I could have done both, if you had let yourself value me enough. But you didn't."

When Tabitha would get him backed into a corner while they were dating, they would end up having sex. He's unsure what to do now; a hot emotion rises in him that finds no release. Although he's aroused by Tabitha's body splayed before him, he's also too annoyed to touch her and he senses that to do so would be an obscure betrayal of his growing crush on Olena.

"You know, Tab, you're smart, but you need to let it go. You're basically asking me to settle, and I won't. The right relationship, the right girl, will be large enough so that it affects how I see the world. It'll involve more than me and more than her."

Tab strokes his leg, tugs the soft black hairs of his calves between her fingers. "Okay, okay, settle down." They talk for a while longer, but eventually Tab begins to doze against her pillow. The sexual charge is gone, and Noah is left sullen and cranky. He lets himself out.

When Noah wakes up the next morning the apartment is empty, but he is thinking of Olena. Hera roped her into going shopping that morning; he imagines Olena lounging bored outside a discount department store while her mother browses inside. She might be smoking and scrutinizing her new countrymen as they promenade before her. The image makes him smile. Hera has left bread and fig jam on the table, and Noah makes himself breakfast. He wanders through the apartment as he eats, carries a chunk of dark peasant loaf from room to room. He stands in the doorway of Olena's room, glances at the Modernist poster on the wall. He steps inside. The top drawer of Olena's clothes trunk lies open. Noah glances over the contents, careful to catch the crumbs from his bread in his palm. The clothes are minimal—worn T-shirts and a few pairs of jeans. Cradled within them are a cured Albanian sausage and a cheap leather belt with a gleaming yellow buckle. A few plastic razors and a bundle of tampons lie next to an old pair of sneakers. The rest of the trunk is devoted to books. On the top are novels by Tolkien and Forster, the former translated into French. Noah carefully turns them with his bare foot as he rips off another morsel of bread. Beneath lies a cluster of mismatched yellowed hardcover books probably published in the seventies or eighties—*Tests of Logic and Intelligence, English Grammar for the Student, Test Your Level: English, New Recruitment Tests: Skills and Strategies.* Noah picks up and flips through the last one. It is a catchall standardized test manual, giving examples of convoluted reading comprehension questions and math problems far more difficult than the SAT's, such as finding the volume of an inflating sphere. Someone, presumably Olena, has heavily annotated the book, writing marginalia in three different colors, alternating Albanian and English: "Confirm: Velocity of train acceleration constant?" and "Past tense of passage indicates narrative distance from subject matter." Both good points, but evidence of thinking that will be useless on the SAT: she is being too abstract, too advanced. The test assumes a less rigorous level of thinking—when it says that Train A travels from Stamford to Ironville at thirty-five miles per hour, the student is to assume the train mystically starts moving at thirty-five miles per hour, that it doesn't start at a standstill and then speed up. Olena, assuming the test to be harder than it is, has used calculus to try to derive a likely acceleration rate for the train. Noah has heard about cases like Olena's from other tutors but has never before had one himself—the "far too bright" student, the one who gets the right answers too easily and so bullies herself into the wrong ones.

Beneath the *Skills and Strategies* book lies an actual SAT. At the edges the booklet has gone as brown as burnt pastry. Noah opens it gingerly and sees the date imprinted inside: 1971. Somehow the test found its way to Tiranë and Olena has administered it to herself repeatedly—the paper where the arithmetic of each question is supposed to be worked is soft and thin. She has solved each problem again and again, neatly erasing her computations each time. The reading passages are peppered with allusions to other texts Olena has read. She has written second and third definitions alongside the vocabulary words in the analogies section. Next to RAINBOW:COLOR she has printed: *Must refer to 2nd definition of color: "to shade with meaning," not simply "hue"?*

The test has no answer key, and so Olena has worked herself into a frenzy of self-doubt. Answers are marked and then erased and then marked again. Noah scans one math and one verbal section. She has gotten all the hard math problems right. But she went through contortions to make the medium problems harder than they are, and thus managed to miss many of them. Her verbal sections are weaker: she knows most of the words, but seems able to find ways to make even the most improbable answer choices work. She has filled the blank of:

> The professor asked the class to work more _____ in preparing for the coming test, as scores on the last exam had been abysmal.
>
> A. diligently
> B. conservatively
> C. lackadaisically
> D. historically
> E. belatedly

with "historically," writing in the margin: *If the latest exam results were remarkably low, results in the past have typically been higher: the professor therefore wants the students to perform as they used to—that is, historically. Better than clear wrong choice, "diligently"—much too obvious.*

Noah arranges Olena's drawer as he found it and sits down at the living room table. He stares out the window at the sunny morning, watches a group of kids chatter as they lean against the wall of an abandoned building. He thinks about Olena, first about her sulky, sexy demeanor, then about the slope of her back, then what he would advise her were she his student. The SAT is a fairly accurate test—that is, geniuses tend to score very well, and less intelligent students score poorly. There are exceptions, however: while students with Noah's style of thinking (brash and instinctual) tend to do very well, students like Olena, who may be just as intelligent, tend to think more profoundly, in a more nuanced manner, come to answers by circular means, identify the correct choice by deliberating its position within the broader world. These more spacious thinkers tend to do poorly. Their test books are filled with furious scribbles, their bubble sheets show the scars of multiple erasures. They may finish only half a section before time is called.

When these students are wealthy—that is, for all of Noah's students—the problem isn't too grave. Such students go through a battery of psychological tests with an M.D. that cost thousands of dollars, and then secure the school's recommendation that the student receive extra time. Roughly half of Noah's students receive extra time. Nationwide the proportion is two percent. Between receiving extra time and intensive tutoring, such students can pull through with scores that reflect their intellect. But less wealthy abstract thinkers, without access to similar resources, take the test with regular time and only ever see half the questions. These particular geniuses wind up attending less prestigious schools, or don't attend college at all. Olena looks to fall in this category. Her math score is satisfactory—something like a 610, could be much higher if she realizes her overthinking, but her verbal score is around a 450 or 460. He has no idea about the writing section, since the practice tests she took were old SATs that didn't yet include an essay or grammar questions. Between the math and verbal she might eke out an 1100 or 1600, above the national average but nothing that will get her into a very selective school.

Noah finishes his bread with a final dollop of fig jam, picks up the crumbs with his finger, and sucks them into his mouth. He showers and tries to force his thoughts away from Olena, back to the students who will pay for his loan payments. He emerges from the steaming tub, slicks his hair and puts on a dress shirt and his one pair of expensive slacks, and heads for the Upper East Side. But his thoughts remain in Harlem.

The doormen of 949 Fifth Avenue seem agitated today. Normally they slouch when Noah enters, accord him no more reverence than they would one of their own. Noah is usually happy for their friendly informality, but today they are alert and direct Noah upstairs formally, as if they had never met him before. Noah thanks them, confused and a little hurt by their primness. He soon realizes the reason for their reserve after he rides up the elevator and knocks on the broad Thayer door. For who should appear on the other side but, presumably, Mr. Thayer himself.

"Hello," he says, guarding the doorway. "Can I help you with something?"

He is tall and dense, athletic, a mass of entwined wire wearing a dress shirt and pin-striped trousers. He stares along his sharp nose at Noah.

"You must be Mr. Thayer," Noah says, holding out his hand.

Mr. Thayer ignores his hand, instead continues his attempt to insert a silver link through his French cuff. "Yes, I am. But you still haven't told me who you are."

Noah lets his hand drop. "Oh, sorry. I'm Noah. I tutor your children."

"Really? What in?" Mr. Thayer leans his head back and looks at Noah curiously, a small smile on his face, as if he has just read something intriguing in the *Times*.

"I tutored Dylan for his writing section. Tuscany for the ISEE, and now for academics."

"Oh right! Noah." Mr. Thayer squints at the cuff, slides the silver bar through, and then holds out his hand. A guardedness remains in his eyes—Noah is fairly sure that he still doesn't know who Noah is. Noah places his hand in Mr. Thayer's and lets it be shaken. Mr. Thayer's palm is rough and dry; Noah can feel its ridges.

"I'm sorry I can't stay and talk to you about Tuscany and Dylan, but I've got a flight in a couple of hours. How are they doing, though?"

"Well, I don't—"

"Do you want some orange juice or a Danish or anything? Fuen is in the kitchen, I think."

"Oh no, that's okay. I was just going to say I actually don't tutor Dylan anymore. But Tuscany's doing well."

"She did great on that test to get into school. Good job. Dylan, though, I really want him to break 2200. If it doesn't happen, well, I won't be too happy. But if so, good job, good job!" He puts his fist and thumb together when he says "Good job," as if he were a politician at a rally.

Either Mr. Thayer is totally out of touch or Dylan is still being tutored for the SAT, just not by Noah. He remembers Cameron's saying that Dylan was still being tutored. Noah files the information away, plans to see if there is a way to get specifics out of Tuscany. But he cannot afford to think about it in front of Mr. Thayer.

"Tuscany's going on a little field trip next week," Noah says.

"That's great," Mr. Thayer says. He picks up his briefcase, slings his suit coat over his arm. "I'm off to London. A company I started is being publicly offered."

"Congratulations," Noah says, sidestepping Mr. Thayer's rapidly departing form.

"It's nothing," Mr. Thayer says. "It starts to get boring after a while. We'll talk when I get back, okay?" Mr. Thayer speaks as if to a peer, in a tone that he might have used if

Noah were a CEO, not a tutor: "We'll talk" must be Mr. Thayer's reflexive way of saying goodbye. Noah nods, pleased to be respected. The door closes.

~

"So, Tuscany, I met your father," Noah announces halfway through the session. Tuscany has pulled her chair away from the dining room table and has begun picking at her nails and feeling her thighs, a sure sign that she is ready for distraction.

Tuscany screws up her face. "My dad? Dale was *here*?"

"I assume so. I just had a conversation with him by the front door."

"Oh," she says, returning to the nails. "Weird."

"He was flying off to London for an offering of a company."

"Sounds pretty normal."

"What does he do?"

Tuscany starts packing her Parliaments, striking the base of the box with her palm. "I dunno. He started like a dozen magazines and after that all sorts of other companies that don't really do anything. He's always buying and selling stuff, but it's like none of it really exists, you know? Stuff like bonds and commodities and trading shit. I don't get it."

Bored again, Tuscany pulls out a shopping bag she carted from upstairs. "Look what I got for our trip!"

She pulls out a jacket that looks like the result of a collaboration between North Face and Victoria's Secret, with fleece bands that crisscross over the bosom. Noah presumes it was at least designed to be used for hiking. He gives a thumbs-up.

"And this!"

Tuscany presents a pair of polyester pants, loose, designed to wick away moisture, convertible into shorts—a great idea for a week outdoors. But the zippers where it converts into shorts go diagonally across the crotch—it converts into a bikini bottom. "Cool, huh?"

"Wow," Noah says.

"I am *so* ready." She puts the contraption down on the table. "What's up? You seem all preoccupied."

Noah can't find a way to artfully phrase the question he wants to ask. "Hey, Tuscany," he says, "is Dylan still getting tutored for the SAT?"

"I don't know. How the hell am *I* supposed to know? No one tells *me*."

So much for that.

~

That evening when Noah returns home he is greeted by the heavy smell of burnt olive oil hanging in the air. The heavy splashes and splatters of her deep-frying render Hera deaf; she doesn't turn around when Noah enters and drops his bag. Olena, however, looks up from her spot on the couch. She closes her book and smiles at him.

"How did the shopping go?"

Olena glances at the kitchen, and then holds Noah's gaze. She lowers her voice to a conspiratorial whisper. "Horrible. It lasted six hours, Noah. Six hours of *clothing shopping*. It went so terrible. Or do I say *terribly*? No, terrible."

Noah smiles. "Terribly. You're describing a verb, 'to go.' "

Olena nods. "Thank you. Let me tell you, I would have preferred to even stay here and study my grammar or work at the cleaner's rather than go there, all those girls flooding with laughter in the dressing rooms. Two were in the cabin next to me, and one said to the other, 'I can't even get them over my thighs!' and the other said, 'So what? Buy them anyway, at least you can say you have Diesel jeans!' It was foul."

Noah laughs. "So what are you doing tonight?"

"What am I to do? I have no friends here. I will wait for

my mother to finish cremating dinner, and then I will read my book. There are not too many options."

"I'm going to dinner with some friends later. You're welcome to join us."

Olena puts her book down and raises her eyebrows in mock surprise. "Roberto just got finished complaining to me this morning that you do not ever invite him to go out with you and your Princeton friends. What makes me special, hmm?"

"I just think you'd like them."

"Oh. Perhaps I would." She shoots a dismayed look toward her room. "But I am to stay here and study for my SAT, I'm afraid. It is in only a pair of months."

"A couple of months, you mean."

"Why not 'a pair'? That means two, no? Ech, I hate English! Why couldn't the French have dominated the world commerce, instead of the Americans with their irrational language?"

Noah laughs. "Are you sure you wouldn't like to come out with us? My friends would love you."

"No," Olena says firmly. "Thank you, but no. I will need to be a nerd for two months. And I have no money."

Noah is about to protest when Hera emerges from the kitchen. "Noah! You are home! You would like to join us for dinner?" Hera holds up a frying pan layered with blackened oily creatures that shine in the early evening light.

"I'm afraid I already have plans. But I'll sit with you, if you like."

Hera turns toward Olena and puts on an aristocratic air. "Have you heard the way he speaks? 'I'm afraid I already have plans'—it is like one of the books we used to read with our English tutor in the good days. Lovely. Noah does not speak like those dark boys in the street, all 'Nigger, it's on, take it and shit!' "

Hera lays the frying pan on the table, opens the freezer

and pulls out a tray of ice cubes, then extracts the ceramic bottle of Albanian alcohol from under the sink. "Come, Noah," she says, gesturing to the head of the table. "Come sit with us, keep us company, tell us of your life there at the top of the world."

And so Noah takes a seat at the table and, over the acrid licorice fumes rising from his tumbler of grain alcohol, relates his hope to show Tuscany that there is a world beyond the one in which she is already living.

"Surely, Noah," Olena says, "she already knows there exists another world. It is a little condescending, no, to think that you are the one who can tell her how to live?"

"I am her teacher," Noah says. "That's what we *do*."

"I always thought of my teachers as not being the best guides for advice—they do, after all, complain about their hard work and little pay. But in your case you have little work and high pay, so I will cede. Your philosophy must be correct." Olena takes a sip from her tumbler. She rushes to the sink and spits out the sip of alcohol. "Ech! Ma, even Albanians do not drink this anymore."

"Titania, please!" Hera says. "That is not very decorous."

Olena rolls her eyes when Hera says *decorous*. "Who *are* you?"

"What?" Hera says. She turns to Noah and says jovially, "Titania is jealous of my mastered English."

"Ha," Olena says, sitting back down. She spears a charred piece of food. "Something like that."

"Anyway," Hera says, "I think you do the good thing. Perhaps you could introduce Tuscany to Titania, make the same relation that you made between Dy-lan and Roberto."

"Oh yeah," Olena says dryly, "I'm sure we would be the best of friends. Oh, Noah, please do!"

"I think Tuscany could learn a lot from you," Hera huffs.

"Yes," Olena says. "Such as her multiplication tables." Her eyes glint with wicked merriment as she takes a bite of food. Noah watches her lips, imagines brushing his own against them, and ponders how to convince her to go out with him that night.

"And more importantly," Hera continues unabated, "you could learn a lot from her, Titania. She is in a good position here."

"There is a term in French for this behavior, is there not, Noah?" Olena says. *"Être arriviste.* The problem is, Mother, that such social climbing is outdated in America. Here one succeeds on one's own."

Both Hera and Noah look doubtful.

"Noah," Olena implores, "what I say is true, no?" She is earnest, has dropped her usual ironic distance—her belief on this point must be critical to her. And, Noah realizes as he thinks about the amount of time she puts in waiting tables and working at the dry cleaner, that makes sense. Her curtness and angry distance come from a consuming fear of being trapped in her current class. They are alike that way, she and Noah, both trying to surmount the social barriers placed in front of their abilities.

"It is true," Noah says slowly, laying his hand on Olena's—he wants to fall into the softness of her, to comfort her—"that it is easier now to work hard and advance than it was before."

"Very carefully stated," Olena says, removing her hand from beneath Noah's, picking up her tumbler, glumly staring into the clear liquid, and putting it back down. "Very, very careful."

"Olena will go to a school, and that school will be great," Hera says, entwining her daughter's slender arm in her own heavy one.

"And it is also true," Noah continues, "that for better or worse, your SAT score is going to be critical. I have to tell you, honestly, I knew a handful of former Eastern Bloc students at Princeton, and all of them went to boarding schools somewhere else. I'm not saying that American schools are going to put you at a disadvantage when you apply, but it does probably mean that they're going to disregard your transcripts. They have no experience with Albanian schools. They won't trust your grades."

"My marks are perfect. I worked hard for them," Olena protests.

"It's my professional opinion," Noah continues, "that your SAT score is going to be the single most important part of your applications."

"I have already taken the Test of English as a Foreign Language, and did well."

"That's great, but of course you did; you're fluent. The SAT is totally different."

Olena hangs her head between her hands. "This is ridiculous. Why should one test count more than four years of work? I have two months to prepare. Two months."

"Actually, Noah," Hera says, "this is something I want to talk to you about—"

"I think I know what you're going to ask," Noah interrupts. "And I'd be happy to help."

"Well . . ." Hera casts a sidelong look at Olena. "The thing is, we don't have the kind of money it would take . . ."

Olena stares at Noah frankly. "It would be a big drain on you, and we couldn't offer you anything."

Noah looks at Hera, tender and impassioned about the prospect of her daughter having the best chance possible. Then he looks at Olena, who appears coolly uninterested, almost barbed, protecting herself.

"I have Tuscany at nine in the mornings—"

"Olena could work with you on the weekend!" Hera says.

Noah shakes his head. "That wouldn't work. She's going to need something a lot more intensive than that. If I'm going to take this on, we'll need sustained effort. Every day."

Olena nods guardedly.

"I was going to say that I have Tuscany at nine in the morning. After Tuscany I have other students, and won't return until ten at night most nights.That's too late to concentrate."

"I could do it," Olena protests.

"No, it's going to have to be the mornings. I leave the apartment at eight, which means that we'll have our sessions from six-thirty to eight A.M."

"I will make strong coffee," Hera offers. "And I will also halve your rent."

Olena fixes Noah in her stare, turning her napkin in her lap. "Why are you doing this for me?" she asks softly.

"Can you put in the time?" Noah asks. He hopes Hera won't bring up the rent again—of course he won't let her halve it, but he doesn't want to embarrass her.

"Of course I can put in the time," Olena says. "I would get up at three A.M., if I needed to."

"You might need to. You're going to have to take a three-and-a-half-hour practice test each day until the May test."

Olena nods.

Noah reaches into his tutoring bag and pulls out two slim booklets, blue ink on newsprint. "These are real SATs, obtained by my agency through special arrangement. I need you to do both tonight. That's seven hours. Time yourself. Mark any vocabulary words you don't know. Skip the hardest three sentence completions. You'll need to buy yourself time for the reading comp."

Noah stands. "I've got a date with my friends," he says, then taps the booklets in front of Olena. "And you have work to do."

chapter 8

It is six forty-five A.M. and Olena, somehow, is fresh and energetic. Noah is not faring as well. His eyes prick, and his hair shoots from his scalp in tufts. He takes a large mouthful of coffee, slowly releases it into his throat. He breaks Olena's practice test results to her. She takes the news stoically.

"So, 1620 out of 2400. This does not sound good."

"It's above average. The math score is quite good."

"To be honest, Noah, I am considered to be very smart. I want to go to the best."

"Then yes, we're going to have to work on this." He is careful to keep his voice neutral. The key to keeping her motivated is managing her expectations.

"What would I need if *I* wanted to go to Princeton? Or even Harvard?"

Noah bites the toast and speaks around the mass of crumbs. "Those are pretty hard schools. Harvard rejects something like two hundred students a year who had perfect scores."

"I would need more than 1700, then. More than 1800 or 1900, I would imagine. What is the average score there?"

"I'm not sure," Noah lies.

"What did *you* get on the SAT, then?"

This question comes up with most of Noah's students. It used to be that he refused to tell them, because he didn't want his students to start comparing themselves to him. But when he didn't tell them they either saw it as a sign of Noah's not trusting them, or that his score wasn't so high after all. Noah has taken to telling his students his score quickly and simply. If anything, it bolsters their confidence that he knows the SAT well. "I got 1580 on the old test. Would be something like 2370 on the new one."

"Oh! You did not get a perfect score!" Olena taps the side of her coffee mug for emphasis. "I will get a 2400."

Noah smiles. "Not leaving us much room for error, are you?"

"Enough talk. Start teaching."

They cover some overarching math strategies. Noah gives her a set of worksheets to complete and a list of four hundred words to memorize, then bids her goodbye and starts his morning commute to his number one paying customer.

"It's only five days!" Tuscany says. "Five days until I go! Thank God, it's colossally boring here." She has stacked her books on an antique dining room chair and placed her bare legs on the mound, so her narrow thighs stand in front of her face like bars. She blows air over her toenail polish.

Noah yawns. Olena is in the middle of her practice test, Noah imagines. He envisions her with headphones on, lean arms akimbo as she massages her temples, processing a paragraph about the formation of nebulae.

"You said I could bring like friends, right? 'Cuz Octavia's on spring break too. She's from camp, we don't hang in the city much 'cuz she's from Connecticut. I checked with Mom and she said sure, why not, bring Octavia! Agnès's already like bought the tickets."

"Agnès said ok? Can this girl hike?"

"What does that have to do with it?"

"It's a hiking trip. You're going to cross mountains."

"You didn't ask *me* if *I* could hike. But don't worry, she does Pilates."

~

When Agnès delivers their breakfast and lunch she moves wordlessly, like a surly servant. Although she has never snapped at him, Noah has always detected a moodiness around Agnès, the possibility for bursts of fury. After he finishes with Tuscany he immediately goes to search for her. He finds her hunched over Dr. Thayer's desk, barricaded behind piles of paper like a *révolutionnaire.* Her back is to him.

"Hi, Agnès," Noah says cautiously. "Have you gotten all your supplies?"

"Yes, the trip," Agnès says, not turning around. "I have gotten supplies, yes." She pauses and points to the piles of paperwork. "Somehow Dr. Thayer expects me to manage all of this while I am on a mountaintop in France. Perhaps you know how I will do this?" Her head cocks to one side, angrily, expectantly.

"I'm sure Dr. Thayer understands that you'll be away for a week, so you can't possibly do all this as well, right?"

Agnés turns in profile and shoots Noah a withering look. "Noah. Please."

"Do you want me to talk to her?" Noah asks.

The cheek visible to Noah stiffens in anger. "No. What I want is to not go on this *odieux* trip."

Noah shifts his weight from one foot to the other. "I'm sorry I roped you into this."

Agnès turns to face Noah fully. She is pale and quivering, and with her white skin and shock of red lipstick she has the coloring of a plucked wildflower. Noah is taken aback by her furious beauty. "I am sorry you did as well," she says in French. "I thought it might have been fun before, but Dr. Thayer has not relented in my work, I don't know how I will even get through this day without her yelling at me—I did not go to *Princeton,* Noah, she is not so nice with me—and I have no desire to spend five nights in a tent with"—her voice drops to a whisper—"Tuscany and her *putain* friend Octavia!"

Noah just stands in the doorway, his arms crossed, speechless. Agnès looks about to get out of her chair and strike him.

"This job is hard enough," she continues, "without our turning on each other. That was a really low thing to do. Why didn't you just let me do my job, and you yours? In fact, I have work to do now, why don't you just go play cool to some other asshole for two hundred twenty-five dollars an hour? I've got some accounts to figure out by twelve."

"Whoa, Agnès," Noah says softly. *"Désolé."* He intended it in a general sense, but he immediately regrets that the word sounds like consolation for her lower wage.

"You're *sorry.* Oh, how *généreux.* Thank you, Noah. I don't need your pity."

"I didn't mean that, maybe it was my French."

"*Noah,* I am with *mauvaise humeur.* You should leave." Agnès swivels back to the piles of paper. Noah stands there and stares at the back of her head for a few moments, trying to think of what to say. Her straw hair quivers.

She turns her head, just far enough to squint at him out of the corner of her eye. "Go away, Noah. And if that sounds rude, perhaps it's my French."

The next day, Agnès has called in sick. And the next. "Strep throat," Tuscany reports derisively. "Yah, right," she continues, eyes dancing with the slim shred of gossip to have wandered into her cloistered life, "maybe her boyfriend actually did get her preggers this time. What's gonna happen if she like gives birth on the trip, huh? *What's gonna happen?*" Her eyes dart about maniacally.

The flight to Marseille leaves in two days.

~

"I don't understand," Olena says, holding up a reading comprehension passage that she has annotated and highlighted in three colors. "If they want to know which answer choice, if accurate, would 'detract least' from the author's argument, do I want the good answer choice, or the bad one?"

This question trips up kids whose parents are Columbia literature professors, never mind recent Albanian immigrants. Noah ponders how to explain it. But his thoughts are on Tuscany and what Agnès's absence means for the Marseille trip. He seems to spend his sessions with Tuscany thinking about Olena, and his sessions with Olena thinking about Tuscany. If only he had more time between the two. As it stands, he has to race through Harlem to make it to the Upper East Side in time, and his brain is slow to catch up with his person.

"You are not concentrating today," Olena chastises, tapping Noah on the arm.

"Oh, please," Noah says, pouring another cup of coffee. "Give me a break. Let's see. Tell me what the passage's about."

"The hierarchical differences between certain means for—"

"Stop being smart. I've told you, reading comprehension doesn't reward brilliance. Imagine yourself a perfect reader with no intellectual capacity. Don't analyze, just do plot summary. Two words, what is the passage about?"

"Colors of flowers."

"Good. Now which answer choice has nothing whatsoever to do with flower colors, either for or against?"

"Okay, okay, Mr. Clever American. I see it. This choice about geology is the one for me."

"Good."

Olena has nailed her vocabulary today, everything from *soporific* to *disrobe.* She has shown true disdain for the test, but is intellectually intrigued by the challenge of it, as if she has decided that the SAT is actually a thirty-five-page crossword puzzle.

"The verbal sections have this very American sense of inclusion," she notes. "Every test, there is a passage about Native Americans or perhaps the Harlem Renaissance. Then there is one science passage, preferably about the accomplishments of a woman. I have also noticed a ridiculous amount of memoir by Chinese immigrants."

Noah nods.

Olena scoffs. "Obviously the verbal part is written by boys like you, smart and guilty white persons. But the math! Those nerds have not caught on. Like this question: 'Carlos is delivering pizzas. If he can deliver nine pizzas in an hour, how many can he deliver in forty minutes?' Yes, Carlos is delivering pizzas, but in the same section Ingrid rides her horse to tennis lessons and walks back and wonders about her average speed. Who is the equestrian, who is delivering pizzas? This is a very American test, I think. All the conscious things are so careful, and all the subconscious things prove what the conscious tries to hide."

Noah agrees entirely. But it is too early in the morning for insightful commentary. He stares dazedly at the delicate curves of Olena's breasts beneath her threadbare shirt, and then snaps his gaze into his coffee.

"Perhaps my English didn't make sense," Olena says, waiting for him to react.

"No, you made perfect sense. I'm just a little sleepy."

"The SAT is crap. That's my message."

Noah perks up. "No way, it's essential. Before the SAT only kids from elite high schools stood a chance of getting into good colleges—Harvard had no way to evaluate a kid from Oklahoma. His high school was so different from Exeter that there was no way to know if his grades were accurate. The SAT changed all that. I couldn't have gone to Princeton without it."

"I am thinking you like it mainly because you did well on it. With a 1620 on 2400 you might be less thrilled."

Touché. "Yeah, maybe."

"I am not going to do well."

"We'll be able to work intensively while Tuscany's away. You're going to be fine."

A rumbling sound comes from Noah's bedroom. Roberto thumps to the floor and enters the living room, scratching beneath his boxer shorts. "What the hell?" he says. "You guys are doin' this like so fuckin' early."

"This is my *future,* Rob," Olena says. She spits the words at him.

Roberto makes a mocking cooing noise and then approaches Olena, gives her a brotherly squeeze. "She's like totally brilliant, huh, Noah?"

"Yeah," Noah says. "Your sister's pretty damn smart."

"Boys, boys," Olena says, pretending to struggle against Roberto's arms. Then she submits. "Okay, I guess you're right, I *am* pretty damn smart." She turns her head pointedly to Roberto. Her nose bumps his biceps. "Smart enough not to hang out with rich assholes who treat me like a zoo exhibit."

Roberto freezes, then releases her, shrugging his frame toward the ceiling. "Whatever. Dylan and his buds and me had like a really killer time last night. I'm having fun. I'll leave you to be all 'smart' about it."

"He plays dumb," Olena says to Noah, "but he's got a master plan somewhere inside all that underarm odor."

Noah has no doubt that Roberto has a "master plan," that both he and Olena do. Noah has noticed that Roberto has stopped asking him to go out now that he's entered Dylan's circle. Roberto has already advanced into a tenuous position in Dylan's league, just as Olena hopes for the high society of the Ivy League. Roberto and Olena are taking separate paths—one social, one academic—to scale the same society. Noah just wonders which of Hera's children will succeed.

~

Noah arrives at the Thayer household to discover that Agnès is still AWOL. Tuscany is gleeful at the heightening intrigue. "What're we going to do, huh, Noah? The trip's *tomorrow.* Tomorrow! And Agnès is like dying in bed. Or else driving around the Hamptons with her boyfriend. I think that's probably it, don't you? I mean, she's totally not sick."

Like a caged bird, Tuscany has turned manic and fluttery since she began spending her days at home. She sits on the dining room table in the middle of her piles of textbooks, running her hands over her feet.

"I have no idea," Noah says. "I don't know what's going to happen."

"I'm still going to go, right? The trips not like canceled?"

"I hope the trip's not canceled. I need to talk to your mom, though. Is she home?"

"She's off visiting clients or something. You should like call her cell phone," Tuscany says, nodding sagely.

~

Noah leaves Dr. Thayer a message, and doesn't receive a response until the early evening. The voicemail graphic of his cell phone is lit when he leaves the gym. The glowing envelope seems disingenuously genteel, as though Dr. Thayer has just messengered a sealed letter. He punches in his password as he jogs up Riverside.

The first message is from a Thayer—Mr. Thayer. Noah stops in his tracks.

Hello, is this Noah? There wasn't a beep. Regardless, this is Dale Thayer; we met last week. Listen, I wanted to talk to you about something, a little business proposition. I've just learned what extortionate *rates your agency charges and, well, I imagine I would run things a little better. I wanted to discuss possibilities with you.*

Mr. Thayer wants to start his own tutoring agency? Noah has no time to think about the implications before the second message begins:

Noah, hi, this is Dr. Thayer. I got your message about Agnès and yes, I'm concerned. I've given her a few calls throughout the day and, well, they haven't been returned. I suspect I'll have to call it off. I'm afraid this simply won't work. So do give me a call.

Noah sprints past his apartment, up a few blocks, and then back down again. This will take some thought. He vows to keep running until he comes up with something.

"Olena," he asks breathlessly when he enters the apartment. Sweat drips from his shirt and begins to pool on the floor. "How's your French?"

"Parfait, courant. Et pourquoi?"

Noah tells Dr. Thayer that he has a friend who is from Europe, with perfect French, and lets the doctor assume a Princeton connection. Dr. Thayer jumps on the opportunity—the reality of Tuscany's hanging around for ten days instead of being far away and out of her hair has apparently made Dr. Thayer willing to hear alternatives.

"Noah," she says into the phone, "I'm sure this girl is very sweet. But I don't know her. And who's going to make sure Tuscany continues her studies?"

"Olena's very responsible, Dr. Thayer."

"I'm sure she is. But I'd like you to go as well."

"Me!"

"Of course."

Noah's thoughts race—France with Tuscany and Olena? But then again, Olena was excited about being paid for the time abroad but reluctant to give up her time tutoring. They would be able to work together during any down time in France. It seems both improper and completely reasonable for him to go.

"I guess I can move my appointments. Okay. Why not?"

Suddenly Dr. Thayer is laughing.

"What is it?" Noah asks.

"It's just funny because you're not, well, a *teacher.* You're just a young man, hardly older than Tuscany. I can only imagine all the trouble you'll get into. And with her friend there as well! She can be a very difficult child, wicked."

Noah is frustrated by Dr. Thayer's tone. She did, after all, ask him to go. "I think she'll be fine."

Noah calls Air France and has Agnès's ticket canceled and reissued.

Two days later the four of them are in Marseille.

~

The trip . . . well, the trip.

On the return flight Noah snuggles against a dozing Olena. They are seated in coach, while Tuscany and Octavia giggle and luxuriate in first class. Noah is happy at the division, glad that the velvet curtain prevents him from taking any responsibility for what Tuscany and Octavia might be up to.

Which, considering the ordeal they have undergone, is probably just sleeping.

Justifiably feeling her role on the trip to be vague, Olena made herself official recorder. She declared that she would involve herself in taking pictures of the girls, ostensibly for the Thayer photo album, an object Noah is fairly sure does not exist.

Noah kisses Olena on the top of the head, powers on the digital camera display, and scans through the pictures.

1. *Tuscany and Octavia stand at the departures curb of JFK Airport, arm in arm. Taxi driver is engaged in the extensive process of unloading Octavia's luggage.*

The blur at the left of the frame is Noah, who flung open the door of the driver's black Mercedes SUV and dashed inside in order to find out about alternative flights, since they are two hours late. Said lateness arose mostly from the styling of Octavia's hair. Her hair is, admittedly, stunning. Octavia and Tuscany pose like demigoddesses of international departure.

2. *Tuscany and Octavia now stand before massive window at Air France departure gate. Stance is identical to previous picture—must have been rehearsed and ingrained in memory the night before. Photo might have been intended to capture girls alongside plane, but Octavia has shifted position and voluminous hair now obscures aircraft.*

Octavia Carotenuto, originally of Milan but presently of Greenwich, Connecticut, is the stepchild of an influential but generally despised Italian politician. She and Tuscany seem to complement one another—Tuscany the slender teacup, Octavia the considerably larger saucer. She has the squarish, rugby-player build Noah generally ascribes to a certain type of lesbian, but Octavia carries her solidness with such a voluptuous sense of sexual possibility that her large muscles and flat chest seem fully intentional, like this season's hot look.

3. *On plane. Girls hang over seat backs, with toothy and pouty grins, and give wild thumbs-up signs. Nearby French businessmen keep eyes firmly closed.*

The very photo seems to carry a sense of the girls' volume. Their iPods hum with a sort of demonic energy, the girls' open smiles hint at the peals of laughter they emit as they explore the possibilities of the cabin. The nearby passengers all sit at forty-five-degree inclinations, angling away from the girls. Noah's mental note: crop out miniature bottle of wine on Tuscany's tray table.

4. *Marseille Airport baggage claim. Octavia lies atop piles of her luggage, unceremoniously asleep, her body jumbled, looking as if dropped there from the ceiling. Tuscany is posed beside her, headphones still in her ears, body clenched and torso extended, as if a mermaid posing on a wave-swept promontory. Note gaggle of French boys staring from corner.*

Noah's backpack took its own route to Marseille, via Milan. It will be four hours before it arrives. Not pictured: he and Olena work on a practice SAT on the carpet of the arrivals lobby.

5. *Final dinner before six-day overnight trip begins.* Le Roi de Couscous *in Marseille: Noah's arm is visible at edge of frame as he energetically lifts a spoonful of meat, cauliflower, and broth to his mouth. Tuscany and Octavia stare mournfully into their bowls.*

The girls are never able to adjust to the fact that in France, the food one eats still looks something like the animal it was. The pig in the couscous doesn't become pork, the cow doesn't become beef—it stays pig, it stays cow. Bones and phlegm-colored stripes of cartilage stick out of the bowl. Octavia, in desperation, orders a chicken soup. It is a slain chicken in broth—strategically severed, but with almost all the parts floating in the bowl. Later that night Octavia forages a meal of a McFlurry and acceptably processed chicken from McDonald's. Tuscany, it seems, ingests only a diet Coke. Olena ventures into the girls' hotel room that night to talk about food (mainly, Olena dryly summarizes to Noah, that it should be consumed). Olena goes in concerned and leaves frustrated and angry. That night she re-names the pair "No-Eats" and "Italian Princess."

6. *Breakfast in the hotel. Noah has taken this picture: Olena, No-Eats, and Italian Princess are seated around a table in a beautiful, sun-filled atrium. Olena is smiling, but the smile does little to mask the look of mild horror that she will wear the entire trip.*

Noah has encouraged the girls to eat up, as this is the last meal that they won't have to carry themselves. Tuscany, encouraged by his speech, has taken her croissant and peeled off each layer, arranged them in a star pattern on her plate, and then eaten half.

7. *Shopping for supplies. Noah pushes a giant grocery cart through a* supermarché. *Tuscany and Octavia are nowhere to be seen.*

The girls arrive at the checkout. They discovered a clothing section upstairs, which reportedly "sucks worse than the Gap."

8. *Morning, on a trail leading up out of the foothills of Marseille. Tuscany wears her pack like an accessory, ignoring its weight through force of will, treating it as though it were only a prop on a photo shoot. Octavia is red-faced and sweating beneath her own.*

9. *Benoît, the guide, adjusting Tuscany's strap. A gallant pose: one muscled hand is perched on a boulder; the other reaches around Tuscany's waist. His fingernails glow pink at the tips of his tan fingers. Olena and Octavia stand a few feet away, watching him intently.*

Tuscany and Octavia (as well as Olena, Noah suspects) developed an instant crush on Benoît. Noah reminds himself that perhaps this is over nothing more than the fact that he is French and in control. He's a father of two. Maybe they feel protected. Whatever.

10. *Benoît on top of a rise, leading them up their first mountain. He exhibits an erect, purposeful attitude, not unlike that of a border collie.*

Benoît, Noah hears through Olena, was thrilled at the challenge of having been assigned an English-speaking group. Though he has conquered most of the mountain ranges of the world, he has not had a chance to use English since his years at *lycée.* And so he picked up some advanced English texts and learned some important phrases. Unfortunately, since *lycée* Benoît has forgotten all of his basic English, so these advanced phrases are the only words he knows. Three or four times a day Benoît will stop the group and announce that "It might be better if . . ." and be unable to complete the sentence.

11. *Lunchtime. No-Eats and Italian Princess nap on a rocky promontory in bikinis, having shed their fleeces. The Mediterranean glows blue far below. Benoît and Noah munch slices of sausage. Benoît looks crestfallen.*

Noah has just informed Benoît that one purpose of the trip is for the girls to speak French, so his English won't be necessary.

12. *Noah and Benoît on a ridge ahead of the group, looking out at the horizon.*

Although they appear noble and apprehensive, like rangers determining the best trails for the womenfolk, Noah and Benoît are still squabbling over languages. Benoît is cowed by Olena's language skills, and has conceded to speak to the girls only in French, but obviously doesn't want to see the English on which he has worked so hard go to waste. As a result he reserves his nonsensical, if sophisticated, English for Noah. Noah, made cranky by the hot sun and his heavy pack, parrots Benoît's earnest suggestions such as, "It might be better if no earth do!" back to him in similarly broken French.

13. *Campsite, the first night: No-Eats and Italian Princess sit on stones staring into a small fire, looking mutinous as Benoît stirs half a soup packet into a pail of iodized water.*

14. *An artsy photo of the night sky, taken by Olena. The silhouette of Noah and Benoît's tent cuts a triangular swath of black out of the swirl of stars.*

Noah shared a tent with Benoît, who, voluble and somewhat annoying during the day, is voluble and highly annoying at night. His snores have a prodigious, practiced quality to them. At the beginning of the night they are rapid and rhythmic wheezes, like Lamaze breathing exercises. Then Benoît segues into his full might, emitting great whooping snores that have a slight Doppler effect, like he is swinging a length of plastic tubing about his head. Noah, after tossing and turning for a few hours, tries to jostle Benoît into a lighter sleep. He shakes the sides of the tent. He shakes Benoît. Eventually he takes to vocalization. He whispers, "Quiet." Then shouts, "Quiet!" Finally he finds the trick—translation into French. *"Silence!"* does it, when pronounced with a Parisian accent. Benoît quiets, and Noah finally falls asleep.

15-48. *A few dozen pictures of the Calanques—fjords hemmed in by verdant flora, iridescent blue water, primeval trees clutching sandy rocks like wave-swept gnarled men, blah blah.*

49. *Another picture of the scenery. Olena and Benoît can be spotted at the horizon, eagerly mounting a rise. Octavia is a few hundred feet behind. Tuscany, filling half the frame, is a thousand feet behind that.*

Benoît assigned Noah to the position of rear guard, and since Tuscany is stopping every few feet to complain, "rear guard" is certainly very far in the rear. Noah's replies to Tuscany's complaints are all of a kind: "No, we can't turn back . . . no, there's no road nearby . . ." They follow the coastline from above, twisting around canyons filled with Mediterranean water. By the end of that day Tuscany's complaining lessens, and she apparently comes to the grudging realization that this hell can be escaped only by plodding forward. Noah, meanwhile, watches Olena and Benoît enviously. He wants to be in the lead as well, to be the one to share each new vista with Olena. His jealousy is a hot, incisive sensation—like gripping a hot stone close in his fist—and a novelty for a guy who is always the first to leave his girlfriends. For Olena to be inaccessible makes him want nothing more than to abscond with her into the surrounding hinterland.

50. *Tuscany scaling a cliff. Scaling a cliff! Note Noah standing below, body tense, ready to catch the flurry of blond hair and slender limbs should Tuscany fall.*

Since Tuscany winds up surviving the trip, this is the image that Noah will enlarge and give to Dr. Thayer. Tuscany is scaling a cliff. A cliff is being scaled by Tuscany. And, conveniently, Noah is there to catch her. Good PR.

51. *The campsite, night. Olena has snapped the picture because it is a warm, touching moment: Tuscany and Octavia are eating handfuls of powdered milk. They giggle and make as if to attack one another with hands covered in yellow clumps of powder. Note Noah and Benoît standing behind the campfire, arms crossed and locked, in tense discussion.*

The group has nearly run out of food.

52. *Morning: Noah and Olena, wearing packs streamlined to the essentials, wave goodbye to Tuscany, Octavia, and Benoît. Their cheerful smiles are cotton fabrications with a gray undercurrent of guilt and anxiety. In Noah's mind they look something like the woodcutter and his wife leaving Hansel and Gretel in the woods.*

The Calanques are inaccessible by car, which, yes, makes them serene, but also means that as far as the hiker is concerned the modern world might as well not exist. It is decided that Noah and Olena will go forage, like pioneers. Or better, find a road and hitchhike to a town with a store. Benoît will hang back with the girls. The official word is that they are taking a day's break to relax. Noah and Olena leave them with the remnants of the powdered milk and half a liter of water.

53. *Wooded French countryside. Wide horizons, the land green and beautiful and empty.*

54. *Again.*

55. *Again.*

56. *What appears to be a citadel of some sort rises from the emerald hills of Provence. Olena has raised her arm in a cheer.*

The citadel turned out to be France's only maximum-security prison. They approach the razor-wired walls slowly and in plain view, hoping not to be mistaken for marauders or escaped convicts and shot, or chattered at, or whatever the Provençal reaction to escaped prisoners is.

57. *Noah standing in front of the prison, scratching his head.*

There is no doorbell.

58. *Hours later: Olena, smiling resiliently, climbs a cliff. Full black garbage bags are tied around her waist.*

A guard finally came out and seemed mystified, even after Olena explained their situation carefully and explicitly, that anyone should come to a prison for nourishment. He finally brings them into the holding area, where they meet with the chef. He laughs for a good minute at the Albanian and American come to a penitentiary for handouts, and then finally sells them powdered potatoes and water, which they carry back to the campsite in bulging garbage bags.

59. *Noah reaching the group's campsite. The garbage bags tied around his waist give the appearance of a fat suit. A piece of paper is in his hand.*

The paper reads:

> ***Chèr*** **Noah et Olena:**
> **Seeing as long you were took, thankful a canyoning expedition to cross our path! Upon knowing badness ours, having joined them. (sake of girls). Your road to continue upon/along water. It might be better if meeting at Hôtel Alizé à Marseille (we are?).**
> ***Avec salutations*****, Benoît**

60. *Olena sits outside tent overlooking the Mediterranean. Sun is setting. She stares at the horizon, chewing a glob of crusty mashed potatoes. At the corner of the frame: Noah's hand entwined with hers.*

This would seem to have been their lowest moment—Tuscany and Octavia, lost and without provisions, have been carted off into the French wilderness. But Noah trusts Benoît—his overweening sense of duty, which rankled Noah so much earlier, is now a source of relief. And to be alone with Olena! Having her near to him the past week, away from the pressures of work and her family, and yet perpetually a few hundred yards ahead, has crazed him. She is finally next to him, and yet he can't pull the moves he would normally try on a girl he had a crush on. To seduce or charm her at all seems obliquely condescending, to approach her as a challenging game that, however complex, he will eventually master. He can't treat her like other girls. She strips him of his cockiness, consumes him with the fear of unwittingly doing something to displease her. He wants to know every part of her and, in their tent hundreds of feet above a barren and beautiful stretch of Mediterranean water, he learns a great deal, just by talking to her. Then he kisses her good night. They wake up in the same sleeping bag.

61. *Hôtel Alizé (interior), Marseille: Noah and Olena sit perched at opposite ends of the gloomy reception area, staring out the windows on either end of the room, like concerned bookends.*

Olena has informed Noah that canyoning involves climbing to the top of a mountain and then throwing oneself down a river, rappelling cliffs beneath torrents of rushing water, diving dozens of meters into rocky pools, and otherwise inviting maximum bodily harm. The idea that Tuscany will be doing this fills Noah with alarm and also something not unlike pleasure. Canyoning is, after all, not Wednesday nights at Pangaea.

62. *Hôtel Alizé (exterior): Noah and Olena have rushed outside upon arrival of Tuscany and Octavia (note frantic and sloppy angle of shot—the picture is composed in a diamond). Tuscany and Octavia approach in canyoning outfits, which are full-body wet suits topped with smart red plastic helmets. The girls look like crash test dummies, or members of an avant-garde rock band.*

Octavia arrives first, stomping the ground like a four-year-old in a tantrum, and slams past Noah and Olena without a word. Tuscany approaches second, gamboling down the gray and littered road. She whips off her helmet and out comes a stream of excited words: oh my God, that was the most fun ever, has Noah ever been canyoning? She jumped off this huge cliff, she was scared at first but then she did it and everyone was watching and Octavia was totally lame about everything and did Noah plan to tell her that they had run out of food? That was so crazy and made the whole trip like a life-or-death thing, and so awesome, and did you see this? (Tuscany pulls down the shoulder of her wet suit at this point to reveal a tremendous bruise, purple ribbed with khaki-colored broken veins.) She has to run inside now, they need their wet suit back.

63. *Close-up of Tuscany's bruise, taken at her request. The clotted hemorrhage is multicolored and extensive, an antique map that stretches from below her earlobe to the point where her pronounced collarbone terminates in her shoulder. The broken veins are lakes and tributaries, the regions of yellow, blue, and purple mountain ranges and forgotten lands. Note hint of a proud smile at the beginning of her lips, at lower left.*

Tuscany is thrilled to have been left with this souvenir, this proof that she has been on a quest, that she has met with some distant and powerful realm, and that it has touched her, struck her, and wrapped its image around her throat.

Noah's thoughts at time of taking of picture all focus on Dr. Thayer, and alternative sources of employment.

chapter 9

Noah. Is it my understanding that you had Tuscany jump into a river and throw herself off waterfalls? Call me as soon as you get this. This is Dr. Thayer.

Noah received the voicemail before he even arrived home from the airport. He sits at the kitchen table. He has gotten his arsenal of information in order: itineraries and flight information, hotel receipts, guidelines sent to him by the hiking company, copies of Tuscany's score reports, his work contract, his training manuals. Olena offered to serve as his second, handing Noah whatever weapons he should need during the phone battle, but in the interest of sounding as casual as possible it was decided that Noah will make the call alone while Olena showers. The sound of the water hitting the plastic of the shower curtain and echoing within the thin walls of the apartment soothes him. Or perhaps it is just the knowledge that Olena is nearby.

Dr. Thayer picks up immediately.

"Hello, Noah," she says. She is gruff, but there is a razor edge of mirth within her voice.

"Hi, Dr. Thayer," Noah says. "I guess you've heard what happened. Can you believe it?" He has put on his crazy-world routine (*What an amazing turn of events!*)—best to start with his most powerful defense.

"Yes. I have heard about it." Noah listens as Dr. Thayer's breath makes static against the receiver. "What are your thoughts?" she continues.

"My thoughts?" His mind leaps about as he tries to determine if Dr. Thayer is playful or serious. "I think . . . the trip went very well."

"Very well? What do you mean?" The doctor is on the offensive.

"Yes, Tuscany seemed to really enjoy herself. She wasn't too willing at first, but the outdoors seemed to really grow on her."

"Grow on her. What does that mean to you, exactly?"

They are in a session, like Noah is the latest intake at a mental ward. He stares furiously into the kitchen table. "How does Tuscany seem?" he finally asks.

"Tuscany seems like she slammed into a rock at forty-five miles an hour."

"Yes, that might have—"

"Octavia was horrified when she saw it. She said Tuscany spun around in the waterfall, hit the rock, and then fell over a cliff, her arms and legs 'going all over the place.' "

"I'm sure there was a lot of water at the bottom . . ."

"I guess my question in all this is: Where were you?"

"You see, I was out with Olena—"

"Olena?"

"The other chaperone who came with us on the trip."

"Oh yes. Tuscany didn't mention her name. Please, go on."

"Olena and I were out . . . in the hills . . . doing . . . has Tuscany told you about any of this already?"

"She might have."

"Then I guess you know we ran out of food. Olena and I went to find some."

"Let me fill in the rest here." Dr. Thayer's voice breaks, and she sobs. Or no—it's a laugh. The laugh continues. It sounds like a dry extended cough. "Oh, sorry, oh dear." The laughing dies down, picks up, and dies down again. "You and this girl just wandered into the woods hoping to . . . hoo hoo, spear a rabbit or something, or find a fairy godmother, hah hah, and instead you find France's maximum-security prison, this fortress just sitting there out in the wilderness, and you just walk up and knock on the gates. And meanwhile, the real tour guide Ben-Hwa thinks you have died or gotten lost—"

"We were gone for a while, yeah . . ."

"So when he comes across a bunch of people taking a canyoning trip, he just decides, why not? We'll join up, and float Tuscany and Octavia down the river like logs in a flume!" Dr. Thayer breaks into unrestrained laughter. Her laughs, bizarre as they sound, loosen Noah's anxiety, and he is soon laughing along with her.

"I'm telling you," Dr. Thayer says. "You don't get adventures like that in the Hamptons. Maybe I should have gone."

"I was worried you were going to be angry," Noah says.

Dr. Thayer's laughter stops. "Who said I'm not angry?"

Noah's own laughs take on a restrained, nervous quality.

"I mean, really, Noah, I could slap you with a lawsuit so easily over this."

"A lawsuit!"

"Oh, settle down, Noah, I'm only teasing you. Don't take it all so seriously." Dr. Thayer begins to laugh again, but her laughs seem hollow, as though she is only remembering the good feeling. "No, the truth of it is, Tuscany had a good time. I don't know how much French she learned, but she had a good time. I suppose that's what matters. Octavia seems a little scarred, but that's the Carotenutos' problem."

"I'm glad to hear that Tuscany enjoyed herself."

"But you see, there is something somewhat more grave to come out of all this. I'm afraid Agnès is no longer with us."

"Oh," Noah says. "She's not?" He speaks slowly, trying to decide which tone to adopt, mournful or cheerful. Speaking with Dr. Thayer is all about planning his state of being, rather than actually feeling—if he said what he was actually thinking, he'd start yelling and not stop.

"I saw this coming a long way down the road," Dr. Thayer says. "It's not as though it's strictly your fault. But planning this trip did a number on her. She's stopped returning my phone calls. And even if she did, at this point it's too late. Terminated, disengaged."

"Oh, I'm sorry." Mournful it is.

"Yes!" Dr. Thayer starts laughing again. Noah cringes. "I'm sure she'd have some choice words for you. But as I said, it's not strictly your fault. I'm just not sure what to do at this point."

"It must be hard to find someone last-minute, huh?"

"Oh, there are agencies, it's not a big deal, but thanks for the false sympathy." She laughs again, like a raven's cry. "But I have some other ideas percolating. I'll have to see if they'll work out, then I'll get back to you."

"Uh, okay," Noah says, mystified.

"Good night, Noah. See you on Monday."

Noah shuts off his phone and takes a deep breath. Aside from Dr. Thayer's unsettlingly aggressive laughter, the call went well. He feels regret for Agnès, and thinks of calling her. But he doesn't have her number, or even her last name. Like all the employees of the Thayer household, they float through with partial identities, unable to locate one another in real life.

He dials Mr. Thayer's number. A chirpy secretary answers.

"Oh, hi," Noah says. "I assumed I would get voicemail." It is nine P.M.

"No, we're always available. Tell me what I can do for you."

"I was hoping to talk to Mr. Thayer, please."

"He's in a meeting. Name, please?"

"Noah."

"One moment."

Noah is put on hold. Then a man's voice: "Noah, hello. This is Dale Thayer. What can I do for you?"

"You asked me to call you."

"I did? Oh yes! Noah, I wanted to discuss a proposition with you. Would you be available to come by Monday afternoon?"

Noah thinks of his loans, still somewhere around $50,000. A proposition from a billionaire sounds nice indeed. "Yes, of course. What time would work well for you?"

"Let's say two-thirty."

"Where should I meet you?"

"Umm . . ." He hears a muted rustle from Mr. Thayer's end, then from a distance: "Darlene, which office will I be in Monday?" then, loudly into the receiver: "Five-twenty-one Fifth Avenue, twenty-sixth floor. See you at two-thirty. Bring your tutoring materials."

~

Tuscany and Noah meet in Tuscany's bedroom on Monday.

"Mom's getting the dining room redone," Tuscany says. "We're having like some big party for some business of Dad's and she wants to get the walls done. The party's not for like two months, but whatever."

Tuscany sits on her bed, which means Noah gets to sit in the executive chair, instead of the tiny embroidered teddy bear throne. Tuscany is wearing a mustard shirt that has only one shoulder; its color and shape serve to highlight and outline the khaki stripes of her bruise. The wound adorns her throat like a corsage. The official subject at hand is hydrogen bonding, but it is, of course, really the trip.

"And that Olena girl," Tuscany says. "Where did you *find* her? She was so like serious, and weird."

"I think she's pretty great," Noah says defensively.

"Yeah," Tuscany says slyly. "I could tell."

Noah coughs. Tuscany laughs. "It's okay," she says. "You like her. Big deal. She's like your age and everything." She smirks derisively. "With hair like hers, she'd be lucky to have you." She smacks her gum a few times, stares at a molecule diagram in the textbook, and then pulls a box from behind the "When in Doubt, Just Don't Eat" pillow. She bounces with excitement. "I was going to wait until our morning session was over, but I can't. So here you go."

It is a stiff cardboard Façonnier box. Noah opens it and gently folds the tissue paper aside. Inside, pressed to be nearly as stiff as the box itself, is a button-down shirt.

A pink oxford. The fabric is sail-thick, as if made from the very stuff of yachts. The sleeves can be rolled up when watching a regatta or worn down for cocktails on the lawn. Now Noah has one.

"Put it on! Put it on!" Tuscany squeals.

"It's so nice," Noah says, folding it neatly back in the box. He is not the pink oxford type.

"Put it on! It'll look so good."

Tuscany's mouth is wide open, her hands clasped. Her eyes gleam. For Noah to wear this shirt would really thrill her. Noah, clutching the box like a shield, excuses himself to Tuscany's glowing frosted-glass bathroom.

The bathroom mirror fills a whole wall, and when Noah takes off his shirt he is disoriented to see himself shirtless in the Thayer apartment. His tanned skin doesn't belong against the brocaded fleur-de-lis walls, and the muscles of his upper arm, enlarged since he began his afternoon workouts, look too virile next to the Provençal soaps and embroidered toilet seat cover. He pulls the shirt across his naked torso. It feels rough against his skin, each thick thread of the fabric announcing itself as it slides over his form. He wears the shirt open, and looks for a moment in the mirror. It is even more strange and overwhelming to see himself half dressed in this environment. His thoughts leap to horrible places: the tingle he would feel had it been Dr. Thayer who just undid the buttons of his shirt, or the ignoble bliss he would feel should he have ducked into the bathroom after having slept with Tuscany. Noah hurriedly does up the buttons. His fingers tremble against the embroidered holes. He strides back into Tuscany's room without looking again into the mirror.

"No, Noah," Tuscany says. "You have to do it like this." She bounces off the bed and approaches him. He involuntarily leaves his hand on the doorknob, paralyzed by the conflict of desire and fear within him. She takes his arm. He watches as her little fingers work against the marbleized buttons of the sleeve. She undoes it and rolls the fabric once, then twice, so that it rests in a sloppy cuff halfway up Noah's forearm. She then lets that arm fall and moves to the other. She tucks her blond hair behind her head and then undoes the button, her lips slightly parted as she works. She folds the second cuff once, then twice, until it is roughly as high as the other. She stands back, puts one hand to her bruise and the other to her hip as she appraises him. She shakes her head and squints, her downy eyelashes locking. "It's not right yet. Hold on, sit down." She points to her bed. Noah obeys, sits with his hands clasped in his lap.

Noah watches in the mirror on the wall as Tuscany kneels on the bed beside him, reaches up her hands, and scratches through his hair, rubbing his scalp and mussing his hair. It no longer shoots up vertically, but falls in tufts over his forehead. She pats the hair forward, so that it hangs sleekly and messily over his eyes. He now looks like a prep school kid at summer camp. She looks with him in the mirror, and makes a professionally optimistic face, like a beautician. "That's better."

She stands in front of Noah, and he can tell she isn't wearing a bra. "And one last thing." She leans forward. Her lips are inches away from Noah's; he can smell the fruit smoothie she had for breakfast: papaya or mango. She is focused on the base of his throat. Her fingers fumble with the button on his chest, skate across his pectorals. The button is undone. Tuscany lingers at Noah's chest for a moment, as if testing, waiting to see what he will do. Her hair smells light and fresh, of tree oil. Noah is tempted to embrace her. It would be so easy, to fold her smallness against him, just to hold her. He puts his arm down so it is almost around her. He senses her slender carriage, the lean and warm muscles of her back. But he removes the arm immediately. The last thing she needs is another grown man "holding her." Noah is sickened at himself, at his own desire. Tuscany stands back. Her face is collected. "Get up," she commands.

Noah stands, and together they look in the mirror. The transformation is complete. Noah looks like he could be one of Dylan's friends, or Dylan himself. The shirt sits neatly over his shoulders, exaggerates the new triangularity of Noah's form. The forearms that poke from the shirt have tanned in the southern French sun. The ends of the shirt fall in neatly curved lines below Noah's waist. The heavy fabric rustles loudly when he moves.

"Wow," Noah says, "well chosen."

"Thanks. Mom and I wanted to thank you for taking me on that trip. Well, I picked it out and everything, but she wants credit too. You look really good."

Noah looks at Tuscany. The last time he felt this drawn to a student he wound up offering to take the SAT for her. He can't let this attraction grow any further. It is a fleeting, wasteful version of his more solid feelings for Olena. He could never be drawn to Tuscany in any real way. He is not Roberto: knowledge of the consequences of his actions restricts how Noah feels. Tuscany stares back at him, then reaches for her cigarette and scans the room for a lighter. Noah decides they will work at the kitchen table that morning, for the official reason that they are making molecular models and Tuscany's desk "isn't big enough." Tuscany raises an eyebrow, immediately seeing through the deception. But she seems relieved when they move to the comparative safety of downstairs.

~

Noah is glad to hear the clock chime two. He stuffs his old shirt in his bag, says a quick goodbye to Tuscany, and hops into the subway. He buys a hot dog from a corner vendor (there was no Agnès to fetch his lunch today, and he didn't want to trouble Fuen), and races into the elevator of Mr. Thayer's building. He is guided deferentially down a chrome-and-wallpaper hallway into Mr. Thayer's office. He is still wearing the pink oxford.

Mr. Thayer is on the phone, his feet up on the desk. He smiles to Noah, rolls his eyes toward whoever is on the phone, and gestures him to a seat. Noah waits in the chair, staring at the reflective glass of the building across the street and listening to the man-prattle of Mr. Thayer: all of his sentences seem to contain the words *leverage* and *commodity*. Finally Mr. Thayer hangs up the phone and reaches over to shake Noah's hand.

"Noah. Thanks for coming."

"Of course." Noah is tempted to add a *sir*. He censors it out just in time.

"Listen, I wanted to talk to you about a few things. And don't worry, none of them have anything to do with Dylan and Tuscany!" Mr. Thayer laughs loudly, a business-lunch laugh; Noah waits for him to offer a cigar.

"One thing you'll notice about me, Noah, is that I get to the point. And the point, in this case, is this . . ." He pauses. It seems he has yet to come up with the point. Then: "I've started a few companies in my time. Some have bombed, others have taken off. And the thing is, a bomb costs you a million, maybe, but a success can net billions. So if you have one success for every thousand bombs, then you're still in money. Look at my history: for every *Northern Airlines* or *Car and Girl Magazine,* there's a *Calvi Fashion* or a *Fish and Girl Magazine.*" Mr. Thayer sits back, gauging the effect of his words on Noah. This is a pearl of business advice that Mr. Thayer has obviously cultured over the years, a conversational tidbit that he throws out when he hasn't decided what he really wants to say.

Unfortunately, these names mean nothing to Noah. "Yeah, I guess bombs are okay," Noah says. He feels incredibly stupid. Perhaps, he suspects, this has been Mr. Thayer's intention.

"Yes. I started in newspapers, did an airline, and now I'm in discount apparel. Looks like crap, but pays well. Though, with labor markets these days, who knows. Anyway, I saw the family expense statement for a few months ago, I think it was August—were you working for us in August?"

"Some of August."

"Let's say September, then. And I see that your agency bills three hundred ninety-five a session."

"An hour."

"Right! That's the thing—it's more like, what, five-ninety-five for a ninety-minute session?"

"Six hundred and sixty." Whoops. That number slipped out far too quickly.

"And once you've learned the material, it's not as though you even need to do any lesson preparation!"

"That's right." Noah feels grudgingly proud now. It does seem like a hell of a business model.

"But you, of course, earn only a fraction of what is billed."

"Correct."

Mr. Thayer plucks a stress ball from his desktop and squeezes it absently as he reclines in his chair. "And why haven't you thought of just going out on your own?"

"Well, my company trained me, and I feel loyalty to them, and they get my students for me, so I don't have to worry about running out of work . . . let's see, um, there's also this clause in my contract that I can't work on my own."

Mr. Thayer looks up sharply. "There is?"

Noah nods.

"Do me a favor, would you Noah, fax me a copy of that contract later today?"

"Umm, I—"

"Right on, Noah, don't agree to anything yet, sorry, I forgot to make my proposal first. Here it is. I'm willing to take whatever your yearly salary is and triple it. Or I don't know your salary, let's not be reckless, but let's say this: I could offer at least a hundred and fifty K for a year of your consulting. You're a smart kid, and you know this stuff enough to make even *my* children good at it. I want to start an agency that will compete with yours. But the only hitch is, I don't know how to tutor. You would be the content side of things, and I'd take care of all the business."

"Wow." There is nothing more to say. Noah would have been just as dumbfounded had Mr. Thayer stood up and done a triple back flip.

"This is all assuming it works with your contract. But I suspect they just forbid you from teaching for a certain time after working for them, and say nothing about doing business consulting. And even if they did—from my wife's accounts your office seems crafty, I wouldn't be surprised—I don't think it would be enforceable. Send the contract. I'll have a lawyer look it over."

"Okay," Noah says. After all, it's just faxing a contract. It's not as though he's agreed to anything yet. A hundred and fifty thousand dollars. He could buy his mom a new car. He could spend the summer far away from Fifth Avenue. He could convince his brother to enroll in a specialized school. He could throw a lavish party.

Mr. Thayer grins at Noah from across the desk. "Send it tonight, okay, Noah? And I'll give you a call when I hear back."

Rafferty Zeigler. Outside of the hundred minutes a week that Noah is actually with him, Noah has come to disregard him. Sullen and forgettable Rafferty, with the panicky mother. Noah dreads their appointment—Rafferty's score has gone down. Sunday is looking to be one hell of a day. On his way to Rafferty's apartment, Noah opens his tutoring notebook to the Fieldston page:

	Starting Score:	**Latest Practice Test:**
Cameron Leinzler:	M650, V660, W670	M760, V760, W730
Rafferty Zeigler:	M680, V520, W540	M620, V520, W550
Garret Flannery:	M700, V520, W490	M750, V650, W600
Eliza Lipton:	M480, V480, W510	M530, V520, W550
Sonoma Levin:	M480, V590, W540	10th grade: not yet testing

It is a mess of numbers, seemingly meaningless and inconsequential, but Noah immediately sees the seeds of a crisis, a set of scores that makes him dread the coming of four P.M. Rafferty hasn't seen his score go up after five months of tutoring. In fact, he has gone down. The Zeiglers have spent $17,000 for a fifty-point decline in Rafferty's score. They live on York Avenue: they must earn less than $400,000 a year, are really slumming by Upper East Side standards—for them, $17,000 is a significant amount. Mrs. Zeigler will be beside herself, Noah knows. Fieldston is a very competitive school, and all the kids gossip about their practice tests. *This is so bad for Rafferty's self-esteem,* she will say. And she will be right—Rafferty, always reserved, has been plunging the depths of sullenness, showing less and less of his already underwhelming enthusiasm. Noah spends his morning sessions wishing that no one tutored, that he wouldn't have to go see Rafferty dejected and his mother hysterical.

"This is so bad for Rafferty's self-esteem," Mrs. Zeigler says. She was waiting in the hallway to ambush Noah, sprang at him from the shadows of the recessed doorway. The walls have been torn apart to fix water damage from a broken pipe, and as a result the hallway is like a Roman grotto, all damp air and scored cement.

"A lot of the students work on plateaus," Noah says. "They'll hold steady for a few tests, and then start to go up."

"Yes, but he didn't hold steady, right? He went down." She whisks her hands through her hair a half dozen times.

"There's deviation between tests. Or sometimes the initial diagnostic test is artificially high. Those are the hardest cases."

Mrs. Zeigler hugs her tiny designer T-shirt close to her ribs. "These kids are so competitive," she says mournfully. "They're always talking about their scores. Is there any way you could say something . . . like that his test was lost this time? He's been down all this week, and he has a science project due tomorrow. I'd hate for him to go into a funk."

Noah shifts his bag to the other shoulder. He can see a vein in Mrs. Zeigler's neck pulsing, see the silk of her shirt tremble with the rapid pounding of her heart. "I don't think I should do that. We'll go over what went wrong, don't worry."

Mrs. Zeigler puts a tremulous hand in front of her mouth and nods slowly. She waves Noah into the apartment with a resigned flick of her wrist. Someone seeing her pose might assume Noah has just suggested finally cutting off Rafferty's life support.

Rafferty is sitting on his bed, watching a football game on the television mounted on his wall. His gaze flicks to Noah when he enters, and then back to the screen. "Hi, Noah," he says. He points to a bowl of chips. "You want some?"

"No thanks," Noah says as he arranges himself in his seat. Rafferty turns off the game and sits at the desk. "How did you feel about the test this weekend?" Noah asks. This is what he always asks when the score is bad—the students invariably say, "Awful," because it always feels awful, it's the *SAT,* and then it seems like the score just confirms that it was an especially hard test. Noah is surprised his students haven't caught on yet.

Rafferty grunts, then says, "I don't want to talk about it," as he clicks the television off.

"I'm not going to lie, it wasn't fantastic," Noah says. "But you'll see that there were problems in only a couple of sections. Section Three was really good."

"What do you mean, there were problems? What was the score?"

"Umm," Noah says as he pulls out the score report. "It was 1690."

"I went *down?*"

"I told your mom, it could be fluky. A lot of students go down at first, it's not—"

Rafferty covers his eyes. "Oh my God. Oh my God."

"It's okay, Rafferty, it's just one score. There are plenty of other practice tests. Let's look at the broad picture."

"You don't tell the other Fieldston kids my scores, do you?"

"Of course not."

Rafferty pulls his hand down so it covers his mouth instead. It might have just been from the pressure of his hand, but Rafferty's eyes are red; he could be about to cry. With his hand over his mouth he looks a lot like his mother, stricken in the hallway. "I *hate* this! I hate it!" He pushes his chair away from the desk, spins angrily. "Why do I have to even take this stupid fucking test? I don't even want to go to college. Which is good, since I won't get in anyway! Fuck!"

"Seriously, man," Noah says, "don't start worrying about scores yet. Seriously. We've got time. Let it run off your back."

Rafferty clenches his hands into fists, strikes his thighs. "Crap! Everyone else is getting like 2100s. And I won't even be able to get into like SUNY Buffalo." He stares at his red fists, and then something catches in his head. He turns to Noah. "*Let it run off my back*? Who the hell are you to tell me that? You're the one who's screwed up here."

"Look," Noah says. "There's no need to place blame, because there's nothing wrong yet. We've got a while before the test."

"Yeah, save your ass, Noah. Six weeks. That's not 'a while.' "

"And the May test isn't your last chance. There's always October, or November."

Rafferty stares at the blank television screen. "What is Cameron getting? Eliza and Garret tell me their scores, but she never tells me."

"You know I can't tell you that."

"Is she bombing too? Are you like doing something wrong?"

This is a delicate turn: Noah's impulse is to tell Rafferty

the truth—that Cameron's doing well—to get him off his back. But then it will seem that Rafferty is the only one doing poorly. And so Noah makes a choice that he instantly regrets: he keeps silent.

"Ah!" Rafferty cries. "She is! Cameron's totally not going up either!"

"Jesus," Noah says sharply. "Stop it."

Rafferty's door opens. His mother is in the portal, clutching another bowl of chips. "I thought you might want some more," she says, her voice quavering. She doesn't enter the room, holds the chips close to her. "What are you two talking about? Why are you so excited, Rafferty?"

"*Why are you so excited, Rafferty? Why are you so exciiited?* Because I'm not fucking going to college, Mom."

"Of course you're going to college," Mrs. Zeigler says, her hand to her throat. Then she looks unsure. She looks to Noah for confirmation.

"Of course," Noah says. "As I said, this—"

But Rafferty has spotted his mother's uncertainty. "See, even you don't think I'm going to go to college!"

"Well, honey," Mrs. Zeigler says, clutching her throat, "I don't know much about these things. We have to trust Noah on this."

"Yeah," Rafferty says, hurling himself deep in his chair. "I have to trust *Noah.*"

Noah glances from Rafferty to his mother, and back again. How could she insinuate that her son might not get into college? "Come on, Rafferty," he says. "Of course you're going to college. You're a smart kid. Stop worrying about the big picture. Today we're going to think about ratios. I need you to concentrate on just that."

"Yes, think about ratios, honey," Mrs. Zeigler says, then mercifully departs, carrying the chips with her.

Rafferty does manage to come around and concentrate on the proportion of pigs to cows on Mr. Cowell's farm, but he spits his answers at Noah hatefully, like sling stones. The hundred minutes are some of the longest Noah can remember.

~

When Noah's alarm goes off at five forty-five on Monday morning he can barely drag himself out of bed. He was up until eleven P.M. tutoring, in bed at one, and tossed and turned most of the night, all the time remembering Mrs. Zeigler's fluttery, worried goodbye in the grotto hallway. When he wakes he lingers in his bed, staring at his sheet, counting the frayed threads in his pillowcase. It takes Olena's soft, concerned voice at his bedside to rouse him. He takes a quick shower and drinks three cups of coffee while guiding Olena through arithmetic sequences. He is gladdened by her resolve and enthusiasm, gives her only a peck goodbye (she is his student, after all), and arrives at the Thayer household somewhat heartened. He has not turned on his cell phone, however, dreading the panicky phone call that Mrs. Zeigler is sure to have made.

As he enters the foyer Noah hears Dr. Thayer's voice call from somewhere within the cavernous apartment. He finds her in the portion of her office that has been converted into a mini-gym. She pounds away at a treadmill, her sharp legs jabbing at the running belt as if trying to pierce it. She is wearing an ill-fitting sports bra, and every other step causes a hint of her aureole to become exposed. Noah concentrates on the bookshelf behind her. "Good morning, Dr. Thayer," Noah says.

"Good morning, Noah," she says, breathing heavily. "Maim any teenage girls yet today?"

Noah wonders how long she spent crafting that line. "No, no." He feigns a chuckle.

"Well done," she laughs. The machine kicks into a

higher speed. She grips the sides and gasps, her legs scurrying beneath her.

"So . . ." Noah says. Why has she called him in here? "How are you doing?"

"Oh," Dr. Thayer says, breathless. "Fine, thanks. Ready . . . to finish this!" She repeatedly punches a button on the machine, and slows to a power walk. "That's better. Ah. So, Noah, I understand my husband has called you." She gives a wink, as if to say, *That scamp!*

"Yeah," Noah says. "I think he wants some advice on starting his own tutoring firm."

"Yes," Dr. Thayer says. "That. Use your judgment, there. Don't feel obligated to help him."

"Okay," Noah says. He stands still, staring at the bookcase. She is hinting that he should rebuff her husband—what is there to say?

"And how is Tuscany?" Dr. Thayer asks.

"She's doing well. Very good."

"We think we've found a school for her in the fall. Mount Oak, probably."

"Sounds good. She'll be happy there."

Dr. Thayer slows the machine even further, so that she is barely moving. She turns around and starts walking backward. "But there's something more important that I need to talk to you about. Dylan. I've made a mistake. He got into George Washington yesterday."

"Okay . . ." Noah says, bewildered. Sounds okay to him . . .

"He got in for athletics. But in order to play, NCAA guidelines say that each recipient needs a certain combination of GPA and SAT score. Dylan's GPA, as you could imagine, isn't very good. So he needs at least a 1580 to play. But his SAT score is a 1540."

"That's from last spring?"

"Well," Dr. Thayer says, smiling as sweetly at Noah as if he were the co-op president, "actually, that's from last month."

Noah suspects where this is going, but plays ignorant to see Dr. Thayer squirm. "Dylan took the test again without tutoring?"

"Yes . . . well, that is to say, he might as well have."

"I'm sorry, I don't understand what you're saying." He stares at Dr. Thayer straight on, exposed aureole or no.

Dr. Thayer's smile drops, and she looks at Noah shrewdly as she marches backward. "I think you do, Noah."

Noah shakes his head resolutely. "No, I really don't."

Dr. Thayer sighs, as if totally discouraged at finding Noah's head so muddled. "I engaged another tutor. Dylan had someone else help prepare him for the SAT, some guru from the Princeton Review. He was written up in the *Times Magazine.*"

"You're perfectly free to do that," Noah says, in what he hopes is his most magnanimous tone.

Dr. Thayer smiles slightly, impressed: she must think Noah is playing this ignorance game well. "Well, the truth is that he was awful. I didn't realize it at the time, of course. I mean, I obviously got someone brilliant—Ph.D. in applied math from CalTech, Rhodes Scholar, all that. But he was an actual *teacher.* He didn't bother being friendly with Dylan, he just pushed him. And I don't know if you've ever seen Dylan pushed, but it's not pretty."

"So Dylan didn't do any work?" Noah asks.

"Yes. And from what I can tell he would have bombed the SAT just to spite his teacher."

"Would have? Why do you say 'would have'?" Noah takes on a casual and distant tone, as if they were discussing an abstract point.

Dr. Thayer gives another impressed smile. "I suspect that, again, you know where this is going. I imagine you are even already familiar with the exact mechanics of how this works."

Noah has a suspicion, but this time his ignorance is mostly genuine. "No, you're going to have to tell me."

Dr. Thayer gauges her pulse for a few moments and then speaks. "Not all tutors have become as morally . . . upstanding as you. This Princeton Review guru fellow, when he saw how much he was being paid and that Dylan was going to do horribly, came up with an alternative. He became a sort of broker, if you will. He found us another student willing—are you going to make me spell this out, Noah?—to take the test in Dylan's place. A simple matter of the purchase of a fake driver's license."

"And you were in support of this?"

Dr. Thayer begins jogging backward. "Perhaps you'd like to fill me in on my other options. Dylan wasn't going to do well enough on the test on his own. There was a spot at George Washington open to him, and all he needed was a better score. And some struggling recent graduate, a boy much like you, would make some money to further his *art,* or buy a car, or what have you. I'm Dylan's mother. I have the chance to see my son go to college, or take some obscure moral route and kill his future. It didn't harm anyone, Noah."

"And so what happened?"

"The idea was this: Dylan obviously couldn't get a 2400. That would be absurd. So the young man who wound up taking the test knew he needed to have Dylan just scrape by. As you know, the curve on each test is different, so it's never a sure shot. He intentionally missed many problems, but . . ." The treadmill speeds up, and Dr. Thayer starts sprinting backward. She is a jumble of limbs moving at awkward angles. "Maybe he missed even more problems because of his own errors, or maybe he didn't know the test well enough. Not as well as you. Whatever it was, Dylan got a 1560, not a 1580. And he can't enroll at George Washington this fall without that 1580."

"And there's only the May test left."

"Exactly."

"So what are you going to do?"

Dr. Thayer steps off the treadmill, wipes her brow with a plush white towel, although she doesn't seem to have perspired. "I think what you need to figure out is what *you* are going to do."

"Sorry?"

Dr. Thayer moves slowly toward Noah. The skin of her fatless abdomen pouches slightly over the band of her spandex shorts. She stops inches in front of Noah. He can smell her breath—like Tuscany's, it has the flavor of melon on it, but beneath it lurks the long-standing yellow stench of tobacco. "Tuscany told me you live in Harlem, Noah. And Dylan, I believe, has met your roommate. Some foreign man. And he told Dylan about your professor ambitions. Good for you, you'd be great! And it is clear, Noah, despite your clothes, that you are not originally from around here. So you deserve another pat on the back, making it this far! But that also means that you have some debt, no? Princeton is not inexpensive. What if you didn't have those loans anymore? If you had your own apartment in Union Square, or Greenwich Village? All for doing what you were trained to do."

"You want me to take the SAT for Dylan?" Noah didn't need to ask, but he can think of nothing else to fill the stunned silence.

"Don't get a righteous tone here. Whether or not you want to confess about Monroe Eichler, you've been on this . . . slippery slope for some time. I'm offering you money for a service. And that service is raising Dylan's SAT score. That is how we've always operated, no? Money pays for higher scores. You're helping those who can pay to get ahead. What I'm proposing may sound immoral, and to some maybe it is. But that's not the point—you've been tutoring for years. Obviously you've been fine with this equation. All I'm asking is that we take it to its natural limits."

"I can't do that. I'll be happy to teach Dylan, but I can't do that. Couldn't you find someone else?"

"Princeton graduates with astronomical SAT scores and willing natures are hard to come by. This first one messed up. And I trust you. You're good at this. You know exactly how many questions to miss."

Noah quickly loses his feeling of moral righteousness. He has a 'willing nature'? What does that *mean*? Whatever it is, he doesn't want it to be true. "No," he says firmly.

"Is it a question of how much money?"

"No."

"Don't forget, Noah, that you've also worked with Tuscany under the table. Your company wouldn't want to hear about that, or anything else that you've done. I had a few therapy sessions with Mrs. Eichler's little boy last year—he was so distraught over his father's death. And so, apparently, was Monroe."

They are veering into nastier territory. Even though he never took the test for Monroe, there's sure to be a damning paper trail behind that cashier's check he deposited. She has far too much she can use against him.

She shrugs and puts on her hostess smile. "It's something to think about."

He hates her. He wants to claw into her exposed abdomen. "I'm sorry, Dr. Thayer, but I'm not thinking about it. The answer is no." *And,* he almost continues, *what would your children's schools do if they heard about your plotting? Your clients?* But Dr. Thayer would see through the threat—she knows he wouldn't ruin Dylan's and Tuscany's futures just to get back at her.

Dr. Thayer grips Noah's arm and smiles affirmatively, as if in complete compassionate support of Noah's rectitude. But Noah doesn't miss the anger flashing at the backs of her eyes. "I assumed as much, Noah. I don't think your answer would have been no a few months ago. But you have become so . . . kind." She gives the compliment the sharp edge of an insult, like calling an unattractive girl sweet. "Maybe you're just worried that your graduate schools would find out. But they wouldn't, really they wouldn't." She sighs. "Perhaps you would still consider tutoring Dylan to see if you can get him where he needs to be by teaching him."

Riding on the exhilaration of having said no, Noah feels a swell of euphoria at the challenge of guiding Dylan down the right path, of showing the Thayers that the good thing can be done. "I'd be happy to work with Dylan."

"He's going to need as much time as you can offer," Dr. Thayer says. Her voice is sugary, repentant. "Perhaps you can teach Tuscany in the morning, and Dylan in the early afternoon?"

"We can work something out like that," Noah says.

"And we can continue to do payment for this just between us?"

It is time to do this aboveboard, particularly after Dr. Thayer's vague threat of blackmail. "No, I think it's best that we go through the office if I'm working toward a standardized test."

Dr. Thayer shrugs. "Okay. It's your money you're losing." She stares at Noah, her hard brown eyes vital within the tired rumple of her face.

"I assume Tuscany is waiting for me?" Noah asks.

A smile ripples across Dr. Thayer's lips. "Tuscany and Dylan both."

~

Tuscany is late for her morning session. Noah uses the time to respond to Mr. Thayer, who left him a message saying that his agency contract was worth "less than the paper it was printed on."

Mr. Thayer is in Chicago. Would Noah like to leave a voicemail? He would:

Hi, Mr. Thayer, this is Noah. I was glad to receive your message this morning—however, I have thought it over and unfortunately don't think I'm going to be able to go ahead with this. My agency has treated me pretty well, and I'd rather not leave at this point. Thanks, and if I can be of any other help, let me know. So long.

It's time to regain the high ground.

Tuscany finally comes in, fifteen minutes late. Her mascara seems to be double thickness today; Noah can barely see her eyes. He wonders if she has worn it for him, and realizes she must have—she is grounded, and the only other people here are her mother and Fuen. She is chipper and eager to work, and happily lets Noah guide her in the construction of a cardboard molecule of caffeine.

"I hear you're going to Mount Oak," Noah says as they pack up their books.

"Yeah," Tuscany says mournfully. "I bet it sucks there."

"Oh, I don't know," Noah says. But his words come slowly: from what he's heard, it does "suck there."

Tuscany picks up on Noah's ambivalence. "I should be going somewhere better, huh?" Tuscany says.

Noah pauses. "Do you still have your school application forms?"

Tuscany nods solemnly. They're in her bedroom. She gets up and waits for Noah to follow. He asks her why she doesn't just bring them downstairs.

Ever since Noah stopped working with Dylan, he's heard nothing but stories about him from Roberto: Dylan danced with some middle-aged woman at a club in the Hamptons, and she kept grabbing his butt and buying everyone drinks. Dylan stopped the car service and peed behind a tollbooth on the Jersey turnpike. Dylan bought both his girlfriends the same ring, and then they ran into each other at Bungalow 8. So when Noah enters Dylan's room, it feels like he has never left. Dylan, however, seems to have trouble remembering who Noah is. He glances up blearily from his bed.

"We worked on what, like that writing test, right?"

"Yes. The writing section of the SAT."

"I bombed."

"Yup."

"But still, you're so much better than that asshole my mom bought from the Princeton Review. He was like all"—Dylan lowers his voice into bass range as he shoots a sponge basketball into a hoop behind the door—" 'Dylan, you didn't do your homework. How are you going to improve if you don't do your homework, the test is in a month?' and I'm like Jesus, fuck off, you know? You're not like a teacher, dude, so don't get all severe. You can't assign *homework,* it's not like I'm getting a *grade* here!"

Dylan glances over and grins, proud of his rhetorical skills. Noah is tempted to admonish him, but he's happy to be considered the better tutor, even if it is just because he didn't make Dylan do any work.

Dylan reclines on his bed. A half dozen glasses at his bedside are coated with the residue of chocolate protein shakes. He bounces with repressed energy, and the cover falls away from his ankle. Noah notices that it's in a splint.

"What happened?" Noah asks, pointing to it.

Dylan looks at Noah slyly. "My mom thinks it's from basketball. Hilarious."

"What *is* it from?"

"Oh God. It was this totally wack night. I think it was like a few nights ago. There was this crazy private party at this club, right? And I go with a couple friends, Siggy and this guy Roberto."

"I know Roberto," Noah says, smirking at the understatement. He did, after all, introduce the two of them. It burns him, briefly, that Roberto has so seamlessly infiltrated Dylan's circle, while Noah is still an employee.

"Okay. Anyway, Roberto, he's like Italian and he starts talking to this guy who's like wearing big shades and this fly polyester suit, like he just made a movie or something. Anyway, the guy owns this apartment in the Meatpacking District. The apartment was the bomb. We went there after the club? He had like four plasma screens put together. So we watch a game. Siggy and I are like totally set, watching basketball on TiVo at like four A.M., but Rob wasn't into it, so he wandered around. I think it might have been the drugs the guy had. I stuck to coke, but Roberto mixed it up with like these light green pills, and I was feeling fine, but Rob was feeling like antsy. So anyway, Rob wanders off, and I guess the guy is in the other room, the one that Roberto wanders into."

Dylan pauses to make another shot at the hoop. He misses. The ball rolls near Noah and he returns it to Dylan. He tries again, scores.

"Umm . . ." Dylan says, scratching his chest.

"The guy was in the other room?"

"Right! Umm . . ." He continues scratching.

"With Roberto?"

"Oh yeah, okay. Right. So he's in the other room with Roberto, and then after a few minutes the door slams open and Roberto is looking all wild and crazy, like he's been nailed with a Taser or something. He's like, 'Guys, we're leaving.' And Roberto's a big guy, so it was trippy as shit to see him freaked out. So Siggy and I are like, but dude, what are you talking about, it's awesome here, but we were kind of quiet about it 'cuz he was buggin' so hard. And so anyway, the guy comes out after Roberto, still wearing his suit, and his fly shirt all like unbuttoned. He's all tan and suave, looked like some guy in a Tanqueray commercial, you know? And he's like, Jesus, chill man, it's cool, it's cool. And Roberto heads towards the door, and the guy just stands there, smiling, like Rob's being a total moron. Rob tries the door and it won't open. You know, it's the solid kind, like my bedroom door, that needs a key to open, no matter what side you're on. And I guess the dude had the key. So the three of us, me, Rob, and Siggy, are standing next to the front door, like idiots, and the guy's standing in the living room. The game's still going on, I can hear it. It was the Knicks, so I was still like halfway listening, 'cuz there were like ten minutes left, even though I already knew the Knicks won 'cuz the Clippers suck. And Roberto brushes past the guy and like opens a window! Siggy and I just look at each other and say, 'Shit, what the fuck? We're on like the sixteenth floor.' "

Dylan picks up one of the protein shake glasses and stares in for a moment. He holds it up to his mouth, but nothing dribbles in. "Mom!" he yells. "I'm thirsty!"

He turns back to Noah. "Shit, that was dumb. I better hurry, 'cuz my mom totally can't know about this. So anyway Roberto opens a window. And now the guy's like really mad, and he goes over to Roberto and like grabs his arm. Now this is where it's the bomb"—Dylan leans forward excitedly—"Roberto turns around and gives the guy this huge punch. I mean, like Roberto's gigantic and weird-looking and sorta like a video game character anyway, and it totally looked like a secret move from Mortal Kombat. And the polyester dude *flies.* He hits the table in the living room, and his head just sits on the corner, like he's propped against it, and there's some blood coming from it. Not a lot, like the dude wasn't dead, but he wasn't feeling too good either. Passed out. Roberto comes back from the window and stands over the guy, we all do, like the three of us. And then suddenly Siggy turns all girly and is totally blubbering. So he's useless, but Rob is totally in charge and says we gotta find the key! I say it's prob'ly in the dude's pocket, but Rob says no way I'm touching that faggot. That's when I figured out what prob'ly happened in that other room. But I'm like, whatever, dude, we need to get out, so I look through the guy's pockets. Even the back ones, but since the guy was like totally passed out I didn't have to worry about him mis . . . mis . . . misconstruing me. But anyway, *there's no key*!"

The bedroom door opens. Dr. Thayer appears, wearing a bathrobe, her face slick with cold cream, carrying a bottle of Pepsi and a glass. "Oh, Noah. I forgot you would be here. I would have brought you a glass. How is the lesson going?"

"The lesson," Noah says carefully, "is going well."

Dylan snorts. Dr. Thayer looks from one to the other of them resignedly, and then, suddenly, she metamorphoses into a maternal figure. Her face glows with benevolent energy as she strokes Dylan's hair, arranges it into sweet pageboy lines. "Both of you know how important this is, right?"

Noah and Dylan nod. Noah's jaw hangs open as he observes the complicated maneuver going on before him. He has known Dr. Thayer long enough to identify her stratagems—she's decided to give solicitousness a shot. She's trying to win Dylan over, keep him as the primary man in her life. She cups his face in her hand, gives him the same earnest, goofy, and lovingly admonitory face young mothers give to infants who gargle their food. Dylan looks at her inscrutably, and for a moment it seems that he might give a sign of the love that she is so desperate for.

Then Dylan bursts out in a laugh.

"Oh, this is funny, is it?" Dr. Thayer says. She looks like

she is about to spit at them as she slams the glass down and turns to leave. "Jesus. It's like I'm the only one who gives a crap here."

"You got it," Dylan says, pointing his finger at his mother like a gun. The door closes.

Noah smiles at Dylan, but the smile turns into a grimace at the corners. He knows he should be more worried about Dylan's score, about getting to work. But he can't muster the feeling. Dylan will never be happy studying, and Noah's honestly not concerned whether he gets into college or not. Whether Dylan spends the next four years straight partying or partying while nominally in classes seems arbitrary. "So what happens next?" Noah asks.

"I was at the point where I went through the guy's pockets, right?"

"Ye—"

"So there's no key! And Siggy's like, 'We're stuck here! We're stuck here!' all high-pitched, and Rob looks like he's about to hit him too. But instead he walks to the window he opened. I walk over too. Siggy just hangs back in front of the plasma screens. It's really cold in front of the window, even though it's April there's like a lot of wind, 'cuz we're way up. And there's a fire escape out there. Roberto steps on it to test it, and he like knocks over a hookah pipe on the ledge, but it holds his weight, so I know it will hold mine. And then Rob just starts going down. I'm like, 'You're not serious.' We're like hundreds of feet in the air, in front of all of Chelsea Piers, and the steps are really small. But he's just going down. I look back. Siggy is just staring at me. I'm like, 'Come on!' and he nods, but he doesn't move. I think he was sorta buggin', maybe he just took the green pills too. So I climb the fire escape. Once I start it's actually kind of easy. I kept looking for cops or people on their balconies or somethin', but there was like no one, I guess Chelsea people are all lightweights and in bed by then. But there's no bottom floor to the fire escape. So I'm like dangling above the street, and Roberto is below me waiting to catch me, and I drop, but I was a moron and kind of jumped as I dropped, like threw myself forward a little, and I missed Rob and hit the curb, and so my ankle is all sprained. We got in a cab, and I woke up my mom, and we went to the hospital, which is, you know, just a couple blocks over, on Park." Dylan sits back, elated.

"And you told your mom you sprained it playing basketball downtown at four A.M.?"

"Uh, yeah! She's dumb as shit sometimes."

A tightness has been growing in Noah's chest as Dylan told the story. What is it? The coke Dylan took? He's guilty not to be working on the test, but that's not it . . . what is it? Is he jealous not to have been there? Surely he doesn't wish he had been there? But he can't tell. And then he realizes the missing piece of the story, and the unhappy feeling in his chest blooms. "What about Siggy?"

"Siggy? Siggy's a wuss. I haven't talked to him since. That was like two nights ago."

"I mean, did he climb down the fire escape?"

Dylan shrugs. "Beats me. My ankle was like really blue, so Roberto and I got in the cab and took me home."

"Roberto didn't wait for him? And you didn't call to make sure he was okay?"

"No. I don't think Roberto likes him, anyway. I told you—Siggy was being a total moron."

"You just up and left him in the apartment? Jesus Christ, Dylan!"

"Siggy's a grown-up kid. And the guy was not moving. I'm sure Siggy just went down the fire escape too."

"But why didn't you call him to make sure he was okay?" Noah persists. His sense of horror grows—Dylan abandoned his friend without a twinge of regret. Noah has condescended to Dylan for so long, has seen him as some amusing exaggeration, a caricature. But as he watches Dylan smile, he can't get it out of his head—he is truly awful. And so, it seems, is Roberto.

"Listen, morality policeman. Siggy was the one being totally lame. I'm not going to call *him.*"

"But—"

"*Dude.* Stop. Why are you being such a hard-ass?"

"Wow," Noah says. He cannot stop himself. "That is truly awful. You don't know what that guy was about. Anything could have happened to Siggy."

"No, Noah. It was *funny.* Siggy was being such a total scrawny wimp, totally girly. If you were there, you'd see. It was so funny."

Noah's hands shake. If he were in Dylan's room as anything but an employee, he could leave. But just to get up and go would be to leave his job as well. He is paid to be there. Like a prostitute with an unpleasant trick, he has to see it through. He pulls out the worksheet on basic math strategies and stares at it. He has worked it through hundreds of times, but he can't make the problems come into focus. The numbers jumble against one another. He takes a deep breath. "Okay," he says. "Number one—"

"Uh-uh," Dylan says. "Be cool. No worksheets. Don't start being like that other guy my mom bought."

He wants to continue to push Dylan, to make him see the wrongness of what he has done. But he knows from his dealings with his own brother that he can't push too much at once. He has to drop it, for now. Noah's voice wavers. He is too upset for the words to come out right. "Number one. If Jonah draws a rectangle and then reduces its width by ten percent and increases its length by ten percent, by what percentage does the total area decrease?"

He looks up at Dylan. He is leaning against the headboard of his bed, his head stuck at an awkward angle. He scratches beneath his splint and stares at Noah coldly.

"How would you start?" Noah asks.

"Why the fuck are you doing this?" Dylan asks. Now he is scared for Siggy. His eyes dart about with the fear that he has done wrong. "Be cool."

"Try drawing it. Pretend you're Jonah."

"I don't want to pretend I'm fucking Jonah. Stop it." And then Noah hears Dylan say, almost inaudibly, "Asshole."

"What was that?" Noah asks. The words are shrill, powerless in Dylan's world. Protestations are doom for cool kids. Noah stares angrily at his fist.

"Nothing," Dylan mutters. "You know what, I don't want to do tutoring today."

"I don't care," Noah says. "You're going to do this problem."

"Like hell I am," Dylan says. His words are cold, entirely passionless; there is no fury behind them.

"Do you want to go to George Washington?"

"I don't know. I don't fucking care."

"Well, leave yourself the frickin' option, at least!" Noah yells. "You're going to have to work really hard to satisfy the admissions committee. We have three weeks. You can make it easy, or you can make it hard."

"'Frickin'.' That's so lame. You sound like a frickin' camp counselor." A hint of a smile plays at the edge of Dylan's features.

"I *am* a frickin' camp counselor!" Noah says. The words are furious, and sound ridiculous as soon as they're in the air. He stares into Dylan's cool gaze. And then Dylan laughs, hard. Suddenly Noah is laughing too.

"Dude," Dylan says. "Why don't you just give up on me? Just go home."

"Let's see a frickin' rectangle. We have three weeks." Noah hands Dylan a pad.

And slowly, with angry and sloppy strokes, Dylan starts to draw.

chapter 10

Noah's progress with Dylan that day is slow. They will compute a problem together, Dylan seeming to lead the way, and then when Noah asks Dylan to describe what they just did he refuses and turns on the basketball game. The problem, Noah realizes, is massive insecurity. Whether Dylan is intelligent or not is moot. Since he knows that he failed years ago when he last attempted anything on his own, he simply will not try. Getting him to reason is like leading an animal into water. He can be dragged, but no amount of coaxing will get him to wade in on his own.

By the time he finishes with Dylan, Noah is yawning and irritable. He is glad to leave the Thayer household, that cavernous twilit opulence, and transfer himself instead to Cameron Leinzler's Pier 1 West Side tackiness. He tries to perk up as he rides the elevator. Most of his students are not like Dylan, he reminds himself. They respect him and learn with him.

But his session with Cameron is hardly reassuring: she seems as irritable as Noah. She begins by complaining about her mountains of homework. And then, after Noah corrects her definition of *dissemble,* she utters the words every tutor dreads: "Are you sure?" The whole tutoring industry is based on "sure." The SAT is an unknowable, terrifying beast. If the student doesn't have complete trust in her master, the quest is lost.

"Of course I'm sure," Noah laughs.

"I really think it means 'to take apart,' " Cameron says. Her vocabulary quiz skates across the table as she jabs it with her pencil.

"Well, it doesn't," Noah says. The words come out harshly. Cameron looks up at him in surprise. Her eyes are inky black in the dim light of her dining room. "It means to not be what you seem," Noah says, more gently.

Cameron looks down at the words scrawled on her quiz and stares at them for a few moments. "You just used a split infinitive. And I talked to my boyfriend—I talked to Rafferty today," she says.

"Oh yeah?" Noah asks jovially. "How is he doing?"

"He's really scared. He keeps going like, 'My score's not going up, my score's not going up.' "

"It will go up. He shouldn't worry."

Cameron's eyes narrow. "But you don't know for sure it will, do you? So you really can't say that."

"Tutoring's a mysterious process," Noah says. "But it works. You can trust me."

"Because it's not like *my* score is that great either."

"You've gone up 270 points. That's pretty awesome, actually."

"Yeah, but it's still just a 2150. Not like 2350."

"You started at 1880. You have to keep that in mind. Going up to 2350 is a big leap."

"Huh," Cameron says, opening up her workbook. "You don't sound too confident anymore. It's like suddenly everything might be coming apart."

"What do you mean by that?" Noah asks. He chokes down a rising nastiness in his throat.

"Well, Eliza hasn't said anything, but Garret's not too happy either. We go to a really good school, Noah. We all have to go to like good colleges. And his verbal is still pretty low."

Garret has never read a book, Noah wants to say. He tries to control the urge to argue his case. Seeming defensive could sink him now. The good tutor is dedicated but carefree. Dedicated but carefree.

"Come on, Cam. Does anyone ever call you Cam? Like 'Spam,' only, 'Cam'?" Noah laughs nervously.

Cameron looks at him in disdain. "Why don't we just work?" she says, opening her notebook to a random page and hunching over it.

~

Noah shuffles to the subway entrance and rides in glum silence with the other hourly workers returning to Harlem. By the time he picks his way along the littered and neon-lit street to his home, it is eleven o'clock. He hopes that Olena will be there, that he can recount his day to her, share his struggles. He is desperate for her wry humor, her power to make his concerns seem gray and distant. But she has taken to studying her SAT materials late at a coffee shop near City College. Hera generally accompanies her, reading the paper and guarding her daughter from any imagined advances by men. What Noah gets instead when he returns home is Roberto.

Roberto has just stepped out of the shower, is slicking his hair back with one hand and eating a cold sausage with the other. "Noah!" he exclaims as Noah drags himself into the room. "What's going on? *Qué pasa?*"

Noah stares dumbly at Roberto for a moment. He is exhausted, and numb with concern over Tuscany, Dylan, Cameron, Garret, and Rafferty. Or, more specifically, over the question of his continued employment, of his mother and brother's predicament, of his student loans. He can't remember how he feels about Roberto. Angry, maybe. Jealous, some. "Not much," he says, sitting at the table.

"Whoa," Roberto says as he sprays body cologne on his chest. "You look like you got smashed by somethin'. What's been goin' down, homey?"

Noah doesn't want to talk things over with Roberto; he is certain of that much. "Oh, not much. Hard day of work."

"I hear you, man, I hear you," Roberto says distractedly. He stands in the bathroom doorway and squints as he passes a razor over a few stray nipple hairs.

"Where are you off to tonight?" Noah asks.

"A party, you know, the usual shit."

"Who's throwing it?"

"This guy Siggy. You know him?" Roberto blows the stray hairs off the razor. They swirl to the floor.

"Yeah. We met him together at Pangaea." Noah pauses. "So I guess he's alive, then?"

Roberto examines his chest for strays. "Alive? Oh, you musta heard 'bout our night at that guy's apartment. It was so fucked."

"Why didn't you make sure he was okay?"

"Ya know, I thought 'bout that? The next day I was like, 'Shit.' But right then I was just, ya know, worryin' about Dylan's ankle, right? He's all yelling and everythin'. Turns out that Siggy got out okay. The key was in some bowl by the door."

"And the guy?" Noah keeps his voice under control, barely.

"The guy? Siggy said his head had like scabbed over by the time he was gone, and he was breathing and everythin'. The guy was a fuckin' pervert. Who the fuck cares?"

"Roberto," Noah says slowly. Roberto, hearing the strained note in his voice, pulls on an old T-shirt and approaches the table where Noah is sitting. "Dylan Thayer is my student."

"I know, man, I knew that before I even met the kid, right, *Capitan*?"

"You can't take him to some random guy's apartment who gives you *coke,* and other drugs you don't know what they are, and then beat the guy up and scale the outside of a building."

"Noah, dude, chill. You were the one drinkin' with Dylan at a club."

"That's totally different. Your lives were in danger."

"No," Roberto says flatly, flexing his arms as he crosses them over his massive chest. "They weren't."

"He could have OD'd. He could have fallen."

"You're just his tutor. He's not your responsibility. And I *like* the guy. I wanted to show him what's badass."

"That was badass?"

"We had *fun.* Maybe you don't understand that. But Dylan and I are like close now. And we have a good time. He's a grown guy. Stop worrying! Shit!"

"He's not a grown man. He's seventeen."

"You know him, man. It's like he's not *really* seventeen. There's nothing that would surprise him."

Noah stammers in response. He has too much to say; the words jumble on his lips.

"You used to be cool, Noah," Roberto says. "You used to just like let everythin' roll off your back, like you never actually cared. But now, ooh, it's all about consequences. You're like paralyzing yourself, man."

Noah's mouth hardens. "Go to your party. *Man.* They'll love you. You're great fun. Just make sure you keep it up."

Roberto seems confused, hurt. Not angry, as Noah would have expected. "I am great fun," he says. "Okay?"

Noah's attention is caught by a stray, panicky tone in Roberto's voice. He turns toward where he stands, wearing a towel and suddenly shivering, in the center of the room. "What's wrong?" Noah asks. "Is everything okay?"

Roberto nods and starts across the room, his mouth clenched.

It is one of the rare moments of instantaneous truth, when Noah's conception of a person crystallizes, when all the evidence that never seemed to fit together suddenly locks into a coherent image because the design, the plan behind all the contradictions, is suddenly projected over. Roberto's over-the-top masculinity, almost a performance, the way he latched so quickly on to Noah and then Dylan, more like a crush than a slowly progressing friendship . . . "Rob," Noah says softly. "That guy didn't just suddenly come on to you, did he?"

Roberto stops in his doorway, facing away from Noah.

"Did you come on to him?"

Roberto shrugs again. Noah pauses. He doesn't want to push Roberto too far, but he also sees how desperately he needs to talk to someone. He wouldn't just stand there, shivering and staring, otherwise. Who else can Roberto talk to about this? Not Dylan or Siggy. "Are you attracted to men?"

Roberto stares down at his calves. Then, softly: "Fuck no." Noah can see him only in profile.

"That's fine, you know, right? It's totally okay. It would be nothing to apologize for, anywhere, but especially not here. No one's going to judge you." Noah approaches Roberto, wants to prove to him that he's not put off by him.

"I had a fight that night, with Gavin," Roberto says. "That's the guy in the apartment. He ran into me with Dylan and Siggy, and we played it like we didn't know each other. So he sets Dylan and Siggy up in the living room, and we go into the other room, you know?"

Noah nods.

"And we're talkin', and then it's like we're not talkin' anymore, you know? But then he tells me to stop and I do and he turns around and he's smiling and I can tell he's all excited and shit by Dylan bein' in the other room. So I get pissed by what he's, what he's all playing, that we're all goin' to have some big orgy. So suddenly we're fightin', and I wanted out of there anyway, but I, you know, deck him."

"So you're not into Dylan?" Noah asks.

There is suddenly a fire in Roberto's eyes. "Jesus, what the fuck are you, some homophobe?"

Noah shakes his head. "No way, man, I would ask the same thing if I thought a female friend was in love with one of my students. I'm just making sure."

"I'm not." A pause. "He doesn't know nothing, so don't tell."

Noah nods.

"And so what if I was?" Roberto asks, suddenly angry again. "You couldn't stop me."

Noah narrows his eyes. "No, I couldn't stop you. But just don't? Don't give him any drugs. Don't get him into any other dangerous situations. Just leave him alone."

Roberto clenches his hands on his hips menacingly, as if palming a revolver. "I'm goin' to this party, okay?"

"Hey, listen—"

Roberto whips around. "Don't fuckin' tell me what to do!"

"If you do anything to get that kid in trouble—" Noah yells. The door slams. Noah wanders into their room and stares blankly at the Anna Kournikova poster on the wall. His eyes scan the rip in the corner over and over until he hears Roberto leave. Then he sits on his cot and blankly surveys the room. His belongings all sit neatly in the corner. The rest of the room is all Roberto's, littered with his sweaty, synthetic clothes and full of his musky scent. Noah lies down and scrunches his eyes shut. He will take a nap, he decides, and wake up when Olena gets home. They can take a walk around Harlem if they feel brave, or just sit in the living room and talk. He imagines her eyes on his, the ferocity of her gaze. He stares at the phosphorescence of the overhead light shining through his eyelids and concentrates on her, wills her to return home.

~

But when Noah wakes up, daylight is streaming in his window. His dress shirt has rumpled and twisted beneath his arms during the night. His crotch is sweaty beneath his dress pants. He stands and glances at the clock: 7:50 A.M. He has half an hour to get to the Thayers'. He throws open the bedroom door.

Olena, showered and dressed, is working on an SAT as she sits on the worn tweed couch. She is surrounded by highlighters and pens. One of the highlighters has leaked a pink stain on her slender forearm. She looks up at Noah and smiles, relieved. "Noah! I was concerned for you. You did not get up for our session." She laughs. "I was beginning to fear that, you know, you had perished."

"I'm so sorry," Noah says, blinking in the bright sunlight. He rubs his face. "I meant to just take a nap. I really wanted to talk to you last night, to see how you were doing."

"I am fine, thank you. But I sense that you are not."

Noah lays a hand on her shoulder. "I'm not. And I missed our session. We'll work extra hard tomorrow, okay?"

"Of course, Noah. You can make it up to me right now, even, by defining *elegiac.*"

Noah does, and dashes into the shower. Olena has toasted him a thick slice of bread and hands it to him as he races out the door.

Yellow cabs aren't often found in Harlem, so Noah hails a gypsy cab. He and the driver agree on $20 for the trip and then they are off down Riverside. Noah sits back in the vinyl seat of the unmarked car, concentrating on the blue glints of the Hudson, trying to focus enough to think of what he will teach Tuscany today. He vaguely remembers having given her a French translation to do for homework; they can begin by reviewing that.

He powers on his cell phone—two new voicemails. He hates the morning messages, generally from parents who have concocted some fresh hellish concern as they slept. And indeed, the first message is from a parent:

Oh, hello, Noah? This is Mrs. Leinzler, mother of Cameron. I hope all's well with you. I have a little issue to speak to you about. I was talking to Cam yesterday, and she's really concerned about her progress. I tried to ring you then, but your phone was off, and I guess I wanted to talk to someone sooner rather than later, so I called the office. I spoke to a very nice man there, Nicholas, I think his name is, and he tried to reassure me. But, well, after I got off the phone with him, I realized that it doesn't look too good for you that I called them. Sorry. I just wanted to let you know, in case they call you. Regardless, I wanted to thank you for your services so far. Nicholas and I are going to work out something today, and he'll probably let you know. Sorry for the long message! Have a good one!

Noah has no time to think about the implications before the second message begins. It is from Nicholas. Noah leans his head against the cab window.

Hi, Noah. Look, we've got a little issue here. I just got a call from a Mrs. Leinzler. Cameron Leinzler's mom? And she was pretty upset. Apparently Cameron's not happy with her progress, and her mom's worried about her. I looked at the scores, and tried to reassure her that Cameron's progress is good, but she's still concerned. Apparently Cameron wants an-

other tutor. Now, this happens all the time, people requesting tutor switches . . . but there have been some other calls about your performance this week, and . . . look, you're going to have to call me as soon as you can. Okay, Noah? Don't worry, but call me as soon as you get this.

Noah closes the phone and holds it tight in his fist. He continues to stare at the river. He is losing his job. He has $900 in the bank. His monthly loan withdrawal will come in a few days. He will have no money in the space of a week. He opens the phone again and dials the agency, tries to smile into the phone. The whole company operates on voicemail rather than actual conversations: he leaves Nicholas a message and, while Noah rides through a tunnel, Nicholas leaves him a message in return:

Hi, Noah, good morning. You got my message, huh? Well, Mrs. Leinzler is worked up. I've tried to encourage her that everything's fine, and I think she's okay. But she does want to look into other tutors. I told her it's extremely late in the process, but so be it. I'll try to dissuade her. If I were in your shoes I wouldn't sweat it—normally. But we've had a phone call from a Mrs. Zeigler, and a Mr. Lipton. Rafferty isn't doing so hot, huh? And Eliza is doing well, but is panicked because she heard from Cameron and Rafferty that they weren't doing well. And apparently one parent in particular has been calling the others, getting them riled up. So it's an odd case. You're doing a good job with these kids, with the one exception of Rafferty—and one student didn't go up right away, that's okay—but since I had so many complaints I had to call Hannah. And she's decided to put you on lock, which basically means she's investigating. She's going to call all your families and make sure that everything's okay. But until she finishes, unfortunately we have to put your appointments on hold. We just hired a bunch of new tutors. We'll field your kids out to them. Don't worry, they'll be taken care of.

The cab has arrived at the Thayers' building. Still clutching the phone between jaw and shoulder, Noah numbly pays the driver and steps out onto the street. He stands under the awning of 949 Fifth Avenue, staring at its gold supports, seeing nothing. Nicholas's message continues.

. . . anyway, Noah, try not to worry about it. There's nothing you can do now. Just sit tight, enjoy your time off.

Noah snaps his phone closed. The doormen are staring at him. Noah nods at them, smiling hollowly. He enters the building and calls the elevator.

As he rides up Noah feels as if floating in the cube, like a fish in a tank. Fuen lets him in and he glides past her. He stops halfway up the stairwell. He is in a complete daze of preoccupation, concerned by nothing except the bleak enormity of his predicament. The glossy banister feels unreal under his grip, and the pristine walls of the Thayer apartment look artificially unblemished, as if digitally rendered. He can't think of where he is supposed to meet Tuscany. Has the dining room refurbishing been completed? Is he even supposed to meet with Tuscany this morning? Or is it Dylan? Dylan is at school; Tuscany must be his student. And upstairs. He takes a step up.

Dr. Thayer's bedroom is at the head of the stairs. Noah sees her brittle form, swaddled in green silk, emerge from the dark chamber and turn the corner into the bathroom. The silvered door closes. He feels just like her, that he embodies the same glassiness. He always assumed that she was under the dulling influence of some narcotic, but perhaps she has just perpetually been what he is now—chronically preoccupied. Her mind is perhaps simply too active. Every conversation she has with her family, with Noah, is overshadowed by some tumultuous decision-making process raging in the back of her consciousness. There is always some grander worry, some unfulfilled need monopolizing Dr. Thayer, and she is only able to devote a fraction of her thoughts to the people around her. Noah wonders what her grand worries are. Or if her constant air of preoccupation is indeed just the result of too much Valium. Valium. Might be nice.

Noah sits on the stairs, hugs his knees to his chest. He thought his Fieldston students really liked him. But they have worked themselves into a hysteria the likes of which only a group of competitive and gossipy teenagers could achieve. If only Rafferty had confided in him, rather than spent the year acting as if everything were fine and then finally throwing an angry fit. Cameron, he imagines, might be joining the frenzy just for the drama of it, to find some way to compete with the exaggerated craziness of the Thayers—Noah should never have confided in her about them. And Eliza—well, once the other two start spending all lunchtime discussing how Noah might be going wrong, she doesn't want to be the one stuck with the dud tutor. But they have all called the office now: he has been shut down. There is nothing he can do.

Tuscany's door opens. Noah glances up, startled. He wills himself to stand, but feels unable. Dressed in a fluorescent tank top and pajama bottoms, with headphones in her ears, she dances down the hallway, past the point of the landing directly above Noah's huddled form, and disappears into her own bathroom. She hasn't noticed him, and Noah is once again alone on the stairs.

He has to get up. He has to teach Tuscany. She is in the bathroom, so he has a few minutes to collect himself. He leans his head against a faux Grecian column on the banister. He can't ask his mother for money; she doesn't have any. Neither, of course, do Hera and Olena. Even though he doesn't have to help support his brother anymore, he is still recovering from Kent's counseling costs—his account is nearly empty. He will have to call his credit card company to raise his limit. He wonders how long the agency will keep him on hold. But he knows that's not the real point. Once there is the appearance of bad tutoring, the damage is done. He's already effectively been fired. His students have been reassigned to other tutors; he won't get them back. And the office will be reluctant to assign new students, knowing that he has had a series of complaints. He'll be lucky to get even one student next year.

Tuscany emerges from the bathroom. She sings tunelessly along with the music on her headphones, turns once in the hallway and raises her arms sexily, as if dancing at a club. Then she sees Noah. "Oh!" she says. She slides the headphones down around her neck. "You're sitting on the stairs!"

Noah looks dully from Tuscany's bedroom to Dylan's. These kids are his employers now, his only work; this is it. Better make it count. He lurches to his feet. "Yeah," he says. "I heard you go into the bathroom, and thought I'd wait here for you to come out."

"Oh," Tuscany says. She looks confused. She raises a hand limply and points to the bathroom. "Well, I'm out."

"Great!" Noah manages to say. He clambers up the stairs. "So, how did the translation go?" he asks chirpily.

"Uh, fine." They take their seats in Tuscany's room. "Is everything cool, Noah?"

"Yeah, why?"

"I dunno. You just seem a little jumpy."

For Tuscany to lose confidence in him would be the final blow. He can't let it happen. "No, I'm okay. Too little coffee today. Or maybe too much." He laughs.

"Okay," Tuscany says. She draws out the word.

She hasn't finished her French translation. Noah gives her an hour to complete it. He sits on the bed, staring at an open novel and serving as dictionary whenever Tuscany doesn't know a word, which is roughly every ten seconds. The hour of passive activity gives Noah a chance to collect himself. A solution forms itself in his head.

"Hey, when's your dad's big IPO party?" Noah asks.

"Next Tuesday. Mom was going to have it on a Saturday but then I was like, 'Mom, everyone's going to be in the *Hamptons*.' So we're having it on Tuesday, 'cuz Dad's going to be out of town the rest of the week. You're totally invited, by the way. You should wear that shirt I got you."

Mr. Thayer. A hundred and fifty K a year. Noah can think of nothing but Mr. Thayer. He chatters aimlessly about the man: what does he like, what does he wear, where does he travel, what are his interests? Tuscany doesn't seem to know much about him. She has a vague idea of his having gone to Princeton but, she confesses, she might be confusing him with Noah. He worked in entertainment for a while, she knows, and has a law degree. He might or might not have green eyes. And that's about it; Tuscany can think of nothing more.

Noah has an hour off between Tuscany and Dylan, and spends fifty-five minutes of it walking up and down Madison Avenue plucking up his poise and courage, and the last five leaving a long message on Mr. Thayer's machine ending in, "So that's about it. Hope you're still interested!"

Dylan is in better spirits during today's sessions: he is just impassive rather than actively disagreeable. He focuses on an instant-messaging conversation while Noah recites the most important math formulas. When Noah suggests turning off the computer Dylan glances up passionlessly and then returns his focus to the screen. Noah's options, he knows, are either to be satisfied with half of Dylan's attention or get none of it at all. So he continues to recite formulas. When he quizzes Dylan on what he's learned, the afternoon's achievements are revealed to include πr^2, $a^2 + b^2 = c^2$, and nothing else.

When Noah turns on his cell phone in the elevator there is a message from Mr. Thayer's secretary. Will Noah be available to meet Thursday at six? Since Thursday at six was Cameron's time slot, Noah leaves a message to affirm that he will certainly be available.

Noah pauses beneath the building's canopy: it is four in the afternoon, he has prospective employment, and there is nowhere he needs to be! He is struck by the odd fact that, although he is losing his tutoring job, he is thrilled by the consolation of free evenings. He knows exactly whom he wants to see. He eagerly calls the house and gets Hera:

"Hello, Noah! I was just telling Olena that it seems we never cross paths no more! I am sad to not be seeing you, except for making morning teaching coffee!"

"You'll be seeing me around more, don't worry. Is Olena there?"

Noah hears static as Olena comes to the phone. She barks at her mother in quick, harsh Albanian. Olena breathes into the phone a moment, collecting herself, then says: "Hello. We are talking on the phone. This is irregular for us, is it not?"

"It is," Noah says, stopping in the sidewalk and staring coyly into the pavement of Fifth Avenue. He can't stop smiling. Olena has called their speaking on the phone "irregular"—she is impossibly charming. "How goes the day's homework?" he asks.

"I have considered selling my SAT materials on the corner. You will find me next to the pleasant Dominican woman who sells mangoes."

"Not good?"

"I am not being as brilliant as I should be."

"Want to get some coffee? And we can put a moratorium on conversations about the SAT."

"I do not know what you have said. But coffee is nice.

Et en plus, comme ça je peux échapper à ma mère. Tell me where to go."

They meet in a busy East Village coffee shop. This is Olena's first American coffee that hasn't been from a Starbucks. "In fact," she says as they sit down, "I did not know there existed others."

Noah rips open a sugar packet and smiles.

"I like it here," Olena announces. "Even if they serve cappuccino in cardboard silos."

"How is coffee served in Albania?"

"How is coffee served in Albania? Did you truly just ask me that? There is nothing of note to be found in my answer. Try again."

Noah laughs. Olena looks at him and takes a sip of her coffee. She tentatively raises it to her lips, holding the cup lightly in her fingers as if she were a princess sipping her first glass of champagne. Her fine dark hair falls around the mug. She touches the liquid to her lips and it scalds them. She cries out and presses a napkin to her mouth. She pulls the napkin away and laughs at herself, once. There is no mark on the napkin—she is not wearing lipstick—but the hot coffee has brought a splash of pink color to her lips. She explores them tentatively with her tongue. She clearly enjoys the new sensation.

Noah leans forward and kisses her. She returns it.

"Perhaps we have fallen into a type," she says after they pull apart, a mock-worried expression on her face. "Student and teacher fall in love. It happens all the time, no?"

Noah shakes his head.

Olena runs her tongue over her lips again. Her expression is quizzical, self-aware, curious. Noah kisses her again.

"If we are to kiss again," Olena says, "I assume we will do it regularly. And if we do it regularly, we will not have created our destinies."

Olena is often difficult to understand—Noah loves the

challenge of speaking to her. But this last part was incomprehensible. "Created our destinies?" he asks.

"Uh," Olena says. "How can this be said? The future we may be entering, provided that we do, both of us, decide to kiss again, and frequently, is not our own. This is what my mother has wanted from the start. Long before you moved in, even."

"She told you that?"

"Told me that? No. But every word she says tells me that, no? Does that make sense?"

Noah nods. He is holding Olena's coffee cup tenderly. He wants to be holding her. He smiles at himself. He takes her hand under the table.

"Good." She grins slyly. "Now, there is something on your mind, not having to do with me. Tell me what it is, so that your thoughts can then again be wholly on me."

Noah explains the day's events. He is so thrilled to be holding Olena's hand, excited by the play of her slender muscles beneath his fingers, and so dismayed to have basically lost his job, that the words come out in a sort of terrorized euphoria. He is both elated and nervous, bombastic.

"Noah," Olena says, massaging his fingertips. "You are not in a good place right now. I want you to not be so worried. Your job has been either lost or retained. There is nothing you can do. So you must stop wondering what to do. Just maximize what you still have available."

Noah nods.

"There!" Olena laughs and puts down her coffee, as if the matter were settled. "We should go back to me now. I am, after all, available."

Hera is home when they arrive. She immediately refers to them as "you two," and takes an uncanny interest in their evening, as though she had been along the whole time, hiding in the shadows as they kissed. Or perhaps, Noah realizes, this is how Hera has always maneuvered, treating them as a couple until they capitulated and finally became one. The three of them eat a late dinner together. Hera expresses an earnest concern for Roberto:

"He is never home, always out—he is flying!" she says.

But Olena will have none of it. "You know, Mother, whom he is spending time with. This is what you always wanted for him, no? This *advancement.*"

"Titania, darling," Hera says, an exaggerated pain on her features, "that you should suspect me of having such ulterior motives for my children. It is your happiness that I concern. Perhaps," she says, fixing wide eyes on Noah, "he is happy now. Perhaps I am wrong to worry. Is Roberto happy?"

Noah thinks to Roberto's drugged episode of crawling down a fire escape and racing to the hospital. "He seems to be enjoying himself."

Hera sits back. "Okay, I am content. See, Olena? If you two are happy, that is best."

Olena rolls her eyes. When dinner is over she and Noah step around each other as they brush their teeth in the tiny bathroom, and then shyly duck into Olena's bedroom. She is already on the bed, pulling her T-shirt off as Noah closes the door.

~

In the morning Olena is back at the table. Four SAT booklets sit in front of her, each papered with Post-it notes. Her pens are arranged in neat rows. It is six-thirty A.M. Noah groggily pours himself coffee. He is wearing Olena's T-shirt beneath his own, and the constant scent of her pleases him. But romance is far from his mind.

Noah looks over Olena's recent tests. Olena is unable to

contain herself, stands behind him and massages his shoulder as he grades them. "Is Section Two okay? I was not sure how I felt taking it. There was a lot of coordinate plane material, and you know how I feel about that. If Section Two is not okay, I am still okay. But Section Three, I really think I aced the passage about Amelia Earhart. Perhaps, when you grade Section Five, you can keep in mind that I had not yet finished the vocabulary list on which *refractory* is found. But I know it now."

Noah finishes grading. He looks up at Olena.

"Well?" she asks. She sits and tries to keep her hands calmly on either side of her face, but a pulse of nervous energy flings one of them to the table and scatters her pens. She begins to tidy them up. "How was it? Swarthmore-good? Cornell-good? Perhaps just Boston College–good?"

Noah shakes his head. "I can't let you take the real test on Saturday."

"Oh no. How bad?"

"Not bad. You've gone up a hundred points. But you're not testing anywhere near your ability level. You need more time."

Olena shakes her head once, and then becomes impassive. "I have no more time. Saturday comes in just a few days."

"You're going to have to forget about the May test."

Tears wet the corners of Olena's eyes. "I am not used to disappointment like this. I am always working very hard. I have spent so much—" She coughs. "So much time preparing for this. I am thinking it was better that I not do this at all."

Olena's English gets a little weaker when she gets emotional. Noah is unable to tell if she wishes she hadn't come to America, or wishes she hadn't chosen to work with him. He doesn't want to ask. He just wants her to be happy. He stands behind her and wraps his arms around her. She sobs once into his elbow, then pushes it away. She sits rigidly in her chair, staring blankly into the blue newsprint of the test booklets. She wipes her nose, then says, "I am sorry. I believe I have drained my nose on your shirt."

"It's okay," Noah says.

"Oh. Oh!" Olena says. "I am getting emotional. There is not time for that. Let us have our session. I will be fine."

Noah pulls his chair next to her and sits down. "No, let me know what you're thinking."

Olena looks at him flatly, and then fakes spitting on the table. "Pah, that's enough, gushy American."

So, Noah teaches her how to factor special quadratic equations instead.

~

Noah arrives at the Thayer household ten minutes early, hoping to catch Dr. Thayer. She is right in the hallway where Noah emerges from the elevator, perched high on a ladder, frantically waving a lightbulb over her head.

"Dr. Thayer?" Noah asks. "Can I help you?"

She looks down from the ladder and nearly loses her balance. She grips the metal rungs. "Oh," she says on seeing Noah. She shakes the lightbulb accusingly. "Just imagine, the day Fuen has to take her kid to the doctor is the day the hallway light goes. I have a book club coming in an hour."

"I'm sure one of the doormen could help you," Noah says.

"Sometimes," Dr. Thayer snaps, "one likes to do things oneself."

"Or," Noah says, "I could help you."

"Would you?" Dr. Thayer says, instantly sweet. "That would be kind."

She climbs down with overly elaborate grace, as if she were actually a mime performing the descent of a ladder. The gesticulations have caused her bathrobe to loosen. The center of her emaciated torso is exposed down to the navel, like she is wearing a dress for the Oscars. "Um, Dr. Thayer," Noah says.

"What? Oh!" she exclaims when she notices the open robe. She tightens it. "Sorry. And really, Noah, who'd have thought you were so prudish?" She laughs at him and proffers the lightbulb. He takes it. By raising her arm she has caused the slippery silk of the sash to loosen again, exposing the jutting lines of the ribs between her breasts. She makes no effort to tighten it.

Noah mounts the ladder. Dr. Thayer stands below and stares up. Noah wills himself to concentrate on the light fixture, despite his terrified curiosity over how much of Dr. Thayer is exposed. He removes the spent bulb.

"Just toss it down," Dr. Thayer says.

Noah pauses. He can't just drop the bulb without looking. He looks down, and basically sees all of Dr. Thayer's front, from collarbone down to the knees, within the loose sheaf of her bathrobe. He drops the bulb. She catches it.

Noah concentrates on the fixture. It is almost out of reach, and the screwing of the bulb will take some time.

"So, Dr. Thayer," Noah says. "I wanted to ask you something."

"Really?" Dr. Thayer purrs. "Do tell."

"I was thinking about your offer to do Dylan's tutoring just between us, without the agency. And I think I was stupid to have said no. Do you think we could work something out?"

"You just simply . . . changed your mind?" Dr. Thayer asks.

Noah can't determine her tone. Seeing her expression would help, but he daren't look down. Her bathrobe probably opened even more when she caught the bulb. "Yes," Noah says. "Is it still possible?"

"Well, accounts are more difficult now, without Agnès. I

still haven't found a replacement. But we could work something out. You'll still want, I assume, two hundred twenty-five dollars?"

"That sounds fine to me."

Dr. Thayer gives a raspy laugh. "I'm sure it does."

Noah continues tightening the bulb. The glass turning in the socket gives little metallic screeches.

"But really, Noah, there must be a reason for this change of heart."

Noah looks down and instantly wishes he hadn't. Dr. Thayer registers the shock on Noah's face, misattributes the cause to something other than her exposed form: "Ah," she says, "you see that I know why you're asking."

"What?" Noah says, confused, his attention back to the bulb.

"I got a call from your agency. Apparently they just wanted to make sure that I was happy with your services. That is not normal behavior . . . why *shouldn't* I be satisfied? It's not hard to realize that something's gone wrong."

"No," Noah says slowly. "Things with the agency are not perfect at the moment."

"I'm sorry to hear it. Perhaps they heard about Monroe Eichler. If there's anything I can do, let me know."

"No, I think it's going to be fine. They're just doing a check on me. Totally normal."

"You must be low on money, then."

The bulb is almost finished. "It's okay, don't worry."

"I know you wouldn't have asked to do this under the table if not."

Noah is tired of Dr. Thayer's insinuations, her detached analysis of him. He glares down. "What are you after?" he snaps.

Dr. Thayer's eyes widen, and she smiles. "I was just wondering if you were reconsidering my request that you, you know, be of more direct assistance to Dylan's SAT."

Noah leans heavily against the ladder. "No, I'm not reconsidering."

"Oh," Dr. Thayer says. She sighs as Noah begins his descent. "I'm not sure if we'll need your services otherwise."

Noah steps off the ladder. She hasn't moved to make room—he is forced to stand inches in front of her. "What are you saying?" he asks.

Dr. Thayer laughs. "I'm just 'saying' that surely we both realize Dylan's not going to get his score through *tutoring*. He needs you to take this test for him. His future is resting on it."

"Dr. Thayer," Noah says. Extortion on top of everything else—his voice comes out weary and on edge. "I can't. I won't."

"I'm sorry to have upset you, Noah," Dr. Thayer tuts condescendingly. "Pretend I didn't ask. But it does seem, don't you think, that all of this is coming to an end? It's almost summer, so Tuscany doesn't need teaching, and Dylan's just hopeless, or so you make it seem."

"I would never act as if Dylan were hopeless."

"Regardless, Tuscany doesn't really need you anymore. I just hate to see you without any source of income."

"Really," Noah says firmly, "don't worry about me." But the thought of having no money at all is horrifying. Dr. Thayer reads the anguish in his face, takes a step closer. She is almost pressing into him.

"What I do expect," she says, "is for you to be present in my children's lives. Dylan needs you badly, but if you're not willing to give him the kind of help he really needs, then at least you can tutor him as much as possible until the test on Saturday. And Tuscany doesn't need a teacher now that it's practically summer, but what she does need is an Agnès. I'm lost without a personal assistant. I can't keep track of appointments myself—I'm concerned that her extracurriculars might be slipping through the cracks."

Noah can feel the heat of Dr. Thayer's body radiating through the thin silk of her robe. "So what are you proposing?" Noah asks.

"I need a personal assistant for a few weeks. All the time you can give. We have a spare bedroom; you could even stay here if you're scared to travel back to Harlem late at night."

"I'm not scared," Noah says.

Dr. Thayer stares at him. The larger question has been left unanswered.

"So it's all or nothing?" Noah asks.

Dr. Thayer shrugs. "We need a personal assistant now. Not a tutor. Take it or leave it, Noah. I have to get ready for my book club."

"Just for a couple of weeks?"

"A couple of weeks. Yes."

"Fine," Noah says.

"Oh, good," Dr. Thayer says. "We'll figure out exact hours later. Just make sure you keep your cell phone on. Fuen will bring you sheets on nights when you need to stay."

Dr. Thayer slowly pulls the silken folds of her bathrobe over her ribs and torso, staring into Noah's eyes the whole time. "And I hope, after this family has invested so much in you, that you will still consider being of more help to Dylan."

Noah stares at Dr. Thayer, unable to formulate an answer. She turns and stalks up the stairs. Noah picks up the used lightbulb and goes to find a trash can, and then to begin Tuscany's lesson.

~

It is obvious that there is little to no communication between Mr. and Dr. Thayer, for when Noah arrives for their appointment Mr. Thayer's first question is a sanguine and direct "How is Dylan doing?"

"Fine, Mr. Thayer. He finds the test difficult, but he's doing okay."

"And Tuscany?"

"Fine as well. She's very bright."

They segue, with swift and brutal civility, into the topic of starting an SAT company. Noah details the hiring processes, the training of employees, the materials created and used, practice test schedules, various rates charged, the means of managing parents' expectations. Mr. Thayer records it all, nods and motions for Noah to continue when he reaches the end of a point. After about an hour he reaches forward and snaps off the digital recorder.

"That's very good, Noah, very good. Because what I'm interested in is not creating another Princeton Review or Kaplan. I want to go to the top, run a boutique agency like yours. My question for you now is this: since we're in this together, partners, can you release your materials to me? Give me a copy of your training manuals, SATs, memos, et cetera?"

"Um, sure, I suppose so," Noah says. They're sitting in the bag at his side; he certainly doesn't have need of them at the moment. And surely he should accede to a billionaire's judgment. He's the one with the enormous desk, right?

"Great, great. I'll need to look those over to come up with a business strategy. We can meet again in a few weeks and determine where to go from here. And then there's the matter of your compensation. I assume the hundred fifty K rough figure I quoted earlier sounds acceptable?"

Noah nods. A hundred and fifty thousand would be just fine.

Mr. Thayer stands and holds out his hand. "Okay, then! We'll be in touch."

~

"You didn't get a contract?" Olena asks.

Noah shakes his head. It suddenly seems like the most foolish thing in the world.

"Oh, Noah," Olena says. "I do not know how businesses run in the United States, but it seems like you should have gotten one. Can you call him and ask him for one?"

~

Noah does call that evening. Mr. Thayer is "in a meeting." Noah leaves a message. It isn't returned.

chapter 11

Noah wakes early the next morning, wanders into the living room in his boxers, and blinks at the light. Olena has already been up for hours: she is showered and neatly dressed. Crusts of bread litter the table, and the caps are off all her highlighters. Her freshly scrubbed face peers up at him from her array of workbooks. "Wow," he says.

Olena laughs. "Sleepy and boxer shorts. You have a very American cuteness today."

Noah nods numbly, stumbles into the shower. Olena parts the curtain and watches him frankly. "I was looking at the SAT website," she says, "and there is a June test. Do you think I could take the June test?"

Noah has just lathered his face. He takes a few moments to wash the soap off before speaking. "I think you have much more of a chance for June than May."

"You are not being a very good cheerleader for me, even if you are cute."

Noah chuckles. "No, I am not. But you can trust me to be honest."

"I will be ready for June. Mark that."

"Aye-aye, Captain. Could you pass my towel?" Noah's towel appears over the top of the railing. He rubs his wet fingers up Olena's arm as he accepts it.

If it were any time later than seven A.M. he would try to pull her in. He dries off in the bathtub, wraps the towel around his waist, and then presses Olena against him. She laughs gaily at the wetness of his skin. "Hi," she says.

"Hi."

They stare at each other for a moment, and then Noah's phone rings. Olena toyed with it in bed the night before, and jokingly set it to squeal loudly for Dr. Thayer's calls. The pitch itself sets Noah's heart constricting.

"What the fuck?" Roberto grumbles from the bedroom. "Turn that shit off."

Roberto arrived home late, and sounds none too happy. Noah grabs the cell phone and silences it. The display reads *Thayer, Home.* Noah stands for a moment, dripping onto the linoleum before the streaming morning sunlight, and debates whether to answer. But Dr. Thayer is his one and only employer: he has to answer. He flips the phone open.

"Hello?" Noah says.

"Rrr," Roberto roars, drowning out Dr. Thayer's reply. Noah closes the bathroom door.

"—you on your way?"

"Um, no, am I supposed to be?" Olena leans her head against his bare chest. He feels her breath against his skin. He strokes her long neck once and then, distracted, lets his hand lie there.

"I thought I told you. I'm sure I told you. I have to leave here at seven-thirty and there is a medications delivery scheduled for eight. I need you here for it, and then you'll have to get Tuscany up in time to be ready for your lesson."

"Oh. You never told me."

"Well, who's going to pick it up, *Dylan*? Whether I told you or not, I need you. So take a cab. I hope you're already showered."

"Yes," Noah says, feeling oddly proud to announce this small victory. Dr. Thayer hangs up.

So this was Agnès's life. No wonder she ran off. Noah sits on the sill of the bathtub for a few moments, until the towel is soaked through. Olena sits beside him, wraps an arm around his arm, and sighs. "What did *she* want?"

Noah feels awful. Olena needs him, has been up and ready for him, and instead he has to race to Fifth Avenue to wait around for a medications delivery. "She wants me to go there now," Noah says.

"Oh," Olena says. She tries to hide her disappointment, but her thin dark eyebrows sag. "For the whole day?"

"I assume so."

"And it will always be like this?"

"I don't know. I'm sorry."

Olena stands and opens the bathroom door. "Don't be sorry, it's your job, you have to go. I know I am unable to pay you."

"Stop, it's not about money, you know that. I would love to be here with you instead."

"I will take another test today, then. Is that what I should do?"

"Take SAJ 2001."

Olena nods, and sits in the center of her array of test materials. She doesn't look up when Noah leaves.

~

Noah runs into Dr. Thayer beneath the lush canopy of her building. It startles him to see her outside, to see her slight frame outlined in sunlight. She looks younger, almost bonny. "Hello, Dr. Thayer," Noah says to her. The doormen look on. She gives a slight, formal nod in return and slides into her car service.

Noah ascends to the Thayer apartment. The door is, as usual, unlocked. This early in the morning the air inside is dead, motionless, black. Noah walks up and down the foyer for a few moments, idly examining the miniature statues arranged along the wall. It feels uncanny to be alone inside the apartment, like seeing the interior of a closed music box. There is no sound from Dylan's and Tuscany's rooms; they must be sound asleep. Dylan probably arrived home when Roberto did, just a few hours earlier.

Noah sits on the firm leather bench by the front door, takes out his phone, and calls Olena. He has time to guide her through two problems before the doormen buzz. "The doctor's got a delivery."

Noah hangs up with Olena, accepts the drug shipment, and carries the black zip-bag into the kitchen. And then, curious, he opens it and peeks inside. Dozens of prescription bottles are lined up within the insulated plastic: Xanax, Dexedrine, Valium, Ritalin. Noah zips it back up and inserts the container into the refrigerator between a bag of imported mozzarella and a half gallon of orange juice.

The monolithic fridge makes a solid suction sound when he closes it, like the door of an SUV. He returns to the foyer and calls Olena back. They try to work through another problem, but it frustrates them both that Noah is unable to see where Olena has made her mistakes. It is Olena who somewhat sulkily decides to end the call. Noah is left by himself in the impeccable luxury of the Thayer apartment. He runs a hand down the smoothness of the steel kitchen cabinets, wanders through the hall and touches the statues. He examines the bindings of the books arrayed on the sole bookshelf: a leather-bound Great Books series, in perfect chronological order and bindings immaculate. Living here is like existing inside the characterless perfection of a catalogue. How, he wonders, would he decorate this place differently if the Thayer wealth were his?

Noah considers calling his mother and brother. But he knows calling them from the Thayer apartment would be a bad idea—they would somehow sense the quiet grandeur around him, which would only further the unreality of his situation.

Tuscany doesn't need to be up for another hour. Noah wanders past Dr. and Mr. Thayer's offices. Both rooms have been cleared of papers, the desks removed. In their place stretch driftwood tables and polished birch tables in the oblong shape of yachts, covered in lace tablecloths and adorned with champagne flutes. Each setting contains a small arsenal of cutlery with handles as solid as swords'. The molding around the ceiling has been relacquered driftwood-tan, and the walls are peach. The whole effect is ostentatious and disorienting, as though a Provençal exterior has been inverted and placed on Fifth Avenue.

Noah continues down the hallway, toward the dining room. Plastic sheeting and masking tape emerge from the entrance. A dropcloth crinkles as Noah approaches. The family portraits have been taken down, and the walls painted a baked ochre. From the window stretches a painted horizon of blue streaked with sunny yellow. Mr. Thayer is evidently to have a theme party: yachts on the Riviera.

The plastic drop crinkles again. Noah turns to see two Hispanic men in painter's smocks standing apologetically at the entranceway. They hold their painter's caps at their waist, as if in respect for the passing of the dead.

"Mr. Thayer?" one of them says. "Hello, Mr. Thayer." The other nods frantically.

Noah's first impulse is to say, *I'm not Mr. Thayer,* but he realizes his true position in the household would be too complicated to explain. Also, he doesn't really mind being considered a Thayer for a few seconds. He runs a hand through his hair.

"It's fine, I'm just seeing what's here. It looks great."

The men still look terrorized.

"I'll just get out of your way," Noah says. He crinkles across the dropcloth and leaves the dining room.

He stands listlessly in the foyer. He no longer feels comfortable wandering the apartment, not with the two workmen there to witness his conflicting contempt and admiration. It is too bizarre to be here without any of the Thayers: he feels that he is being illicit and naughty, as though he were locked in a museum at night, with free rein over a forbidden place. He has to share the feeling with someone, even just to break the artificial solitude of the apartment. Maybe Tuscany is already awake. Noah makes his way up the stairs. He can't hear a sound from either her room or Dylan's. But there is a piece of heavy paper taped to Tuscany's door. Noah leans forward to read it in the dim light:

Noah,

Thank you for accepting the delivery (provided, of course, that you have come on time). T will need lunch. Please see that it is provided. I will need you to stay here tonight. I can't attend to the children. Also, I'll expect you to be here tomorrow evening to help take care of D and T during Mr. Thayer's IPO party. Feel free to bring someone who would find conversing with our guests interesting (and vice versa, of course!). You will need to wake D up in the morning to go to school.

Dr. Thayer (Susan)

Noah takes the note, sloppily folds it, and wedges it into his pants pocket.

Tuscany, sleepy-eyed and big-haired, emerges from her bedroom to find Noah in front of her door. "Hey," she says slowly. "What are you doing?"

"Just got the note from your mother."

"She's a crazy bitch sometimes, isn't she?" Tuscany says.

She brushes past Noah and wanders down the hallway.

Noah is about to reprimand Tuscany, but bites it back. Her point is, after all, pretty accurate.

"Hey," Tuscany says on returning. "There's some guys in the dining room."

"Yeah, they're redecorating for your dad's party."

"Oh, cool." Tuscany disappears into her bedroom. "Come on in."

Noah enters. She is sitting on her unmade bed, wearing a worn tank top and sweats. She throws herself back among her pillows, stretches her arms. "You know," she says, her eyes closed, "Agnès always made me make my bed first thing." She giggles. "You make a crappy au pair."

"Maybe you should make your bed, then."

"Mmm. No thanks." She stretches in her comforter and stares at Noah. One side of her shirt has fallen, and she breathes against the bare skin of her shoulder as her eyes meet his. She is seducing him; he feels his pulse race in his wrists. "So what are we going to do today?" she asks.

"You're getting a unit test in chemistry," Noah improvises.

She pouts. "I thought you said I don't have to take tests."

Noah crosses his arms and backs toward the door. "Well, today you're going to take a unit test. Come on, get dressed and come downstairs. I'll be at the kitchen table."

Tuscany sits up again. "What the *fuck*?"

"I'm serious. I'll be waiting." He leaves the room and closes the door. He leans against it for a moment, feels his blood pounding within his fingertips. He listens for a moment to the rustling of her bedsheets as she gets ready. Then he goes down to the kitchen.

Tuscany arrives fifteen minutes later wearing a baggy shirt, quiet and abashed. Noah administers a test from the textbook. They pass the rest of the session going over her outline for her next essay. At lunchtime Tuscany announces that she wants tomato and mozzarella slices. Noah extracts the mozzarella from the fridge, and as he does so Tuscany laughs derisively. "You put the *drugs* in there?"

"Yes. They're supposed to go in the fridge."

"In *Mom's* fridge. That's upstairs, in the bedroom. There's a combo. It's fifty-four, sixteen."

How do you know the combination? Noah's raised eyebrows say. But it is futile to pursue the point—and regardless, the time is long past that he can be shocked by the Thayers. "I'll put them there after lunch. Now help me and cut a tomato."

Tuscany seems taken aback at being asked to help, but then nods. She puts a tomato on the counter and extracts a butcher knife from the block. She holds it unsteadily a foot above the red fruit, as if she is planning to guillotine it. Noah takes the knife from her and replaces it with a smaller one. He shows her how to cut the tomato. Pleased by this new trick, Tuscany passes the lunchtime in pleasant conversation, and then leaves to take the car service to her riding lesson.

Dylan's afternoon session doesn't go as well, primarily because Dylan doesn't show up. Noah passes the afternoon in Dylan's room. He calls Dylan's cell a few times. There is no response. He watches TV for an hour, then calls Dr. Thayer's cell. She must be in sessions: he goes straight to voicemail. He has done what he can. Noah idly watches $225 worth of *Oprah* and calls Olena during a commercial.

"*What,* Noah?"

Noah mutes the television. "Wow, what's wrong?"

"You can't just call me when you are free, in these idle minutes."

"I have a lot of free time right now. Dylan didn't show. I just wanted to help you."

"It doesn't work on the phone." There is a pause. "I got another 1730."

"Oh, sorry. Can you see why?"

"No. I can't without your showing me."

"Listen, I have bad news. I'm going to have to stay here tonight."

"Oh."

"Is that okay?"

"Yes, of course." Olena's tone convinces Noah of exactly the opposite.

"There's going to be a party here tomorrow. Do you want to come? We might be able to do some work here beforehand."

"A Fifth Avenue party? Sounds awful. No, thank you. I should work."

"I'd really like it if I had you here to talk to. I want to see you."

"I'll think about it." Olena hangs up.

Noah spends the afternoon loafing in Dylan's room. Effectively, he *is* Dylan: he lazes on the bed, scratches himself, watches television, and surfs the Internet. The three hours of sumptuous solitude are both pleasant and deadening. At first he is preoccupied with Olena, but then he thinks of nothing. He begins to move more and more slowly; the whole room seems as if invaded by some foreign and heavy gas. When the door opens Noah turns his head lethargically to see who's entering.

"What the fuck?" Dylan says, grinning broadly.

"Hey," Noah says. He looks at the television and then back at Dylan. "We were supposed to have a session this afternoon. We have a week left."

"Oh yeah?" Dylan says, putting down his bag. "Move over." Noah slides a few inches on the bed. Dylan sits next to him, turns the television volume up. He watches in silence for a few seconds, then speaks: "It's not as though I'm actually going to take the thing, you know? This is all a total joke, just to make my mom feel better."

"It's just a 1580, Dylan. If you tried you could do it."

"No way, I'd fuck it up. You know that."

"No, I don't know that. Just stop second-guessing yourself."

Dylan looks at Noah blankly, then returns to the television. "Yeah, whatever. So what's for dinner?"

"I don't know, I'm supposed to make you guys something."

Dylan laughs. "I'm ordering Chinese."

~

Fuen leads Noah to his room before she retires for the evening. It is small, tasteful, and sterile, all scented soaps and L'Occitane toiletries. Noah's crisply ironed sheets smell of lavender and stale potpourri. He reads a book for a while and then turns the lamp out. Pale filtered light from the Fifth Avenue street lamps illuminates the polished edges of the furniture. Noah doesn't know how long he lies awake, puzzling through his finances, his job, Mr. Thayer, Dr. Thayer, Tuscany, Dylan, Olena. He sleeps fitfully, but when he awakes, cleansing sun is streaming through the window. He sits up in his bed, disoriented and unable to remember where he is. As the stiff scented sheets fold around his torso it takes him some time to realize that he is in the Thayer apartment and not a hotel.

~

Tuscany leaves for riding practice well before Dylan returns from school, giving Noah enough time to race home, change clothes, and get back to Fifth Avenue for the evening's party. He hopes Olena will be home when he arrives, but she isn't.

Noah rushes into the bedroom and scans about his closet. He will wear the pin-striped pants, his tutoring standbys, and . . . the pink oxford gleams in the evening light from the corner of his closet. It is the only clean garment he owns. His hand closes around the heavy fabric.

Noah is almost out the door when Hera spies him. "Noah!" she exclaims. "You can't go to high society like that!" She tugs at his shirt.

Noah removes it and stands shirtless by the counter as Hera hurriedly irons the shirt. "There," she says, "much better." Noah buttons the hot fabric over his torso and bolts out the door. He hopes he doesn't need a tie.

~

Noah takes a cab down to the Thayer apartment and gets trapped in a mini traffic jam, as three caterers' trucks are parked in front of the building. He has to be left off on 79th Street and walk over. He would have liked to have opened the cab door in front of the Fifth Avenue apartment, to have slid his legs out of the car and onto the sparkling pavement, strolled out beneath the luxurious awning. Dropped off where he was, for all anyone knows he could have taken the subway, could be going to work. If it weren't for the pink oxford, he would just be another tutor on the job.

Dr. Thayer is already in her evening dress. She has been massively made up, and her weighty black velvet gown hangs flatly on her narrow form. With her pallid complexion and teased hair, she looks like a doll mail-ordered from the Franklin Mint.

"Noah!" she exclaims. "I'm *so* glad you came." She gestures Noah inside, sweeping her arm to indicate the panorama of the apartment, as if he has never been there before. A few guests speak in low murmurs in the next room. Dr. Thayer's fulsome performance is probably for their benefit: *He's not just a tutor—he's a friend.*

"The apartment looks nice," Noah says, because he feels Dr. Thayer is expecting him to. The foyer looks no different than normal.

"Thank you!" Dr. Thayer laughs lightly. "I'd offer to take your coat, but you don't *have* a coat!"

Noah laughs with her at the world's unpredictability. He offers a wrapped bottle of wine. It only cost $8, but he thought the label looked expensive. After frowning at the gaucherie of Noah's having brought wine, Dr. Thayer accepts the offering and, forgetting the stage of the hostess ritual in which she is supposed actually to invite her guest inside, wanders off into the kitchen.

Noah steps to the edge of the dining-room-cum-yacht. Ragtime music has been piped throughout the room. A small group of men and women in business suits cluster around a baby grand and chat about their excuses for having arrived so early. "Really?" Noah hears one of the women say. "I'm here because the London Exchange has already closed!" The rest laugh uproariously. Noah wonders whether to plunge in; he stands at the edge of the room, bobbing in and then bobbing out, like a kite at the end of its string. He doesn't know a thing about the London Exchange. He didn't even know there was one. Maybe Tuscany needs help. He starts to the stairwell.

Dr. Thayer swoops in and grabs Noah's arm. "You're not leaving already?" she says. "They're not being entirely too boring? Not intellectual enough? Some of them probably went to Princeton too, you know."

"No, I just thought I'd check on—"

"Stop worrying about Tuscany! People will suspect you're perverted. I'm sure my guests will be interested in what you have to say. I'm proud to have you here! I want them to get to know you. Come on, I'll introduce you."

Dr. Thayer steers Noah toward the yacht room. He tries to think of things to say to businessmen.

"Noah!" Tuscany's voice comes from the top of the stairs. Noah turns around gratefully.

She has stepped to the landing and then posed there, like a fairy-tale princess making her grand entrance at the ball and waiting for the guests to remark on her beauty. She is wearing a red silken dress, ribbed in a darker red, that crisscrosses in the front and ties low in the back. Her hair is tied simply behind her head. She no longer looks like a teenage starlet, but is instead a beautiful young woman. Then she claps gleefully, and is a teenager again. "Noah! You wore my shirt!"

Noah glances down at the oxford. "Yes."

Dr. Thayer entwines her arm around Noah's elbow. Her limb is impossibly lithe and strong, a vine. "*I* bought the shirt," she says. Then she laughs to lighten the severity of her words. The arm hooked in Noah's constricts. She clutches him urgently, pulls him to her, as if she were drowning.

"Yes, Mom," Tuscany says, descending the stairs. "*You* bought the shirt. Jesus."

Dr. Thayer leans into Noah's ear as Tuscany nears. "I need to talk to you later tonight, when she's not around. Come find me."

"What are you say-*ing*?" Tuscany's voice becomes shrill at the end, almost a shriek.

"Nothing about you," Dr. Thayer says.

Tuscany pauses in mid-step and glares at her mother, makes an ill-concealed effort to contain herself, then takes the last few steps newly calm and poised. She takes Noah's other arm. "You look so good," she says. "Doesn't he, Mom?"

"Yes," Dr. Thayer says sulkily. "He looks very respectable."

Their conversation unnerves Noah. They are not speaking as a mother and daughter—they are rivals. And he realizes that, despite Dr. Thayer's nominal attempts at parental authority, they have always been rivals. Dr. Thayer's preoccupation with Dylan and dismissal of Tuscany make sense: Dylan, the son, can succeed in areas that don't threaten Dr. Thayer. But Tuscany . . . where she derives the most attention—her looks, youth, spirited nature—are the very areas in which Dr. Thayer is fading to gray. Dr. Thayer can't stand to see her daughter come to the landing poised and lovely, when she is haggard and lost. She sees in Tuscany the animus that has already faded from her, the very vitality she most wants to recover, her own ghost.

"Who's here?" Tuscany asks. She pivots to see into the dining room. This turns the whole trio and wedges Dr. Thayer against the banister of the stairwell. She detaches from Noah's arm.

"I'll leave you two," she says.

"When's Dad going to get here?" Tuscany asks. Her chewing gum pops.

"Who knows? Who knows." Dr. Thayer unsteadily wanders off.

"Wow," Tuscany says. "She's really fucked. I wonder what she took."

"Do you want to grab some food?" Noah asks brightly. "I think I saw trays in the kitchen."

Tuscany grips her flat abdomen. "No way, I'm so full. But I'll go with you."

They stand in the kitchen while Noah eats a few bruschettas. Tuscany is eventually lured away into the dining room by a chatty uncle, and Noah is left alone with the appetizers. In time Dr. Thayer weaves her way into the kitchen. She opens the fridge door. Then she sees Noah.

"Noah!" she says loudly. "What are you doing in here again?"

Noah's mouth is full of olive paste. He shrugs and points to the dining room, as if that explains everything.

"I'm glad I caught you," Dr. Thayer says. She leans in, and Noah smells the foul scent of vermouth on her breath. "Dylan hasn't been doing well on these practice tests. We're very worried. Are you sure you're not willing to step up to the challenge?"

"If," Noah says, "you're referring again to taking the test for Dylan, no. I'm not 'up to the challenge.' "

"Can't blame a girl for trying," Dr. Thayer laughs. She slams the fridge door closed. She leans backward, crosses her arms, and stares at Noah quizzically, an icy smile on her face. "How about some wine? Would you allow me to have a waiter bring you some wine? We have a nice little Pinot Grigio that might suit your palate."

"That would be fine, thank you."

Dr. Thayer snaps her fingers sharply. Her smile turns into a snarl as she does, as if she has just ordered someone beheaded. She lurches out of the kitchen.

Noah sucks olive paste off his finger, stares out the window. Dr. Thayer doesn't return. No wine arrives.

He spies Tuscany at the head of a driftwood table, engaged in conversation with men in business suits. They form an admiring circle around her. She catches Noah's eye and waves him over. The businessmen follow her wave and nod respectfully to Noah. He straightens his shirt and dives in.

Each of the men has a name that is instantly forgotten, the kinds of names that appear so often in newspapers or the subtitles of C-Span that Noah just glazes over when he hears them. Solomon X, X Lidden III, Powell X, Peter X Stockton, and a half dozen Andrews. Within a few minutes of speaking to any one of them, the conversation is prodigiously steered to alma maters. Princeton always gets smiles and nods, and warms up the conversationalist immediately—it effects as much intimacy as at least three months of acquaintance. Noah feels he has made a host of best friends within twenty minutes.

The conversation turns to politics: everyone waits patiently for his turn to spout off on the topic at hand, then paints a fascinated face for the next person's monologue. The stern undertone of each jolly conversation is an old boy's search for *truth,* for essential meaning. Jokes are spoken with unchanging and serious faces, philosophers trained to be comics. Everyone has plenty to say, plenty of meaning to impart, except for Tuscany, who has made it her role to be the receptor of everyone's self-indulgent wisdom. She laughs bonnily, receives as many admiring glances as possible, demurs when asked for her own opinion. Noah wishes she would express herself, not focus on her image instead, but he doesn't know how to make it happen. Perhaps the seeds have been planted, and in a few years she will have the confidence to hold her own ground and not fall back on her looks. But not yet.

The party is filling. The caterers have arrived in full force, and Noah is thankful for the constant distractions of wine and hors d'oeuvres. Tuscany squeals when Octavia arrives, dashes over to the front door to greet her. Octavia, wearing a very short dress, makes the rounds of the party with lips glossed and erotically parted. She and Tuscany face down unsuspecting thirty-year-old bachelors arm in arm, giggling and laying their hands on the unwary men. Dr. Thayer is nowhere to be seen.

Then Noah does see her, unsteady, at the door of her bedroom at the top of the stairs. She sniffs visibly. Noah thinks she might have been crying, but her eyes are lively. He realizes she might have snorted something instead. She surveys the room, takes a few deep breaths, and then lowers herself down the stairs and disappears into a throng of party guests.

A caterer opens the front door. Mr. Thayer enters with a springy, athletic step. A cheer goes up from those scattered members of the party who were paying attention. He ricochets through the crush, among and between his guests. Noah, standing at the other end of the long foyer and obscured by the geisha statue, plucks another glass of wine from a wandering caterer. And then he sees who has entered behind Mr. Thayer—Olena. He steps out from behind the bronze statue to see her better.

Her hair has been pulled back into a neat French braid. She wears a dove-gray dress that falls in artless lines from her narrow shoulders. In the midst of so much gold and perfume, she looks simple and lovely. She stands politely at the entrance, a bottle of wine in her hand, and scans the crowd about her, looking for a host. Noah starts to make his way toward her, but the crowd is packed in tightly around him. Olena slowly walks into the kitchen, maintaining the same cautious, gracious smile on her face. The bright orange price tag from the Harlem corner store glows at the neck of her wine bottle.

The animated, half-drunk party guests seem to conspire to prevent Noah from reaching the kitchen. An older woman with pronounced clavicles leans against a table, hemming in one route. When Noah adjusts his path a rotund man in an ascot begins to gesticulate, blocking another course. The physically expansive laughter of his audience forms a further roadblock. By the time Noah reaches the kitchen, Olena has disappeared. Noah refreshes his wine and picks up a cracker globbed with crabmeat.

Finally he spies Olena. She is in the midst of animated conversation with a handsome man wearing an expensive peasant-style linen shirt. His hair forms a dramatic black wave on the top of his head, and is flecked gray at the crests. He asks Olena a question, which she shyly answers. Whatever the answer is, he is charmed.

Noah feels a hot splash of jealousy. The man has such a constructed and distinguished appearance that he looks like he just walked off a print ad for Aston Martin. Noah would assume him to be self-absorbed—but he's posing Olena plenty of questions. Surely he has nothing interesting to say—but Olena seems enraptured. She finishes a sentence for him, raises her glass to toast one of his remarks.

Suddenly Noah is aware of his powerlessness from his perch at the edge of the kitchen. He wants to be active, not observing. Tuscany and Octavia aren't far away, chatting up a pair of guys. Noah approaches them. Tuscany greets him effusively. Octavia pretends she doesn't even know him, her heavy arms locked in front of her chest. Noah stands at the edge of their conversation, hearing none of it, his thoughts on Olena. He looks over at where she stood. She's no longer there, and neither is the guy.

Noah turns, trying to hide his panic, to convince himself that he is being irrational. Where is she, though? Then he feels a light touch on his arm. He turns; it is Olena.

"You came," Noah says.

"Of course I came. I thought I would surprise you. This apartment!" She shakes her head.

"I wasn't sure if you were going to come say hello!" He sounds pathetic, needling. What is with him?

"Did you see who I was talking to? The guy with the crazy laced-up bodice?"

"Yes," Noah says darkly.

"He's very interesting—"

"I could see that."

"Don't be stupid, Noah. Stop it. He's a *dance teacher.* He's head of the youth division of the Dance Theater of Harlem. I was telling him all about your tutoring. Did you know that 'No Child Left Behind' funds tutoring for kids at failing schools, a couple thousand dollars for each kid? I told him how very awesome you are at SATs and he's really interested. He's going to get a drink now, but then he's going to come over. He knows a couple of guys who . . . Wait, talk about something else."

The man has arrived. He flashes a broad, tan smile at Noah. "So, you must be the star tutor."

"I don't know what Olena told you . . ." Noah laughs.

"She's got a high opinion of you. Tell me what you do."

Noah hears the gravel in the man's voice, his grit. His snobby affect vanishes: Noah can easily imagine him observing a dance class in a T-shirt and Birkenstocks. He senses that the man's costly dress shirt is, like Noah's, a temporary disguise. And so Noah barrels into a description of what he's been doing. The man is interested: a lot of his kids will end up at conservatories, but those who don't make the cut will end up at dance programs at larger universities, and haven't received the right education to succeed on the SAT. If he could secure federal funding, would Noah be interested in conducting a private class?

Olena has been following along excitedly, but suddenly her hand on Noah's arm tightens. He follows her gaze. Dylan has arrived, and with Roberto. Next to Roberto's bulk, Dylan looks like a teen pop star with his bodyguard. Roberto roughly pushes his way through the crowd to clear a path to Dylan's bedroom. The pair disappears upstairs. Olena excuses herself and follows them.

Noah tries to plunge himself back into the man's rapid shifts in thought. New federal programs allow funding for tutors in underprivileged communities, or they could go through existing nonprofit organizations like Prep-for-Prep. He's been looking for academic tutors for his dancers but hadn't even thought of getting them SAT tutoring as well. Would Noah please call him to talk further? Noah asks for a card. The man gives him one, shakes Noah's hand, and disappears into the crowd.

Noah stares down at the card, the fruit of a connection effectively earned through his work with the Thayers. It is brown ink on tan paper: he finds the numbers difficult to read through the haze of the wine. But this is *something,* the start of *something.* He imagines what it will be like to feel good about his work, to earn money and also be happy doing it. It seems indulgent and blissful. He wants to share the feeling with Olena, to thank her. But he can't find her.

He scans the crowd, sipping his wine. The apartment is nearly full. The guests stand wedged into corners, perched at the entranceways to rooms. For all the Thayers' wealth, this is still Manhattan, and an apartment party always makes for cramped conversations. They either stand still, as if ordered to pose, or move through the rooms purposefully and indirectly, like chess pieces.

Dylan and Roberto are upstairs. Olena is likely with them. He'll go say hello.

A tight ring of stylish Orthodox Jewish women blocks the path through Dr. Thayer's office. Noah decides to pass through the kitchen instead. He enters, only to find at the other end the one man he most wanted to avoid. Mr. Thayer is crouched over, a champagne bottle between his knees. A piece of its wire mechanism has broken off, and he strains to extract the cork. The silk trouser fabric covering Mr. Thayer's thighs shakes with the effort. The neck of the bottle is directed at Noah. He sidesteps quickly, and slams into an open cabinet. It closes noisily. Mr. Thayer stands up quickly, immediately defensive, as if the champagne is a prostitute who has been giving him a blow job. He sees Noah, and the two of them stare at each other from across the gleaming open space of the kitchen. There is no one else here; this is their own private arena. Noah's pulse quickens.

"A friend brought this," Mr. Thayer says unsurely, holding up the assaulted bottle.

For two men well versed in pleasantries, one of them should figure out how to start up a conversation. But a long and silent charge passes between them. Noah sees in Mr. Thayer's eyes not a hint of apology, and yet he empathizes with him—Mr. Thayer has no idea what to say, is so obviously uncomfortable, that Noah sees himself in him. He feels like excusing himself and leaving the kitchen. But he knows how angry Olena would be for his sake were she standing here next to him, how angry he would be later if he let this moment pass without confronting Mr. Dale Thayer.

Mr. Thayer has placed the bottle on the counter and is fiddling with the foil. Apparently he has decided that the bottle will make for a less nerve-wracking conversational partner. "Can't . . . seem . . . to . . . get . . . you . . . open . . ."

Noah's impulse is to ask if he can help. Instead he leans against the counter. "Looks like you're having some trouble there."

"I am, I am," Mr. Thayer says. Then, apparently sensing some inherent weakness implied in his bent posture, to be so concerned over a bottle, he stands up and puts it down. "I'm glad you could make it, Noah."

"Are you?"

"Of course." He pauses, and looks searchingly into Noah's eyes. "Did Mindy call you?"

"That's your assistant? No."

"Oh," Mr. Thayer says. "She should have."

Noah pulls himself up to his full height. He sees, now, that he is slightly taller than Mr. Thayer. "What did you want her to tell me?"

"Oh. I really wish Mindy had called you. You should have known by now. I've been looking at the market, and I'm just not sure if this is going to happen. And even if it does, I don't think I'll need help with the actual materials for some time. I've got your number at the ready, though, for when I do."

"What about all the materials from my company? Are you finding those helpful?"

"I'm not sure what you're getting at, here."

"What I'm 'getting at, here,' is that you've played me. You've used me to get confidential materials, and then dropped me."

"In business, Noah, nothing is as simple as that."

"Bullshit."

Mr. Thayer's eyes light up. "*Bullshit?* I wasn't going to tell you, Noah, but since you're obviously so into being so *honest,* here, let me tell you this—your agency's materials are crap. Your 'learning' processes are crap. Those training manuals are worthless. All you do is teach seventh-grade math to eleventh-graders. I had expected some magical formulas, some brilliant tricks that crack open the test. But all you're paid to do is to be friends with my children and photocopy words out of the dictionary. It's a sick industry, creating a need where there wasn't any. And yes, that's business, that's good economics. But I don't need your help on the academic front because there *is no* academic front. I can create my own group of wunderkind pseudo-shrinks without anyone's help. If families want to pay for the privilege of inviting young Ivy League men into their homes and being able to chat about their newest employee at cocktail parties, I'm willing to oblige. I just don't see how you'd have anything to offer to that venture."

Despite himself, Noah is struck by Mr. Thayer's honesty. His words are ruthless but heartfelt. He is brilliant and self-absorbed, feels free to speak his mind if the thought is interesting enough. There is no appealing to compassion here.

"What I do here . . ." Noah says. His voice falters, so he starts over. The cork flies off the champagne. Mr. Thayer smiles wanly as he fills flutes. "What I do here *is* teaching, Mr. Thayer. I wouldn't do all this if it were all tricks and special strategies. My job here isn't to teach how to cheat the test, and it isn't figuring out how to find the quickest way to college. I'm taking your kid, who went to one of the best schools in the nation, has all the resources in the world, and somehow doesn't know how to reason, has never read a book, forgot algebra as soon as the grades were in, and I'm filling in the gaps. I'm showing him how to add fractions and to derive equations. My question for you, sir, is how children of genius parents at the very best schools are just scoring average on a nationwide test. Average. Or, in Dylan's case, well below average. Do you ever wonder why? Well. He was never read to as a child, never encouraged to take the hard road to solving a problem, never had to make sure his own needs were covered. And how do successful parents raise average children? By focusing on their own genius, by looking after their own goals and ignoring the better good of their kid, by raising a child for the sole reason that finally there will be someone in the world whose duty will be to be impressed with them."

Mr. Thayer has finished filling the flutes. "Someone brought this bottle of champagne as a gift," he says jovially. "I thought it would be polite to serve it right away." He takes a glass off the tray and sets it down on the table. "Maybe you'd like one." *Now now,* his manner says, *you didn't have to get personal.*

Then he picks up the tray, nods to Noah, and leaves the kitchen.

Noah is left clutching a glass of champagne. It has been handed to him like a consolation prize for having been dicked over. He holds the flute tightly in his fingers, wonders how it would feel if he crushed the glass in his fist, felt the glass cutting into the lines of his palm. He wishes that Mr. Thayer were still in the room. He wants to tell him about Cameron, Sonoma, all the students who understand the gift of their privilege, who take advantage of the resources offered them and try to rise to the higher challenge. Instead everything is focused on kids like Dylan, the glamorous disasters. *Other parents managed,* he wants to say. *Why couldn't* you *pay any attention to your kid?*

He wants Olena, her rationality, her goodness. He needs her to ground the eccentric world that has spitefully placed a glass of champagne in his fist. He slams it down and strides into the foyer. He sees, out of the corner of his eye, Mr. Thayer in heated discussion with Dr. Thayer. She has crossed her narrow arms over her chest. Noah knows he doesn't have much time left before they ask him to leave.

He takes the stairs two at a time and knocks on Dylan's door. "Go away," comes Dylan's voice. Noah hears Roberto laugh. He opens the door.

Dylan is on his knees in front of his desk, his crutches on the floor at his side, his thick lips dripping spittle into the trash can. Roberto is sitting on the bed, reading a *Maxim.* "What the hell?" Noah says. "What's going on?"

Noah sees a flash of irritation cross Roberto's face, annoyance at Noah's prudishness, and then sees him force himself into friendliness. "Hey, Noah, don't worry, man, I've got it covered here."

"Got what covered?"

Dylan looks up. His eyes are bloodshot; Noah can barely see them through the wet mess of his hair. "I'm fine," he slurs.

Noah kneels next to Dylan and holds his head back, grips his forehead. Dylan's face is smooth and cool in his palm. His skin isn't clammy; Noah wishes he knew whether that was a good sign. "What did you give him?" Noah asks.

Roberto shrugs. "Nuttin' serious. Xanax, I guess. He must have taken a few shots before that, or snorted something. I've seen him like this before, he gets over it quick, huh, Dylan?"

Dylan groans affirmatively.

The door opens. Olena appears with a glass of water and a wet washcloth. "Noah!" she says. "You have seen what my asshole brother did to Dylan?"

"I didn't do anything. He did it to himself," Roberto growls.

Olena hands the water to Noah. He presses it to Dylan's mouth. Dylan gums the lip of the glass. His pale lips move without coordination, like grubs. "He's not okay," Noah says.

Dylan manages a sip of water. Olena presses the washcloth against his forehead as Noah holds him. "You're a good-looking guy," she says to Dylan with exaggerated sweetness. He smiles and gives a little laugh. "I think he's going to be okay," Olena says.

Noah spins on Roberto. "You should get out of here, man. You've already gotten a seventeen-year-old fucked up. You have the balls to just walk into his house during a party? Leave him alone, let him just be, okay?"

Roberto puts his magazine down. He adopts a pissed-off thug voice. "What, like I'm not *allowed* to be here? Look, you're not the one to be telling me what to do, okay?"

Olena says something cross in Albanian. Roberto stands and leaves the room. Noah hears the door creak, but it doesn't click closed. He turns. Dr. Thayer stands in the doorway. She takes in Dylan's kneeling form, Olena in the middle of administering the washcloth, Noah crouched next to her with the glass of water in his hand.

"What happened to Dylan? What did you do to him?" she asks softly.

"He's taken something," Noah says. "I think he's probably going to be okay."

"What the fuck?" Dylan groans. "What is *she* doing in here? Get out! God!"

"Do you want me to leave?" Dr. Thayer's voice is cool but shaky. She closes the door behind her.

"Yes!"

"Hold on," Noah says. "Let her help you."

Dylan brushes the washcloth out of his face, tries to sit

up but can't. Olena steps back into the corner. "What the hell? I don't need her to 'help me.' Shut up, dude."

"You've really gone and screwed it up this time, huh?" Dr. Thayer says to Dylan, suddenly vitriolic; she is probably scared.

"Just get her out of here," Dylan cries. "Please. I just want to sleep."

"Let's give him some space," Dr. Thayer says. "I'll keep checking in on him." She holds the door open. Noah and Olena have no choice but to go through. She closes it behind them. The three stand huddled outside the door. Noah expects Dr. Thayer to be angry or worried, to want a hushed conference about Dylan, but she has a perfect hostess veneer. "You must be Olena," she says. "I recognize you from the trip pictures."

"P-pleased to meet you," Olena says.

"Thank you for coming," Dr. Thayer says. "Your dress is very pretty."

"Thank you."

Dr. Thayer stares Olena down. Catching the dismissal barely hidden in the doctor's gaze, Olena announces a need to use the restroom. Dr. Thayer and Noah are left alone in the hallway.

She jabs her finger into Noah's chest. She is smiling, but she wields her bony finger like a dagger; it really hurts. Noah takes an involuntary step backward. "You," she says, "shouldn't have put my medications bag in the downstairs fridge."

"What?"

"It turned up upstairs eventually, but missing the entire contents of Xanax." She laughs harshly. "I can recognize a Xanax-alcohol mix when I see one."

"Jesus!" She has made it sound like an amusing anecdote. "What about Dylan? What are you going to do? It could be something more serious than alcohol, I don't know . . ."

Dr. Thayer looks into Noah's eyes. Her gaze is mesmerizing; it holds a vestigial power; she is using some move that at one time was seductive. Now her gaze is equally compelling, but only because it holds a lost grandeur, the same horror and mystery of a ruined temple. "My husband," she says, "is angry that I invited you here."

She speaks the line with a breathless wickedness, as though the two of them are at the climax of an illicit and doomed affair.

"Truth be told," Noah says hesitantly, "I'm angry with your husband."

"I warned you to think twice about working with him. He's merciless. All of our friends have been burned by him at one point. The strong ones remain, the weak ones leave. I'm glad I invited you, though," Dr. Thayer says rapidly. "He needs to face what he does. And apparently you gave him quite a little showdown. You broke through to him, I think. He seems thoughtful." Dr. Thayer gives a little golf clap.

Noah nods. The array of artificial blond highlights in Dr. Thayer's hair, shining above the iron gray beneath, is beguiling.

"He's quite angry," Dr. Thayer repeats, lost in some ecstasy. She couldn't seem to find anything more pleasurable.

Noah nods. He is being prodded toward some great assault, sexual or verbal, and within the haze of wine he cannot think of how to prepare a defense for it. "And Noah," Dr. Thayer breathes, "he has a lot of right to be angry."

"Hardly."

"I saw your big friend, that roommate of yours, 'Rob,' leave. I believe he's the one who just showed up with my OD'd son. I don't think that's really someone my son's tutor should have introduced him to, do you?"

"I didn't introduce them, not intentionally, and the reason for his—"

"Let me continue, if you will. We've paid you quite a bit, Noah, and you haven't really come through, have you? All Tuscany has to show for her spring semester is a big yellow bruise that doesn't seem to go away. And you managed to chase off her au pair, and aren't making a very good replacement. And Dylan, well! He didn't go up at all on his writing score, and it doesn't look as if he's going to improve on the rest of his SAT. So really, what have you done for us, other than soak up forty thousand dollars? Oh, of course you've been a good *friend* to our children, we both can't thank you enough for that."

Dr. Thayer is both so feeble and so cruel—Noah wonders how it would feel to strike her, to smother her.

"But Noah," she continues, rubbing a hand against the ridges of her rib cage, "we've paid you this money in good faith. And we do expect results."

"I know what you're referring to. And you can forget about it."

"Here's the thing. You've got a number of strikes against you. One, you've introduced my son to an . . . indecent lifestyle. Two, you've tried to enter into an illegal contract with my husband. Three, you were assigned both Dylan and Tuscany through your agency, and proceeded to work with them under the table. I don't think they would be happy to hear about any of this. They don't even know about Monroe Eichler, do they? And they were so unhappy to hear about your lackluster results with the Fieldston kids."

Dr. Thayer called the Fieldston parents, all in her push to get Noah in the position where he would have to accept her offer. It's boggling. His rage at Dr. Thayer now has too many targets; he sputters. "*You're* the one to suggest I work under the table. I didn't even—"

"*I'm* not the one whose job is hanging by a thread. Why should your agency care what *I* do?"

"You told them—you ratted me out! And introducing Dylan to an 'indecent lifestyle'? What the hell? He's been dipping into your drug supply for years. You've destroyed his ambition—he has nothing else to turn to. You've hired tutors illegally, cheated for your kids, you— How would everyone in your world react if they knew what you've done? What would happen to your reputation, your practice? You're more vulnerable than you think, here."

Dr. Thayer blanches for a moment, then flushes again. She is threatened and thrilled: Noah can see the excitement, the arousal, in the twitching lines of her usually deadened face. She glances at the unaware guests arranged below, then grips Noah's elbow and pulls him toward her bedroom. Momentarily stunned, he allows himself to be led to the lip of her sanctum, then he pulls back and stands in the doorway, arms crossed. Dr. Thayer reaches around him to close the door, but gives up when Noah doesn't move. They stand inches apart and breathe at each other.

"You know I would never allow my own children to get high from my own prescription meds. Why would I do that?" She speaks the words quickly and anxiously, into the parted triangle of fabric at Noah's throat.

Noah falters. The reason is obvious, but is also too complex for him to articulate in his agitated state. "You prescribe him enough on your own. He's got a quadruple dosage of Ritalin, you've given him a huge stash of Unisom to go to sleep every night. He doesn't even have to steal to be doped up."

"You've got some nerve to accuse me of—what, exactly?—my son doesn't concentrate well, so I help him concentrate. He doesn't sleep, so I help him sleep. I don't quite understand what you're getting at."

"Forget about it," Noah says. "It's not my business."

Dr. Thayer grabs Noah's wrist. The cold lines of her

hand close on his flesh like forceps. "I want to know what the hell you've got going on in your head. I've sensed this weird condescension from you since you arrived here last year, as though you can't believe what you see. Tell me. What *do* you see? What would you do differently?"

Words and feelings rush through Noah's mind. But he has suppressed his reactions for so long for the sake of his job that he can't speak into Dr. Thayer's face. Finally he makes an attempt. "You've . . . destroyed him," he chokes.

"I've *destroyed* him? Tell me how I've *destroyed* him." Dr. Thayer is aroused by the swell of feeling within her. She rubs her ribs more energetically.

"He doesn't have any desires. He's been helped for so long—by drugs, by tutors—that he can't do anything on his own. You haven't allowed him to try anything, to make mistakes and learn. People are only happy when they're achieving at something, right? And he has nothing to gain. You've met all his needs, and whatever he could produce now can't compare to the output of his tutors. So he's stuck. He can't produce anything." He is, Noah thinks, an idle and nasty prince.

"So what do you expect me to do now, shut it all off?"

"No," Noah says. "It's too late."

Dr. Thayer's hand is still on his arm. It has slowly worked its way up from the wrist to his shoulder. "Why are you telling me, then? Just out of spite?"

Noah is immobilized before her. He wants to push her away, back onto the bed. "I don't know," he says. He doesn't know. How bad is it, after all? The family has enough money to pay people to help Dylan forever. He can remain an infant for life. He will always be an inferior being surrounded by more able men, like a king and his ministers. Many have lived out their lives that way.

"I could say *you've* been mean this whole time," Dr. Thayer says, "working on a hopeless situation just to get paid, keeping me content just to make sure you can get as much money as you can from us. You've really used this to your advantage, Noah. And now that there's no more to be gotten, your true nastiness comes out." She stands back and stares at Noah with wide eyes, in breathless anticipation of the effect of her words. She is looking to catch an emotional charge, anger or lust, wants to get as far as possible from her deadened state. Noah could slap her across the face with all his might and she would turn back toward him, bloodied and smiling.

"You employed me to do a job," Noah says, "and I did it the best I could. No employer can blame an employee for that."

"So finish the job!" Dr. Thayer breathes. "You're getting paid to help my son get ahead. He hasn't gotten ahead—so you haven't done your duty. But you can. You're this kid's only hope for going to college. How can you just turn it down? You get paid, Dylan gets a college education, gets away from this hellhole, or whatever you think it is. All for doing what you've been doing already. What's the big difference, helping a kid pass a test the week before or during the thing itself?"

"It should be based on merit . . ." Noah says.

"It is based on merit," Dr. Thayer says. She cackles. "You live in America, Noah. Money is the only proof of merit we have."

In the haze of alcohol Dr. Thayer's words have a certain allure—how different would taking the test for Dylan be from what Noah's already done for him? One way or another, he's been selling spots at elite colleges to the upper class for three years now. Outright cheating changes the mode, but the overall effect is the same. It's because of Noah that the moneyed elite still congregates at Harvard and Yale, that old boys' clubs persist in Cambridge and New Haven, just as they do in Boston and New York. Because of the work Noah does, dozens of students like him won't get into Princeton this year.

Dr. Thayer steps into her bedroom, beckons Noah farther in. He doesn't budge. She leans over her dressing stand and plucks a business-sized check from the glossy surface. She holds it out to Noah.

"What's that?" Noah asks.

She just stands at the center of her bedroom, holding the check limply. Noah leans forward to take it from her. He looks at the check, then presses it away against his shirt. His credit cards are overdue. He hasn't been able to eat out. "You can't be serious," he says.

"Eighty thousand dollars," Dr. Thayer says.

Noah holds out the check. "Take it back. Take it back or I'll rip it up."

Dr. Thayer shrugs, smiling and running a hand up and down the silk covering her hip. "Rip it up, then."

Noah holds the heavy paper between his fingers. Then he unfolds the check and looks at it again. It fades from blue to white, is numbered 19563 and emblazoned with Mr. Thayer's company name. It would be as if Mr. Thayer actually paid him for his consulting after all. He could buy his mother a real house, or put a down payment on an apartment in Union Square. Or—and this is what makes his thumb caress the check—he could pay off his loans once and for all, and use the rest of the money for tuition. At the very least he'd have savings. No one in his family has savings.

"You're considering it," Dr. Thayer says. Her voice is much too close. He looks up from the check and she is right in front of him. She smells, like the whole apartment, of old fabric and lavender.

"Of course I'm considering it," Noah says tearfully. "This is more than three years' income, when I was growing up."

"Your mother would be so happy," Dr. Thayer breathes. "That Olena girl could use the money too . . ." Her voice trails off. Suddenly her hand is clutching the opening of Noah's shirt, and then—he suppresses the revulsion that convulses through him—one of his buttons has popped off, and her head is leaning against his bare neck. He looks down in horror at the top of her head, looks at the minute gray discolorations of her skin where the hair parts, the redness where the scalp has burned at the Hamptons. "Just take it, Noah," Dr. Thayer whispers, "I want you to have it. I don't want it back."

Dr. Thayer's weight pulls at his shoulders and, partially drunk from the wine and champagne, Noah stumbles. Dr. Thayer is dragging him down. They are nowhere near the bed, and Noah nearly loses his balance, lurches over the floor. Noah stares, stunned and beguiled, into the dark plush carpet. Dr. Thayer hangs from his neck, disoriented, her eyes black. He pries at her fingers—he can either throw her to the ground or risk falling on top of her. Her lips part, and she looks about to swoon. She closes her eyes, and seems unable to reopen them. She dangles from his neck, almost weightless, like a sleepy infant. She is going to pass out. Noah staggers over to the bed. He pulls at her fingers, but they have tightened fast around his neck. He frantically digs at them, but they are as chill and impervious as chains. A moan of pleasure escapes Dr. Thayer's lips as she feels Noah's nails dig into her flesh. His touch—even though he is only desperately trying to free himself—is arousing her.

"What the fuck?" It sounds like a little girl, but the voice behind him strengthens into a scream, and Noah then recognizes the owner—Tuscany. He hears a rush of fabric and then feels muffled pounding against his vertebrae as Tuscany pummels her mother's fingers. She emits little animalistic screeches, like a bird flying at the bars of a cage. Then Dr. Thayer is off him and lying supine on the bed. Her inky eyes are open and staring at her daughter. In the semidarkness, Noah sees only a momentary disappearance of their gleam when she blinks. Tuscany is next to him, breathless, her hair in disarray.

"What the fuck, Mom?" she sobs. "What the fuck? Leave him the hell alone."

"*You* leave us alone," Dr. Thayer says. "You shouldn't be in here." But her words are small, without force. She curls into a fetal position on the bed.

"You're a crazy bitch! Why do you have to be that way? He's my *tutor.*" Tuscany is shaking with rage. Another cry escapes her.

Dr. Thayer is paralyzed before her daughter's anger. "I'm sorry," she says dreamily, "I just need to sleep."

"You're a crazy bitch!" Tuscany repeats. The intensity of her voice has subsided somewhat. An adult tone—rancor—has crept in. "You only think about yourself."

Noah doesn't want to see Tuscany having to come to his defense any more than he wants to see Dr. Thayer stricken and moaning. The whole situation sets him on edge, gives him a distorted sense of his position. He suffers a loss of balance verging on vertigo. He staggers to his feet and spins around to look down the hallway.

"Where did Olena go?" Noah asks Tuscany. She looks at him blearily, glances at Dylan's door, shrugs.

Noah throws open the door to Dylan's room. He is lying on the floor, ashen-faced, his head in Olena's lap. She looks up at Noah worriedly. "He's not okay," she says.

Noah kneels next to them. Dylan is breathing, but slowly. His eyes are closed, his lips slack. A wet patch of urine has spread over his crotch. "We have to get him to the hospital," Noah says.

Olena shifts her weight beneath Dylan in preparation to lift him. Feeling her move, Dylan raises his head. "What?" he asks sleepily. Spit bubbles at the corner of his lips.

"Where do we take him?" Olena asks.

"Lenox Hill. It's just a few blocks away."

Dylan has sat up halfway and then fallen back down. "Come on, man," Noah coaxes, lifting Dylan beneath his shoulders. "Come on up with me."

Olena and Noah maneuver Dylan to the door of the bedroom, and then out onto the landing. "His parents?" Olena grunts from beneath Dylan's weighty arm.

"His mom's out of it," Noah says. "His dad . . . I don't know, let's see if we can find him."

They lug Dylan down the stairs to the front door. Noah scans the room—Mr. Thayer is nowhere in sight, but Tuscany bounds out of her mother's room and hovers over them. "Are you taking him to the hospital?" she calls concernedly. "I wanna come too."

"I need you to find your father for me," Noah says.

"Why? You'll take better care of Dylan than he would."

"Now. Go find him for me," Noah says sternly.

Tuscany disappears. Noah and Olena stand silently by the front door, Dylan half conscious and hanging between their arms. The room is crowded enough to render them inconspicuous: the party guests are careful not to notice.

And then Mr. Thayer turns the corner, a tumbler in hand. He has rolled up his shirtsleeves and wears a broad smile. But within the smile his eyes are cold, pure fury.

"What did you do to my son?" he asks, his fingers white around his glass.

"Your son overdosed on your wife's drugs," Noah says.

Mr. Thayer looks to the pale face of Dylan and then up at Noah and Olena. "Are you going to take him somewhere?"

"You need to take him to the hospital," Noah says. Dylan's leg is wet next to his.

"*I* need to take him?" Mr. Thayer laughs.

Noah leans forward slightly and loosens his grip. Urine-soaked Dylan falls into his father's arms. Mr. Thayer goes totally rigid, holding his son stiffly, like a poker hand. He has managed to keep his drink intact in one hand.

Noah opens his mouth and then closes it. He is unsure how to voice the anger in him and still make sure that Mr. Thayer will take Dylan to the hospital. Olena lays a hand on Noah's arm. "Good night, Mr. Thayer," she says.

Olena opens the front door and leads Noah through it. Noah glances about the apartment wildly one last time, and catches Tuscany's eye from where she stands at the landing. She nods: she'll make sure Dylan gets to the hospital.

Noah and Olena walk a few blocks up moonlit Fifth Avenue before they hail a cab. Noah sits back in his seat, strokes Olena's head, and stares out the window. Dr. Thayer's check sits crisp and flat in his shirt pocket. The corners press into his chest. It is the only power he has left over them. In his rage he wants Dr. and Mr. Thayer to pay for the negligence of their children, for their wealth, for their sense of superiority, for his own sense of inferiority. He deposits the check at the ATM before he and Olena get home. He will decide what to do with the money later.

chapter 12

"I can't do it, man, there's no way." Dylan has pressed himself against the door of Roberto's car.

Noah's knuckles are white where they bear down on the steering wheel. He turns to Dylan in cordiality but also dread, nervously scans the green campus of Horace Mann High School. Despite his determination that he is doing right, he is equally convinced that he has done something very wrong. "You totally can. You just need to score twenty points higher. That's two questions more than usual, three at most."

Dylan stares intently at the glove compartment door, glances at the greenery of Horace Mann, lit by early morning light. "This is so fucked. You're going to be in such shit for this."

Dylan went through a brief fit of rage the previous night after Noah picked him up, before the Unisom took effect. But his body reacted well to the familiar narcotic, and this morning he woke up in Noah's apartment well rested and alert. "This is your last chance to take the test, Dylan. I'm not going to take it for you, and now it's too late for your mom to pay someone else to. And I'm already 'in shit,' so it's too late for that too. Go take your damn test."

"Why are you doing this to me?" Dylan asks.

"You're going to pass this on your own. If you don't do it yourself, your whole time in college is going to feel like a cheat. Start this out right."

"Just drive me home. You've fucked me over royally. You've made your stupid message. But now I'm not going to get into school 'cuz of you. So just take me the fuck home." Dylan fiddles with the glove compartment latch.

"Look, just concentrate. You've had a good night's sleep, we've gone over this—"

"What? I'm totally unprepared! I've got like no chance."

"We don't have to shoot the moon here. You just have to get a 1580. And here's how you're going to do it. Each math section is about twenty problems. Skip the hardest five. Just do the easy fifteen, and do them well. On verbal, only do half of the sentence completions. You'll need the extra time on reading comp. Just try. You're going to do fine. Really."

Dylan plucks at his seat belt. "You're an asshole."

"You can do this. And more important, you have to. You're here now, and I've already registered you. This is it. And this time you're going to do it."

Dylan pounds the car door. "You're an asshole," he sobs.

"Stop it. Just go there and do it. You're taking the SAT. Big deal. So are two million other kids."

"This is like extortion or something."

"Extorting you into taking your own SAT? Okay, then. Extortion."

Dylan opens the car door, puts a foot on the pavement. Noah starts the ignition. Dylan turns to him. The door swings and rests against his splinted ankle. "Wait. For real. Please, won't you just take it? We already got you the fake."

"No way. Get in there."

Dylan punches his uninjured leg, then looks toward the

school. A girl passing by recognizes him. Dylan impassively returns her wave. He looks back at Noah. "At least wait here for me? So I know you're around?"

Noah turns off the ignition, slowly removes the key. "Yeah," he says quietly. "I'll stick around, if you want."

"Cool." Now that he has given up on wheedling Noah, Dylan seems to have found some reserve of strength. He takes a deep breath, extracts himself from the car. Since his ankle is still in a splint, it takes some maneuvering to get to the curb with calculators and pencils intact in his grip. Noah hands Dylan his crutches from the backseat. Dylan flashes a gray and perfunctory smile. Noah gives a wave in return, but Dylan has already turned toward the school. Clutching his registration ticket over the handle of the crutch, Dylan hobbles toward the building. The girl who waved earlier has been waiting for just such an opportunity, and comes over to help Dylan inside. Together they disappear into the building.

Noah unclasps his seat belt, leans back heavily into his seat. He gave up smoking years before, but wishes he had a cigarette on hand. The older guy sitting in a beat-up car in a high school parking lot—the cigarette would complete the image, make him a perfect vision of seediness.

He watches the Horace Mann overachievers file into the school. They scan through flash cards as they walk; a pair compares definitions for *somnolence.* Everyone is wearing casual gear, sweatpants and T-shirts, but everything is too fitted, the hair too constructedly sloppy. Everyone tries hard, no one wants to seem to try hard. They each go to great lengths to look as slovenly as possible.

After the students finish filing past, Noah eases open the car door and walks through the pastoral private school campus. He takes his time, listens intently to the crunch of gravel beneath his feet, the distant sound of a lawn mower. He has three and a half hours with nothing to do but wander the campus and think.

He didn't sleep well the night before, and drank too much. Roberto had been a hard sell on being an accomplice, and required half a dozen beers before he assented. But Noah knew his help would be essential—the doormen knew Roberto as Dylan's friend, would let him up at ten P.M. without calling to check with the Thayer parents. And Dylan would take whatever drugs Roberto passed him, even if the drugs turned out to be sleeping meds and beta-blockers so he would be alert for his SAT. Noah had Dylan get a good night's rest in Harlem, and then drove him to take his test. There had been no other option. Dr. Thayer had no faith in her son. She wouldn't have let him take the test on his own; she would have just found someone else to pay. So agreeing to her plan and then working on his own seemed the only way to set things right. But it was still subterfuge, and Noah shivers each time the magnitude of his actions rolls over him.

Noah sits beneath a tree. His mind turns in a soon-familiar loop—fear over the repercussions of what he has done, pride at the moral path he has taken, doubts whether he has been that moral after all, fear over the repercussions of what he has done, pride . . . He lies flat on the soft, wet grass and falls asleep.

He is awakened by the buzz of a nearby power edger. He bolts upright, a leaf and a pair of rotten acorns bouncing off his body. He looks at his watch—the SAT has been over for an hour. Dylan left without him. He stands unsteadily, ducks past the Hispanic gardener, and makes his way back to the Datsun.

There is no easy way to find out how Dylan did on the test. Dylan will answer the phone for neither Noah nor Roberto. Calling Dr. Thayer is out of the question. And there is no way to find out from the rest of his students, because Noah doesn't *have* any more students. He got a call from Nicholas early Monday morning: an anonymous parent claimed that Noah requested payment under the table, and that he was trying to start his own company. Noah wouldn't be receiving any more students. One of Dr. Thayer's parting shots, her specialty.

That message was paired with another:

Hey, Noah? This is Cameron. Hey! Remember me? You tutored me for the SAT for a while? Anyway, we got this crazy letter from your company, and it sounds like you're really sick or something, and I wanted to make sure you're okay. Also, they gave me this other tutor, and it's like this old woman, and she's got like bad breath? And she's just so boring, it sucks, and anyway, I'm taking the math IIC in June, and wondered if you could come for a few sessions anyway, even if your company says you're dead or something. So give me a call, 'kay? See ya.

Noah meets with Cameron the same day. Dr. Thayer's $80,000 is still in his bank account, but he hasn't had the nerve to spend any of it; his bills are overdue and he could really use the money from a tutoring session. Besides, he is excited to see Cameron again. She is amazed to find out that Noah isn't sick at all.

"But look at this." She points to the letter she received from the agency: "*Unfortunately, for reasons out of anyone's control, Noah will no longer be able to continue his tutoring duties. We would be happy to provide you with tutoring coverage during his period of absence.* 'Period of absence'? What the hell? It sounds like you have leukemia or something."

"I guess it doesn't make the company look too good that a tutor got fired."

"But why would they? You're like really good." Cameron has always been moody, as various and obvious in her feelings as any high school theater star should be. Today she is quiet and earnest.

"A lot of you guys freaked one another out," Noah says. "It happens. And I guess I was a bit equivocal about the whole thing anyway."

"Equivocal. 'With ambivalent feelings,' right? I'm sorry about the freaking out too. We're crazy stressed about this shit. And there was that call from Dylan's mom, just checking to see that we were happy with you. It made us all kinda nervous. I guess we got all *Crucible* on you."

"Dr. Thayer called you?"

Cameron nods. "Yep, she talked to my mom. Anyway, if you want I could like write a letter saying how all my friends think you're really good, and we don't care if you secretly think tutoring is crap, because we do too. Would that help?"

"Definitely not. And I don't think I want the job. It's not that big of a deal. I'm kind of happier this way."

"So I'm like your last student ever?"

"You're it."

Cameron sits back. "Wow. That's so cool. I'll do you proud."

Noah shrugs. "Make yourself proud. I'm already proud. You're going to do fantastically."

Cameron smiles shyly at the crumbs caught in the gnarled and polished wood of her table.

"Hey," Noah says, "have you heard anything about either of the Thayer kids?"

"Dylan Thayer? No, I have no clue. He's like off the radar screen, doesn't hang out with high school kids anymore."

"What about Tuscany?"

"Oh right, that's his bitchy sister, right? No, I haven't heard anything. She liked dropped off the earth too."

They cover subject-verb agreement and parallel sentence structures. Cameron has to be at her *a capella* group practice, so they pack up early. As Cameron opens her giant handbag, Noah sees a glint of shiny paper inside, with a sheen that he recognizes. "Hey," he says, "what's that?"

"This?" Cameron extracts a magazine. "Some magazine they distributed at school. It's not too bad. Everyone's reading it. Someone around here made it, I guess."

"Can I look?"

Noah opens the cover of *It's All You* (an amateur photo of a Central Park tree before the Fifth Avenue skyline) to the table of contents. Only two of the articles, this time, are by Tuscany Thayer:

I. Rushing Rivers and Rushing Heads: The Pleasures of Outdoor Sports, pg. 5
II. Getting In: Managing Boarding School Admissions, pg. 24

Noah flips to the second article. It shows a picture of Tuscany in a library, wearing a tight tank top and rhinestoned eyeglasses, and peering over a book that she just might be holding upside down. At the bottom are biographical credits: *In the fall the author will be attending Hampshire Academy.*

She did it. She got in.

~

The development head of the Dance Theater of Harlem arranges to meet Noah in the downtown office of a foundation he works at during the week. Noah turns the corner and pauses on the wide avenue—he has been here before. Then as he scans the street he glimpses a familiar curved velvet rope. The office is up the block from Pangaea. Or what used to be Pangaea; the club has closed and been replaced.

Noah pauses in front of the old Pangaea door. He remembers the milling beautiful of his night at the club. Clutching his legal pad, wearing a floppy hat over his flat hair, Noah feels like he did in elementary school: nerdy and ignored. He smiles as he surveys the two doors to the club. He also feels the same righteousness he felt in elementary school, the conviction born of his mother's consolations and his teachers' exultations that the geeky individual will be the one to come out satisfied, the one to live a life that is more than mere participation.

Not every dork, he knows, is a latent success story. And the sophisticated Manhattan kids like the Thayers know this from the start. It is a safer gamble simply to become popular and do whatever it takes to remain popular. In the upper ranks, the ability to make yourself liked is more important than the ability to analyze sonnets or lead a community service project. But perhaps, Noah thinks, his triumphant geek and Dylan's eternal cool kid can coexist.

It is, he realizes, a Wednesday, Rich Bitch Wednesday. Noah pulls his hat tighter over his head and enters the office building.

~

The June SAT arrives. Noah and Olena have been studying in the mornings, with Olena taking practice tests in the afternoons while Noah teaches his SAT class, and somehow they feel prepared. Noah drives Olena along with his six student dancers to the test site in the Dance Theater van, watches Olena disappear into the crowd of Horace Manners, surrounded by a ring of black and Hispanic kids. They are a foreign body, an odd parcel sent into the elite mass, jubilant and nervous live versions of the minorities of the reading comprehension passages. Noah spends another three and a half hours wandering Horace Mann High School as they take the test. When

Olena bounces into the van afterward she is quiet for a moment, tentatively asks Noah about a few troublesome questions, and then a victorious smile spreads across her face: she thinks she has nailed it. Noah's students chatter with her about troublesome questions as they ride back to Manhattan. Noah and Olena check her score on the Internet ten days later. A 2120.

"Maybe," Olena says excitedly, "maybe I can go to Dartmouth!"

"You'd be next to Tuscany," Noah observes. "You could tutor her."

They won't know for a year where Olena will get in. Until then she is happy to concentrate on her applications. Although Olena can't yet quit her job at the dry cleaners Noah brings in enough money to pay his rent to Hera and his own student loans. His own Ph.D. applications lie to one side. He's not excited about them, not anymore, and his teaching keeps him distracted.

The summer passes, but still neither Noah nor Roberto can reach Dylan.

When the fall SAT crunch begins, Noah expands his SAT course and adds a section of Upper East Side kids, tutoring a few of Cameron's friends who didn't score well enough in the spring. He meets with five Fieldston students in a spacious living room, circled together on an Oriental rug a few blocks down from the Thayer apartment. After class Noah must walk down Fifth Avenue to his bus stop, and so once a week he passes beneath the green canopy of their entrance. He looks up at the windows—they are still shuttered tightly enough to reveal nothing of what is inside. Each time he passes the building the sting of his tangled memories of the Thayers fades. He is no longer struck by a tumult of conflicted feelings, doesn't suffer a minute's depression after passing. By October he is able to walk by without thinking of them at all. Instead his thoughts remain on the grant applications to expand his nonprofit, or the prospect of hiring another teacher, or the crisp quality of the air, or Olena, or whatever random musings come naturally to his freed mind.

But then, one late autumn evening, he sees Dr. Thayer. He has just entered her block, is two awnings down. She stands on the corner, clutching a briefcase, as firm and angular a figure as the street post next to her. She waits for the doorman to hail a cab; her finger stabs the air impatiently. When she sees Noah she reflexively pivots toward him, and suddenly it looks like she is hailing him instead of a taxi. She drops her hand to her side.

Noah strides down the rest of the block. She waits for him patiently, resignedly.

He stands in front of her and she in front of him. Like Olena, she is able to communicate wordlessly with him. He infers that she wants to tell him something, and that at the same time she wishes she were anywhere but there.

A doorman, seeing Noah and Dr. Thayer face each other down, steps around them and into the street. He squints down the length of Fifth, his expression inscrutable under his captain's cap.

"How are you?" Noah asks.

Dr. Thayer nods in response. The move is polite and public, but tells Noah that were she to use words, they would be cutting.

"I heard that Tuscany is going to Hampshire Academy," Noah says. "Please congratulate her for me." The formal manner he now has to adopt with Dr. Thayer frustrates him. Seeing her is like seeing a lover months after a breakup—it is what cannot be said that is hardest to take.

"She's thrilled," Dr. Thayer rasps. And then, with a cough: "Thank you."

"She did it herself, she deserves the credit." A furious depression wells inside him. These platitudes are killing him.

"She's taken plenty of credit, I think, not to worry," Dr. Thayer says. A weak smile plays on her gray features.

They stare at each other for a moment, polite and nonsensical grins on their faces. "And Dylan?" Noah asks.

"Dylan," Dr. Thayer says. A passing cloud seems to darken her features, but then Noah realizes they are under the awning; it is instead some internal light that has faded. "Dylan won't be attending college this fall."

Noah wraps his sweating hands around the strap of his messenger bag. "No?"

"No!" Dr. Thayer exclaims with sudden, horrifying lightheartedness. "Your little scheme didn't work. How wild, that I should have known best. Oh *yes,* he took this test on his own! But he *failed* on his own, Noah. And we have only you to thank for it. And it's not as though we can sue you for our eighty thousand, you fucking little criminal."

Dr. Thayer stops, openmouthed. She is about to continue, but she clamps her mouth shut. She has been maintaining her artificial smile as she spoke, which causes a line of spit to fall out of the corner of her mouth. She wipes it daintily with the edge of her designer sleeve.

"I'm sorry," Noah says. "But he had to do it on his own."

"Who do you think you are?" Dr. Thayer says. There is flame in her voice; the smile has dropped. "You are an *employee,* Noah, not a family member, not a friend. A worker. It's not your place to play God. I'm so mad I could—" She cuts herself off again, snaps her mouth closed.

"Where is he now?" Noah asks softly. He sees, behind Dr. Thayer, that the doorman has succeeded in hailing a cab. Its turn signal on, the taxi waits for traffic to clear before sailing over.

"Oh, he'd thank you, I'm sure! We just got him his own apartment downtown. He's taking the year off to 'relax.' I've washed my hands of it."

Dr. Thayer stares at him. Noah stares coolly back. Guilt

and anger swirl in his head, the coolness and fire of the feelings canceling each other out. "Your cab's here," he says.

She steps back toward the curb. "Thank you," she says, as curtly as she would to the doorman himself.

"Goodbye," Noah says.

Dr. Thayer steps into the cab, slams the door. The light has turned red, and so the cab just idles in front of the building. Noah begins to walk downtown toward his bus stop. As he reaches the next block the cab races past. Noah can feel the hot exhaust of its passing, wonders where Dr. Thayer is going. He is out of her life, so he will never know.

So Dylan is living on his own, has finally dropped his parents' aspirations and officially become what he was all along: a dissipated young man. Not happy but not depressed, sheltered from ambition and thus also from discontent. Smooth and intentionless. Noah feels a chill kernel of guilt for what he has done, but knows this is only a tiny amount compared to what he would feel had he actually taken the test for Dylan. He made the right choice. The grim, unhappy, unendearing right choice.

Noah pauses on the next corner, turns around. It isn't far to get back to the Thayers' building. He enters the lobby, flashes the staff card Dr. Thayer gave him so many months ago, and then he is riding up in the sleek elevator. The door, as always, opens directly onto the apartment. The front door is unlocked, he is sure, but he stands before it as before a fortress wall. He can't will himself to turn the heavy knob, to see the familiar gleaming foyer, to gaze up the stairwell leading to Dylan's and Tuscany's rooms. He runs a hand down the smooth white surface of the door, the antique silver knocker.

He opens the flap of his messenger bag, extracts a stiff envelope. He doesn't hold it in his hands, doesn't dare; as soon as it is out of the bag he slides it under the door. Inside: one check for $80,000, made out from Noah's bank account to one Dr. Susan Thayer. The fortune, heavy in his hands for months, has been returned to its owner.

Noah just stands and breathes in the narrow vestibule for a moment, fills his lungs with the circulated, air-conditioned air that has been passing for years through all the apartments of 949 Fifth Avenue. Then, with a concerted effort, he turns his back and calls the elevator.

He rides down to the gleaming lobby, then walks past the bored and staring doormen into gloomy Fifth Avenue to catch the bus home to Harlem, where he will teach. It's what his mother always encouraged him to do.

Acknowledgments

I owe a great deal to my best teachers: Mrs. Anselo for being there when I wasn't quite ready for first grade, Mr. Polack for being there when I was too ready for fifth. And later on, Margery Shoaff and Camille Lizarribar for demonstrating that insight is always a worthy goal.

My kind friends who read drafts, I will continue to put upon you. Caroline Hagood, you were my big break, baby. Thanks to my editors: Rob Weisbach for picking up *Glamorous Disasters*, and Amanda Murray for keeping it aloft. I am most indebted to my agent, Richard Pine, for always knowing just what to do.